# Ultimate Error

# Ultimate Error

James D. Tesar

Editing: Writer Services, LLC (WriterServices.net)
Cover Design & Book Layout: Writer Services, LLC

ISBN 10: 1-942389-18-3
ISBN 13: 978-1-942389-18-7

# Table of Contents

# Prologue

***

## Aswan Valley, Ethiopia

## World Population: Three

The dry savanna winds blew across the barren remains of the once great Cretaceous lake—now a dried, windswept crater of tall grasses, meandering streams and mud-filled waterholes.

Lucy sat cradling her child in a grove of trees with her mate. Together, they had already survived three dry seasons, but this one was the worst. She feared they would not survive the fourth.

After months of scorching heat and dry winds, only a mud-filled watering hole remained—the remnants of the raging waters that had filled the rocky gorge during the wet season, but now the watering hole was a deathtrap. The competition for food and water had become fierce, and three little hominids were no match for lions, hyenas, and buzzards. Every day, the lions and hyenas sat in wait. With the herds gone, they knew that sooner or later the little creatures would have to come down out of the trees.

Lucy sat cradling her little boy. If it didn't rain soon, they were going to die.

The sun had reached its peak hours earlier and was now heading in the direction of the far side of the lakebed. Lucy and her mate had learned long ago that late afternoon was the safest time to make their way to the water's edge. By then, the lions and hyenas would be sleeping in the shade of a large tree.

Finally, Lucy said, "Let's go. We can't wait any longer."

Lucy's mate climbed down onto the open plains and sniffed the air. Then he motioned for her and the little boy to follow. As they walked further out onto the open plains, the grasses grew taller and Lucy was scared. Pulling on the thick long hair on her mate's back, she cried, "This is bad. The grass is too tall. We can't see."

He turned and barked at her, "No! No! Stand up. Stand upright."

Lucy was only about three feet tall, even when standing upright. He pointed at the child. "Make the boy stand up. We have to walk upright; it's too dangerous to walk like the others. We can't see over the tall grasses down on our hands." Suddenly, he stopped, holding up his hands. "Shhhh. Quiet. Don't move. Don't move."

Lucy and her little boy crouched down in the tall grass

while her mate, standing on his two legs, stretched up to look out over the tall grasses. He sniffed the air in all directions.

Suddenly, the tall grass parted. "Noooo,..." he screamed. Turning to Lucy, he yelled, "Run! Run!"

Lucy grabbed her child and stood upright, and they all ran for a lone tree ahead on the open savanna. It was a planned ambush, and others were waiting. The lions knew they would head for the tree, but in their starving state from the long dry season, their timing was off and they missed their prey. Lucy's mate scrambled up the tree first. Lucy handed him the little boy and just made it up herself as a group of lions circled the tree.

Lucy, her baby, and her mate were dying of thirst. The lions were dying of starvation. It was a standoff. The future clan of Homo sapiens hung in the balance.

Suddenly, off in the distance, Lucy's mate heard a rumbling. "Listen! Listen!" he said, pointing off to the far side of the gulch. "It's a storm. Maybe rain is coming."

Lucy was weak, and her little boy was breathing very hard. It was the same every year; life was on the brink of extinction again.

"Will the rains come soon enough?" Lucy whimpered. "They'll just sit there and wait until we either make a break for the woods or fall out of the tree from weakness."

Lucy's mate looked at her. "We should never have come out here. We should've stayed in the trees like the rest."

Lucy shook her head. “No, we can’t be at the mercy of the winds, the rains, and the dry seasons forever. We can’t stay in the trees.”

Lucy’s mate caressed her hand as he looked at the patient felines below. “They won’t go away. They’re too hungry, and they know we have no way out. This is the Law of the Land. They are bigger than us and stronger. We have no choice in what awaits.”

Caressing the little boy’s head, he continued, “I’ll go down. Once they’ve eaten, they’ll go away. Then you and our child can make it back to the woods with the others.”

Lucy cried, “No! That’s the way it always is. And then the same thing happens again, all the time.” Lucy pleaded; she couldn’t bear watching them tear him to pieces.

Suddenly, a bolt of lightning struck the ground only a few yards from the tree, setting a stand of dry bushes on fire. Lucy screamed, “Oh! That was too close. We could have been killed.” Then she looked beneath the tree. “Look. Look. They’re running. The lightning has set the bushes on fire, and the lions are afraid of the fire.”

Lucy’s mate started down the tree. “Let’s get down now while they’re running. We can make it to the woods before they come back.”

Lucy grabbed his arm. “No, they’re afraid of the fire.” Climbing down, she walked over to the flaming bushes, picked up a burning stick and handed it to her mate. “Here. If we stand upright, we can carry the burning sticks. They’ll be afraid of us as long as we have the fire.”

Lucy turned and pointed to hundreds of sticks and tall grasses scattered about as far as the eye could see. “As long as we have sticks, and there are so many we’ll never run out, we don’t have to stay in the trees.”

Then Lucy pointed to a large mound of rocks and a small cave. “There, let’s go to that cave. Bring the fire. The lions can’t get in if we keep the opening with fire.”

Lucy’s mate looked back at the woods. “What about them, back there in the trees?”

Lucy shook her head. “Leave them in the trees. They are fools.”

# Chapter 1

***

## International Space Station

In a matter of months, the total biomass of the planet had shifted from that of seven billion upright bipeds to a creeping mass of slime molds and festering piles of fungi. Looking down from the International Space Station, large black clouds of flies could be seen swirling over the major cities. The air that blanketed the planet was foul and heavy with the smell of sulfur and methane. The surface of the planet was barren, stripped of every plant and animal by the marauding masses of pillaging bipeds. Fourteen billion years of carefully crafted evolution had been undone in a matter of months. The bipeds' reign of terror over the planet was almost finished.

# Chapter 2

***

## Two Months Earlier
## New Orleans, Louisiana

From the moment his alarm had gone off and he'd inadvertently gotten out of bed and put his left foot down onto the cold floor, Budd knew that he was going to have a bad day. His mother had always told him, "If you get up in the morning and put your left foot down first, you're getting out on the wrong side of the bed."

Interstate 10 heading toward the airport was backed up for miles.

"I knew it! I knew it from the minute I got out on the wrong side of the bed," Budd moaned aloud as if there were another passenger. "I should just turn around right now and go bury my head in my pillows."

Though there hadn't been an incident in weeks, to Budd the littlest things in the world were catastrophic, and there always seemed to be something just waiting to blindside him.

As he looked ahead through the long line of backed up cars, he could see that this wasn't just another simple breakdown. Today's debacle involved a guy in a so-called "Smart" car who apparently didn't understand the laws of physics. He thought he could fit between two 35-foot semi-tractor trailers. From what Budd could see, the miscalculation, along with the fact that he was in a sardine can on wheels, wasn't looking good for the guy.

Although the accident was across the median heading in the opposite direction, broken crates of fruit and cases of Triple-C Bushwakker beer lay strewn across both sides of the highway.

As the traffic slowed to a crawl, Budd noticed a bystander wearing a black T-shirt with bright yellow letters stenciled across the front. With each strobing cycle of the emergency vehicle lights, the bold letters lit up below a "smilie" face: "HAVE A NICE DAY."

Budd grimaced, taunted by the sarcastic message that seemed to be directed right at him. He clenched his teeth, mumbling to no one, "Boy, this guy definitely got out on the wrong side of the bed."

As his car creeped up to the heart of the wreckage, his stomach turned. A bitter taste of bile rose in his throat. The scene was gruesome. With the array of red, blue, and white flashing lights from all of the emergency vehicles, it was hard to tell whether he was looking at blood, flesh, and brain tissue or chunks of watermelon.

Budd was shaken over the thought of the driver who, only minutes earlier, had been very much alive and breathing, his heart probably beating to the rhythm of the music blaring from his radio. He was likely on his way to work after kissing his wife and kids goodbye, telling them, "See ya tonight."

As the vile taste rose further in his throat, Budd had the eerie feeling deep in the pit of his stomach that there wasn't going to be any, "Seeing ya, tonight," by this guy. He was definitely going to be having a closed casket.

As he waited, he thought of the many all-too-familiar times when he had been late for work, willing to take similar daring chances as this guy had. Then, the nausea intensified as he watched the firemen peeling back the twisted steel with huge metal sheers—the Jaws of Life.

Rolling his eyes, he mused, "How ironic, the Jaws of Life." As the traffic started to creep forward, he shook his head, "Not this time."

Relieved that the traffic began to move again, Budd tried to shrug off the reality of life's tenuous thread, telling himself that it was only one person of more than seven billion. To Budd, these were pretty good odds. Somehow, the large numbers and statistical probabilities made the gruesome truth a little more palatable.

The darkness of the sky began to bleach upward as the sun approached the horizon. Budd reached the sign for his turnoff for the back entrance to Armstrong International Airport—Aircraft Support Service Road.

Five minutes later, as he was getting out of his car, he put his hands up squinting against the early morning sun. The horrible images of the morning accident had left him with a pale and pasty look. From the angle of the sun, he knew he was already late. Pushing the car door shut, he could only wonder at what earthshaking problems were waiting for him inside.

Budd's route to his office took him past his favorite food stand of glazed donuts, creamed cheese croissants, and huge cinnamon buns topped with nuts. Swiping his service badge on the magnetic lock to the door of his office—the Office of Maintenance and Ground Crew Operations—he heard the electronic device click. With his arms filled to capacity: a gooey Cinnabon glazed bun swimming in an amalgamation of butter, precariously balanced atop an extra-large Venti Starbucks cup of coffee in one hand, the morning newspaper in his armpit, and his keys and briefcase in his other hand, he leaned into the door with his back.

The old janitor at the end of the hall stopped what he was doing to watch the morning ritual, smiling as Budd cursed, "God damn light switch." He watched as Budd leaned in and tried to hit the light switch with his elbow, while at the same time fixing his gaze on his very tall cup of coffee. When that didn't work, he turned, attempting to push the switch up with his tongue, which actually worked.

Finally, with the door open and the lights on, Budd headed toward his desk. He couldn't wait to sink his teeth into that cinnamon-sweet pastry.

Caffeine and sugar were at the top of his food chain, along with fries, burgers, soda, pizza, and chewing gum. They were his solution to maintaining the energy that he needed for his type "A" personality. Although he knew that the sugars, cholesterols, and preservatives were slowly killing him, they were a much more pleasant way to go than something like being squished between two semi-tractor trailers. Such comparisons made him feel better about his atrocious diet.

The old man had just gone back to mopping the floor when he heard a high pitched scream, "Ahhhhh! Goddamn it! Shit, that's hot!" The door of Budd's office swung open, and Budd burst out, holding his crotch as he scurried to the bathroom. "Shit! Shit! Why the hell does that coffee have to be so damned hot?"

The old man struggled to keep a straight face, gazing at the floor as if he didn't see the steaming cloud of coffee that covered Budd's crotch.

Budd's string of profanity continued as the bathroom door swung closed. A few minutes later, the old man heard the buzzing sound of the hand dryer. Turning back to his mopping, he mumbled to himself with a painful grimace, "The boys ain't going to be hanging too good today."

A short time later, Budd was back at his desk, sipping on what was left of his coffee and biting into his now coffee-soaked Cinnabon bun.

Hitting the "enter" button on his computer's keyboard, three large wall screens came to life. Budd scanned the screens to see the current condition of things. Concourses A and B were green, but Concourse C had five red flags. This meant there were delays. "What the heck's going on with C?" Budd mumbled.

All five planes were waiting to be serviced. Glancing at the flight destinations, they were all East Coast flights—Kennedy, La Guardia, and Jersey. Glancing up at the wall clock, it was almost seven, and these planes should have been off the ground over an hour ago. Nearly choking on his breakfast, his blood pressure spiking to somewhere near critical and the veins in his forehead popping, he cursed, "God damn it … God damn it. What the hell is going on down there?"

Budd was the supervising manager for the ground crews for all three terminals, and no matter what the reasons were for flight delays, in the end, it was his responsibility. Flight delays to Montana, North Dakota, and Nebraska never caused much of an uproar by the airlines; but because of international flight connections, Kennedy, La Guardia, and Newark were critical.

Still cursing, Budd swiveled in his chair and reached for the intercom phone. "Aw, shit!" he griped in frustration as the rest of his cup of coffee went streaming across his desk, soaking a stack of quarterly reports. He watched the coffee pool under the phone as he held the receiver to his ear. Waiting for his fate, he wondered if the death by electrocution would be quick and painless.

When nothing happened, he pushed the button for the Concourse operator. As he waited for an answer, he watched as the coffee now started heading in the other direction toward the edge of his desk and another close encounter with his groin.

Pushing his chair back, he impatiently mumbled, "Come on. Come on. Answer the damn phone." It had actually only rung twice to this point.

"Good morning! Ground Crew Operations; east terminal. I hope you're having a wonderful day. This is Sheila. How can I help you?"

God, how Budd hated hearing that damned chipper voice every time he called. He just didn't understand how anyone could be so energetic that early in the morning.

"This is Budd. Get me the ground crew for Concourse C."

"Well good morning to you, Budd. Yes, I'm fine. Thanks for asking. And how are you?"

Sheila was all of nineteen, maybe twenty—a Generation Z, into multitasking, motivated by success, cynical, ultimately private. Her only care in the world was that her earplugs fit into her ears, and she drove Budd nuts.

Budd rolled his eyes and let out an exasperated breath, "God! It wouldn't matter if the world was coming to an end!" Thinking to himself, *This kid would probably be just as bubbly if it were.*

Before he could say anything, Sheila calmly reminded him, as she did just about every day, "You know, Budd … you're going to have a heart attack one of these days if you don't chill out. Remember, positive energy is the way to go."

He tried his best to stay calm, but the clock was ticking on those five planes still sitting on the ground. "Why the hell hasn't the ground crew for Concourse C checked in yet?"

"I don't know," Sheila said quizzically and a little sarcastically. "Would you like me to connect you with them?"

Frustrated by the insouciance of youth, he barked, "Of course! Yes, I want you to connect me. Why do you think I called you? Those planes—"

Before Budd could finish, she snidely interrupted his rant. "Just one moment, please. I'll make that connection."

As he waited, he started to sop up the spilled coffee while holding the phone between his ear and shoulder. Mumbling incoherently as the canned music played tauntingly, he knew that God forsaken melody would be looping in his head for the rest of the day.

After what seemed like half an eternity, Sheila came back on, perky as could be. "Here you are, Budd. I have Larry Johnson, ground crew for east terminal, on the line."

Budd started bellowing at Larry before Sheila had time to disconnect herself from the call. "What the hell is going on down there, Johnson? You've got five planes, and all of them are delayed!"

Larry started to explain, "We—"

Budd continued, "That was a rhetorical question! I need those planes in the air, now!"

Larry took a breath and started talking. "We—"

Without giving Larry a chance to get a word in edgewise, Budd went on, "Flight 260 to JFK should have been off the ground over an hour ago! What the hell is taking so long to pump oil into the reserve tanks?"

Silence came over the line.

The rest of the ground crew stood watching Larry's facial expressions. He shook his head and mouthed to them, pointing at the phone, "It's Budd."

The ground crew figured as much and pointed to the speaker button so that everyone could hear.

"Johnson!" Budd yelled.

"Oh … I figured that was a rhetorical question too. You see, we—"

Budd didn't wait for an explanation. He threatening that if the planes weren't off the ground within twenty minutes, Larry and his entire crew would be fired before the end of the day.

"Look, *Budd*," emphasizing his name, "we're working our asses off down here. Some numb nuts parked the reserve oil refueling trucks in a back hanger on the other side of the terminal. We spent almost an hour just driving around trying to find them. And before you try to give me any more shit, the oil is in barrels!"

That stopped Budd cold. He gazed around the room, perplexed, trying to make sense of things. "What the hell are you talking about, it's in barrels? We don't get oil in barrels anymore!"

"No shit," Larry responded. "We have to dump the stuff into the hydraulic pumps, the old-fashioned way. Oh yeah, and there's no light out here. So, if we can manage to do it in the dark, then we have to pump it to the terminal's main tanks and then to the planes."

Rubbing his temples, trying to ward off a headache, he looked up at the "DELAY" status on the screen. "Okay, okay." Budd tried to calm himself. "How long before you get those planes off the ground—JFK 260 first?"

"Considering the barrels are on four trucks, and each is double stacked, there must be over two-hundred barrels, and we only have two forklifts. So, *at least* an hour to get JFK 260 filled." Then he added, "I'm not sure how long it's going to take to dump them all into the hopper."

Budd shook his head and thought, *Could anything else go wrong.* Looking back up at the board, he responded, "Okay, Larry..." trying to think of what to do next, "what's done, is done. Unload the barrels. Dump them. Then get back over here. I'll deal with the airlines."

Dropping the receiver without touching the phone, so as not to get electrocuted, he headed toward the bathroom. The coffee was taking a toll on his bladder. As he headed out of his office and down the hall, the old janitor heard him mumbling to himself, "Who the hell delivers oil in barrels anymore?"

# Chapter 3

***

## Office of Maintenance and Ground Crew Operations

## Armstrong International Airport

Larry slipped his cell phone into his pocket and told everyone to get started. As two of the men headed to the forklifts, Jeremy walked over to Larry. "Damn, it sure is creepy out here," he said, pointing to the dark swamp that rimmed the outer perimeter of the terminal.

Larry laughed. "You ever seen that movie, *The Monster of Boggy Creek*? Filmed right here—right out there in that swamp. Ripped a bunch of guys to pieces."

Jeremy looked at him, not sure if he was kidding. "They ever catch the monster?"

Larry pulled up his shirt sleeve and showed Jeremy a huge

scar on his arm. It was actually from a pedal bike accident that happened when he was a kid, but he was having too much fun. "Nope, still out there somewhere."

Larry said something else, but Jeremy couldn't hear him over the sounds of the forklifts, so he just turned and started working on the hydraulic pumps.

A few minutes later, the forklifts started setting down the first of the drums in front of the hopper to the pumps. Taking the lid off the first barrel, Jeremy jumped back. "Whoa! What the hell?" He motioned to Larry, who was counting drums on one of the other trucks.

"What's up?" Larry asked, walking over.

Jeremy pointed at the open drum. "Smell this stuff."

Larry leaned in, sniffed, and jerked his head back. "Whoa!"

"What the hell is it?" Jeremy asked. "Does this stuff always smell like that?"

Larry shrugged his shoulders. Neither of them had known what it really smelled like—never had had a whiff of an entire fifty-gallon drum before. Oil always came in tankers and was pumped directly from the trucks to the terminals.

Jeremy looked down at the thick, black surface. Staring at his faint reflection, he asked Larry, "You ever smelled anything like that?"

Larry looked at him and smiled. "You ever been to Iowa?"

Jeremy laughed. "Yup. Pig shit, right?"

While Larry and the crew were struggling with the barrels of oil, Budd was back in the bathroom, struggling with a personal health issue. Over the last hour, his groin had been burning and itching as if it were on fire. He had pulled down his coffee-soaked shorts to get a good look at his boys.

Alarmed at the sight of his genitals, he cursed, "What the hell's in that coffee?" His scrotum looked like a shriveled up prune, as if it had been soaking in a bucket of water for a day. His entire groin area was beet-red, and the skin was chaffing off.

Pulling his shorts back up, he headed out in the direction of Terminal B. He knew of a bathroom for the handicapped that had a dispenser for adult diapers. After that, he headed to a bathroom near Terminal A that had dispensers of baby powder.

Twenty minutes later, the painful burning subsiding, he was back at his desk doing his usual morning activities: filling out forms, coordinating with the other ground crews, and stamping out fires here and there. His blood pressure had just started to stabilize when his cell phone started to buzz. Pulling it out of his pocket, he snapped it open without looking at the caller ID, and barked, "Budd."

To his surprise, the ringing continued. Looking at the caller ID, it was blank. It wasn't his phone that was ringing.

Looking around, bewildered, he finally realized that the

sound was coming from somewhere in his desk. After pulling open a number of drawers, there in the bottom drawer sat a cell phone, the incoming call light flashing and buzzing.

Picking it up, he mumbled, "What the hell?" Looking at the caller ID, it showed, "Blocked Caller." Hitting the speaker button, not sure who was going to respond, he answered, "Budd Stringer, Office of Maintenance and Ground Crew Op—"

Before he could finish, a scrambled voice that sounded like something out of a Clancy movie said, "This is official business. You need to listen carefully. Do not interrupt, and do not ask questions."

Furrowing his eyebrows, he gave his typical knee-jerk reaction by blurting out, "Don't ask questions? Who the hell is this?"

There was no response to his question. The cold gravelly voice just continued. "There are two-hundred barrels of oil on four trucks at the perimeter of the east terminal. You are not to touch them. There is a crew coming to pick them up."

Trying to remain civil, Budd interrupted, this time a little more perturbed. "Who the hell is this?"

Instead of an acknowledgment, the caller continued. "This is Federal business. Classified."

Budd wasn't sure if this was a prank or what, but he was now beyond trying to remain civil. So confused at the moment, he could do nothing but repeat the caller's last words. "Federal! … Classified!" Rubbing his temples, his blood pressure back on the rise and now gritting his teeth, he said, "What the hell are you talking about? Who is this? And what office or department are you calling from?" Without a pause, he continued. "Are you sure you got the right number?"

With no acknowledgement to his stream of questions, the caller calmly continued. "If you interfere, impede with this project in any way, you could be charged and prosecuted at the Federal level for interfering in national efforts."

Budd damned near choked, repeating the word, "Prosecuted," in disbelief.

Flopping back in his chair and rolling his eyes up at the ceiling, he couldn't even comprehend the meaning of the words—prosecuted, national efforts, federal, treason.

"What the—" Budd started to stutter, attempting to argue, but the caller interrupted.

"The following is very important. Listening clearly?" Before Budd could say anything, the caller continued. "When this call ends, you are to put the phone back in the desk drawer where you found it."

Budd wanted to argue, but the caller repeated, "Do you understand?"

Before he could say anything, the phone went dead.

The confusion of it all, and the threats, caused Budd's adrenaline to flow. He was trembling. "I'll find out who that was. Tell me what to do, assholes!" He slipped the phone into his pocket. This would prove to be a bad idea.

# CHAPTER 4

***

## Maintenance Operations
## Ground Crew
## Concourse C

The sun had just started creeping up over the horizon, and the crew had about half of the barrels unloaded. As Jeremy emptied another drum into the pump system, one of the forklift guys shut down his rig, stood up, and pointed out across the tarmac. "Hey boss! Someone's headed our way."

Larry climbed onto the forklift and looked off into the early haze. It looked to be a small caravan of trucks. As the vehicles got closer, he could see that they were not airport vehicles.

Doug, the forklift driver, asked, "Who the hell is this?"

Larry had no idea. Coming across the giant lot from the west were four vintage 60's trucks with more rust on them than original paint. Larry raised his hand to have the other forklift operator shut down his rig. They all stood and waited.

A few moments later, the four trucks parked side-by-side, not more than thirty yards from the crew, with their headlights shining directly into their faces. Then, nothing. The trucks sat idling while the crew stood silent.

Finally, Larry, holding his hands up over his eyes to shield the glare, approached the trucks and yelled out, "Hey, what about cutting the headlights?"

An arm came out of the open driver's side window of the first truck, waving to the other trucks. The engines and lights shut off one by one.

With spots in his eyes, Larry heard the door of the first truck squeak as it opened. A vague outline of a tall, lanky person stepped out of the truck. As the guy approached, Larry strained to see who it was. A distinct sound knocked on the pavement as he walked. Larry looked to see mud-crusted alligator boots. The man stepped in front of his truck, facing off with Larry. Larry was taking it all in—the bandana on his head, a beard that came down to his chest, a distinct punch of body odor.

Doug, still sitting up on the forklift, bent down and whispered to Jeremy, "Looks like this dude's from 'Duck Dynasty.'"

Jeremy nodded in agreement. Then, just like an opening scene from the television show 'Duck Dynasty' the lanky guy put his foot up on the bumper and spit a big glob of tobacco on the ground. Wiping the remaining drip off his chin, he asked, "Who in charge here?"

"I'm in charge. What the hell is going on?" Larry asked.

The doors opened on the other trucks, and a bunch of similar-looking men stepped out and walked around to the front of their trucks.

Doug bent down again and whispered, "What the hell? There gonna be a shootout like at O.K. Corral?"

With another spit of tobacco, this one slithering down onto his beard, the grungy-looking lead guy looked over at the unloaded drums. "What in the hell you doing with those barrels of oil?"

Larry looked at him, confused.

Without answering his question, Larry asked, "How the hell did you guys get into the airport? This is government restricted, Homeland Security-controlled property."

Since 9/11, you pretty much had to be strip-searched and interrogated to get onto the terminals of an international airport. Larry had no idea how this lost tribe of Neanderthals in a bunch of rust bucket trucks had managed to just drive onto one of the most secured airports in the country.

The guy didn't answer Larry's question. He pointed and said, "We's supposed to pick up them there barrels of oil that y'all messin' with."

Larry, beginning to get frustrated and feeling a bit antagonistic, repeated the word, "We's?" He suddenly felt a flush of anger as he remembered that the clock was still ticking on those delayed planes in Concourse C. He blurted out, "Who the hell are you? Why is this *your* oil? And what the hell would *your* oil be doing on the back lot of an international airport?"

Jeremy came up behind Larry and, in a low voice, said, "These guys must be nuts. Maybe they're terrorists."

Larry looked at Jeremy.

The guy with the bandana exploded, "What the fuck is this, ten-thousand questions?"

Taking his foot off the bumper, he headed toward Larry while reaching into his ragged hunting vest with its rows of shotgun shells lining each lapel.

Larry heard Jeremy mumble, "Oh, shit."

They both were expecting the worst, like a knife or gun, but the man pulled out a wadded up piece of paper. He handed it to Larry, but he wasn't sure he wanted to even touch it. The guy's shirt cuff was stained with tobacco juice and, God, did he stink. He could only wonder how long it had been since this man had taken a bath.

Unravelling the piece of paper and tilting it toward the light that was a block away, Larry could see an official looking government emblem stamped across the top. The paper was stained with either coffee or tobacco juice, and he couldn't quite make out what the seal said. Looking toward the bottom, there were no signatures. Then the guy tapped his finger on the paper and said, "See those numbers right there? They the same numbers as on them barrels."

Before Larry could compare the numbers, his cell phone started to buzz. Holding his hand up, actually trying to get the guy to back off a little because the smell of his breath was burning his eyes, Larry told him, “Hold on.”

He answered his cell phone.

“Hey, it’s Budd. How is it coming along?”

Larry turned away and spoke quietly into the phone, “Budd, there are four trucks here with about a dozen rough-looking characters saying the barrels are theirs.”

Budd suddenly got a sick feeling in the pit of his stomach. “Oh shit!”

“Oh shit? What do you mean, oh shit, Budd?” Larry started to feel like he was in the middle of something outside of his job description.

“Listen, Johnson. Give them the barrels!”

“What do you mean? We’ve already dumped most of them!” Larry heard fear in his boss’s voice—something he’d never heard before. He’d always gotten an earful of anger and frustration, but never this. He started to panic but held it together. His men were looking on, and the Cajuns were watching.

“Larry, just get your crew and walk away. Come to my office, now! Do you hear me?”

Larry started to say something, but Budd interrupted him, “Don’t argue with me. Just get in your trucks and get back over here.”

Larry put his phone into his pocket, then he handed the crumpled up piece of paper back to the guy. "It's all yours."

The crew looked at each other, surprised at the sudden change of events.

Larry definitely didn't care. The stuff smelled like pig shit, and if these guys wanted it, it was all theirs.

As he turned, he pointed to the forklifts, "The keys are in the lifts if you guys need them."

As Doug climbed down off the forklift, meaning nothing by it, he asked the bandana guy, "What the hell you gonna do with a bunch of barrels of oil?"

Getting right up into his face, he told Doug, "Now that ain't none of you're God damn business, now is it?"

Doug stepped back and shrugged. "Sorry. Didn't mean anything by it. Just wondered."

After a spit of tobacco, he said, "We're taking it to the Gulf, Okay?"

Doug put his hands up, "Okay."

A few hundred yards away, while the debacle with the barrels of oil was taking place down on the back forty, up in the control tower, Terry and David were completing their last few days of FAA Academy Training as Air Traffic Controllers. In a few weeks, they would be receiving their assignments as full-fledged controllers.

As they stood watching, they listened as a seasoned controller guided Flight 260—a wide body DC 10—onto the east-west runway.

"Flight 260, this is the tower, Armstrong International. You are cleared for take-off; New Orleans to JFK, continuing on to Germany."

The radio played out the return message. "This is Captain Nelson ... flight 260 ... Copy that, tower."

Inside the plane, Nelson glanced over at the copilot. "Okay, let's give 'er all she's got. We're over two hours late."

The copilot nodded, pushed a few buttons into his computer, and a screen lit up with little rows of green arrows showing the current direction of the winds. He looked over at the captain. "We have good tailwinds all the way to New York. We should be able to make up for some lost time."

Nelson nodded and pushed the throttles full forward.

As Larry and his crew headed toward their trucks, they could hear the roar of a large jet off in the distance. Larry's radio crackled, and he heard a pilot say, "Tower ... 260's out of here."

As Larry and the crew were getting back into their trucks, the boss man of the Cajun crew screamed out, "Hey, half these barrels are empty! Where's the rest of the shit?"

Larry stepped back out of his truck and pointed upward just as a huge DC-10 flew overhead. Screaming back over the thundering noise of the jet, "There's your oil. Heading to New York City—the Big Apple."

Climbing back into the truck, he told Jeremy, "Let's get the hell out of here."

As they drove back to the main terminal, Jeremy asked, "Larry, is there gonna be enough reserve oil? We only emptied half of those barrels.

Larry replied that the terminal tanks were already over half full and that they had emptied more than enough of the barrels to fill them back up. He added, "It's only for the reserve tanks, anyway."

According to the FAA, large jets flying overseas had to have reserve oil tanks that were stored under the fuselage. In the case that, for whatever reason, the main engines lost oil pressure, oil would be available and pumped automatically to the engines from the reserve tanks. As far as Larry knew, he had never heard of anyone ever using the reserve oil. It was just another redundant FAA rule.

As they had made it back to the terminals and were now all crammed into an elevator taking them up to the main floor, Doug, more-or-less talking to himself, quizzically asked, "Why the hell are those guys taking oil to the damn Gulf?"

It had been some time since British Petroleum had blown up an oil rig off the shores of Louisiana and flooded the coastline with a few hundred million barrels of crude in the "Deepwater Horizon Oil Spill." It shut down drilling in the Gulf at a time when the Obama Administration was pushing to actually increase drilling.

# Chapter 5

***

## Dry Creek, Louisiana

The raggedy band of locals finished getting all of the drums loaded back onto the trucks when Silas, another of Dry Creek's lifelong inhabitants, asked the boss man with the bandana, whose name was Darrell, if they were going to get paid since more than half the barrels were already empty.

Darrell shrugged, as he really didn't know. He was so damned tired that, for now, all he wanted to do was turn around and go back home.

The money was so good, it was hard to turn down; especially in an economy as poor as Dry Creek, Louisiana. It was easy for Darrell to round up men for the job. Ten-thousand dollars in bundles of newly printed twenty dollar bills, and another ten-thousand when the job was finished, made it easier to ignore the consideration of whether or not they were getting involved in anything seedy or what they were to do was questionable. Darrell asked no questions, and his handler only told him what needed to be done for the twenty grand.

The whole thing started a few weeks earlier when Darrell was covered in grease, working under a 1954 vintage Ford pickup truck in his repair garage in Dry Creek.

He was trying to get a rusty bolt moving from the bottom of the oil pan when he heard the old Ma Bell coin-operated telephone that hung on the outside of his building start ringing. He was surprised to hear the relic, as he hadn't heard the damned thing ring in probably twenty years. He didn't even know the number for it. Even more surprising was that someone did.

With the mess he was in the middle of, he didn't bother to crawl out and answer it, but it started to get on his nerves when it would not stop ringing. After fifteen minutes, he started cursing it. After almost thirty, he was ready to get his shotgun.

Clemet, the old man who ran the hardware store across the street, had heard the phone ringing and was just as baffled. Being that business was slow, and curious as hell, he crossed the street to get a closer look.

"Hey, Darrell. You want me to get that?"

Darrell rolled his mechanic's creeper board enough to look at Clemet. "Sure, go ahead. How in the hell can anyone be calling that dang phone? Don't even have a dang number to it."

As Clemet headed back out towards the phone, Darrell

shook his head and jokingly said, “Probably the dang Russians.”

Clemet leaned into the garage and whispered, “Darrell … it’s for you.” His brows were as close to his hairline as they could go.

Darrell looked up in bewilderment. “Me? What in the hell you mean it’s for me?”

“Well, I ain’t got no better way in sayin’ it more clearly than how I just did. You better get on up here ’n answer it. Person sound like they got a wicked cold or somethin’.”

Darrell picked up the receiver that was hanging from its cord. “Hello?”

The voice on the other end was scrambled. The caller told him that he had a job for him and would be paid very well.

Somewhat aggressively, Darrell asked, “Who is this?”

He was told not to ask any questions, just follow instructions.

Darrell was getting ready to hang up, when the caller told him to go look in the far right corner of his storeroom, under a gray tarp.

Clemet followed him back to the storeroom as Darrell complained incoherently to himself. “Gray tarp … I ain’t got no gray tarp in my—”

Clemet and Darrell looked at the gray tarp right where the man said it would be. They looked at each other and then approached it. Pulling it off, they saw a wooden crate.

"What in the hell?"

"What is it, Darrell?"

"I ain't never seen it before."

It had no markings and was secured with flat metal bands.

"Well, you gonna open it?" asked Clemet.

"I guess I ought to."

Clemet let out a yelp. "God damn, man."

The box was full of brand new twenty dollar bills.

Darrell quickly closed it and went back to the telephone. "Who in the hell is this?"

The caller ignored his questioning, telling him that he needed some local drivers, probably four trucks, to go to Armstrong International Airport in a few weeks and pick up some barrels of oil.

Skeptical, he asked, "And do what with them?"

The caller told him that they were to take the barrels to a specific location on the coast and dump their contents into the Gulf.

Darrell figured something wasn't right about this, but any misgivings that he had were vindicated by the cash that was sitting in the storeroom. He had no qualms about dumping oil into the Gulf. Though the world was kept in the dark about it, British Petroleum's Deepwater Horizon fiasco was still plaguing the northern Gulf of

Mexico. Wildlife was still being found all gummed up by the residual gunk lingering in the swamps and shoreline. *A few measly barrels wouldn't make any difference*, he reasoned with himself internally. *And, besides, money has been tight since the oil spill.* With the lack of off-shore fishing and tourism, jobs and money, were hard to come by in Louisiana.

"I know a lot of locals … with trucks. That's all we gotta do?"

"After you dump the contents, bring the empty containers to Nevada. You'll be given further instructions from there."

Darrell was starting to have second thoughts. He'd never been out of Louisiana, and as he started to balk, the caller told him that there would be another ten-thousand dollars when the job was finished.

Hearing that, Darrell said, "Okay," but before he could get any specific instructions, the caller hung up on him.

A week went by, and Darrell heard nothing. He'd checked the old pay phone a number of times to see if it was still connected. He and Clemet were hesitant to do anything with the money. They just left the box sitting under the tarp where it had been discovered.

Just when Darrell thought this might all blow over and that maybe he'd end up with some extra free cash, Mary Ann Dobson, a spinster who lived on the outskirts of town, showed up at his garage with a letter that had been mistakenly left in her mailbox.

Wrong letters in wrong boxes was nothing new, it had become somewhat of the norm. Everyone was aware that Jasper, the local mailman who had been delivering mail to Dry Creek locals for forty years, had been getting a little forgetful in his later years.

The letter was addressed to "Darrell's Garage." There was no return address. Inside was a map of Armstrong International and instructions.

Following the instructions, they left Dry Creek a little after midnight and arrived at the outskirts of Armstrong International Airport a little after four a.m. They turned off onto an unmarked dirt road that skirted along the edge of the swamp and ended at a remote, locked service gate leading onto the west edge of the airport tarmac.

As instructed, they turned off their engines and headlights and waited. Someone would come and open the gate. They had sat for about an hour, sweating in the humid air filled with hungry mosquitoes, when someone with a flashlight walked up from the direction of the swamp. It was still dark, and the person's face was not discernible, probably by design in the scheme of things. He walked over to the gate, unlocked it, and swung it open. Then, he turned and walked back into the swamp.

Darrell, knowing the Louisiana swamps very well, sat in disbelief. "Walking into the frickin' swamp in the middle of the night." Looking over at his passenger, Billy, he said, "That guy ain't going to be having balls for long. Alligators just love human testicles."

It had all sounded pretty simple, but now they had wasted

a lot of time arguing with the ground crew, and as Silas had pointed out, half the barrels had been emptied and pumped to main terminal storage tanks.

After looking at Silas, the trucks, the barrels, the crew, a spit of tobacco, and a stroking of his beard, Darrell called out, "Load up, we're heading back."

The drive back to Dry Creek took a fairly long time as they had been directed to stay off of the interstate. Darrell knew that whoever was running this shady operation must have known that you had to have environmental permits to transport "Hazardous Material," even though oil wasn't considered hazardous material in bulk tank trucks, only when in barrels. Also, the interstate was patrolled by state police, and whoever was running this must have wanted to stay clear of them. They were more difficult to influence with a bribe to look the other way and tougher to deal with.

The back roads and good-ole-boy local police were no problem for Darrell. He, and generations as far back as he could remember, had been running moonshine, endangered species, and providing alligator meat to tourists for decades without a glitch.

It was a little after 11:00 p.m. when they finally pulled into Dry Creek. Dry Creek, Louisiana was anything but dry. Its highest elevation was fifty feet above sea level. It was swampland with some dry spots here and there.

They pulled into Darrell's homestead, which looked like something out of the movie "The Deliverance"—rusting trucks with no tires sitting up on cement blocks, the living quarters a trailer covered with hanging moss, and two mange-ridden dogs chained to trees.

Before the trucks barely came to a stop, the men were jumping out, heading for the nearest tree. The multiple cups of coffee and long ride filled bladders to capacity.

Within minutes, swarms of mosquitoes descended on everyone, targeting any exposed body parts. One of the guys, Buford, gave out a blood curdling scream when a huge Louisiana blow fly took a bite out of the tip of his most private part. Everyone laughed as Buford ran to the truck to get a tube of local salve—a home remedy concoction well-known to ease the pain of the Louisiana blow fly.

After everyone had finished with their personal business matters, one-by-one they all sat around on big rotting logs, boulders, and stumps that circled a large fire pit.

As everyone sat puffing and dragging on cigarettes, which helped keep the mosquitoes at bay, Silas looked over at Darrell. "What's next?"

Darrell pushed a large glob of tobacco chew into his front lip. "We stay here tonight and get some sleep. Tomorrow, we head to Nevada to drop off the barrels."

"What about the rest of the oil in some of them barrels?" Silas asked. "We gonna get paid the rest of that ten-thousand dollars?"

"Look," Darrell said, "ain't nobody knows that we didn't take that stuff to the Gulf but us guys right here. In the morning, we head to Nevada. I gotta map. When we get out in the desert, we stop somewhere and empty the rest of the shit in the sand. Bring 'em their empty barrels, and we get our money. Simple as can be."

Silas was a little hesitant. "What happens if they find out we didn't dump the stuff in the Gulf?"

Darrell, spitting out a big chuck of chew, said, "What the hell they going to do, kill us all?"

# Chapter 6

***

Wednesday, September 12th
4:30 P.M. EST

86 Pinckney Street
Boston, Massachusetts

Ricky walked down the rustic red brick sidewalk past the historic Victorian row houses that lined Pinckney Street of old town Boston. Each of the nineteenth century houses were adorned with wrought iron fences, spearheaded with pointed finials, and worn cement steps that led up to tall oak doors. Though he was nearly seventeen now, the kid in him still turned the routine event of walking home from school into a game of hopscotch and skipping tiptoed on only the darker bricks. Although he stopped the tiptoeing whenever anyone else came along, God forbid he'd ever be caught committing such a childish act at almost seventeen.

Finally growing out of the gawky stage cursed by every teenager, his acne had cleared, he no longer looked like a gangly weed ready to be blown away by the slightest gust of wind, and his mother had finally stopped dressing him like a little boy.

His hair was dark brown, almost black, with a tinge of reddish hue when the sunlight shined through it at just the right angle. He had gotten this highlight from his mother, who had beautiful, dark auburn hair. His most exciting trait now, which made him feel like a real man, was the stubble starting to grow on his chin.

Reaching his destination at 86 Pinckney Street, he climbed the worn cement steps of the house that he had lived in for his entire life. Checking the mailbox hanging next to the door, he pulled out two fitness magazines, the electric bill, water bill, and a bunch of junk mail. The fitness magazines were his mother's, Lucy, who spent her days as an aerobics instructor at an elite Boston fitness center.

Tucking the mail under his arm, he pushed open the heavy wooden door and yelled at the top of his lungs, as if his mother were deaf, "Mom, I'm home."

Just as the door slammed shut, shaking the windows, Ricky heard his mother, in a much more subdued tone, call back from the kitchen, "Don't slam the—"

It was too late. She sighed, as she was certain she'd be quick enough today.

Ricky walked into the kitchen where his mother was preparing dinner. A pile of cut-up vegetables, chicken, and a salad were on the counter. Looking over at her, with a shrug, he said, “Sorry, Ma. I know, don’t slam the door.”

Lucy turned, and out of the corner of her eye, she could see the backpack was already hurdling toward the table. She started to say, “Don’t throw your back pack on the,...” but it was also too late. Ricky’s bag was already skidding across the open table, coming to a dead stop within inches of a vase of flowers.

Ricky had held his breath. If that bag had knocked over the vase of flowers, he knew he would be dead. “Oops. Sorry, Ma. I know, don’t slam the door. Don’t throw my book bag on the table.”

Lucy shook her head, scolding him, “God, every day I have to say the same thing. I sound like a broken record.” As she turned back to her cooking, exasperated, she mumbled, “It’s no wonder some animals eat their young.”

Ricky knew that he was walking on thin ice, and he could see that his mother’s chopping of the vegetables had become a little more aggressive, with a touch of anger.

He might be seventeen now, but he still knew when it was time to play the “mommy” card. And he also knew that it worked every time.

With a pathetic look, like a puppy being scolded, his eyes downcast, he said sheepishly, “Sorry.” Immediately, he could see that it was working.

Lucy looked over and smiled. “How could a mother not love that beautiful face?”

Ricky waited, knowing the "mommy" card always came at a high price—the hug, the sloppy kiss—but it was better than the kitchen knife cutting vegetables.

Lucy walked over and held out her arms. "You know, you're never too old to tell your mother that you love her." Then she moved in to give him a big hug.

Before he had a chance, her arms were wrapped around him, and he found himself stuck between his mom and the table. Hoping to avoid a sloppy kiss, which always came next, he squirmed to get free. "Ma, I can't breathe, you're suffocating me."

Lucy stepped back and put her hands on her hips. "Well, excuse me for wanting to give my little baby a hug."

Ricky rolled his eyes, "I'm not a baby anymore. I'm almost seventeen, you know. I'll be a legal voter in about a year."

Lucy turned and walked back to her cutting board. With a deep sigh and an end-of-the-world sadness, she said, "Fine, I'll just have to live with the memories of when you used to want to be hugged."

Ricky sat down at the old wooden table. "Ma, I think you're being a little over melodramatic.

Lucy, trying to play the "sorrow" card, sniffled. "That's fine. I'll just live with the memories."

Ricky rolled his eyes. It was time to change the subject. Reaching for his backpack, he asked her, "Do you want to know how school went today?"

Not giving her time to respond, he said, "It was terrible."

As she got some salad dressing out of the refrigerator, she said, "Let me guess, Physics … or better yet, your Physics *teacher.*"

Ricky nodded.

Lucy had been keeping abreast of the latest trials and tribulations of Ricky and his physics teacher. Pouring the salad dressing in the lettuce-filled bowl, she waited.

Ricky rummaged through his backpack, shuffling through his books and papers before finally pulling out his Physics folder. Pulling it open, looking for a specific piece of paper, he said, "You got it, Mom. There's something wrong with this guy. I'm telling you, he's a nut case."

After finding the piece of paper he was looking for, waving it in the air, he said, "If I get an 'F' in Physics, it's going to be goodbye to Harvard." Lucy didn't say anything. She just let him rant. "I'll probably end up in Montana. I'll be lucky just to get into Little Big Horn Community College in Crow City, Montana," he said, holding up a flyer of Little Big Horn that he had found pinned to the bulletin board at school.

Lucy found his sarcasm amusing and maybe a bit melodramatic. As she wiped the counter with a damp cloth, she smiled. "That might be nice, and maybe you could meet a nice cowgirl and someday herd cattle in Argentina like my brother."

Ricky frowned. "Mom, your brother is in Patagonia, not Argentina. And he herds sheep, not cattle."

Lucy was having fun teasing Ricky. "Minor detail. My

point is, you meet a nice down-to-earth cowgirl, maybe someday have a baby cowboy. You could name him Angus, and we could all live on the open plains in Patagonia, herding sheep." Lucy was having a hard time keeping a straight face.

"Very funny, Mom. And if we had twins, we could call the other one Braveheart." Ricky started to pack up his papers. "If you're not gonna take me seriously, I'm gonna go do my homework in my room."

Lucy laughed. "Ah, just think of it, a grandmother's dream—twins Angus and Braveheart."

Ricky stood up and started to head toward his room, but before he could leave, Lucy held up her hand to stop him, "Okay, okay. I'll be serious … I promise. So, what's the matter with this teacher of yours?"

"Are you going to listen or not?" Ricky asked, stopping and looking at his mother.

She held up her hand. "Seriously, scouts honor. I promise I'll listen."

Ricky sat back down. "I've been telling you for weeks. He is crazy. I think he's schizo."

Ricky was attending one of the most elite preparatory schools in Boston, and Lucy doubted that they had hired a mentally deranged teacher. She wasn't even sure that Ricky knew what schizophrenia was, but she had promised to listen, so she simply asked, "What makes you think so?"

"Not just me, Mom, all the kids know it too."

*Well, if all the kids know it, then it must be true*, Lucy thought to herself, but she didn't interrupt.

"Rumor has it, Mom, that when he was a kid, he was some kind of a boy genius. After only two years of high school, he took the SATs, got a perfect score, and got into MIT."

While listening, Lucy went back to preparing dinner, chopping onions for the salad, her eyes watering, and trying to appease Ricky. "That doesn't sound like a nut case to me."

Ricky was getting himself all in a tizzy. "Just wait. There's more, Mom. I'm not done!"

Lucy wanted to smile. *God he's cute*. But she held herself back. Her little boy was becoming a man.

"Apparently, he didn't stay long at MIT. I bet he was a schizo, and they kicked him out. We're trying to put the whole story together."

A little confused, "*We* are?" Lucy asked.

"Yeah, all of us—the rest of the class. Everybody thinks he's nuts."

*A conspiracy theory. A second shooter on the knoll, of course*, Lucy thought to herself, holding back a laugh. "Okay … continue."

"Okay. We know—well, we think—he didn't finish at MIT. It looks like he went straight from MIT as a kid and got a Ph.D. from Princeton. But, there's a big gap of like eight years that we can't figure out where he was. I'm guessing he was probably in a looney bin."

Taking two plates out of the cupboard, two pork chops out of the fridge, and a container of milk, Lucy replied, "So far, I haven't heard anything that would suggest he's a 'nut case'. He sounds brilliant to me."

Ricky shook his head. "Oh no, Mom, there's even more, and it gets better. Do you want to know what he did for his Ph.D. thesis?"

She raised an eyebrow. "Go ahead, I'm listening."

"Listen to this ... Apparently, he tried to prove that Newton's Laws of Physics were wrong—like when an apple falls off a tree and hits the ground, it's not because of gravity. What kind of crazy talk is that?" In his excitement, Ricky's voice cracked, hitting the higher pitch of his youth. "Mom, gravity's the law! It's *not* just a theory."

Lucy walked to the table and put down two plates of food. "Okay, what else?"

Ricky looked at her dumbfounded. "Mom, what else do you need to know? This guy's a looney. The guy tried to prove that Newton was wrong and that gravity doesn't exist! I'm telling you, there's something not right in the head with this guy. He's an odd duck."

Lucy pondered this for a moment while she took a bite and slowly chewed her food. Then, after she swallowed, said, "You know, Albert Einstein went to Princeton too, and he was considered an 'odd duck.'"

Ricky gave her an exasperated look. "Mom, this guy ain't no Albert Einstein."

Tilting her head, she said, "'Ain't' ain't a word, dear." Ricky rolled his eyes. As they continued eating, Lucy asked, "How old is this guy, anyway?"

Ricky smiled. "Oh, he's *old* ... probably forty, forty-two," he said, looking at his mother with a mischievous smile.

"Oh, that's real funny!"

Ricky knew his mother had less than a year before she hit the big "four-0", but he also knew that for a women of nearly forty, she was, what the kids called, "a good looking babe." Her work as an aerobics instructor had helped to keep her in good shape.

Lucy was about five foot, eight inches tall, thin and trim, and didn't look a day over thirty. It didn't take rocket scientists, but Ricky had seen that whenever they were out-and-about, she turned heads.

She had beautiful dark auburn hair, high cheek bones, and a well-proportioned bust. She could get straight out of bed with no makeup and still look beautiful.

Lucy frowned at the, "He's really old," comment. With a fiendish smile, she said, "Ungrateful child, I knew I should have left you on someone's door step."

"Too late now." Ricky was smiling ear-to-ear. "Like the Cheshire cat in *Alice in Wonderland*, you're stuck with me now."

Lucy shook her head. She knew it was too late now; nobody wanted a teenager. Then, getting back to the business at hand, she asked him what had happened today that had gotten him all worked up.

Ricky held up his index finger in an "I'll show you" gesture. After finding the piece of paper he wanted, he handed her an assignment sheet. As she was looking at it, Ricky said, "Get a load at that. That's the project he assigned us."

The paper read: *The growth and well-being of living organisms acting as a unit will continue to thrive and develop in a straight exponential line until some outside force acts upon that unit, changing the direction of the unit.*

Lucy flipped the paper over to look at the other side, figuring there had to be more. It was a little baffling. Setting the sheet of paper down, she asked, "What else did he say about the assignment?"

"That's just it, Mom. He didn't say anything. He just wrote on the board in big black letters: 'T-H-I-N-K'."

Lucy furrowed her eyebrows. Looking a bit confused, she asked, "Anything else?"

Ricky nodded. "Oh Ya!" Then he handed her a second piece of paper, which had in big bold letters: "INERTIA."

Lucy looked at it, turned it over and then back to the front. "And then what he did he say?"

Ricky threw up his arms. "That's it, Mom! He told us that he would discuss it tomorrow after everyone had time to think about it tonight. And then, just like that, he said, 'Class dismissed.'"

# Chapter 7

***

## Frankfurt International Airport
## Germany

Kurt and his partner for the day, Hans, drove along the access strip heading to Terminal 2 of Frankfurt International. As they passed under the Skyline Shuttle, Kurt could see ahead of them a row of four or five planes that all needed routine maintenance checks before they continued on to their next destination.

They pulled up alongside a large wide-body DC-10. Kurt typed the numbers displayed on the side of the plane into his tablet while Hans sipped his coffee and chomped on a cinnamon bun. A list of codes scrolled down his screen.

"Okay, this one first. Night flight arrival from JFK," Kurt said.

Hans took another sip of his coffee and asked, "What's this thing need?"

Kurt scrolled down the screen of his laptop. "It's a third-leg stop: Louisiana, JFK, and here. So it needs Level 2 inspection—hydraulics, tires, flaps, and electronic circuit checks."

With a last chomp on his cinnamon bun, Hans motioned, "Let's get to it." He headed toward the DC-10 as another plane, a 747, pulled in, adding itself to the row. Kurt opened the back doors of the maintenance truck and pulled out the Electronic Circuit Management computer.

Times had changed. No longer did planes require manual checks. The computers simply analyzed monitored data from the various ports around the plane.

Kurt plugged the laptop into the main lighting systems ports, and as he waited for the computer to run the first check, Hans yelled to him, "Hey, come over here."

"Wait a second. The diagnostics run is almost done," Kurt yelled back. After a moment, the system finished, and the computer indicated that everything was normal—no blinking red lights. Kurt unplugged the laptop and walked over to Hans, who was standing at the open door to the landing gear. "What's up?"

"What's this?" Hans was pointing to a small black puddle of goo under the fuselage.

"Where'd that come from?" Kurt bent down to have a closer look, then he walked under the belly of the plane, shining his flashlight up into the crawlspace of the landing gear. "It's not from the landing gear retractors."

Angling the flashlight, Kurt aimed up to the underbelly

of the baggage holding area. Thinking out loud, "If it's not coming from the retractors, I wonder if it's something leaking from inside the baggage holding area?"

Hans took a closer look at the thick black substance on the ground and said, "It doesn't look like oil." He pulled off one of his gloves and ran his fingers through it, then, spreading it between his thumb and index finger, he brought it to his nose and sniffed. "Whoa! Definitely not oil!" He offered a whiff to Kurt. "Here. Smell it."

Kurt pushed his hand away. "Christ! Don't put it up my nose. I can smell it from here."

Just then, another drop fell from somewhere within the undercarriage of the plane. Where the hell do you think this stuff is coming from?" Hans asked.

Kurt looked at his watch and then down the row of planes, adding the 747 that had just pulled in. "Damn, now we've got 6 planes to check."

"So what do we do?" Hans asked.

"I guess we'll have to check it out. By the smell of it, it's probably a dead bird or some decaying animal that climbed in there when the plane was sitting on the ground somewhere. They got a lot of sea birds in Louisiana—big ones, pelicans and others. Probably one up there rotting."

Hans suddenly became a little freaked out and took a few steps back while trying to wipe the substance off his fingers. "What if it's a dead body?"

"What the hell are you talking about?" Kurt asked, looking at him confused.

"Just a week ago, some kid flew all the way from Hawaii to LAX at 36,000 feet in the landing gear, and he lived," Hans said. He paused for a moment before asking, "Where's this plane headed?" as if suggesting that they let the next ground crew figure it out.

Kurt picked up his laptop and looked at the screen. "Flight 1630 to Bahrain International, Saudi Arabia."

Hans shook his head. "Ah, Jesus, maybe there's some dead al-Qaeda terrorist up there that crawled in to get past Homeland Security, and now the guy is dead and rotting."

"I doubt it," replied Kurt. "The guy would still be frozen solid. The plane only landed a few hours ago. Besides, what kind of terrorist tries to get out of the United States? For Christ's sake, they're trying to get in, not out."

Kurt was trying to think of what to do next, then, handing Hans the flashlight, he said, "Here ... crawl up there and check it out. And if you find a dead body, whatever in the hell you do, don't touch it. You don't want the DNA of some dead terrorist on your body. You know, you mess up some crime scene, like on that TV show "CSI", the CIA, FBI, or Homeland Security finds your fingerprints on a dead terrorist, they might think you're involved." Kurt was having fun messing with Hans. "Man, those Homeland Security guys get hold of you, they'd probably waterboard you to death."

Just as Hans was about to crawl up into the landing gear, he hesitated. "Didn't they outlaw waterboarding, like it's inhumane, or something?"

Kurt smiled. "Well, kind of." He gave Hans a push to get him going. "They only outlawed waterboarding for terrorists, like those guys at Gitmo, but they still waterboard civilians. There's no law against that."

Hans pushed back, "They can't waterboard us. They have no authority over here; we're German."

Kurt gave him a smirk. "Don't count on it, those guys have been known to waterboard their own grandmothers."

"Then I'm not going up there. Let them check it out in Bahrain. One dead body's not going to bring down a plane," Hans said, pushing Kurt's hand away.

"Give me the damn light," Kurt exclaimed. "I'll go." He grabbed the flashlight from Hans.

"Have fun," Hans said, shaking his head disapprovingly. "Don't touch the body, unless you really like water."

Kurt started making his way up into the plane. It was a long crawl. First, with a small stepladder, Kurt got himself up onto the huge tires. Then, working his way up the hydraulic cylinders, he pulled himself into the huge space that held the landing gear during flight. Sitting on an electrical panel, he shined the light upward onto the underbelly of the cargo bay.

"See anything?" Hans nervously called to his longtime working buddy.

Kurt yelled back, "Not yet. I'm still looking." A few minutes later, he yelled down, "Damn! It really stinks up here! Smells like someone took a dump. I wonder if someone's pet crapped in its cage in the bay—diarrhea style."

Hans yelled back up, "I once saw a dog that stuck its butt out the door of its cage, blasted a big load of dog doo, and the stuff leaked down onto the tires. And when the plane landed, it almost skidded off the runway."

Kurt laughed, shouting back to Hans, "Greased the tires good." He added that it not only smelled like something shit, but then died and now is rotting.

Hans thought to himself how glad he was not to be up there, *Better you than me*, then he decided that he'd get Kurt a beer after work. He earned it.

A few seconds of silence passed before either of them spoke. Hans started humming the theme to CSI. "Kurt ... do you see anything, dead bodies, leaks?" Hans started to become worried. "Kurt? Hey ... Kurt!"

After what seemed like an eternity, Hans heard, "I see something."

Hans breathed a sigh of relief. "Jesus, man, keep talking. I thought maybe you died up there."

"There's black stuff oozing out of two places."

"Oozing out of what?" Hans yelled back as he saw Kurt climbing back down.

Once safely on the ground, Kurt replied, "Looks like it's leaking from around the gaskets that seal the reserve oil tanks."

"Those things don't leak."

"Well, something's coming out of both the reserve tanks, and the shit stinks."

Hans looked down the row of waiting planes. "So, what are we going to do about it?"

"Nothing," Kurt said. "It's only reserve oil—just backup stuff that never gets used. Somebody must have overfilled them, or they haven't been cleaned for a while. Either way, this can be handled once this plane reaches its final destination in Saudi Arabia." He pointed to Hans' computer. "Just be sure to make a note of it for the Bahrain crew to flush the reserve tanks and replace them with fresh oil."

Kurt looked at his computer trying to find out the last time the stuff had been changed. "Looks like they just refilled them when this thing was in Louisiana."

Hans laughed. "That would explain the smell."

After checking the other ports of the DC-10, they climbed back into the truck and headed to the next plane. As they drove away, another 747 pulled into the end stall. Kurt commented that at least it was another 747; they were the easiest to check out. Kurt hated the damned old DC-10s, but thank God there weren't many left flying.

As planes continued landing, taking off and taxying, Hans sipped his coffee, which was now cold. They turned into the next plane, and Hans looked over at Kurt, thinking, *I sure hope that stuff's okay.*

About an hour later, as they were working on their fourth plane, Kurt heard the control tower giving Flight 1630 takeoff instructions.

"Flight 1630, this is the control tower, Frankfurt International Airport. You are cleared for takeoff, runway 2-9 to Bahrain, Saudi Arabia."

Kurt's radio crackled. "This is Captain Sheehan, Flight 1630 to Bahrain. Copy that, tower, we are out of here."

Then he heard the tower say, "Have a nice day."

# Chapter 8

***

## 86 Pinckney Street
## Boston, Massachusetts

Ricky was already home from school and sitting in the kitchen doing his homework. His mom was running late. She was an aerobics instructor at Boston's Elite Fitness Center, one of the most upscale fitness centers in Boston. She started working there after finishing school at Bay State Community College, where she majored in Psychology. She had gotten the job through her father who was an Ambassador to South Africa. Her parents were both killed in the Pan Am terrorist explosion over Lockerbie, Scotland. Fortunately, the trauma of losing both parents at a young age was cushioned by the substantial inheritance left behind by her father. He had been in banking before getting into politics, and along with the well-invested stocks, bonds, and gold Krugerrands, Lucy had inherited the old Victorian house on Pinckney Street.

She had an older brother, Brad, with whom she shared the sizable inheritance, but he had disowned his portion of the endowment, instead, deciding to live off the land in a commune in Patagonia, South America. She loved her brother, corresponding a few times a year by mail, but she never understood why anyone would want to live like a pauper on a godforsaken, windswept plateau at the tip of South America. She hoped to someday visit him, but for now, Boston was just fine.

Lucy climbed the rustic steps and pushed open the big wooden door. As she turned back to check the mail, she announced, “Honey, I’m home.”

With a wide grin on his face, Ricky yelled back, “I’m in the kitchen, doing homework. And don’t slam the door.”

A few seconds later, she walked into the kitchen and tapped him on the head with the mail. “Very funny.”

As she went to set the mail on the counter, Ricky added with a smirk, “And don’t throw your gym stuff on the table.“

She walked over to give him a kiss, which she did every night, and said, “Someone is getting too big for his own britches.”

Ricky was ready for the kiss; he knew it was coming. Putting his hands up, thwarting her attempt, he said, “Mom, I’m almost seventeen. I don’t need a kiss.”

Lucy smiled. “You’re never too old for a kiss from your mother.” Then she tossed her gym bag onto the table and watched it slide ever so close to the vase of flowers.

Ricky looked up. "Funny, Mom, I assume you're making a point."

Smiling, she turned back to sort through the mail and asked him how school had gone today. Without giving him time to answer, she added, "Did your physics teacher explain what he wanted you guys to do for your projects?"

Ricky dropped his head down on the table in exasperation. "Oh yeah, Mom, he told us alright."

Smiling to herself, she assumed, at least in Ricky's mind, that it wasn't good. As she thumbed through a fitness magazine, she said, "Okay, let's hear it."

Ricky lifted his head and started rummaging through his backpack. Finally, he found his physics folder, opened it, and took out some papers. He waved them at her and said, "Okay, Mom, pay attention."

Lucy nodded. "I'm listening."

"Okay. Do you remember the movie we watched about that genius mathematician guy who went to Princeton? He was some kind of a schizophrenic nut, but he ended up getting a Nobel Prize in Economics or something?"

Lucy remembered and nodded. "Yeah, I think it was that actor who was in "Gladiator"—that Russell Crowe guy!"

Ricky nodded. "Yeah, that's it! It was called 'A Beautiful Mind.'" Then he held up an outline of the project that had been handed out to the class. "Okay, so here is what he wants us to do. He wants us to apply Newton's Laws of Motion to the dynamics of society."

Lucy put down the fitness magazine and stepped over to look at the paper he was waving in his hand.

Taking the piece of paper from him, she asked quizzically, "He wants you to do what?"

Ricky shook his head knowing that he had her attention. "See, Mom, I told you so. He's a little nuts. He's all into this inertia thing."

She couldn't help but smile. "Now I didn't do great in Physics 101 at Bay State, but if I remember correctly, inertia, gravity, and spooky forces at a distance are kind of their bread and butter. Physicists can be a little strange."

Ricky rolled his eyes. "Little strange? What about nuts?"

She still wasn't convinced that he was nuts, as Ricky put it, thinking his rendition was more than likely somewhat biased. "I'm not sure I understand what he wants," she said, handing the piece of paper back. "He must have explained more."

Taking a sip of water, he replied, "Oh, it's real clear, Mom. I think he wants us to help him prove that Newton was wrong and that gravity doesn't exist!"

As she turned and started preparing dinner, she asked, matter-of-factly, "I assume you know Newton's Laws."

Ricky was offended. "For cripes sake, Mom, of course I know Newton's Laws. We had that in Earth Sciences last year."

"Well, excuse me. I just thought I'd ask." Then she told him to go through the outline, page by page, and explain it while she cooked dinner.

Ricky held up the outline that Doctor John Christenson, his physics teacher, had handed out. "Okay, the first page is just review stuff. It reviews Newton's Laws, and yes, I know Newton's Laws."

Lucy ignored his sarcasm and proceeded to wash some lettuce at the sink. "And they are?"

Ricky smiled. "Newton's first law says that when a body is in motion, it will continue moving in a straight-line direction until some equal and opposite force acts upon it to change its direction." Then he looked over at his mom and added, sarcastically, "For your edification, Mom, since it's been a *long* time since you went to college, this is called inertia."

Lucy tilted her head and looked at Ricky, trying to hide her grin. "It hasn't been *that* long since *I* went to college, and I do know what inertia is. So you keep up the smart little innuendoes about my age, and you might not live long enough to go to Harvard."

"Sorry, Mother," he said, keeping his eyes on the paper, trying to hide his grin. "Okay," he turned to page two of the outline, "do you remember on that sheet he handed out yesterday—the one telling us to 'think'—where he wrote about the growth and well-being of living organisms acting as a unit, and how they will continue to thrive and develop in a straight exponential line until some outside force acts upon that unit, changing the direction of the unit?"

As she started to peel some potatoes, she nodded that she remembered and asked him if Doctor Christenson had explained what he meant by that.

Ricky exploded. "Oh yeah, Mom, wait until you get a load of this. Mr. 'Doom and Gloom' says that inertia is a property of matter and that the human race—all seven billion people on the planet—can be thought of as a single unit moving forward in a straight line." With a brief pause to summarize, he continued, "In other words, we're just 'matter'. He doesn't seem to see much difference between us, trees, dirt, and grubs."

Lucy cringed a little. "Okay, continue. I'm listening."

"Okay, here's where it gets creepy. He's referring to us as simply seven billion balls of matter, and he says that we've been cruising along for a few million years at a constant evolutionary rate. Our project is to think of some external force that could act upon this unit—that's us, the seven billion chunks of matter–and change the direction of our society."

With her back to him, she could not help but almost laugh out loud. Ricky was all in a tizzy.

"A little nuts, huh? He's not just talking about changing the direction of society; he's talking about ... like, mankind comes to an end and is replaced by another life form like insects, funguses or slime molds."

God, he was so damned cute. She just wanted to go over and hug him to death, but with all the self-restraint she mustered, she continued cooking. She put some lettuce in a bowl and said, "Okay, I'm starting to get it. He wants you to think of a hypothetical scenario—a force applied to our society that will change the evolutionary direction of the human race. I'm not so sure that's crazy; it kind of ties biology, evolution, sociology, and physics all together. "That's pretty good thinking." As she took plates and silverware out of the cabinet, she asked, "Did he give you any examples of what he means?"

Ricky nodded. "Yeah, he explained the dinosaur dilemma. You know, a few million years ago the dinosaurs were like one of the dominating societies on the planet, cruising along at a constant evolutionary rate. Things had been going along just fine. They were moving forward as a single peaceful unit, eating plants and each other, until 'whammo,' a meteorite smacks into the Yucatan Peninsula, and it's goodbye dinosaurs, hello humans."

Lucy was starting to see the reasoning behind the project, but Ricky would have none of it. He and the class had already made up their minds that Doctor Christenson was a little deranged.

"Mom, are you getting the picture? He wants us to come up with some hypothetical cataclysmic event that ends mankind, like goodbye humans, hello daddy longlegs."

As she put a helping of potatoes, salad, and a chicken breast on each plate, she said, "Okay, he might be a little eccentric, but he is the teacher, and maybe he has a good reason for this. Life isn't always as obvious as it seems. Let's just work on the assignment, and we'll see if there's a lesson to be learned."

Ricky rolled his eyes, but before he could argue, she asked him what he was going to do next.

Pushing his books out of the way, he picked up a scoop of

potatoes. "Well, for the weekend, we're supposed to start thinking about ways to end the human race." Putting the whole scoop of potatoes in his mouth, he garbled, "Nice way to spend the weekend, huh?"

Lucy shrugged. She had to admit, an assignment contemplating the end of the human race was a little different … maybe even a little bit strange.

# Chapter 9

***

## Bahrain International Airport

The skies coming into Bahrain International were clear with a fifteen-mile-an-hour easterly wind. Captain Sheehan of Flight 1630 scanned the panels to identify the source of the flashing red light and the screeching alarm that had just started buzzing.

"There." Andrew, his copilot, pointed to a sensor on the far right panel indicating that hydraulic pressure to the landing flaps was low, and oil pressure in one of the engines was also low.

Sheehan leaned over and tapped the console, figuring it was just a problem in the electrical switch, but the alarm did not shut off. He was used to this; the small sensors in the plane's console were so sensitive that they often short circuited. He had been flying DC-10s for more than twenty years, and he knew the plane like the back of his hand, so he wasn't overly concerned.

Just then, another indicator light showed that the oil pressure in the second engine was also low.

Though he was confident that the pressures in the engines and flaps were normal, FAA rules required reporting any abnormal readings. Before calling the tower, he turned to Andrew. "This damned technology can really be a pain in the ass sometimes."

Andrew laughed. "Like a good woman. Can't live with 'em, can't live without 'em."

Sheehan nodded in agreement. "That's for damn sure. I'm on my third."

Andrew laughed and told him that they better call the tower. Sheehan switched the radio to "Talk". "Bahrain International, this is Captain Sheehan, Flight 1630, origination, Frankfurt. We are experiencing indicator lights in the cockpit and need clearance for emergency landing. We are currently two hundred miles out."

The control tower came back, "Flight 1630, we have you on radar, what is the nature of your problem?"

Sheehan explained that they had warning lights indicating low hydraulic pressure to the landing flaps and low oil readings in both engines. He explained that he had no real concerns and there were no indications of real mechanical failure, confident that it was just faulty sensors.

The controller on the job was fairly new at Bahrain. Not exactly knowing the protocol, he told the captain to hold for a senior controller. Sheehan and the copilot kept their course and waited for further instruction. They continued listening to the Beatles' song "Hey Jude" from their CD player until, after a few minutes, a senior controller responded, "Flight 1630, are you currently on backup hydraulic oil from the reserve tanks?"

Sheehan had never in his career been concerned with the reserve oil tanks. He had actually forgotten that they even existed. They were nothing more than redundant backup systems required by the FAA, and he had never heard of them ever being used.

When he looked down at the indicator lights to the reserve tanks, he said, "Shit."

The controller in the tower said, "What's that? I didn't catch that."

Sheehan reached over and turned off the music. "Sorry, just thinking to myself. I didn't see this, but we switched over to the reserve tanks over an hour ago. There are no indicator alarms for that, just the lights. For whatever reason, the computers switched over to those tanks automatically."

Sheehan looked over at Andrew. "Maybe this is real?" He was a little more concerned now. "Bahrain tower, I think we need to get this plane on the ground as soon as possible."

The tower came back, "That's affirmative! Flight 1630, we are going to divert you to the mainland. Change course to King Fahd International Airport in Dammam. It has a larger runway and is better equipped for emergencies if needed."

"Copy that, Bahrain. Flight 1630 changing course to the mainland airport, King Fahd International."

This was no problem for Sheehan. He had been diverted to that airport a number of times for weather-related conditions. As he started to make his turn, he heard the tower at Bahrain International contacting the tower at KFI. "King Fahd International, this is the tower at Bahrain International. Pick up Flight 1630; needs emergency landing instructions and Emergency Landing Protocol. I repeat Emergency Landing Protocol."

"Bahrain International, we have Flight 1630 on our radar; will take control." The tower at Bahrain International thanked them and signed off.

"Flight 1630, this is the tower at King Fahd International. You are currently coming in from the north. Please circle and make your approach from the south. You will be landing on Eastern Runway 2."

"Understood. Flight 1630 will approach from the south, landing on Eastern Runway 2." After announcing to the passengers that they were diverting to King Fahd International, the plane started banking to the south.

# Chapter 10

***

## Las Vegas, Nevada

Gloria was getting ready for work when she heard the television in the living room screeching. She poked her head out of the bathroom and saw big red letters going across the screen: "THIS IS A KXNT SPECIAL NEWS REPORT." This was followed by an announcer. "We interrupt your normally scheduled programming to bring you this breaking news report."

The screen switched to the KXNT-TV newsroom. "This is Anna Franklin, KXNT Las Vegas, with breaking news. Environmentalists are outraged at an oil spill that occurred in Lake Mead approximately twenty-four hours ago.

"Although the amount of oil spilled was small, all hazardous materials being transported across state lines are required to obtain a hazardous material transportation permit and be escorted by officials from the Department of Transportation. Apparently, according to our sources, none of these were done. The State's Attorney General's Office is trying to identify those responsible."

As Gloria stood buttoning her blouse, Anna referred to her notes. "What we have so far is that an undisclosed amount of oil has reportedly been spilled into the lake, which, as everyone knows, is one of Nevada's main tourist attractions.

"Authorities are reassuring us that the amount of oil is small, isolated, and of no serious concern, but onlookers at the scene are reporting something very different, saying it appears to be spreading." She continued skeptically, "One only wonders who to believe."

Gloria smiled in agreement as Anna continued to explain that the Governor had already called for the aid of cleanup crews that worked the Deepwater Horizon oil spill in the Gulf of Mexico, just off the shores of Louisiana in 2010. Anna turned to the large projection screen behind her. "For more on this story, we go live to the shores of Lake Mead."

The news switched to an on-scene reporter standing a short distance from the lake.

"Thank you, Anna. This is Sheila Blake, KXNT news. We are standing only a few yards from the site of a potential environmental disaster that could have a major impact on the residents of not only Nevada but also Arizona and California. This lake is a reservoir that provides drinking water for nearly 20 million people, irrigation water for thousands of acres of farmland, and millions in tax revenue as a tourist destination.

"As you can see behind me, authorities are putting out the all too familiar floating barriers that are used to contain oil and other hazardous chemical spills."

Pointing to stacks of barriers, Sheila reminded viewers of seeing the miles of these yellow barriers at other oil spills, like the Valdez spill in Alaska, and then just months ago in the Gulf of Mexico off of Louisiana.

As Gloria continued watching, Sheila started to walk over to the edge of the lake to get a little closer look when an FBI agent with dark sunglasses stepped between her and the camera.

Sheila was somewhat taken aback, but, holding her ground, she confronted the agent. "Excuse me. This is public property, and this is a free country." Trying to get around the agent, she continued, "We do have First Amendment Rights."

The agent didn't move and never said a word.

Sheila stepped back and defiantly apologized, "Well, Anna, and to our viewers, apparently the FBI doesn't recognize freedom of speech or the First Amendment. I guess that's as close as we're going to get."

She motioned to her cameraman to let her continue. "Although, from what I have heard here, the slick seems to be small in comparison to the eleven million gallons of crude oil that spilled into Prince William Sound in the 1989 Exxon Valdez accident in Prudhoe Bay, Alaska, or the two-hundred million gallons from the Deepwater Horizon drilling disaster off of Louisiana, cleanup crews here appear to be having some problems containing this spill. Exactly what these problems are, we do not know as we've been unable to get any information from authorities since the FBI has taken over the investigation. And, as you just saw, the FBI isn't very interested in cooperation."

Back in the news room, Anna interrupted, "Sheila, what do we know at this point?"

"Well," she continued, "what we do know is that three or four trucks loaded with unauthorized barrels of oil crossed the state lines into Nevada. From the little we know, I have heard here that they had crossed Texas, up through Arizona, and here into Nevada. I have no confirmation of that, just hearsay."

Anna interrupted again, "Why is oil considered a hazardous material, Sheila?"

She nodded her head. "Anna, I asked the same question. Refined oil in appropriate containers is not considered hazardous material, but crude, unrefined oil is."

Anna asked, more-or-less rhetorically, "Why would anyone be transporting crude oil north, since all the major refineries are south in Texas City?"

Sheila shrugged. "I have no idea. But being that it was crude, and the stuff crossed state lines without the appropriate permits, that's what has prompted the FBI's involvement." Just to be defiant, she looked over at the FBI agent and winked.

As Gloria combed her hair, the screen switched to a split screen with Anna Franklin back in the newsroom. "If you have just recently tuned in to KXNT, I'm Anna Franklin bringing you a breaking story. Sheila Blake is on the scene of what appears to be an oil spill, of all things, in Lake Mead. Surprising, since Nevada does not have oil; we have uranium."

Gloria watched as she could tell that Sheila had just been given the cue that she was back on. "Sheila, do we know the destination of the trucks, who they were, and why they were transporting barrels of crude oil?"

"No, Anna, we have no information as to where the trucks came from or where they were headed. The drivers and passengers have been taken into custody—we think by the FBI—and are being questioned at an unknown location."

The FBI agent with the dark sunglasses came over and again stood between Sheila and the camera. "Well, Anna, let me step over here a little." Then the agent turned and put his hand across the lens of the camera. Although there was no picture, the TV viewers could still hear Sheila. "Don't push me. What the hell is your problem?"

Back in the news room, Anna was a little perturbed. Knowing that Sheila could still hear her, even though there was a hand across the camera lens, she said, "You could tell that guy, FBI or not, that the First Amendment says something about freedom of speech."

Sheila continued, "Anna, even though there's no picture, I hope you're getting all of this transmission." Then Anna heard again, "Stop pushing me. You're hurting me. Anna, I don't think this guy cares too much—" Sheila's microphone went dead.

Anna turned to the main camera. “It seems that we have lost our connection. That was Sheila Blake on the shores of Lake Mead in Boulder City, Colorado. We’ll bring you more on this breaking story as it happens.”

An announcer came back on, “We now return you to your normally scheduled programming.”

# Chapter 11

***

## 86 Pinckney Street
## Boston, Massachusetts

Ricky spent the weekend Googling the past mass extinctions of the world. On Friday, Doctor Christenson had explained to the class that there had been five major mass extinctions in the world so far, starting with the first one 450 million years ago, to the last one—the well-known demise of the dinosaurs—65 million years ago.

The assignment for the weekend was to review the last five mass extinctions, think about which society had dominated at the time, what outside force had been applied to change the direction of the existing society, and what new society replaced the former one.

Lucy climbed the stairs and walked into Ricky's room. Ricky was sitting on the bed with his computer on his lap.

"How's it going, honey?" She expected Ricky to complain

about Doctor Christenson, be confused about the assignment, frustrated, discouraged, in a grumpy mood, and ready to give up.

Surprisingly, he was upbeat and in pretty good spirits. "Going good, Mom. I'm starting to get it."

Lucy, delighted by her son's response, sat down on the edge of his bed. "Do you want to share it with me?"

Ricky smiled. "Okay." He went on to explain that Doctor Christenson wanted them to understand that physics and the *laws* of physics could be applied to something other than gravity, friction and motion, like the Princeton mathematician who applied mathematics to economics, from which he received a Nobel Prize. "So, sorry; no Little Big Horn Community College, no Montana, no twins, no Angus and Braveheart."

Lucy feigned disappointment with over-exaggerated pouting lips. "Shucks, I was hopin' for riding and wrangling the Big Sky Country."

Ricky laughed. "Sorry, Mom. Besides, you wouldn't survive the 'Big Sky Country.' You're a Boston girl."

Lucy raised an eyebrow. "I don't know; I once killed a whole streaming bunch of ants, right down there in the kitchen."

Ricky had no response for that and just shook his head.

Picking up his yellow note pad, Lucy stated, "So, you have to think of some outside force that could change the direction of our existing society that's currently cruising along."

Ricky nodded, "Uh-huh. Inertia. Goodbye humans, hello ... I don't know yet. I haven't gotten that far."

Lucy laughed. "You know, your professor doesn't sound so crazy after all, does he? This kind of thought-provoking assignment is what schools like Harvard, Yale, MIT and Princeton want. They want visionaries who look when everybody else is wearing the blinders of past theories, you know? 'Out of the box' kind of thinkers."

Ricky tilted his head and raised his eyebrows showing agreement, but he still wasn't completely sold on the soundness of Professor Christenson's mental state.

Lucy looked at the nearly blank yellow pad and asked, "You want some of my ideas?"

Ricky replied, "Not really,... but I'm sure I'm going to hear them anyway, so I might as well say yes and be done with it. Let's hear it."

Lucy was all excited; she was sharing quality time with her baby just like she used to do. She thought back to the times when he would cuddle up next to her, learning to count or singing the ABCs song. For a mother, watching her baby grow up was like a two-edged sword. From the memories of the past—hugging, cuddling, and dependence; to adulthood, defiance, self-confidence, and development of an independent personality. Lucy knew that there would be less and less opportunities as Ricky grew up, and she was going to take advantage of every opportunity she had.

"Oh, boy! This is exciting," she said, writing "#1" on the yellow pad.

Ricky rolled his eyes. He was not sure whose project this was going to be, but he knew there was no stopping his mom now.

"Okay! Number one!" Lucy was beaming. "Ah, what about invaders from Mars?" Before he could say a word, she continued, "Let's say we find life on Mars. Not some worm or amoeba, but humanoids. And by finding that we discovered them, they decide to do a preemptive strike, come down to earth and wipe us out. Goodbye humans, hello Martians."

Ricky shook his head, hoping that the phone would ring or someone would ring the doorbell.

"Come on, Mom, get serious. That was done eighty years ago—*War of the Worlds*. Boring. It's not original. Remember, thinking outside the box?"

Not giving him enough time to suggest that she just let him work on it himself, she wrote on the yellow pad, "#2". "Okay, what about this? What if we create a virus that kills all the humans on the planet but not the pets, and they take over the world. Goodbye humans, hello puppy dogs."

Ricky shook his head, "Ma, you're wasting my time. *Animal Farm*, *Planet of the Apes*, and Matt Damon in that virus movie *Contagion*." Ricky shook his head. "This has to be something original—none of these meteorites, Martians, or other 'been there' ideas."

Just then, Lucy had an aha moment and pleaded with all the drama she could muster, "Okay, please, please just one more. I've got a good one!"

Ricky, knowing there was no stopping her, said, "Go ahead."

Lucy took the yellow pad of paper and wrote idea #3. His head dropped. "Okay, you're going to like this. This one is good and unique."

Ricky let out a deep sigh. "Let's hear it." He knew he was going to hear it anyway.

"Okay, but you have to hear me out. Don't interrupt," she said, holding up her finger.

Ricky gave a halfhearted shake of his head as if to say, "Fine."

As she scratched notes on the yellow pad, she explained her latest brainstorm. "What if, instantly, all the cell phones in the world quit? It would be so devastating that all the teenage girls would kill themselves. Then, with no young women left to reproduce and repopulate the world, mankind would eventually come to an end."

Lucy was beaming. She was serious and so excited about helping her little boy. Looking at Ricky, who sat dumbfounded, she asked, "What do you think?"

Ricky wasn't sure what to think or say, but he realized that, in all of her exuberance, she was serious. After a short pause, he said, "I think I know now why you got pregnant in college, Mom."

Lucy frowned and got up off the bed somewhat perturbed. "Fine, you don't want my help. I'm gonna go down and cook dinner."

As she was leaving the room, she turned and looked at Ricky. With a haunting smile, she said, “You know, they haven’t found Jimmy Hoffa’s body yet.” She tilted her head. “Just a warning.” She laughed to herself as she went down the stairs.

# Chapter 12

***

## Federal Branch FBI
## Lawrence Baily Memorial Building
## Las Vegas, Nevada

Agent Kelly sat at his desk reviewing a stack of casino ledgers for any anomalies. The Federal Government was not that worried about tax violations by the casinos themselves because with major banking and accounting firms, the flow of money was easily tracked. What the Federal Government was ever so diligent about was looking for any signs of organized crime. It had taken J. Edgar Hoover and others years to roust the American Mafia out of Vegas, but now it was the Russian Mafia that was trying to cut in on the action.

Kelly had gone to college at George Washington University—GW they called it for short—and had never really chosen a major, more-or-less just aimlessly taking a series of courses with no real focus or direction. During his senior year, he saw a recruitment poster for the FBI promising opportunities to work in Intelligence, Counterintelligence, Terrorism, Counterterrorism, and Cyber Intelligence. At a whim, since he was in his fourth year of college and still clueless as to what he wanted to do with his life, he applied and got an interview. After scores of personality profile tests, urine samples, and even a rectal exam, he was accepted. If college had done nothing for him other than racked up thousands in student loans, it had gotten him into the FBI.

Surprisingly, for someone who had spent four aimless years at GW, he finished near the top of his class at the Academy at Quantico in Virginia.

He applied for a spot in the Cyber Intelligence Division since the poster had promised "an exciting future." As he soon learned, nine-tenths of what the Bureau did was anything but exciting, unless one considers freezing your ass off near the Arctic Circle exciting. Fresh out of Quantico, he was assigned to the Federal Bureau of Indian Affairs in Crow Agency, Montana—home of the Little Big Horn Indian massacre.

He spent the next two years in the "teepee" capital of the world, bored to death and freezing his butt off, dealing with Indian Affairs. Within months, it became obvious that "Indian Affairs" pretty much dealt with alcoholism among Native Americans and reviewing fraud cases throughout the Indian-run casinos.

After two years of roping and wrangling in the Big Sky Country, an opening became available in Las Vegas. Kelly applied, figuring that anything had to be better than his current location. Now, ironically, he sat only a few miles from Dante's Inferno, still reviewing the same casino ledgers. As far as he was concerned, the only difference between the Little Big Horn and Vegas was that instead of his testicles turning blue from the cold, they were now red and chafing from the prickly heat.

As he sat looking at his millionth ledger, his desk phone rang. It was his secretary, Kathy. "There's some guys here to see you."

Kelly was taken aback, a little surprised at her tone.

Kathy had been his secretary since he came to Vegas and was usually more forthcoming with information and more formal when announcing that someone was waiting to see him, like, "There are two guys here from the Bellagio who would like to see you."

Kelly set down a bundle of ledgers from the Sands—the old Rat Pack Casino—and asked her, "Who are they? What do they want?" Kathy was very hesitant, and Kelly noted a hint of fear in her voice. "They wouldn't tell me. They only said they're here to see you."

Kelly had no time for this. In the past week, his prickly heat rash had erupted into a burning Inferno, so he was a little testy. He snapped at Kathy, "What the hell is this cloak and dagger bullshit? Find out who they are and what they want."

Kathy turned in her chair, away from the men and whispered, "Listen, you better just see these guys!" Then she turned and smiled uncomfortably at the guy who appeared to be in charge. She could not see his eyes behind his black sunglasses, and he didn't smile.

"Fine, they don't want to tell you who they are or why they're here. Tell them to go away. I'm busy."

A few seconds later, the door to his office opened, and three guys dressed in black with sunglasses walked in. Kathy poked her head around the biggest of the three guys. "Sorry, they just pushed their way in. I told them you were busy."

Kelly nodded to her that it was okay, and she left, closing the door.

"Gentlemen." As he looked at the three guys, he was uncertain if they were government or Tommy Lee Jones and Will Smith from "Men in Black". "Can I help you?"

The one who appeared to be in charge, the Tommy Lee Jones guy, stepped up to his desk and dropped some papers in front of Kelly. He didn't seem to have much in the line of social graces. With no "Hello," no introduction, he just pointed at the papers. "We're here to get these guys."

Kelly looked at him, confused. "And we're talking about what guys?" The man in black didn't answer, just pointed at the papers. Kelly picked them up trying to get some idea of what they were talking about.

The heading at the top of the first sheet stated THE DEPARTMENT OF HOMELAND SECURITY. Immediately, Kelly now understood the lack of social skills. As he shuffled through the papers, he couldn't help but think to himself what assholes these Homeland Security guys were. He looked up at the man who was front and center and said, "You know, you guys can all take off the sunglasses. There's certain to be no more sun in here for the rest of the day."

The man slammed his fist on the desk and barked, "Where are they?"

Kelly had no idea who he was talking about. Pushing back in his chair and crossing his arms, he said, "What we have here is a failure to communicate. Why don't you start by telling me who the hell you are and what guys are you talking about?"

All three reached into their jackets and pulled out Homeland Security IDs, but before Kelly could even get a look, they snapped them closed and put them back into their jackets.

Shaking his head, he leaned forward. "No, no, let me see them." The lead guy was getting pissed. He reached into his jacket and shoved the ID into Kelly's face, then threw it down on his desk.

"That wasn't very nice," Kelly said as he looked at the ID. "So it's Officer Billows. Is that 'Billows', like, ya know, billowing a lot of hot air, or is it Officer Blooowws like, well, ya know, blow me?"

The other men snickered. The lead guy turned his head slightly and looked at them, immediately straightening up and trying to suppress their grins.

Kelly wasn't about to just roll over and give into these assholes, so he continued to bust the man's balls. "Do you guys *really* need those jackets? I mean, come on! You know it's like … 117 damn degrees out there. You must be sweating like pigs. Are they made of wool? Man, you must be roasting."

That was the straw that broke the camel's back. Like a grizzly bear during mating season, the guy slammed his fist on Kelly's desk. "You have eleven men from an oil spill that happened day before yesterday. We're taking them."

Even though the FBI was now part of Homeland Security, Kelly hated these guys. They were pompous asses who never got the message that they were all on the same side, working together.

After 9-11, the President had vowed to consolidate the intelligence services and to coordinate intelligence operations between the various departments. But somehow a rogue group of these guys worked independently and had no intentions of working with anyone.

Kelly took out his cell phone and was about to make a call when the man in black snapped, "You don't need to make any calls. Just get the men, and we'll be on our way."

Kelly closed his cell phone and looked up at his own reflection in the sunglasses. "You talking about that bunch of Cajun guys from the oil spill in the lake? What the hell do you want with a bunch of Cajun yahoos? They're probably carrying moonshine." Kelly sat forward. "Here's what they do; I saw the Indians do it in Montana all the time. They put moonshine in barrels way in the back and on the bottom of a truck. Then they stack barrels full of grain, corn and whatever on top of the moonshine barrels.

If they get stopped by the troopers, they know they're not going to unload the damn trucks to get to the back barrels. You must already know this, so what aren't you telling me? Why do you want these guys?"

The man pounded his fist on the desk again, this time even more demanding. "I don't have to answer to you. You get those guys now. All I need to do is make one phone call, and you'll be stationed some place worse than this cesspool." He straightened up and patiently said, "Now where are these guys?"

Kelly had learned long ago that if you wanted to get anywhere in the Bureau, you didn't rock the boat. He really didn't care what they did with these guys or the fact that they wanted to take them from his jurisdiction. He wasn't going to risk staying in this inferno forever.

Kelly leaned back in his chair. "Hey, you want 'em, they're all yours." He picked up his desk phone and called his secretary. "Hey, Kathy, please come in here." As they waited, Kelly picked up his cell phone and pressed a couple of buttons. Just as Kathy opened the door to his office, the three men turned to look at her. Kelly quickly snapped a picture of the Homeland Security ID that the guy had thrown on his desk.

"Yes, Sir." Kathy nodded.

He asked her to call the holding area and have them get the guys from that oil spill thing ready and that they were being moved.

Kathy looked at the three men and then at Kelly. "Where

are they being moved to, Sir?"

The man in black didn't say anything. He just bent down, picked up his ID, and pushed past Kathy. As the three waited for Kelly to lead the way, the man in black scowled. "Just make the call."

Kelly walked them through the corridors to the holding cells in the basement area. By the time they got there, all eleven Cajuns were standing in a row, handcuffed.

Darrel looked at Kelly. "Where are we going?"

The lead guy told him to shut his mouth, and just move it, giving him a shove down the hall. Kelly followed them outside to where two diamond-black vans with black windows stood waiting. The men pushed the Cajuns into the vans and, without another word, drove off.

Twenty minutes later, Kelly was sitting in his office looking at the photo ID that he had snapped of the Homeland Security guy. He turned to his computer and punched in the man's Homeland Security ID name and number on the FBI's secure database. After a few minutes, the computer screen lit up. "No match."

Kelly leaned back in his desk chair and rubbed his temples. He had the sinking feeling that no one was ever going to see those Cajun guys again.

# Chapter 13

***

## 86 Pinckney Street
## Boston, Massachusetts

Ricky looked up from his history book and was surprised that it was dark already. He had been so engrossed in his studies that he had lost track of time. Glancing at the clock next to his bed, it was almost 6:30.

He threw his history book on the bed, grabbed his yellow legal pad of paper, and headed down the hall.

As he ran past his mother's room, Lucy yelled out, "What are you doing, dear?"

Lucy had gotten home a little early from the fitness center and had decided to clean up before cooking dinner. She was sitting on the edge of her bed in a bath robe, a white towel wrapped around her head, putting moisturizing cream on her face.

Ricky moonwalked back and poked his head into his mother's room. "I have to watch the world news tonight."

Lucy lowered the small handheld mirror from her face. "The nightly news? What's this all about? I don't remember you ever being interested in the news."

Ricky frowned. "Trust me, Mom, I'm not doing it because I've all of a sudden become interested in world events. It's an assignment for my Civics class—a new assignment. We have to watch the world news every night. Then, every day, our Civics teacher is going to pick someone at random to stand up and give a three to five-minute summary of the previous day's world events."

Lucy smiled, "That's a pretty tricky way to make sure you watched. If he calls on you, and you haven't watched, you're going to be standing there looking pretty dumb."

"Yeah, I know. And it counts for fifty percent of our grade."

As he turned to head downstairs, he gave her a grimacing look. Then, sarcastically, he said, "You look real nice tonight, Mom." Laughing as he ran down the hall, he yelled, "Gotta go, it's 6:30."

Lucy held the little mirror up to her face. She had to admit, with the turban towel wrapped around her head and the white face cream outlining her unadorned eyes and lips, she looked a little scary.

Ricky bolted down the stairs and into the living room. In one fallen swoop, he grabbed the remote, pressed the "on" button, plopped onto the couch, yellow legal pad and a pen in hand, and waited for the television to light up.

The local news had just finished, and Ricky heard the announcer saying, "From NBC World Headquarters in New York, this is the 'NBC Nightly News' with Sawyer Clark."

The tall, slender journalist appeared on the screen. "Good evening, this is Sawyer Clark, and here are our top stories tonight.

"We are waiting for an update on the commercial jetliner that crashed in Saudi Arabia three days ago. Diplomatic difficulties have hampered the release of information.

"Riots have once again erupted on the streets of Los Angeles. A routine traffic stop resulted in the fatal shooting of an African American male in Los Angeles last night. At approximately 11:40 p.m., Officer John McKinley and Walter Bennigan stopped a car for a routine traffic violation.

"When asked for his license and registration, Tyrone Williams, a 33-year-old man from Inglewood, became aggressive and started shouting racial slurs. According to police reports, Williams came at the officers, and he was shot and killed.

"Williams was unarmed, and the incident is being viewed as another senseless police-shooting incident of an unarmed African American man."

"Residents of the Florida Keys are up in arms after the Food and Drug Administration gave the okay to field test a genetically modified Zika-killing mosquito into the Everglades.

"The project is being spearheaded by the giant biotech company Oxitec, and opponents argue that lobbyists for the drug company care more about money than environmental safety. Unfounded accounts claim that a bite by the genetically altered mosquitoes can cause the devastating neurologic syndrome 'Guillain-Barre.' Spokesmen for the drug company point out that 'Guillain-Barre' results from a viral infection, not the bite of an arthropod such as mosquitoes. This will most likely be argued out in the courts.

"In the political news, the President is currently in Europe meeting with world leaders at the G-20 World Economic Summit. We will have that story live from our correspondent Chris Davis in Germany."

Sawyer, looking to a different camera, continued, "And closer to home, a potential environmental mishap has emerged in one of our major western economic states, which could have dire consequences to the water that supplies most of the tourism and agriculture of the West."

He turned back to the main camera. "We will have more on this, and other stories, when the 'Nightly News' continues."

Just as the TV went to a commercial, Lucy came down the stairs wearing a bright yellow fitness jumpsuit and large puffy Yogi-the-Bear slippers. Standing between Ricky and the television, she smiled and said, "Well, how do I look now?"

Ricky frowned. "Where'd you get those slippers?"

Lucy smiled, seemingly proud of her shopping coup. "They were on sale."

Ricky nodded. "I'm sure they were," he said and then motioned for her to move away from in front of the television, explaining that the slippers were a little distracting.

Lucy shrugged. "Anything interesting in the news?"

Ricky shook his head as he looked at his notes on his yellow pad. "They're going to have more on that American airplane that crashed in Saudi Arabia the other day."

"Huh, I heard about that! Any survivors?"

"It was a huge jumbo jet. There's usually not too many survivors." Then he went down his list and told her about the shootings in Los Angeles, the Zika-mosquito thing, the G-20 summit, and some environmental disaster somewhere in the West.

Lucy nodded. "I'm gonna go get supper ready."

As he turned his yellow pad to a fresh page, Sawyer reappeared.

"In our lead story tonight, very little is still known about the commercial jetliner that crashed in Saudi Arabia a few days ago. Apparently, it has sensitive political ramifications for the Saudi government, and details have not been released yet. FAA officials are working with Saudi officials to recover the black boxes from the downed DC-10.

"We have a correspondent, Karin Hadad, in Riyadh, Saudi Arabia and hope to have more on that story tomorrow night."

After Sawyer covered other stories of political and social

unrest, she turned to the large projection screen to her left. "Tonight, a potentially sensitive environmental disaster threatens us, right here, close to home, in the United States."

A large photo of Lake Mead in Nevada appeared on the screen. "During the early hours a few days ago, four trucks carrying barrels of oil through Nevada collided with each other, overturning into Lake Mead, spilling an untold amount of crude oil. It is speculated that the driver of the lead truck may have fallen asleep causing the accident. Although the spill is considered minor, authorities are concerned because Lake Mead is the only source of fresh water for all of Las Vegas, for the turbines that produce most of the electricity for much of the western seaboard, and for the billion-dollar agricultural industry of California."

As Ricky finished taking notes on the environmental story, Sawyer announced that they would be taking a commercial break and that when they return, they would see how one person could make a difference on their nightly "Making a Difference" segment.

Sawyer smiled and said, "We'll be right back."

Ricky put down his pad and pen. He was starved. He went into the kitchen where his mom was setting the table. "What's for supper?"

Lucy was just filling two glasses of milk as she pointed to the plates. "Chicken, bread, salad, potatoes and gravy."

Ricky reached into a bowl of chips and was about to put a

handful into his mouth, when Lucy scolded, "No, no, not before supper."

Ricky dropped the handful of chips—all but one. When Lucy turned, he popped it into his mouth.

With her back to him, she said, "I'm not deaf. I hear someone chewing something crispy."

Ricky didn't say anything; he just chewed his chip.

As Lucy came back to the table, she asked him, "Any earth shaking news?"

Ricky shook his head. "Nothing much. The world's not coming to an end or anything."

# Chapter 14

***

## Georgetown, Washington, D.C.

He didn't like going into this area of D.C., but since everyone had a portable phone, there weren't many of the old Ma Bell coin operated phones left. After driving past the Circle K convenience store, he pulled around to the side of the store avoiding the security cameras in front.

He punched in the area code and 7-digit phone number and waited. An automated operator's voice came on, "That will be three dollars for the first two minutes." After reaching into his pocket and taking out a handful of quarters, he dropped in 12 quarters. After a few rings, a voice at the other end said, "Yeah?"

He looked around. "You got 'em?"

"Yeah, I've got 'em."

"Any problems?"

"Nope."

"Get rid of them." The phone went dead.

# Chapter 15

***

## 86 Pinckney Street
## Boston, Massachusetts

Since it was a nice afternoon, Ricky decided to take the long way home. As he walked along the Esplanade of Ducklings Walk, he heard the chanting of the Harvard rowing crews: "Stroke … stroke … stroke." He stopped and looked out toward Ducklings Island, where he could see three rowing teams pushing their long boats up the river. He was going to be on that rowing crew someday, that is, providing Doctor Christenson didn't land him in Little Bighorn, Montana.

Eventually, he made it around to Pinckney Street. He loved Boston in the fall—the wind in the large maple trees, the rustling of the leaves, the bright colors … but he knew it was only a prelude of what's to come: Boston's cold, wet, dreary winter.

After a meandering walk past the long row of Victorian

homes of Pinckney Street, he climbed the old cement stairs of number 86. Turning the old ornate handle of the big wooden door, he gave it a push. It was locked. Shaking his head, he figured his mother either had an extra session at the fitness center, had stopped at Haymarket for fresh veggies, or was stuck on the Boston T—the infamous Green Line.

Ricky rummaged through his backpack, fished out his copy of the house key, and got out of the cool fall air.

After about an hour of doing his homework, he heard the front door open. "Honey, I'm home."

Ricky yelled back, "Okay. I'm home too. In the kitchen, doing my homework."

Lucy walked into the kitchen and straight over to Ricky. Before he knew what hit him, she'd bent down and gave him a big wet kiss on the cheek. Ricky quickly wiped it with his sleeve. In defiance, she threw her warmup jacket on the table. Ricky looked up at her, shook his head, and with much fanfare popped a huge potato chip in his mouth and chomped with added emphasis. Smiling, he figured they were even.

Lucy pulled out one of the chairs and sat down to take off her tennis shoes. As she untied them, she asked, "Did the teacher call on you today in Civics class?"

Ricky shook his head. "No, but it was a close call. He called on Katie right behind me." Then, with a brief thought, he said, "Maybe it would've been better if he had called on me. I was ready. The chances of him calling on the same person two days in a row are pretty slim. Now Katie's off the hook. She doesn't have to watch the news for the rest of the week."

As Lucy got up and walked over to the refrigerator to start preparing dinner, she said, "Yes, that's true, but maybe the point is that you'll learn something from watching the news."

Ricky wasn't sure about that. He rummaged through his backpack and took out a sheet of paper with big black letters printed across the top: "PARENT-TEACHER CONFERENCE."

Ricky walked over and handed it to his mother.

Lucy looked at it and, with a big smile, said, "Ah! A parent-teacher conference, next Monday."

Before she could say anything more, Ricky interrupted, "Ma, we don't have to go if you don't want to. I know you're tired after working so hard at the fitness center all day. So, if you have to stay late or you want to rest, we can skip it."

Lucy looked at him. "Are you kidding me? I wouldn't miss this. Besides, I can meet this infamous Physics teacher of yours."

Ricky shook his head, trying to paint a gloomy picture of the upcoming encounter. "Ma, you don't want to meet him. He'll probably start talking about the outer edges of the universe or something."

Lucy smiled. "Well, we're going, and that's that. I'll leave work early, come home and get ready, and we'll go together."

Ricky hated being seen at school with his mother. She always wanted to do something embarrassing like hold his hand or walk with her arm over his shoulder as if he were a first grader.

Lucy looked up at the clock. "It's almost six-thirty. You better get ready to watch the news."

Ricky rummaged through his backpack, found his yellow legal pad and pen, and headed for the living room.

Lucy followed him out of the kitchen. "Honey, I'm going to take a quick shower before I finish fixing dinner."

Ricky nodded, then he stopped, turned, and pointed. "Don't leave your warmup jacket on the table. It goes in the dirty clothes hamper. Oh! And don't wear those Yogi-Bear slippers. They're very distracting ... maybe *irritating* is a better word."

Lucy gave him a grimacing look. "I like my Yogi-Bear slippers. I think I'll get you a pair for Christmas."

Ricky didn't say anything. He just headed for the living room, found the remote, and turned on the TV.

After a few minutes of commercials, the news came on. "From NBC World Headquarters in New York, this is the NBC Nightly News with Sawyer Clark."

Sawyer appeared on the screen. "Good evening, I'm Sawyer Clark. In our lead story tonight, after three days of silence, the Saudi Arabian government has released information on the American commercial DC-10 jet airliner that crashed on its approach to King Fahd International Airport in Dammam, Saudi Arabia. The government has confirmed that all 361 passengers aboard were killed. We'll have on-the-ground coverage of that story from our local correspondent Karim Hadad in Dammam.

"Explosion in Turkey kills at least thirty people, another ninety-one injured, when a suicide bomber detonated a bomb in the middle of a large crowd.

"In Economics, the national debt has risen another 1.7 trillion within the first two quarters of this fiscal year. What that means for the American dollar when we continue."

Sawyer turned in his chair, "Please stay with us; we'll have more on all of these stories and our 'Making a Difference' segment after this break."

Ricky scratched a few notes on his pad as a commercial played about cosmetic surgery, then Sawyer reappeared. "Thank you for staying with us. And now for breaking news out of Dammam, Saudi Arabia. We'll go to our local correspondent, Karim Hadad."

On the monitor to Sawyer's left appeared a young Middle Eastern man holding a microphone. "Karim, what can you tell us about this horrific crash?"

After a short pause for the time link, Karim said, "Thank you, Sawyer. I'm standing on the southern perimeter of King Fahd International Airport." The camera zoomed outward as Karim turned and stepped back. "As you can see behind me, it's pretty dark right now in Dammam since we're eight hours ahead of you there in New York.

"A little over two days ago, an American commercial jetliner crashed on its approach to King Fahd International. The wide-body McDonald Douglas DC-10 had been diverted from Bahrain International Airport as a precautionary measure. According to the Bahrain tower, the pilot of the DC-10 had reported warning lights going off in the cockpit. From sources I've talked to here, with the sensitivity of newer high-tech microchips, this is not an uncommon occurrence, but as a precautionary measure, Bahrain's tower followed protocol and diverted the plane to King Fahd Airport.

"As directed, the plane circled to make an approach from a southerly direction to land on eastern runway 2. For whatever reason, Sawyer, the plane undershot the runway and went down two to three miles out, crashing into one of the largest oil ports and oil storage facilities in Saudi Arabia."

Sawyer interrupted, "Why would they divert the plane to King Fahd Airport?"

Karim, shaking his head, said, "That's a good question, Sawyer. Bahrain airport is more frequently used for commercial flights, like this flight from Germany. It's located on the island of Muharraq on the northeastern tip of Bahrain. King Fahd International is used more often for larger cargo planes because it has longer runways than Bahrain, and it's better equipped to handle emergencies, having more and better emergency ground equipment."

Looking at Karim on the large monitor, Sawyer asked, "Karim, do authorities suspect terrorism?"

"Nothing can be ruled out until the black boxes are located and reviewed. I have unofficial information that minutes before the crash, the pilot reported an automatic shutdown of one of the engines. According to engineers at McDonald Douglas, the automatic shutdown of an engine of a DC-10 is a nearly impossible. This does raise the concern of possible foul play. We can only speculate at this point; no one is going to know what went wrong with Flight 1630 from Frankfurt until the black boxes are recovered."

Sawyer asked, "Why haven't they reviewed the black boxes? What's the delay? It's not like they went down over water."

Karim replied, "The challenges of recovering the black boxes would've been less challenging if they had crashed into the nearby ocean. The situation we have here is like nothing I've ever seen." Turning and pointing off into the dark, he continued, "I know it's dark, but let me try to point out what happened here.

"For planes approaching King Fahd International from the south, they fly over Ras Tanura—Saudi Arabia's largest oil facility. This facility is known as Saudi Aramco, and it accounts for over twenty-five percent of the world's oil exports. Planes approaching King Fahd International in this direction normally fly somewhat low over this facility, but the facility is located far enough away from the airport that it has never been an issue."

Ricky was hurriedly scratching down notes, trying to get the details of the story, but the geographic layout of the area was confusing. They had never studied this geographical area in much detail in school. He knew that Saudi Arabia was in the Middle East, a lot of oil came from there, and that it ran along the ocean. He finally decided to just get the details of the story, and he would look up the area on Google Earth later.

Karim was still on the large screen. "Authorities feel pretty confident that this was not a situation of pilot error; not a case of misjudgment or accidentally undershooting of the runway. This plane just simply dropped out of the sky, whether it was a mechanical malfunction, an intentional grounding, or as we have already alluded to, an act of terrorism.

"The reason they haven't retrieved the black boxes…" Karim briefly looked at the notes on his pad. "Sawyer, this is where it gets bizarre. The plane actually went down in the center of a large oil storage facility, an area where there are rows-upon-rows of enormous storage tanks. Each tank holds millions of gallons of thick crude oil that's waiting to be pumped offshore to tankers sitting in the Straits."

Ricky scratched down the word *Straits* with a question mark. "Straits of what?" He knew he would have to know that if he was called on in school.

Turning, Karim pointed in the direction of the Straits of Hormuz, where, off in the distance, the lights of oil tankers could be seen bobbing in the ocean swells.

"Crude oil, Sawyer, is a thick, black gunk; like what we saw on the beaches in Louisiana after the Gulf oil spill, or on the shores of Prudhoe Bay in Alaska a few years ago. Now, keep in mind that crude oil doesn't burn, so there was no fire or explosion when the plane crashed. If crude did burn, they would've just lit a match to what was covering the shores in Louisiana and burned it off."

Sawyer interrupted, "So, if there wasn't an explosion or fire, and they didn't land in the middle of the ocean, they should've found the boxes by now. Where are the black boxes?"

Karim shook his head, taking in a quick, deep breath while attempting to keep his composure and his last meal down. Pointing off into the darkness, he said, "Over there, at the bottom of an enormous moat."

Sawyer's head tilted. "I'm not sure if we're hearing you clearly with our link. Did you say *moat*?"

Karim explained that, for environmental reasons, the storage area had been surrounded by a reinforced concrete ditch with a depth of a couple hundred feet and hundreds of feet wide.

Sawyer, still not understanding, interrupted, "You mean a moat, like we used to see around medieval castles in Europe?"

Karim nodded. "One and the same. It even has a few drawbridges."

Karim described that the facility was surrounded by this containment area in the event there were ever a rupture of one or more of the tanks. "Being that the storage facility is only a few hundred yards from the Straits of Hormuz,..."

Ricky scratched down the word "Hormuz".

"...an oil spill would not only be environmentally catastrophic, it would have economic ramifications worldwide."

Before Karim had hardly finished his sentence, Sawyer blurted out, "So the plane's in the cement containment area?"

Karin shook his head. "Not just the plane." He explained that the plane had made a near perfect landing, sliding straight down the center row. As the plane slid between the tanks, the wings clipped storage tank after storage tank on both sides, rupturing one tank after another, releasing millions gallons of crude oil.

Then he paused, "Here's where it becomes horrifying. Eventually, the wings snapped off the plane, leaving the fuselage sliding along between the tanks like a high-speed train. At the very end of the facility, the fuselage with its 361 passengers dropped off and came to rest at the bottom of the moat."

Ricky sat mesmerized by the story. This was like something out of a movie, like Harrison Ford, sweat pouring off of his face, tension building, as he takes control of Air Force One trying to avoid crashing into the White House.

The show's director switched the screen to Sawyer. She had a solemn expression, intently listening.

The screen switched back to Karim. "Millions of gallons of crude oil from the ruptured tanks filled the moat, engulfing the plane." Karim paused briefly. "The fuselage is sitting at the bottom of a few hundred feet of thick, black crude oil."

Sawyer gasped. Horrified, she shrieked, "*Were they dead? Were they still alive?*"

Karim was trying to avoid the gruesome details of what might have happened. Nodding, he said, "Most likely; the fuselage ended up in the moat intact and still pressurized."

Sawyer, being less seasoned as a reporter than the regulars on the show, was not as equipped with her composure for something as horrifying as this. Sickened by the very thought, she gasped. "The passengers are down there? They're still in the plane? Alive at the bottom of an ocean of oil?"

Karim attempted to allay the situation. "No."

But before he could get another word out, Sawyer blurted out almost angrily, "So they all sat there alive as the oil slowly rose over the top of the plane?"

Now tearful, she tried her best to suppress her emotions. The director didn't know what to do.

Ricky set down his yellow pad and just watched. Sawyer was losing it. The director called for a closeup.

"My God, can you imagine sitting there watching the oil rise over the windows and then being plunged into total darkness?"

After apologizing to her viewers and regaining a little of her composure, she asked submissively, as if not really wanting to know, "How long did they live?"

Karim just shrugged. "No one knows. It could've been hours, it could have been half a day, but it's unlikely they're still alive at this point. Eventually, as the weight of the oil increased, the pressure would've crushed the fuselage like a soda can."

Sawyer totally broke down and announced that they would be back after a commercial break.

Ricky got up and went to the kitchen where Lucy was cooking something on the stove. "Anything exciting on the news?" she asked.

Ricky didn't even hear his mother's question. He was shaken by the report. He couldn't help but think of the people sitting in total blackness, screams filling the cabin of the plane as the sounds of twisting metal creaked and buckled while the structure slowly imploded. Then, slowly suffocating, drowning as their lungs filled with the black gunk.

Lucy could see that his mind was elsewhere. "Hey, you here?"

Ricky came out of his trance. "Oh! Sorry. I was just thinking."

As an afterthought in frustration, he said, "I don't know why oil disasters should even be news anymore. They should just announce whenever there isn't one."

# Chapter 16

***

## Las Vegas, Nevada

Gloria Johnson walked over, found the remote, and turned up the volume on the television as high as it would go. At one time, getting to live near the strip in Vegas seemed like a dream come true, but now the continuous noise, the flashing lights, and the never-ending honking of horns was getting old. She wondered what it would be like if it all just stopped—the cars, the horns, the lights, nothing but the sounds of the cool desert breeze. Knowing that wasn't going to happen, she set the remote down on the coffee table and went to the kitchen to fix dinner. As she rummaged through the refrigerator, she could hear, "Good evening, this is Anna Franklin KXNT with the evening news, live from the Las Vegas strip."

Gloria liked Anna Franklin; she was her favorite newscaster. When she finished her degree at UNLV in Communications, she was going to be just like Anna. No more working these sleazy casinos. No more wearing tights so tight that it cut off the circulation to her legs, the stupid bunny ears, and no more having to push her breasts up so that drunk and obnoxious men could gawk at her. Only six more months before she finished her degree, but for tonight, she had to work the blackjack tables at Caesar's.

From the kitchen, she could hear Anna. "In the news tonight, environmental concerns continue to grow over the oil spill that occurred in Lake Mead almost a week ago. A simple clean-up project that should've taken as little as a day has become a major challenge. Specialized clean-up crews that worked the Deep Horizon oil spill in Louisiana have been called in. For more on this story, we go to the shores of Lake Mead above Boulder City with KXNT reporter Sheila Blake."

Sheila appeared on the screen. "Thank you, Anna. I'm standing here at the site of the oil spill which occurred a week ago with Doctor Carl Jacobs, a chemical engineer and the Director of Research Facilities at BP Amoco PC Oil Refineries in Texas City, Texas. Texas City is the United States' third-largest refining facility, which is located just across the bay from Galveston."

"Doctor Jacobs. Thank you for being here with us. Let me start by asking you, why are they having so much trouble cleaning up what seems to be a small amount of oil? I mean, these guys cleaned up the whole BP oil spill in Louisiana."

Doctor Jacobs nodded.

Sheila couldn't help but smile; he was so darn cute.

Doctor Jacobs was a short, pudgy little man with classic wire-rimmed glasses that hung halfway down his nose, and he wore a jacket that had easily been in style in the forties.

"Well, Ms. Blake, this most certainly does not compare in size to the Gulf oil spill in 2010, yet the crews are having a devil of a time getting it cleaned up."

"Why is that?" Sheila asked, looking back to the camera quizzically for visual effect.

"Well," Doctor Jacobs said, "the oil in these drums seems to have a peculiar density and specific gravity which is affecting its buoyancy." Before Sheila could stop him, he continued, "The viscosity of this oil is not what we normally see in naturally occurring crude. And—"

Sheila politely stopped him. "Doctor Jacobs, I'm sorry to interrupt you, but—density, specific gravity, viscosity—can you put all this into layman's terms? We're not at MIT you know."

Sheila had reviewed Doctor Jacob's background before the interview and knew that he had been a Nobel Laureate from MIT, the Massachusetts Institute of Technology, and was a world's expert on the chemistry of oil.

Doctor Jacobs nodded his head. "I'm sorry, Sheila. As you know, oil floats on water, like melted butter in a pan of water. No matter how hard you stir or shake oil and water, when you stop, the oil floats back to the top. That's density."

Sheila nodded.

"Now," he continued, "the problem here is that this oil is not floating on the surface of the water like normal oil. It's formed an oil slick that is staying submerged about eight to ten feet *below* the surface."

Sheila interrupted. "So those guys can't get at it, and they can't contain it with those yellow floating barriers that we always see at oil spills?"

"Exactly," he responded, shaking his head, "and they can't just use their skimmers. The stuff is hanging there in a long slick of oil submerged about ten feet down, not sinking to the bottom and not floating to the top."

As Gloria listened, she stared into the refrigerator like 'Old Mother Hubbard' who went to the cupboard; it was bare. She turned and started to open cupboard doors to see what she could find.

"Doctor Jacobs, do you have any idea why this oil is different, where it might've come from, and what it's doing here in Nevada of all places?"

He shook his head. "No, Ms. Blake, not at this time, but we'll know when we get it back to our labs in Texas City." Doctor Jacobs went on to explain that not all oils were created equally, explaining that each oil deposit around the world has its own unique "chemical fingerprint.'"

Sheila interrupted him quizzically, "Fingerprint?"

Doctor Jacobs smiled; this was his specialty and where he had won the Nobel Prize. He continued to explain that the term "crude,'" as in "crude oil,'" was just a useful starting point to describe fossil fuel deposits, explaining that each deposit worldwide was a remnant mixture of the plants and animals that had lived and died in that specific area millions of years ago. Keeping it simple, because he knew it was actually plankton at the bottoms of the oceans billions of years ago, for the benefit of Sheila's listeners, the dinosaurs analogy was easier to understand.

Sheila was all excited. "You mean like one area might've had a little higher dinosaur content, maybe more T-Rex's, while another area had more Reuter Raptors."

Gloria stood in the doorway to the living room eating a bowl of Cheerios, shaking her head. "What a ditz." She could do a lot better than that Sheila Blake. She was only there because she was a ditsy blond with big boobs.

Doctor Jacobs smiled. "Something like that, but at MIT, we like to think of it more in terms of the hydrocarbon content." Jacobs went on to explain that hydrocarbons were the things in crude oil that burned.

Again, Sheila was excited; this brought back memories of her days of high school chemistry. She blurted out, "You mean the gasoline content?"

Gloria couldn't stand to watch her. As she turned to go put the bowl in the sink, she mumbled, "Twit."

Again, Doctor Jacobs could only smile. "It's a little more than just the gasoline content. There's the sulfur content, the iron content, and the ratios of those different hydrocarbons." Smiling, he continued, "We like to call it, 'Environmental Forensics.'"

After a little more discussion, Sheila wrapped up the

interview, sending it back to Anna. The camera panned out with the lake in the background. "This is Sheila Blake for KXNT news, live from Lake Mead, Boulder City."

Anna reappeared, thanked Sheila, and announced that after a short break they would hear from Matt Olsen at Nevada's State Department of Justice for an update on the criminal proceedings of the men and the company involved in this environmental disaster.

Gloria headed off to the bathroom to comb her hair and get dressed. She had to be at work in an hour. She hated the late shift; it went on until three in the morning. Looking at herself in the mirror, she announced into her hairbrush, "This is Gloria Johnson sitting in for Sheila Blake, who has been fired for being a ditz." Gloria smiled and started putting on her ridiculous black tuxedo outfit and bunny ears.

Through the mirror, she could see the TV behind her as Anna Franklin reappeared after the commercial break.

"Thank you for staying with us," Anna announced. "And now we'll go to Matt Olsen at the State Department of Justice for an update on the criminal proceedings in this environmental disaster."

As Gloria buttoned up the skimpy tuxedo, she stared at Matt. *What a hunk.* He was another reason she wanted Sheila's job.

Matt thanked Anna, then he said, "Anna, unfortunately I have very little to report. This seemingly minor oil spill has become a very complicated and political issue. There seems to be a lot of friction between the FBI at the local level and the Department of Homeland Security at the National level. Although, theoretically, the FBI is part of Homeland Security, neither the FBI nor Homeland Security are talking apparently—not to each other or to us. From what I could gather, each is accusing the other of holding back information."

Anna interrupted, "Matt, someone must be questioning the men driving those trucks? Do we have any information on the whereabouts of these guys?"

"Well, Anna, this is where things get a little strange. Our sources tell us that the eleven men involved in the oil spill were being held by the local FBI branch here in Las Vegas but have since been turned over to some other branch of Homeland Security."

"Why all of this FBI stuff, and not just the local State guys?"

Matt shrugged, explaining that it must have been because these trucks crossed state lines, and that makes it Federal.

"What about the trucks?" Anna asked.

Matt shook his head. "Gone."

Anna didn't give up. "The barrels?"

Matt shrugged. "Gone."

"The men, let me guess, gone." Anna said sarcastically.

Matt nodded as he unfolded a piece of paper that he pulled out of his jacket. Looking at the name on the paper, he said, "I tried to get an interview with an agent from our local branch of the FBI here in Las Vegas, an Agent Kelly, but he was unavailable for comment."

"Matt," Anna began incredulously, "trucks, people, and barrels of oil don't just disappear."

Matt cocked his eyebrows. "I'm not so sure about that, not when Homeland Security is involved. People have been known to just disappear."

Matt couldn't help but remembering the movie "Rendition" and knew that at times people disappeared at the hands of Homeland Security. He didn't say it out loud, but if that movie was any indication of what can happen, these guys were probably on some South Pacific Island getting waterboarded.

Anna turned back to the main camera and announced, "That was Matt Olsen from the State Department of Justice reporting on the current legal ramifications of the oil spilled into Lake Mead." Then she signed off, "This is Anna Franklin from KXNT news in Las Vegas. We'll have more on our eleven o'clock edition of the news. Thank you for being with us."

Gloria grabbed the remote, turned off the television, and headed out the door to deal Blackjack for the next ten hours.

# Chapter 17

***

## Massachusetts Preparatory School For the Advancement of the Sciences

It was a perfect evening for a walk; the trees were just starting to show a tinge of yellow and orange, bikers were whizzing around, and the ducks that resided on Frog Pond coasted along lazily looking for patrons to throw them some bread crumbs. Lucy and Ricky had decided to take a roundabout route to the Parent-Teacher's Night at Ricky's school by going through the Boston Public Gardens. As they made their way to the corner of Beacon and Arlington streets, Ricky could see the school ahead.

Shaking his hand loose from his mother's grip, he said, "Mom, don't be trying to hold my hand or anything at school. You'll embarrass me."

Lucy put her hands to her cheeks, "Oh, God forbid that anyone would ever see you holding your mother's hand."

Ricky rolled his eyes. "Mom, let's just make an appearance and get out of there."

As they walked along, Lucy told him that they were not just going to make an appearance and get out of there, but that she wanted to meet all of his teachers and discuss his progress.

Ricky frowned and sighed. He just knew she was going to embarrass him. He was sure that none of the other kids were going to bring their mommies.

As they got closer, Ricky picked up the pace, trying to put a little distance between himself and his mother. Lucy smiled to herself, but she understood the pressures of teenagers. Ahead, she could see the cement pillars of the Massachusetts Preparatory School for the Advancement of the Sciences. It was an old rustic Bostonian landmark with wide cement steps leading up to two huge hand-carved wooden doors and topped with a clock tower.

As they neared the steps, Ricky clasped his hands behind his back. He wasn't taking any chances that at the last moment Lucy would grab his hand. Halfway up the steps, he stopped. "Mom, why can't you just see my progress when I get my report card?"

Lucy smiled, "I have a better idea. Let's start with your Physics teacher."

Rick dropped his head in defeat. "I have an even better idea. Let's *not* start with my Physics teacher. Maybe if we leave him till last, you'll be tired, or it'll be too late, and we can go home."

Lucy gave him a little nudge to continue up the steps. "I like my idea better. Lead the way."

As they entered the building, Ricky headed down the hallway making sure he stayed, at minimum, an arm's length to avoid any slip-up of his mother's terrible habit of reaching for his hand at the last moment. Halfway down the hall, a cute little girl named Katie stopped and said, "Hi."

Ricky introduced his mother to Katie and her parents, and then they continued on. Ricky was looking ahead—a few more doors. It was make or break time. Trying to distract his mom, he made small talk pointing out old school photos that were hanging on the wall. Then, Lucy suddenly stopped, all excited. "What's this?"

Ricky gave out an exasperated sigh. She was pointing to a door with frosted windows. Stenciled in black letters was the single word, "PHYSICS."

She looked at Ricky with a cynical smile. "Boy! That was a close one. We almost walked right past it."

Ricky rolled his eyes.

Lucy looked to see if there was a sign-up sheet or any kind of a scheduling sheet. After not seeing one, she asked, "Are we supposed to knock, or do we just go in?"

Ricky shrugged. "Who cares? Just knock and let's just get this over with."

Lucy gave a soft tap that was hardly audible. Ricky looked at her and said, "That wasn't a knock." Ricky stepped over and gave a good rap on the door with his knuckles. At first, they heard nothing. Ricky seized the moment and said, "Must be busy. Let's go. We can come back later."

Then Lucy heard a pleasant, "Enter!"

As Ricky reached for the doorknob, Lucy's hand struck out like a flash of lightning, streaking toward it, but Ricky was ready and whipped his hand back quickly. Lucy grinned with a sarcastic little smile. "Oops, sorry. Habit." Just as Ricky was about to push the door open, Lucy whispered, "He sounds nice."

Ricky shook his head in disbelief. "Mom, he only said one word."

The room looked like a classic Physics room. There were multiple workbenches, weights, pulleys, scales, and a few Bunsen burners. Doctor Christenson stood up from behind his desk and walked over to greet Ricky and his mother. Ricky looked at his mom. "Mom, this is Doctor Christenson, my Physics teacher." Then he looked at Doctor Christenson. "Doctor Christenson, this is my mom."

Lucy extended her hand, thinking to herself, *My, my, this guy is good looking.* With a smile, she said, "My name is Lucy, and I've heard a lot about you. It's very nice to meet you."

Doctor Christenson took her hand and smiled back. Ricky just stood there, waiting. *Geez,* he felt like interjecting, *You can let go of my mom's hand now at any time.*

Ricky may have only been sixteen going on seventeen, but

this didn't take a rocket scientist or a physicist. Doctor Christenson wasn't looking at his mom, he was looking into her eyes, and she wasn't resisting. Ricky wanted to vomit.

Then, not taking his eyes off of her, he said, "You know, I've always loved that name, Lucy. You know, Lucy was the first little hominid to walk the planet. Lucy in the sky with diamonds."

Doctor Christenson finally let go of her hand and pointed to a couple of chairs. "Make yourselves comfortable." As they sat down, he walked around his desk and said, "I hope what you've heard about me so far has been good."

Lucy smiled. "The reviews have been mixed so far." Ricky gave his mother a glare.

Doctor Christenson opened a desk drawer and pulled out Ricky's folder. Then, with just a hint of sarcasm, he said, "I always seem to get mixed reviews," flipping Ricky's folder open, "but not to worry; most of the time, I try to keep an open mind when grading."

Ricky turned slightly toward Lucy and, in a low, hardly audible whisper, said, "Great, Mom, I'll go pack for Montana."

The room was so quiet that you could have heard a pin drop. Doctor Christenson smiled. "Did I hear Montana? Big Sky Country. I didn't know you were considering leaving all of this for the open country."

Lucy could not help but laugh. This guy actually had a sense of humor. Not only was he good looking; he was smart, and he was not wearing a wedding ring.

As she sat grinning, she explained to Doctor Christenson that Ricky was convinced he was going to flunk his Physics class and end up in a small college in Iowa, Montana, or the Dakotas. Before Ricky had time to react, Lucy's hand struck out as fast as a rattle snake and grabbed hold of his hand.

"Personally," she began, smiling, "I actually like the idea of Montana. I told him I could see him meeting a nice cowgirl, herding some cattle, and making his mother a grandmother—a set of twins, Angus and Braveheart."

Ricky didn't think this was funny, looking at her scornfully, his face beet red, "Mom, you're not funny. Let's go."

Doctor Christenson laughed. "I doubt he'll end up in Montana. He's doing great in my class—an "A+" student." As he closed Ricky's folder, he sat forward, putting his elbows on his desk. "We'll not only get him into Harvard, but I know some people, and maybe we'll get him on that rowing team."

That perked Ricky up a little. Doctor Christenson had been aware of Ricky's dream of being on the famous Harvard rowing team, pushing up the St. Charles River.

Sitting back, he continued, "I know I get a lot of mixed reviews. I've even heard through the grapevine that the students are working on a conspiracy theory. They think I might be a little nuts."

Lucy was still grinning. "That's the theory I've heard."

Ricky looked at her. "Mom, my God!"

Doctor Christenson turned in his chair and pointed to a framed quotation hanging on the wall. He said, "A well-known professor from Edinburgh, Scotland once said, 'Attempting to explain a scientific quandary can be a lot more difficult than just reporting scientific facts.'" He turned back and looked at Lucy. "I know I could easily just tell the students to memorize the textbooks and regurgitate the facts; that's what the public schools do. But that's not what Harvard, Yale, and Princeton want. They want thinkers—Bill Gates, Zuckerberg, Einstein."

Lucy liked this guy. Looking at Ricky, she said, "That's why I'm paying all of this money for private school."

After another twenty minutes, during which time Doctor Christenson reassured him that he was not going to end up at Little Big Horn Community College, he stood up and walked them to the door.

Lucy put out her hand. "It was a pleasure to meet you."

Doctor Christenson stood in the doorway and watched as they walked down the hall. After a few doors, they stopped in front of the door for Ricky's civics class. As they stood waiting, one of the hall lights shined directly onto Lucy's dark auburn hair. Doctor Christenson smiled, turned, and closed the door.

It took about an hour or so to see the rest of the teachers. As they stood at the corner of Beacon and Arlington, waiting for the light, Lucy said, "Your Physics teacher is a pretty good-looking guy, and he seems very smart."

Ricky just rolled his eyes.

# Chapter 18

***

## Bayou Cane, Louisiana

Jay, of "Jay and Ray's 'Devil's Swamp Airboat Tours'", was changing the bearings on the big fan of the airboat, getting ready for another busy weekend of tourists. Ray was off in the back room of the "Devil's Lair-Swamp Tours Hideout" putting fresh strips of swamp grass and the skeletal remains of crawfish on the life jackets.

Jay and Ray had landed on hard times after the Environmental Protection Agency had closed the swamp to commercial crawfishing after it had been learned that the country's chemical companies had been using the swamp as dumping grounds for toxic waste for years. According to locals, the waters were so toxic that it had spawned a swamp monster known to thrive on the flesh of children. What at first had been a devastating blow to Jay and Ray, who had known nothing all of their lives but crawfishing, in the end had turned out to be a godsend.

One day, while Jay was working on his airboat, a city slicker-looking guy had somehow made his way through the mud and rapped on the door of his shack, which would become known as "The Devils Lair." The guy said that he was looking for a location to make a "Swamp Monster" movie and wanted to know if he knew his way around the swamps and if he would take him out on his airboat. The guy paid Jay $300 dollars for a one-hour tour, which was more than he made in a week catching crawfish. Now, Jay and Ray had a thriving business taking tourists through the haunted swamps of Devil's Lake.

Ray especially liked the night tours though the swamps. He and Jay had hooked up a gismo to the fuel line, and when they were in the darkest depths of the swamp Jay would cut off the fuel to the engine. It would spit and sputter and then stop. For special effects, they would sit in the darkness, the deafening sounds of the night creatures filling the air, while Jay would frantically be trying to get the engine going. Then, after a dramatic effort, he would announce in defeat that they would have to get out and walk back out of the swamps.

By now, while back at the Devil's Lair waiting for their journey into the swamps to begin, they had already seen the grainy photos of "roux-ga-roux" the green moss-covered monster that roamed the marshes, who, according to the local Cajuns, preyed especially on the flesh of children.

Shining a flashlight up into his face, Ray would go through a dramatic ritual of having everyone tighten their life jackets and explaining the dangers of the perilous journey ahead.

Then, just before stepping out of the airboat, in a very somber manner, Ray would explain what they were to do if someone got pulled under by a gator. While shining his light along the shoreline, looking for the beady eyes of lurking gators, he would explain how immediately after a gator got its prey, there was always a short frantic feeding frenzy—a period where all the other gators in the area would fight over the bounty. That, he told everyone, was the only time and chance the rest had to get away, stressing that at this point nothing could be done for the unfortunate victim. Everyone else had to keep moving.

Ray loved to keep up the dramatics until at least one child was crying, and then, miraculously, Jay would get the boat started.

As Jay was finishing tightening up the bolts to the large fan of the airboat, he heard Ray yelling to him, "Jay. Hey, Jay, come here."

Ray was adding the swamp monster look to the life jackets and listening to Cajun music on their A.M. radio.

Jay walked in. "Yeah! What's up?"

Ray pointed to the radio. "Listen to this."

Ray turned up the volume. "This is WDSU out of New Orleans with breaking news. Last night, eleven members of a local cleanup crew were killed when their boat exploded in a mangrove area somewhere in the Barataria-Terrebonne Estuary."

Jay knew that it was common practice for the big oil company BP-British Petroleum to hire locals who owned their own boats to go into the mosquito and alligator infested mangroves to clean up oil that still resided after the Deepwater Horizon oil disaster months earlier.

"The eleven, whose names have not yet been released, were all from the Dry Creek area."

Jay was wiping grease off his hands. "Geez, man. That's only twenty-thirty miles from here. You know anybody in Dry Creek?" Ray asked.

Jay nodded. "A few. I know this guy Darrell. Used to see him every year at the crawfish bash. Otherwise, I don't know those guys."

Ray shook his head. "Man, they ain't ever gonna find those guys. They're alligator poop by now."

# Chapter 19

***

## Hoover Dam
## Boulder City, Nevada

Philip Rossi hated having to drive into Boulder Canyon for the afternoon shift, especially in the middle of the summer. Being the shift manager for the hydroelectric plant at Hoover Dam was not the problem, it was the damned tourists, the damned unrelenting 110-degree heat, and the damned dust. He had been born and raised in Florida, where windshield wipers were used to clear water off your windshield, not dust and tumbleweed.

Despite having left an extra half hour early, he was still going to be late for work today. It had taken him twice the time it normally took to drive the twenty miles from Boulder City to the access ramp that lead into the power plant. The traffic on State Road 172 leading to the site-seeing O'Callaghan-Tillman Memorial Bridge was bumper-to-bumper with tourists.

As he sat lost in thought and moving at a snail's pace, a piece of tumbleweed the size of a tank smashed into the side of his car. It hardly phased him. A few days earlier, he had run over a jackrabbit the size of a donkey. Now, he watched as the temperature gauge on his dashboard slowly rose toward the red, and, ahead, he could see the greeting sign, "Welcome to Nevada."

After another half hour of turning the air conditioner on and off, praying to God that the damn car didn't overheat, he reached the Employee Parking lot of the Hoover Dam Hydroelectric Power Plant.

Sweating like a pig, he made his way to his office, "The Office of Maintenance and Management," for the eight turbines in the Nevada wing of Hoover Dam. Diego Mendez was in charge of the nine turbines in the Arizona wing.

No sooner had he walked into his office when his phone started ringing. It was an intercom phone from the Turbine Room. He grabbed the phone. "Yeah!"

"Hey, Philip, it's Davis. I'm in the Turbine Control Room."

Rossi looked up at the large screen that displayed the electronic grid which showed the status of each of the eight turbines and their power output in real time. Philip spotted it just as Davis said, "One of the turbines has tripped."

Philip couldn't believe it. Looking at the screen, he mumbled, "Are you kidding me?" Of the eight turbines on the Nevada wing, seven were green, turbine #6 was red. All nine on the Arizona side were green.

Philip knew that they had never had a turbine trip its power supply on its own since the plant was built over eighty-years ago, but now, sure as hell, turbine #6 had shut itself down.

Turning to his computer, he punched in a series of numbers and then said to Davis, "Wasn't that turbine just opened, stripped down, and serviced a week ago?" He did not give Davis time to answer. "Why the hell would it shut down?"

Davis had no idea, but he did remember that when they had opened it, it stunk. No one had thought much of it at the time.

Since the buck had to stop somewhere, Philip wasn't going to have it dropped into his lap. He barked at Davis, "Look, you're the guy in charge of maintenance of those turbines. We've never had one shut down by itself—ever. And now, a week after you mess with it, it doesn't work?" Philip continued his barrage of questions, not letting Davis get a word in edgewise. "So, what's up?"

Finally, "We don't know," Davis said, "it just overheated."

Philip shook his head in exasperation. Five years earlier, he had been sitting in Windsor, a little suburb town of Hartford, Connecticut, climbing the corporate ladder of Con Edison, the giant power company. Then, someone at Con Edison got the bright idea to invest in the power plant in Boulder City, which everyone at Con Edison kept referring to as Boulder City, Colorado, the beautiful, mountainous state of ski slopes and hiking. But, as Philip was to find out, it was actually Boulder City, Nevada—flat, barren, and hot as hell. So much for climbing the corporate ladder. He was transferred to head up the operations at Boulder Dam.

Once Philip got there, it was apparent that no one in beautiful Connecticut had ever actually gone to Boulder Dam, which was more correctly Hoover Dam, and more correctly in Nevada, not Colorado. Only the water came from Colorado.

He hated Nevada. It was a waterless inferno not fit for life other than jackrabbits and tumbleweed. He often marveled at the great deal the government had given the Indians: "We'll keep Connecticut, you guys can have Nevada except for where there are areas of water. And, thanks for inviting us over for dinner. We'll make it a 'national holiday.'" If he was ever to get the hell out of Nevada, he didn't need turbines shutting down all by themselves.

He had now only been in his office for fifteen minutes. He had been run over by a giant piece of tumbleweed and sweated to death for over an hour, and now this. "Look," he shouted at Davis, "those turbines don't overheat. Jesus Christ, they're like jet engines. Those things are almost frictionless, and there sitting in a tub of grease that's almost as thick as cement."

Davis just waited for Philip to get over his ranting and raving.

"And," he barreled on, "they're cooled by a couple million gallons of water a minute from the spillways."

"I know," Davis said, but he didn't want to get into a shouting match with Philip. He had been servicing the turbines for years, and he had no idea why one would trip itself. But when they had opened the thing a week earlier, they had noted a peculiarity, but no one had made much of it.

Philip was looking at his computer. "Why'd you guys service that thing? It wasn't due for six months."

Davis explained that deep within the turbine, some internal sensors had shown an increase in the resistance, so they opened it to check the sensors.

Philip knew that with all the modern technology, the little micro sensors were sensitive little buggers, and it had to be a sensor problem because there wasn't really much to a turbine, just a spinning ball of steel in a bundle of copper wires.

"Did you replace the sensors?" Philip asked.

"Yeah, of course," Davis said.

Davis didn't want to say anything because he didn't really know if it had anything to do with the current problem, but when they had opened turbine #6, the grease in the thing was thin and watery, and it stunk like a pig. Not knowing what to make of it, they just cleaned it out, packed it with new grease, and sealed it up.

"Okay," Philip said, "what's done is done. Open the damn thing up, strip it down again, and get it running."

Davis told him that they had already started.

# Chapter 20

***

## 86 Pinckney Street
## Boston, Massachusetts

Ricky turned off the path along the Charles River and headed east on Pinckney Street. He walked along with his head down, earphones blaring loud music in his ears, and his fingers twitching on his iPad. A bicyclist heading in the other direction screamed at him to watch where he was going, but Ricky, lost in some tweet rant, never even looked up.

Meanwhile, Lucy had gotten off the Green line at Bowdoin Street, walked over to Hancock, and turned west onto Pinckney Street. When she got in front of the little sign for 86 Pinckney, she stopped in the middle of the sidewalk and stood waiting. She could see Ricky coming straight at her from the other direction with his head down. He never even looked up. She braced herself for the collision, and Ricky walked right into her.

Pulling the little headphones from his ears, he looked up. "Oh … hi, Mom."

Lucy told him he needed to watch where he was going as she gave him a hug while trying to slip in a quick peck on the forehead. Ricky squirmed away, looking around and worried that someone might have seen it.

"Ma."

Lucy pursed her lips. "Well, excuse me. I'm your mother, and I can give you a little kiss if I want."

He looked around. "That's fine, but not out here in the street."

Lucy sighed and quickly brushed it off. As they climbed the stairs, she asked, "How was school today?"

Expecting a dismal, disgruntled reply, she was quite surprised. "Great. I came up with an idea for my physics project! It's really, really good, and I think it's gonna get me an A+."

As they walked into the kitchen, Ricky went over and set his backpack gently on the table. He glanced over at his mother, and with a devilish smile, he gave it a little push. Lucy nodded, set the mail that she had under her arm down on the center counter, took off her sweaty warm-up jacket, and gently dropped it on top of Ricky's backpack.

Ricky grimaced, nodding toward the sweaty jacket. "Dirty laundry goes in the laundry basket."

Lucy shrugged. "Backpack goes on the chair." It was a standoff. Lucy pulled out a chair and sat down to take off her shoes. "Let's hear about your project."

Ricky was excited. "Okay, okay, but you might be a little disappointed."

Lucy looked up, a little confused. "Why would I be disappointed?"

Ricky smiled, "Because there's not gonna be any junior college in Little Big Horn, Montana. No cowgirl. No herding cattle. No twins. No Angus and Braveheart. Gonna be right here in Boston … Harvard."

Lucy told him that maybe he shouldn't count his chickens before they hatch and that she was not giving up hope for Angus and Braveheart. "So, whatcha got?"

Ricky pulled a magazine out of his backpack. "Listen to this," he began, holding up the magazine for Lucy to see, "I was in the library today, sitting there, just thinking, and I spotted this magazine." He pointed to the one in his hand.

Ricky went on to explain that some scientists in Belgium had recently discovered that plants emitted electromagnetic waves of radiation in response to stress, pain, and human emotions. He explained to Lucy how the scientists were working on converting the electromagnetic waves emitted by the plants into radio frequencies.

Lucy didn't quite get it yet and how this was going to relate to his physics project. She lifted her eyebrows quizzically. "Aaaand…?"

"Ma," Ricky burst out, "we might end up having a whole new language to learn, just like we learn Spanish, French, or German, but now we'll have to learn 'Plant'."

Lucy tilted her head, her eyebrows furrowed, and with a look of confusion said, "And that's going to change the direction of society?"

Ricky was bursting with excitement. "Can you imagine what it would be like if we could talk to plants? Just like that Dr. Dolittle did in the movie where he talked to the animals."

Lucy smiled. "I remember that movie," she said and then started to sing the little song. "If I could talk to the animals, walk with the animals, sing with an orangutan too." Ricky tried to stop her, but she was on a roll. "I could chat with cheetah, speak antelope and pachyderm and converse with the animals in the zoo."

Ricky interrupted, "Yeah, sounds good, right?"

Lucy nodded; it actually sounded pretty good to her. She told Ricky that having a plant or a tree for a friend would be like having a pet. And, she pointed out that you wouldn't have to clean up after it, wouldn't have to have a smelly sandbox, and if you took it for a walk, you wouldn't have to worry about it biting someone. "I like it," she replied with a smile.

Ricky shook his head. "Nope! Wrong! It would be the event that changes the direction of society."

Lucy kicked off her shoes and went over to the refrigerator to start getting things ready for supper. Taking out a couple of fresh pieces of tuna and pouring a little olive oil in a pan, she asked, "How's that?"

As she had her back turned, Ricky got up, stealthily

walked over, and grabbed a handful of chips from the chip bowl. Before he could get even one chip in his mouth, Lucy scolded, "No, not before supper."

Ricky was always amazed at how his mother did that, like she had eyes in the back of her head. He had been so quiet, and she wasn't even looking. He had come to the conclusion that it was just a mother thing.

"Please, Ma," he pleaded, "just one?"

Lucy rolled her eyes. "Okay, just one."

Ricky pushed the whole handful of chips into his mouth. Lucy looked at him, exasperated. "I thought I said just one."

Ricky, acting surprised, as if he misunderstood, said, "Oh! I thought you meant one handful."

Lucy shook her head. "You know what I meant."

After Ricky had set the table and Lucy had everything ready, they sat down to eat. "Okay, so how is talking to plants going to change the course of society?"

Ricky, with his mouth half full, said, "Can you imagine the psychological impact on society if we could feel and hear the thoughts of plants?"

With a mouth full of lettuce, Lucy just shrugged. She wasn't sure.

"Think about it. Think about the psychological stress there would be on a lumberjack guy that was about to cut down a tree. Can you imagine what it'd be like for him if during the whole time that his chainsaw was cutting into the tree, he could hear the tree screaming and pleading with him? 'Please! Please, don't kill me! Why are you killing me? I haven't done anything to you!' And then imagine as he stood over the dying tree, watching the sap ooze from the open wound like blood squirting from someone's neck after being slit with a knife."

Lucy was almost getting nauseated, but Ricky continued. "And then, think of this, as the lumberjack stood there waiting as the dying tree took her final gasping breath, he heard a baby seedling just yards away, 'Mommy, mommy, don't die.'"

Lucy set down her fork and suggested that maybe they should finish this after dinner, but Ricky plowed on. "What about this? Can you imagine just taking a nice Sunday walk in the park, and with every step you take, as your feet are crushing to death hundreds of little blades of grass, you hear the screams of the rest of the grass in the park, yelling at you, 'Murderer! Murderer!'"

Lucy was getting a little creeped out watching her sweet little boy go from Dr. Jekyll to Mr. Hyde. Pouring a little more oil and vinegar on her salad, she took another mouthful and started to chew.

"Awe!" Ricky blurted out, scaring Lucy half-to-death.

"Do you hear them?"

Lucy looked at him, bewildered. "Do I hear what?"

"Them … the poor little plants. Those little leaves of lettuce that you're chewing. Do you hear them with each crushing bite of your teeth?"

Ricky held his bowl of salad up to his ear. “Shhh … do you hear them screaming?” Then he gave an eerie, “Whooooau,” and leaned forward. “That’s my physics project, Ma, the force that will change the direction of society. With a quivering voice, he said, “Maaaaaad. Everyone maaaaaad.”

Lucy put down her fork, “How am I supposed to eat?”

Ricky nodded. “Exactly. That’s the inertia, the force that would change the direction of society.”

Lucy had to agree that it was a pretty clever idea, but she still liked the cellphone idea better.

Ricky just rolled his eyes. “Yeah, that was a doozy.”

Lucy looked up at the kitchen clock. ”Oh, it’s almost six-thirty. You better go watch the news. I’m gonna go up and shower.”

As they were walking out of the kitchen, Ricky stopped and looked back at the table. ”Aren’t you going to eat the rest of your salad?” Then he smiled.

Ricky got comfortable on the couch, his yellow legal pad and a pen in hand, and waited. After a few minutes, the NBC logo came on. “From NBC World Headquarters in New York, this is the NBC Nightly News with Savannah Guthrie.”

“Good evening, I’m Savannah Guthrie, sitting in for Brian Williams this evening. In our top stories tonight;

“In Zimbabwe, police used tear gas and water cannons on demonstrators who were picketing over the deteriorating economic situation in that country. Many were hospitalized. No deaths have been reported.

"As austerity efforts continue throughout Europe, riots broke out in Italy, Greece, and Portugal in what many are saying is the worst economic crisis to hit Europe in years. The Euro hangs in the balance.

"And, closer to home, in the news tonight, more on the stalemate in Congress between Democrats and Republicans. But first, we're going to go live to our correspondent, Karim Hadad, in Dammam, Saudi Arabia for the continued coverage of the American DC-10 passenger jetliner that crashed last week in the Aramco oil fields—Saudi Arabia's largest oil refinery. Karim."

"Thank you, Savannah. I'm standing only a few hundred yards from one of the worst airline disasters in history. As we've been following this story, a little over a week ago, an American commercial jetliner crashed into a number of gigantic oil storage tanks here on the Saudi peninsula. As we reported last week, the plane ended up sitting at the bottom of a moat that surrounds the storage tanks. This moat is two hundred feet deep, and it was built to contain oil in the event of a rupture of those tanks."

Savannah interrupted. "Karim, have they been able to get to the plane yet?"

Karim turned and gestured to the large moat behind him. "Yes, Savannah, they've been pumping the oil from the moat to three large tankers offshore. You can see the lights of those tankers over my right shoulder. After days of pumping, they're finally to the bottom of the containment area, and most of the plane, as you can see, is now visible."

"Karim, have they been able to get to the passengers inside the plane?"

"Yes, Savannah, they have, and this is pretty horrifying. It appears that everyone was alive when the plane slid into the moat, and it appears that the fuselage stayed pressurized."

"My God," Savannah gasped, "you mean that they sat there alive as the oil engulfed the plane?"

Karim nodded. "That's right, and no one knows how long they sat there in the darkness before the pressure of the oil imploded the windows and the plane filled with the thick, black oil."

She attempted to keep her composure. "It must've been sheer hell, torture, sitting there in the blackness waiting to die."

Karim nodded in agreement. "No one knows how long they may have sat there panic stricken. We can only pray it wasn't long."

"Oh," Savannah gasped, "can you imagine drowning in oil?" Regaining her composure, she continued, "Have they removed the bodies or identified the passengers?"

"Not yet," Karim told her. "As gruesome as this sounds, they have to use degreasing compounds to clean the bodies."

Savannah interrupted, almost angrily, "You mean like cleaning the pelicans in Louisiana after the BP oil spill?"

Karim didn't respond; he just nodded.

Savannah told Karim to hold on, that they were going to a commercial break, and that she had more questions when they returned.

Ricky got up and went to the kitchen to get a glass of water and took a handful of chips. By the time he got back, Savannah was asking Karim about the oil tankers offshore.

"Karim, you mentioned that the oil was being pumped into tankers just offshore. What can you tell me about the tankers?"

Karim turned and pointed out over the gulf. "Yes, Savannah, the oil has been pumped to three tankers that were empty and waiting to be filled. The tanker to your far left is owned by the Indian Oil Corporation from Mathura, India. That oil will go to the Bay of Bengal somewhere. The tanker in the middle is owned by the Nippon Sendaie Oil Company from Japan, and a third one is from Donghai Island in the Guangdong Province of China. So, the oil is safely contained in oil tankers, the Straits were not contaminated, and the containment area, the moat, did its job."

Savannah smirked. "So all's well that ends well, except for three hundred people on an airplane."

Karim could only shrug.

The picture flashed back to the news desk at NBC studios in New York City as Savannah announced that after a commercial break they would return with their "Making a Difference" segment.

Lucy came down the stairs in a bathrobe with a white towel wrapped around her wet hair. "Anything in the news?"

# Chapter 21

***

## BP Amoco Research and Refineries
## Texas City, Texas

Kathy Gregory had been having a good week until now. She had planned on having an even better weekend. She and her girlfriend Nancy were planning to go the Brews Brothers Bar, a local watering hole for the young doctors of the nearby medical school. According to her "Lucky Stars Moon Watch Charts," Venus, the planet of love, was in her constellation, and Jupiter was snuggling up next to Venus. Woohoo! But now, she sat staring at all the blinking lights on her Mass Spectroscopy machine.

The morning had gone well—the Brews Brothers Bar, the stars, Jupiter and Venus were all lining up perfectly. Nancy had sent her a text: "Woohoo! Can't wait."

By ten a.m., she only had eight more oil samples to run—three from an oil field in Nigeria, three from a new offshore drill somewhere in China, and two from a

Canadian shale facility. At fifteen-to-twenty minutes a sample, she had hoped to be done by two in the afternoon. That was until her boss, Doctor Jacobs, had slipped in an extra sample with a pleading note: "Kathy, Doctor Jacobs here."

The extra sample was in an old Coca-Cola bottle wrapped in a napkin with some scribble on it, "Lake Mead," and a hand written note: "Kathy, I know it's Friday, and I know you want to get out early, but could you please squeeze in just one more sample?"

Knowing that he would be calling every half hour asking if she had been able to squeeze in his sample, she decided to just go ahead and run it.

The bottle was half full of oil and half full of a mixture of algae, moss, and mud. After spinning the sample down in the centrifuge, she injected a small amount of the oil into her Mass Spectroscopy machine. Within minutes, red light after red light came on, and the machine shut down. She sat bewildered, staring at the machine. She had been running oil samples at Amoco's Texas City, Texas Research Facility for three years, running hundreds of samples, and had never once had the machine shut down. After multiple tries to reboot the machine with no luck, she sat back and muttered, "So much for getting out early."

Hitting the reboot button one more time, she sat back and paged through her "Lucky Stars Moon Watch Charts" wanting to see just how close Jupiter was going to get to Venus when her cellphone rang. Looking at the caller ID, it was Doctor Jacobs.

Before Jacobs could say a word, Kathy blurted out, "Where did you get this stuff from?"

Doctor Jacobs could tell by Kathy's tone that it was more than just a rhetorical question. He had a pretty good idea of what stuff she was talking about. "Is there something wrong?" he asked quizzically.

Kathy rolled her eyes. "Is they something wrong? The stuff just shut down my machine."

Kathy tried to explain what had happened when she put his oil sample that he had gotten from Lake Mead into her machine. After a few minutes of trying to explain the situation, Doctor Jacobs interrupted, "Just a minute. I'll come over."

A few minutes later, Jacobs came into the lab where Kathy was sitting, reading her daily horoscope. "Jesus, it stinks in here."

Kathy set down her horoscope. "Yeah! It smells like our barnyard back in Iowa." Doctor Jacobs knew what she meant. Before the big city life of Galveston, Texas, Kathy had grown up on a pig farm in Iowa.

Jacobs wasn't actually that awfully familiar with the smell as he had grown up in New England. After getting his undergraduate degree from Yale, he had gotten his Ph.D. at MIT, and then after three Post Doc's at the Czech Technical University in Prague, he had been nominated for a Nobel Prize for his innovative research in oil exploration.

As a young postdoc at Prague, he had developed an "Oil Fingerprinting" database using Mass spectroscopy. Like the FBI's database for human fingerprints, Jacobs had developed a system that could identify the origin of any oil sample, anywhere in the world, by analyzing the particular ratios of the oil sample's hydrocarbon contents. No two oils had the same fingerprints.

Kathy held up the Coke bottle. "It's this oil sample you asked me to run. It stinks, and it crashed my machine."

Doctor Jacobs walked over and looked at all of the blinking lights. He was very familiar with the Thermo Scientific 253 High Resolution Mass Spec. "What happened?"

Kathy, a little irritated because she had hoped to get out a little early, snapped, "What happened?" She held up the smelly coke bottle. "This happened."

Jacobs looked over his half-rimmed glasses. "Did it analyze it at all?"

Kathy reached over to the printer and handed him a printout. "It doesn't recognize it."

Doctor Jacobs furrowed his bushy eyebrows. "That's impossible. Something's wrong with the machine." He took off his glasses. "Did you call the rep for the machine?"

Kathy became a little defensive. "There's nothing wrong with the machine. It's this stuff," she said, pointing at the Coke bottle. "What is this stuff?"

Doctor Jacobs explained to her that some guys had overturned some trucks full of barrels of oil into Lake Mead, and the Department of Transportation and the FBI wanted to know the origin of the oil. He explained that he had scooped some out of the lake into the Coke bottle that he found lying on the shore.

Kathy understood the database fingerprinting system like the back of her hand. "This stuff's not in the database."

Doctor Jacobs shook his head. "Impossible." The database he had developed fingerprinted every deposit of oil on the planet. "Is it synthetic?"

Kathy shook her head. "No, it's not synthetic. It's rotten."

"It's what?"

Kathy explained that there must have been some animal poop nearby, and when he scooped up the sample, some of it must have gotten into the bottle.

Doctor Jacobs shrugged, admitting that it was highly possible; he had not looked around the area. He explained that he hadn't had much time to look around; some FBI guy was breathing down his neck. He told her he just bent down and scooped some up.

Kathy told him jokingly, "They must have wild pigs in the area."

Doctor Jacobs looked at his watch. "I've got a meeting. Call the Siemens rep, and get them over here. Get this thing fixed."

As Jacobs was heading to the door, Kathy said, "I'm going to send a sample to the Physical Chemistry lab." Jacobs just nodded, *fine*. Kathy yelled out, "Have a nice weekend."

As soon as Doctor Jacobs shut the door, Kathy called

Nancy. "Have you ever seen Jupiter that close to Venus in your life? The King of planets and the Goddess of love. Woohoo."

Kathy left a message for the Siemens rep and left.

# Chapter 22

***

## Hoover Dam Power Plant
## Boulder City, Nevada

First, the lights went out in Boulder City and then spread from there. Soon, every electron in Vegas, California, Colorado, and New Mexico turned and started heading back to the great turbines at Hoover Dam. Phil Rossi stood looking down from the control room. The turbines had all started spinning backwards, sucking back the trillions of electrons they had sent out. Rossi could only stand and watch as the turbines began to swell and pulsate, gobbling up electrons like the gluttonous Jabba the Hutt. Then the loud ringing filled his ears, the final warning; like Jabba, the turbines had had their fill and were about to explode.

Rossi woke up in a cold sweat, his phone ringing. After the fiasco a week earlier with turbine #6 shutting down, he had been at the plant every day and gone to countless meetings, reassuring everyone that it had just been a fluke.

He hadn't gone to bed until after midnight. He looked at the clock at his bedside. It was five a.m. He picked up the phone.

"Phil, it's Davis. Another turbine has shut down." Rossi dropped his head back down onto the pillow; he wasn't sure if he was still dreaming.

In a daze, half asleep, he said, "What the Hell are you talking about?"

Davis explained that turbine #3 on the other spillway had shut down. After a fairly short dissertation, Rossi told Davis to hold on and that he would be right in.

If there were any consolation to have to go to work at this ungodly hour, Rossi contemplated, *at least the damned tourists aren't on the road yet, the winds haven't picked up any giant tumbleweeds, and the temperature is only a hundred.*

A short time later, Rossi parked and headed straight to the Control Room.

Davis was on the phone with Mendez, who was in charge of the nine turbines on the Arizona side. Davis pointed at the control panels on the wall. Eight of the nine turbine lights on the left spillway were green, #3 was red.

Rossi was so tired, running on epinephrine only. "You've gotta be kidding me."

Both Rossi and Davis knew what would happen if the lights went out in Las Vegas. Nevada had no economy other than Vegas. First, there would be state congressional subcommittee meetings, a short trial, and then Rossi would be spending the rest of his days in a cell in Carson City with some big bastard named Bubba. He couldn't help himself from wondering whether they had a gas chamber or an electric chair.

Rossi looked at Davis. "Don't tell me this was just recently opened and serviced."

Davis paused and then nodded affirmatively.

Rossi shook his head in bewilderment. "What the hell is going on?"

Davis didn't say anything. He just stared at the board, then Rossi told him, "Whatever you do, don't open any more of those turbines."

Davis told him that he already had the guys opening up turbine #3, trying to figure out why the thing shut down.

Rossi motioned to him. "Let's check it out."

They made their way to the Arizona spillway where eight of the nine turbines were humming.

When they reached turbine #3, Rossi turned his head. "What the hell! Did someone shit their pants?"

One of the workers lying on his back in a puddle of grease looked up. "Right."

The workers hadn't found anything yet. Rossi had to start writing up a report, although he had no idea what he was going to say. As he walked away, he mumbled, "Next thing you know, the goddamned things will start running backwards and suck back every goddamn electron in the world. Right back to here. Then Jabba the Hutt will explode."

The maintenance person on the floor looked up at Davis and mouthed, "I think he's losing it."

# Chapter 23

***

## 86 Pinckney Street
## Boston, Massachusetts

It was a little after five o'clock. Lucy was already home, in the laundry room, putting a batch of clothes into the washing machine when she heard the front door slam.

"Mom, I'm home."

Lucy called out, "Oh, that's very funny. As if I didn't hear the door slam."

Ricky poked his head into the laundry room, ignoring the facetious door comment. "What's for supper? I'm starving."

Lucy rolled her eyes. "Honey, the little kids in Africa are starving. You're just a little bit hungry."

Ricky held up his index finger. "I know, Mom, that's because they live where there's no food and water. If we lived there, we'd be starving too. They need to move to where the food is."

Lucy looked at Ricky. "That's terrible!"

"I know. I was just kidding. There's a comedian guy on MTV who says that. So anyway, what's for supper? I'm a little hungry."

Lucy closed the lid to the washer, hit the Casual button, and told him that they were having potatoes, gravy, salad, and beef from the "Big Sky Country."

"Very funny. Give it up. Not going to be herding cattle, no cowgirl, no twins, no Angus and Braveheart. Gonna be right here in Boston."

As they walked into the kitchen, Ricky looked around for the bowl of chips, but they were nowhere to be found. He walked around, looking in all of the usual places while Lucy stood against the refrigerator, smiling, as if to say, "Go ahead, you're not going to find them."

Ricky studied her face, glancing from cabinet to cabinet, intently watching his mother for any giveaways. Then, with a big grin, he walked over to the refrigerator. "Ahem, excuse me please." She stepped aside. Pulling the door open, Ricky reached into the back of the refrigerator behind a pile of lettuce and pulled out a handful of chips.

"What gave me away?"

Ricky smiled. "All I can say is, never play poker. First of all, you leaned against the refrigerator. That was a dead giveaway. You never lean against anything. Second, you fidgeted. That's called a 'tell' in poker. You're an easy mark."

Lucy became a little defensive. "I am *not.*"

Ricky smiled, and to prove his point, with much fanfare, he poked a potato chip into his mouth.

Lucy turned and started preparing dinner. "Fine. So I'm an easy mark. Who cares?"

Ricky sat down at the table, took some papers out of his backpack and started to work on his homework.

He tried to concentrate on some math problems, but Lucy kept interrupting. "How was school? How was physics? How's your project going?"

Finally, Ricky blurted out, "Mom! I'm trying to work."

She apologized, but no more than a minute later, she said, "Guess who I saw at the grocery store today?"

Ricky gave up and set down his pencil. Needless to say, he had no idea. There were about eight million people in the greater Boston area, so his guess was going to be a stab in the dark.

"Doctor Christenson. I saw Doctor Christenson at the grocery store," Lucy blurted out before he even had a chance to guess.

Ricky had no idea of the bombshell that was about to come. "Oh, that's nice. Was he able to carry on a conversation about something other than the outer reaches of the universe?"

Lucy didn't pay any attention to his snide little remark. "Do you know what I found out?"

Ricky wasn't really interested, but he knew he was going to hear about him anyway. "No. What did you find out? He's an alien from outer space? Time traveler from the future? Reincarnated from...."

Again, Lucy disregarded Ricky's sarcasm and interrupted. "He's forty-two years old. He was married, but his wife was killed in a car accident a few years ago. He lives alone around the other side of the park. He has no pets, and he eats TV dinners."

Ricky turned in his chair. "Geez, Mom. What did you do, waterboard him?"

Lucy pulled out some plates and silverware, poured two glasses of milk, and fixed each plate with potatoes, gravy, and a lean piece of beef tenderloin. "Nope, just basic female observational techniques. We just walked along, grocery shopping and talking. My single most intuitive observation was that his shopping cart was full of TV dinners, pot pies, boxes of macaroni and cheese, and Oreo cookies. I had already observed the other night that he didn't wear a wedding ring." Lucy smiled, proud of her intuitive powers. "Five minutes flat, I pretty much had the whole picture."

As Ricky cleared his papers out of the way, he said, "Maybe you should be an interrogator at Gitmo."

As they started to eat, Lucy said, assertively, "I asked him over for dinner next week."

Ricky's jaw dropped, and he almost choked. "You did what?"

Lucy shrugged. "I asked him over for dinner. That's all."

Ricky was dumbfounded. "Mom, do you have any idea what the kids at school will do to me if they find out? I'll probably get stuffed in a locker. I'll be called a teacher's pet. I'll be shunned. I'll probably end up friendless, psychologically scarred for life. Oh, God, I'm gonna to have to be a cattle herder after all. Thanks a lot, Mom."

Lucy smiled and furrowed her eyebrows, "Don't be silly. He's *only* coming to dinner. It's not like it's the end of the world."

The rest of the meal was consumed with Ricky's doom-and-gloom scenarios of his future, ruined by his mother's crazy actions. As they finished eating, Lucy pointed out that it was almost six-thirty and that he'd better get ready to watch the news.

Ricky packed up his books and headed toward the living room. Turning in the doorway of the kitchen, he said, "If you call me and there's no answer, it's because I've taken my own life. That would at least save me from the miserable future I have in store, thanks to you."

Lucy smiled and exhaled. "What would I do without you?"

# Chapter 24

***

## Bay of Bengal, India

Despite four of his eight crew members coming down with some kind of a gastrointestinal bug, things were going well for Captain Patange of the oil tanker, the *Cretan Star.* The high-pressure systems to the north of the Bay of Bengal were still producing the drier season's northeasterly winds. The heavy monsoon storms of late October and November had not yet started.

The captain walked onto the bridge as the first mate bellowed out, "Captain on the bridge."

Patange nodded to the first mate then looked out one of the large front windows of the bridge and asked, "What is our heading?"

The first mate checked the digital compass settings. "Latitude 18°56.3' North, longitude 72°45.9' East. Right on course for the bay, sir."

Patange nodded approvingly. "Good. Contact Port Authority."

The first mate gave a nod. "Yes, sir," he replied and proceeded to open a communication line.

The captain looked out over the bay, his hands behind his back. It was calm, the skies were clear, and there was a slight northeasterly breeze. Docking would be a piece of cake.

He knew the Bay of Bengal well enough that he could navigate it blindfolded. He had docked here many times at night, with docking lights only, in the middle of the heaviest monsoon rains, and once, coasted the tanker in when the engines had failed.

"Sir, it's Mumbai Port Authority." The first mate handed Patange the radio.

"Mumbai Port Authority, this is the *Cretan Star.* We're en route from Ras Tanura, Saudi Arabia, requesting docking instructions."

He stood waiting for orders, then the radio crackled, "*Cretan Star*, you'll be docking at jetty three on Jawahar Dweep. We're switching you from Mumbai Port to Indria Dock Command on Jawahar Dweep. They'll give you docking and unloading instructions."

"Got that, Mumbai Port. We'll wait for instructions from Indira."

# Chapter 25

***

## Frankfurt International Airport
## Germany

Kurt scanned the maintenance work roster for Terminal 2. Three more sick call-ins. "Damn!" That made seven in the last three days. There was no way he could get all of the maintenance checks done on the morning's planes and get them off the ground on time with only a skeleton work crew.

Kurt took out his cellphone and dialed the Assistant Administrative Director of Ground Operations, Niklas Volder.

Kurt and Niklas had been best of friends since high school and still spent many of their days off together golfing, having backyard cookouts with their families, and their wives carpooling the kids to soccer, dance, and piano lessons. Kurt and Niklas had gotten into their share of trouble in younger days but always managed to worm their way out of impossible situations. Today, Kurt wasn't so confident.

With his mouth half full of a maple-pecan glazed bun, Niklas answered, "Hey, what's up?"

Kurt hesitated; something had been troubling him for the past few weeks. "Nik, you know the plane … the DC-10 that went down in Sadia Arabia a few weeks ago?"

Sipping at his coffee to wash down the syrupy bun, he replied, "Yeah, what about it?"

"Hans and I serviced that plane, you know."

Niklas said nonchalantly, "Yeah, I know. I've got the report here. Everything on our end checked out. What about it?"

Kurt hesitated again, trying to think of the best way to put it. "We kind of left a small detail out. We didn't think much of it at the time, but now … well … now I think it was important."

Niklas shoved a larger-than-life pecan into his mouth. "What? How important?"

"Important, Nik. I'm not sure we should've let that plane fly. I think we should've grounded it."

Niklas almost sucked the whole pecan into his lungs. "Ah, let's not talk about this on the phone. Maybe I'd better come over there."

While Kurt was waiting for Niklas, he rearranged the work schedule. Frankfurt had been hit hard with a gastrointestinal bug in the previous few weeks that had crippled the city. The bug had spread like wildfire. Schools were closed, many work places essentially shut down, and emergency departments throughout the city were overwhelmed with patients. It was being referred to as the "belly bug" in the news media.

Twenty minutes later, Niklas walked into the maintenance building of Terminal 2. He spotted Kurt. "Jesus Christ! What the hell stinks in here?"

Kurt motioned for him to come over, out of earshot of the other workers. "That's kind of what we left out of our report on the plane that went down in Saudi Arabia."

Niklas looked at him bewildered. "What are you talking about?"

"The smell! The stink you noticed when you walked in! When Hans and I serviced that DC-10 that crashed, we noticed the same smell."

Niklas interrupted, "Smells like the 'belly bug'. Maybe it's just everybody shittin' so much around here, they're stinking up the place."

Kurt nodded. "Yeah! Tell me about it. Elsa and all three kids had it two weeks ago. Bad. But I think there's more to it."

Kurt explained to Niklas that when they serviced the DC-10, they found oil dripping from somewhere up in the underbelly of the plane.

Niklas nodded, already well aware of that from the report, which he brought with him.

"So? What're you getting at?"

Kurt motioned for Niklas to follow him. Strewn around the maintenance floor were three or four of the terminal's hydraulic pumps, all broken down into parts.

Niklas looked around, "What's wrong with those?"

"They're leaking oil from around the gaskets and seals. They're overheating and shutting down." After Kurt looked around to be sure that no one could hear, he said in a low voice, "That stinky shit's eating those gaskets. It's dissolving them."

Niklas was getting frustrated, still not following what Kurt was talking about. "What shit?"

"I know this sounds crazy, Nik, but there's something wrong with the oil in these pumps. It's rotten. It's the same stuff that was in the reserve tanks of the DC-10. It doesn't seem like it's oil." Kurt pointed to a puddle of dark slime. "Look! I don't know *what* the hell it is!"

Niklas picked up a screwdriver and swirled it through a small puddle of the slimy stuff. Kurt looked on intently, waiting for a second opinion. Niklas held it up and looked closely as the gunk slowly slid down the neck of the tool. He squinted and shook his head as his eyes started to cross.

"So? What do you think?" Kurt solicited.

Niklas shrugged his shoulders.

"Nik, what if terrorists … or something … or somebody messed with the oil in those reserve tanks? What if it got pumped into the main engines of that DC-10 and did the same thing it did to our pumps?"

Niklas looked around the large service area. He whispered to make sure his voice didn't echo throughout the open space, "But you didn't dump any of that oil from those reserve tanks into our oil, so how'd it get here?"

"I don't know." Kurt was just as exasperated. "When we serviced that plane, the smelly stuff got on our shoes, and Hans had it all over his hands and got it on his clothes. Maybe we … I don't know what the hell to think."

Niklas' phone rang, and Kurt's eyes opened wide as he gawked at him. Nik listened momentarily, acknowledged and then ended the call. "Shit, that was Hedy. The kids are sick … diarrhea."

Kurt rolled his eyes, "Yeah, tell me about it. I think my kids were the first ones to ever get the damned bug."

Niklas was beyond himself. Half of the workforce was out, the hydraulic pumps that serviced the planes were mysteriously breaking down, and now his family was sick. Shaking his head, he said, "Man! What else could go wrong?"

Kurt took in a deep breath and let it out slowly, giving himself time to bolster the courage to tell Niklas what the hell else could go wrong. "The FAA guys took my handwritten log book."

Niklas asked hesitantly, "And?"

"And … I made note of the fact that the oil in the reserve

tanks needed to be changed on the layover in Saudi Arabia."

With the kind of day Niklas was having, his patience was quickly growing thin. He already knew this information as it too was noted in the report. Kurts hesitance made Niklas uneasy. He knew there was something he didn't want to know about but needed to.

"Come on, Kurt. There's something else. What?"

Letting out another deep breath, he said, "After the plane left, I scribbled in an after note in pencil that I had concerns about letting the plane go and that maybe we should've had the plane brought back."

Niklas threw down the screwdriver. "Fuck!"

Kurt tried to reassure him, "Look, it's been a month. Those FAA guys are only going to read the computer report. I didn't put any of that in the computer report. They're never gonna go fingering through a handwritten log book."

# Chapter 26

***

## 86 Pinckney Street
## Boston, Massachusetts

As he sat waiting for the news, he Googled a map of Patagonia. Maybe he could go live with his mom's brother.

Lucy had just dropped the bombshell that she had invited Doctor Christenson over for dinner. Ricky had no idea how he was going to concentrate on the news. He couldn't believe it; his mother was almost forty years old. It had always been just him and his mom. Why'd she need to go asking Doctor Christenson over for dinner?

He hadn't even noticed that the NBC Peacock had come and gone, and again Sawyer Clark was sitting in for Lester Holt. It was no wonder that Sawyer had shaken up the big three nightly newscast; the dull, drab, male-dominated newscasters were just that. Sawyer was radiant. She was wearing a bright yellow dress with a gold pendent and a new Fossil Q Smartwatch, and she was a very competent newscaster.

With her big smile, she began, "In our top stories tonight: Tensions continue to mount in the Middle East as Iran threatens once again to close the Straits of Hormuz, this time over immigration policies. For that story, we'll hear from our foreign correspondent Richard Engle in Tehran.

"Further east, tensions are building again in the Korean Peninsula as Kim Jong-Un tested another missile that may have intercontinental capabilities. For that story, we'll hear from our NBC reporter Jinah Kim along the Demilitarized Zone in South Korea.

"And closer to home," Sawyer turned to the projection screen to her left showing workers picking lettuce, "a food-borne gastrointestinal illness has hit the U.S. Worst hit are Nevada, California, and areas of Texas. At this time, it is unknown if it's a virus or bacteria, but many are blaming California's lettuce crop. We'll have more on that story when we hear from our medical editor, Doctor Nancy Snyderman.

"And, lastly, in our 'Making a Difference' segment, we'll hear how dogs are helping veterans cope with the stresses of Post-Traumatic Stress Syndrome."

Sawyer announced that they would be right back with all of those stories, and more, after a commercial break.

Ricky looked at his notes. He had hardly written down anything. His mom's bombshell was going to be the kiss of death for him at school. She might just as well have invited over the Godfather, Don Corleone, for dinner.

After a few commercials, Sawyer reappeared.

He didn't pay much attention to the first stories. The Iran thing was nothing new. He jotted down a few notes that, this time, it was over immigration. The week before, it had been over shipping rights, and the time before that, he couldn't remember, but he knew enough to wing it if he were asked. The North Korean thing wasn't anything new either; they had just discussed North Korea in class today. It had gotten quite a laugh out of the class when Richard, one of his classmates, not knowing how to pronounce Kim Jong-un's name, called him Kim Dumb-Luck.

Then the cameras zoomed in and Sawyer introduced Doctor Nancy Snyderman. To Snyderman's right, the projection screen had been split. On one half was a picture of what looked like bacteria growing in a petri dish, and the other half showed workers picking lettuce.

After thanking Doctor Snyderman for taking time out of her busy schedule, Sawyer smiled and nodded. "Another food-borne outbreak. Not really news anymore."

Doctor Snyderman nodded in agreement.

Just about every week, it seemed that the nightly news was reporting another food-borne illness. It had been chili peppers from Mexico, raspberries from Guatemala, cucumbers had crippled Germany, and some onions and scallions had killed a woman. Sawyer had covered that story with Doctor Snyderman just a few weeks earlier.

She reminded Doctor Snyderman, "As we said a few weeks ago, who would've ever thought that green onions could kill you?"

Doctor Snyderman nodded and added, "Or that a little animal on a raspberry could kill you."

Sawyer smiled; she remembered Nancy describing the little bug that had infected the raspberries from Guatemala. It hadn't been a virus, a bacteria, a fungus, or a mold; it had actually been a little animal. At the time, Sawyer didn't know it; she had only been a communications major in college, but the raspberries had been infected with a protozoan, and according to Doctor Snyderman, protozoans were classified as animals, belonging in the Animal Kingdom. Sawyer had thought it kind of gross, thinking of it as eating little animals. For some reason, eating bacteria didn't carry the same connotations as eating the family pet.

Sawyer smiled. "So what's it this time? Fungus, mold, or little animals?"

Snyderman smiled. "No, this time, it looks like it's just a common garden variety bacteria that's gone rogue."

"So, if it's common," Sawyer asked, "why is this one making such a fuss?"

"Because his one is shutting down the tourist capital of the world."

Sawyer nodded. "Vegas."

Sawyer then asked Doctor Snyderman what they knew so far about the outbreak, and Nancy outlined that epidemiologists suspected it was a bacteria known as Escherichia coli, a common bacteria found in soil and water contaminated with fecal refuse.

Sawyer next asked why this was so much worse than any of the other outbreaks.

"Because this one's causing abdominal cramping, bloating, and diarrhea. Casinos don't make money when the tourists are in the bathrooms. They make money when they're at the slot machines," Doctor Snyderman replied.

"How serious is this disease?"

Doctor Snyderman explained that it really was not that serious of an outbreak from a death point of view; it was more of an inconvenience and etiquette issue. She smiled, explaining that people would rather stay home than have abdominal bloating and passing gas at the Casino tables.

Sawyer wrinkled her nose. "That's why the news media's calling this one the 'belly bloat.'"

Snyderman smiled.

With the aid of slides on the projection screen, Doctor Snyderman explained that, here in the States with clean water, it was a fairly self-limiting disease, but that the same outbreak in poor countries with contaminated water supplies could be devastating, killing millions.

"I hear a similar bug has hit India," Sawyer said.

A picture appeared on the projection screen of the streets of New Delhi, India, showing the deplorable conditions, human waste running in small streams along the roads, and thousands of emaciated people.

Sawyer turned back. "Do you think it's the same bug?"

Nancy shook her head, no. She doubted it, pointing out that the outbreak in India was an ocean away, and that with India's large slums, such outbreaks were not that uncommon.

Sawyer asked Nancy to stay with her as she had a few more questions, but first they had to take a commercial break.

During the break, Lucy called out from the kitchen, "How's the news? Are you doing okay?"

Ricky rolled his eyes. Other than not being able to concentrate, he was doing just fine.

He yelled back, "Fine," although he was contemplating having to kill himself.

Sawyer and her bright yellow dress reappeared on the screen. "Doctor Snyderman, do we have any idea where this started?"

Nancy shrugged. "Epidemiologists are pursuing two trains of thought. One group is pretty sure that it started in the lettuce fields of California."

Sawyer interrupted, "But Texas is getting hit hard along with Louisiana and Mississippi."

Doctor Snyderman pointed out that that was to be expected since Interstate I-10 was one of the major shipping routes east for California's fruits and vegetables.

"And the second train of thought?" Sawyer asked.

Nancy smiled. "Vegas." She explained that some of the

research pointed to Vegas as the epicenter and told Sawyer that if Vegas was "ground zero," that would be easy to explain. She pointed out that the world was not that big anymore and that thousands of tourists fly here to the States every day. Shrugging, Snyderman added, "All you have to do is jump on a plane anywhere in the world, and twelve hours later you're standing at a slot machine in Vegas. Some epidemiologists think the little rogue bug hitchhiked on an airplane and is now playing roulette in Vegas."

Sawyer laughed at Nancy's little pun and added, "And winning."

Nancy laughed.

After a few more questions as to the origin of the little rogue bug—India, France, Germany, China—Sawyer thanked Nancy and announced that they would be right back after a commercial break.

Ricky set down his pad of paper and leaned back on the couch, thinking, *That's it. If I get sick, I'd have to stay in my room, and Mom would have to bring me supper. She wouldn't want to take a chance on Doctor Christenson getting it. He might never come over again.* Ricky smiled. *Mom's chicken noodle soup.*

# Chapter 27

***

## Jawahar Dweep
## Bay of Bengal, India

Under normal circumstances, when their tanker was being offloaded, a twenty-four-hour shore leave was a welcomed break for Captain Patange and his crew. But this stopover proved to be anything but relaxing.

Half of his crew were sick with abdominal pain, cramping and diarrhea. While time spent on a shore leave was usually in a local bar, pub, or brothel, the crew spent most of their time in the bathrooms for this port stopover.

Captain Patange and his first mate had not been affected so far, and the night before, they had wandered into town, ate at a nice restaurant, and returned to the ship early. It was now almost noon, and the captain sat on the bridge reading a book and waiting for word that the unloading was finished. The radio crackled and startled him, as he had dozed off.

"*Cretan Star*, this is Indria Dock Port Authority. You're next in line for undocking after the tanker *Arabian Sea*, which is currently on jetty four."

Captain Patange set his book down and picked up the ship-to-shore radio. "Port Authority, this is the *Cretan Star*. Understood. We are ready to undock and will wait for instructions."

Patange got up to go find the first mate but felt a little dizzy. Grabbing the wheel of the tanker, he felt a rumbling in his stomach. Then he heard the harbor radio announce, "Indria Port Authority to Jawahar Dweep docking crews, as soon as the *Arabian Sea* is undocked from jetty four, the tanker *AbQaiq* will be docking at jetty two, and the *Cretan Star* will be leaving jetty three. Have jetties three and four ready. We have two more tankers waiting for unloading."

# Chapter 28

***

## Port of Zhanjiang
## Guangdong Provice, China

Captain Xang Pai was on edge. The trip from Ras Tanura to the South Sea of China had taken longer than expected. High winds, rough seas, and a sick crew plagued him for much of the trip. Within the last few days, the ship started to take on a foul odor. Pai assumed it was from the sick crew.

For now, his ship was at the Sea Port of Zhanjiang, latitude 21° 10' 11" North, longitude 110° 24' 36" East. As he sat waiting for docking instructions, he could see the port city of Guangdong province.

Guangdong province was one of the richest provinces in all of China and had the highest concentration of billionaires. The weather was perfect this time of the year being located just north of the Tropic of Cancer.

Pai couldn't wait to get to shore. They had a week's leave before heading back to Saudi Arabia. All he needed was docking instructions.

Finally, at 1:25 in the afternoon, the ship's landline radio crackled, and the Zahnjiang Port Authority told the *Lian An Hu* to prepare for docking.

Captain Pai picked up the radio to confirm his ship's call letters. "Port Authority Zhanjiang, this is Captain Xang Pai, tanker Q6637N the *Lian An Hu*. We're ready for your docking instructions."

The voice at the other end told Pai they were cleared for docking at jetty 2 and that command was being turned over to the docking crew. Pai set the radio down, paged the first mate and began thinking about what he planned to do during his week of shore leave.

# Chapter 29

***

## Port of Yokohama
## Sendai, Japan

Captain Itou of the oil tanker *M Star* was beat. He and his crew were supposed to have had a two-week shore leave when they arrived at Ras Tanura in Saudi Arabia over a month ago, but a few days after arriving, the DC-10 commercial jet went down in one of the oil storage areas. His empty tanker was needed to move some of the excess oil that had filled a security ditch.

The *M Star*, the *Lian An Hu*, and the *Cretan Star* were all empty at the time and chosen, not the least bit democratically, to transport the oil from the security ditch to other refineries around the world. It was an emergency, and they had to get the oil out of the so-called moat because the plane that caused the debacle was sitting at the bottom under a few hundred feet of crude oil with its seats full with dead passengers.

Now, Captain Itou sat in Sendai harbor, in the North Pacific Ocean, bobbing like a cork. At a latitude of 38°16'05" north and a longitude of 140°52'11" East, they sat directly under the continuous torrents of rain that showered down from Mount Funagata.

Finally, after bobbing for a few days, the radio came to life. "This is Port Authority of Sendai. Tanker *M Star*, you are cleared for approach and docking."

Itou couldn't wait. He would finally get some much needed sleep. He grabbed the radio. "Port Authority, this is Captain Itou. We'll start our approach. Thank you."

# Chapter 30

***

## Department of Energy
## Office of Biological and Environmental Research

## James V. Forrestal Building
## 1000 Independence Avenue SW

It was Friday afternoon, and Newhouse was getting ready to leave work for the weekend. Another goddamned week of meetings and pushing papers, and nothing had gotten done, and he knew next week would be the same damned thing. After years of being knee-deep in all of Washington's bureaucratic bullshit, he knew that if you wanted to get anything done in Washington, you had to bypass the damned House and Senate, bypass all of those damned appropriation committees, and for that matter, bypass the President. If you wanted something done, you had to just do it. Take the bull by the horns, and let the chips fall where they may.

This week alone had been an exceptionally taxing week of bullshit. First, they had blocked a new highway project in Ohio because of some owls in a tree, then they blocked a flood prevention dam in Minnesota because of some mutant three-legged frogs, and then they cut funding for Federal land development in Alaska because it was in a flight path for geese flying overhead at two-thousand feet. But he had made damn sure they weren't going to block drilling in the gulf.

As he was about to shut down his computer, he noticed a red flag flashing on one of the messages. As the Director of the Department of Energy, he received hundreds of e-mails a day. Thanks to the generosity of the U.S. taxpayers, he had developed—actually, his geek son at Stanford University in Palo Alto, California had developed—an expensive customized software program that filters through the hundreds of e-mails. Newhouse had learned long ago that all you needed in Washington to get anything done was a sizable slush fund. In that way, you didn't have to bother with any House Ways-and-Means Appropriations Committees.

His nifty government-funded software alerted him to any keywords, like, "The Washington Post is currently looking into energy…" Any e-mails that raised a hint of concern were red-flagged. Greens were automatically deleted, and yellows got a quick glance if time permitted.

Moving his cursor to the little red flag, he clicked the mouse. "To whom it may concern."

The Siemens workers had gotten Kathy's Mass Spec machine working, and she had finished all of the back load of samples. She had not tried to run Doctor Jacobs' sample again but received a report from the Physical Chemistry and Microbiology labs.

As she had expected from the smell, according to the Microbiology lab, the sample was highly contaminated with common fecal bacteria, E. Coli and Bacteroides—common bacteria found in poop.

She had been about ready to file the report when she had noted a P.S. comment. "Note: sample is heavily contaminated, which is unusual considering the minimal amount of organic material. Despite minimal material for which to reproduce upon, the bacteria are dividing at an exponential rate. It is suggested that the sample be sent for gene sequencing."

Doctor Jacobs had given her a wadded up piece of paper that the FBI agent had given him at Lake Mead. The agent told him that as soon as he had the results of the sample, he was to send the report to the e-mail address on the sheet. He told Kathy it was the FBI headquarters, Langley, or Arlighton; he really couldn't remember exactly where the FBI headquarters were located.

Newhouse read the e-mail. "This is Katherine Gregory. Lab Technician at BP Amoco PC Oil Refinery in Texas City. This is the report requested on the oil spill in Lake Mead. Because of unusual properties, our Physical Chemistry and Microbiology laboratories suggested that the sample be sent for gene sequencing. I have forwarded the sample to Cornell University in New York City for sequencing."

Kathy had taken it upon herself to send it to Cornell's labs because she had a friend there and could easily get the results. Sending things to the CDC in Atlanta was like a black hole; things went in and never came out. Kathy left her e-mail address and phone number.

Newhouse looked at the date on the e-mail. Friday the $13^{th}$. He slumped into his chair and stared at the screen. "Fucking Friday the $13^{th}$." All he needed was for someone to sequence the thing.

# Chapter 31

***

## Tri-State Toll Plaza
## Interstate 90
## Sixty Miles West of Chicago

It was still early enough in the afternoon, and Gus was just approaching the Kenosha, Wisconsin exit. Listening to his CB radio, he had ten minutes to decide if he was going to take a chance on cutting right through the city or take the 294 Bypass. His biggest concern was that it was a Friday afternoon, but looking at the clock on his dashboard, it was still early enough that he might be able to make it to the other side. The Bypass took him way out and around the city and was much longer, but if he got stuck in Chicago traffic on a Friday afternoon, it could take him until midnight to reach I-80.

He had made good headway out of California taking Interstate 15 up to Las Vegas because of construction on his usual route of I-10. He had slept for a few hours at a truck stop in Vegas while his rig was oiled and greased before the long haul east. Now he was approaching the outskirts of Chicago on I-90. All of the time he had saved by taking I-15 out of Los Angeles would be for naught if he got stuck in the middle of Chicago traffic on a Friday afternoon.

He knew this stretch of the road like the back of his hand. The 294 Bypass turnoff was just ahead. His CB was full of chatter from other truckers ahead of him. Traffic on the Dan Ryan inbound and the Kennedy outbound were both heavy but moving. The Eden's Express was wide open.

With a hope and prayer, he could connect with I-80 in less than an hour, catch the Indiana North-South Toll Road, and have smooth sailing all the way to Boston.

No turning back now, he sailed pass the 294 Bypass exit and pushed straight ahead. He was going to go for it.

Things went fine for the next thirty minutes. Traffic was getting heavy, but moving. Other than a major accident, nothing was going to stop him now, until an indicator light on his dashboard started flashing. It was indicating that there were problems with the hydraulic brakes.

"Damn. Damn. Damn," he muttered as he tapped the little flashing light hoping it was only a problem with one of the little sensors. He knew there couldn't be a problem with the brakes because they had just been opened and greased at the truck stop outside of Vegas.

Ten minutes later, he was sitting at a small roadside rest stop—a picnic area with a historical marker. The turnabout was so small, he had hardly been able to get the tail of his rig off the highway. Now there were three red lights flashing. One indicating that the brakes were overheating, which he knew had to be false; they had just been re-greased. The second, a flashing light indicating that there was low oil pressure in the hydraulic brake system, which indicated that the seals were leaking. And the third flashing light was not only blinking, but there was a loud screeching warning with an automated voice overlay, "Warning. Warning. Impending brake failure. Warning."

As he climbed down out of his rig, he watched the traffic whizzing by. He knew he wasn't going to make it now. He walked around his rig, kicking and looking at each wheel base. Sure enough, oil was leaking from two of the hydraulic brake systems at the back of the rig. Cursing, he climbed back into his rig and clicked the button on his CB radio.

"Dispatch, this is American Freight and Trucking, rig call number DN3872Q. I'm going to need towing to the nearest full-service plaza."

A young girl with a classic Midwestern accent answered, "This is American Freight and Trucking dispatch service, Midwest coverage, Minneapolis. What's your 20?"

Gus told her that he was about thirty-five miles west of Chicago, a little past the Wisconsin-Illinois border, past Kenosha, and a ways after the I90-94 split.

She asked him a series of questions—if he remembered the last mile marker and if he was blocking traffic.

He told her that he was at a picnic-type road stop and that

he was not blocking traffic. Then she asked him what the nature of his problem was, his urgency code status, load, and destination.

Gus told her that his code status was “Urgent”, destination Boston, and that he had a refrigerated rig with a load of tomatoes, lettuce, and cucumbers.

“Okay,” the perky, little Midwestern voice said, “a towing truck is being dispatching now, and you’re nearest full-service plaza with heavy truck mechanical support is at the Tri-State Toll Plaza.” Then she asked if Gus thought the load would need to be transferred to another refrigerated rig.

Gus told her, “No, the refrigeration is running, and it’s only a brake problem.”

“Okie dokie then,” she told him, “you just sit tight. I’m on it.”

Gus couldn’t help but smile.

# CHAPTER 32

***

## BP Amoco Oil
## Refineries and Research
## Texas City, Texas

Kathy looked at the clock every fifteen minutes. She couldn't wait to go home; she and her girlfriend Nancy were going deer hunting tonight. It was open season on bucks.

Kathy was from a small pig farming area in the middle of Iowa, and Nancy was from Door County way up in northern Wisconsin. This weekend was one of the biggest of the year for the Midwest. There would not be another one like it until the opening weekend for ice fishing. This was the first weekend of deer hunting season.

During their last encounter at the Blues Brothers Bar a week earlier, her and Nancy had met two guys—good looking guys—both from the Midwest. Being that deer hunting at night could be dangerous, and it was Friday the 13th, Nancy had gone shopping that afternoon and bought herself and Kathy a fancy pair of witch's underpants that were supposed to ward off evil spirits.

Kathy looked at the clock—one more hour to go. Scrolling through her e-mails one more time, for lack of anything better to do, she noted that she had gotten an automated reply back from the FBI confirming that they had received her report on the oil analysis. Then she noticed that the reply was from a different e-mail address than the one she had sent the report to. She only noticed because the address on the crumpled up piece of paper that Doctor Jacobs had given her was NH@FBIHB935PA.gov. The reply came back from NH@JVF1000IA.gov. The "IA" at the end had caught her eye because that was the abbreviation for the state of Iowa.

Worried that she had sent the oil report to the wrong address, she Googled the address for the FBI. The FBI was in the Hoover Building, 935 Pennsylvania Avenue, but their e-mail address was HB@FBI935PA.gov. She was confused. Her e-mail had somehow gotten rerouted.

She looked up at the clock. Time had stood still. She still had thirty-five minutes. She needed to get home and start getting ready for deer hunting. Everybody knew that the best time for hunting was at dusk; that's when the young bucks come out.

After sending Nancy a text to see if she had made it home yet, she searched for "JVF1000IA.gov" out of curiosity. JVF was the James V. Forrestal Building at 1000 Independence Avenue. It was the address for the Department of Energy, not the FBI.

Doctor Jacobs was going to kill her if she screwed up and somehow sent that report to the wrong address. She remembered how the FBI agent at Lake Mead had threatened him if they didn't get the report.

She typed back in the NH@JVF1000IA.gov e-mail address. "Dear Mr. NH, I hope I didn't make a mistake and send my oil analysis report to the wrong address. I know it was supposed to go to the FBI. I'm not sure who you are, Mr. NH, but send me a note back that you got my report and that everything is okay. I'll be back Monday morning."

Little did Kathy know that pushing that send button was to be a fatal error.

Newhouse sat staring at the flashing red flag.

# Chapter 33

***

## 86 Pinckney Street
## Boston, Massachusetts

Although it was a brisk evening, Doctor Christenson decided to walk. 86 Pinckney was across the other side of Boston Commons Park. He walked along Frog Pond, which would soon be frozen over and turned into an ice skating rink. As he walked along kicking the autumn leaves, it brought back memories of his walks along the Severn River in Jonas Green Park when he was a Cadet at the Naval Academy in Annapolis. After another ten minutes of walking, ahead, in the dim light of the rustic gas lamps that dotted Pinckney Street, he saw number 86.

Ricky helped his mom get things ready for dinner. He had come to accept his fate, although he wasn't sure who was sixteen going on seventeen. He had never seen his mother so giddy.

He offered to eat in his room so that she and Doctor

Christenson could be alone, but she defensively reassured him that Doctor Christenson was only coming over for dinner, and that was all.

Ricky smiled and gave her a wink. "Yeah! Sure, Mom."

Lucy snapped at him, "Go away, I'm busy. Go watch the news."

As he headed out of the kitchen, he started singing the little song from *The Sound of Music*. "I am sixteen going on seventeen."

Just as he sat down, Sawyer Clark appeared on the screen, again sitting in for Lester Holt. She outlined the main stories that were going to be covered for the evening—more stuff on Iran and the Straits of Hormuz, more stuff on Kim Dumb Luck in North Korea, and alarming news on the gastrointestinal disease that appeared to be spreading worldwide. Doctor Nancy Snyderman, the NBC nightly news medical editor, was again going to be there to discuss the current situation.

Just as Ricky started taking notes, the doorbell rang. Lucy poked her head out of the kitchen. "Oh my God. I'm not ready. Honey, get the door."

As he pushed the record button so that he could watch the news later, he looked back at his mom, who was all in a tizzy.

"Mom, you've got salad dressing in your hair."

Lucy freaked. "Oh my God. Do I?"

Ricky laughed. "Just kidding."

As he headed to the door, all he heard was, "Brat."

Ricky led Doctor Christenson into the kitchen. "Mom, I can eat in my room if you'd like." Lucy gave him the evil eye. Ricky grinned and gave her a little wink, then told Doctor Christenson that he had to go watch the news. Doctor Christenson nodded; he had heard about their Civics class homework.

Lucy was as fidgety as a sixteen year old. Doctor Christenson could not help but smile. It had been over two years since his wife's death, and seeing Lucy standing there brought back memories—memories of his wife standing there in her apron, all in a tizzy. Lucy was beautiful and athletic with dark auburn hair.

Lucy felt the momentary stare. "What? My hair?"

He hadn't realized his momentary lapse in thought and his blank stare. Shaking his head, he replied, "No, no, it's nothing. You just have a little salad dressing on your face."

Lucy freaked. "Oh my God. Do I?"

Doctor Christenson laughed. "No, I'm just kidding. Relax, you're beautiful."

Lucy told him to pull up a chair at the table and that dinner was almost ready. As he sat down, he said, "You know, when I was sixteen, if my mother would've invited my teacher over for supper, I would've probably run away from home, or killed myself."

Lucy smiled. "He considered both, running away from home, Patagonia I think, and killing himself."

They both laughed, and then he asked what they were having for dinner.

Lucy let on like it was nothing special, although she had spent all weekend thinking about it. "Nothing much, just an old-fashioned pot roast, potatoes, gravy, and fresh corn on the cob." Then, very apprehensively, she said, "I hope you like it."

John smiled. Lucy had told Ricky that even though Doctor Christenson's first name was John, he was always to address him as Doctor Christenson.

"Pot roast is my favorite. I have it two to three times a week."

Lucy gasped. "Oh, I'm sorry, I didn't know you had it all the time. I could've cooked something different."

"No, no," John replied laughing. "You see, there's this guy named Morton. I met him in college. He doesn't have a first name; they just call him Morton. You can find him in the frozen food section at the grocery store. He makes this pot roast dish with potatoes, gravy, and peas. Now, it takes a bit of cooking expertise, but I have it down to an art."

Lucy smiled, realizing he was being facetious. She knew very well what Morton frozen dinners were.

"First," he stressed, "you must follow the instructions. You take the pot roast, potatoes, gravy, and peas out of the cardboard box, and then pull the film back at the corner of the container just a smidgen."

Lucy stopped him, “And how much is a smidgen?”

John smiled. “I don’t know exactly. It’s just a little bit.”

Lucy was gaining her confidence and starting to feel a little more relaxed and frisky. “You’re a physicist, went to MIT, and you don’t know how much a smidgen is?”

John shrugged. He had never thought about it; it was just a term everyone used. He told her it didn’t matter and to just make it a little bit.

Lucy waved her hand and went back to cooking. “Fine. I guess they don’t teach everything at MIT.” Then she added, “A smidgen is just a pinch.”

John smiled. “Can I continue now?”

Lucy nodded.

“After you’ve pulled back the plastic film, just a pinch, you put it in the microwave for eight minutes. It’s so simple, a caveman could do it.”

Lucy nodded. “Provided a caveman had a microwave.” Then she told John how a cavewoman would do it. “First, she’d have her man go out and get a big chunk of mastodon or the loin of a sabertooth tiger.” She reassured him that she had already done the hunting, telling him that she had gone out after work and brought down a big water buffalo, dug up some tubers, picked some berries, and started a little fire here on her gas range.

She looked at him with a playful smile. “So, let’s see who’s better, that Morton guy or me.” Then she added, with a coy little smile, “Bet you don’t get dessert with that Morton guy.”

Before John could say anything, Ricky walked into the kitchen. "Mom, I'm hungry. Is supper ready?"

"I'm ready too," John said. "I'm starving."

Ricky smiled. He was finally going to get to use his mother's corny little Atticism on someone else. Politely, he told Doctor Christenson, "According to my mom, you're just a little bit hungry. The kids in Africa are starving."

"Honey," she said, giving him a scornful glare.

John laughed. "He's right. I don't think I'm actually starving."

"What's new in the news?" Lucy asked.

"Not much except some intestinal bug running around the world killing lots people," Ricky replied.

John said that he had heard about that and that India was getting hit very hard—thousands dying.

"Yeah, Doctor Snyderman says it's spreading like hordes of locusts of biblical times. She says it's already here in the United States, out in California, and heading east. Hope I don't have to stay home from school," he said with a smile.

Lucy reassured him that he would be fine.

Then John asked Ricky how his project was going, and Ricky told him that he had hit upon a great idea and that he couldn't wait for him to see it. But he wasn't going to tell him what it was just yet; he needed more data.

John laughed. "Boy, I heard a good one. Someone had a crazy cellphone idea—something about all the cellphones in the world going dead at the same time, driving all the young girls of child-bearing age to kill themselves, and with no one left to repopulate the world, the world comes to an end."

Lucy looked at Ricky and frowned. "Huh, wonder where he heard that from?"

John and Ricky both laughed.

After they finished eating, Ricky went back and watched the rest of the news. Lucy walked John to the front door and thanked him for coming. John told her, "It sure beat Mr. Morton."

# Chapter 34

***

## Interstate I-90
## Tri-State Toll Plaza

Gus was going nuts. He had now sat for four days, waiting. All he needed was for his brakes to be checked, and he'd be on his way. He called Minneapolis just about every hour hoping they could put a little pressure on the guys here at the toll plaza.

Meanwhile, Grant Linwood looked out through the large doors of the Tri-State Toll Plaza heavy trucking mechanical support garage and shook his head. Another rig was being towed in, and he couldn't believe it. He had been working this toll plaza for over twenty years and had never seen this many disabled trucks, and the quandary of it was that the westbound plaza on the other side of the interstate was empty.

As he stared out across the expanse of semi-tractor trailers, one of the other mechanics Greg Alter walked up behind him. "Where the hell to you want me to park this one?"

Grant just shook his head. "How the hell do I know? Go park it over on the westbound side."

In the background, Grant heard the phone ringing and ringing. Finally, already at his wit's end, he yelled back, "Hey, one of you guys get the God damned phone, will ya? My hands are full of grease."

Of course, no one answered the phone, so he walked over, picked it up, and answered politely. "This is Freightways Chicago Truck Route Management, Huehl Road Tri-State Toll Plaza. How can I help you?"

To his surprise, the perkiest little voice in the world said, "This is dispatch American Freight and Trucking, Minneapolis. We are calling in reference to the status of six of our trucks currently at your maintenance facility."

Grant was already so stressed that he wanted to explode and scream, "What six trucks? We have over thirty."

Whenever they got calls from the various dispatch services, it was usually some old argumentative bat on the other end threatening them with lawsuits if their perishable load perished. Without thinking, he asked, "How old are you?"

The young girl, unfazed by his question, said, "I'm Sheila, and I'm nineteen."

He just smiled. He doubted that even Attila the Hun could be nasty. "Well, Sheila, I'd love to help you if you think your trucks look any different than anyone else's."

Grant couldn't believe it. Despite his attempted facetiousness, the little girl stayed as sweet as pie. "Well," she began, perky as perky could be, "I would think that ours look just about like everyone else's, but I could give you the call numbers of the rigs."

In the last week, just about every rig on the interstate was breaking down. They had replaced so many oil pumps, brake shoes and hydraulic hoses that they had run out of parts. Now, they couldn't fix any more trucks, and yet they kept coming.

"Look, Sheila," Grant was getting a little testy, "the call numbers on each rig are twenty digits long. I don't have time to go out and walk around this plaza trying to find your six trucks."

Undaunted by his irate tone, Sheila said, "I can narrow it down for you. The truck I'm specifically interested in is refrigerated. So, you'd only have to check those with refrigeration units on the cab roof."

Actually, she was brightening up his day just a little. "Sheila," he said very nicely, "I have no idea what's going on, but we have every truck from here to California sitting in our plaza, stinking, leaking oil, and it's cold as hell outside." Then he burst out laughing.

"Actually," Sheila said, "from what I hear, hell is very, very hot. Not cold."

Grant explained to her that it was just a figure of speech, that he was just trying to make a point.

"Oh, a point," Sheila began, being just as facetious, "I gotcha."

Grant had to end this call, and soon. He felt his stomach rumbling again, and he had already had one burst of diarrhea that had almost killed him. Now he could feel another one on its way. "Look, Sheila, give me the call number for the truck you're looking for, and I'll go look and see if I can find it."

"Okie dokie then, that would be just great."

Sheila gave him the call number to Gus' truck and then asked if Grant would call back as soon as they got it fixed.

Grant told her he promised he'd try to find it and get it bumped up next in line.

"You promise now? Cross your heart and hope to die?"

Grant laughed. "Cross my heart. I'll go right now and give you a call back within the hour."

"Nope. Won't be here. Going deer hunting. I'm off in twenty minutes. But you promised."

Grant took off running. It was on its way, and he wasn't going to make it.

# Chapter 35

***

## National Security Agency
## Fort Meade, Maryland

Keith Alexander was the Director of the National Security Agency, known as the NSA, the Chief of the Central Security Services—the CSS—and the Commander of the United States Cyber Command. He was also a three-starred general with more bars and buttons on his uniform than almost anybody else in the military. With a snap of his fingers, Alexander could have you standing at the bottom of the Potomac River in cement galoshes next to Jimmy Hoffa if he so wanted.

No one would ever think of walking right up to the door of a three-star general, let alone the Director of the NSA, and just giving a knock, but Sasik was different. Sasik was the general's personal little mole—a sneaky little shit—a Carnegie Mellon computer-geek dropout who helped Alexander get around some of those Constitutional Amendments.

Alexander knew that Microsoft had its Bill Gates—a Harvard dropout. Facebook had its Zuckerberg—a Harvard dropout—and he had his own little Mellon dropout. Whenever Sasik came knocking on his door, he knew the sneaky little shit had something good.

Sasik walked up to General Alexander's secretary's desk and asked if he was in. She nodded affirmatively.

She despised this little worm. She didn't know how or why, but Sasik had more access to the Director of the NSA than the President of the United States did.

She asked, "Would you like me to ring him?"

Sasik shook his head. "No, I'll just knock."

Sasik and the general had a secret little knock. This way, there was never any recorded secretarial record of the comings and goings of Sasik.

"Come in."

Sasik poked his head in the door. "It's just me, Sir."

The general looked up from his desk and motioned to Sasik. "Come in. Close the door."

Sasik had been a Carnegie Mellon dropout, actually, kicked out for what Mellon called "Unethical behavior." Something to do with altering grades.

With his shady background, he would never have gotten his foot in the door in a computer-related field at the NSA, but he had wormed his way in as a lowly coffee boy. On his application for a "support staff position", which, under that heading meant “coffee boy”, he hadn’t mentioned his little misunderstanding at Carnegie Mellon. Being that he had only applied to be a coffee boy, no one had bothered to run across the fact that he was a world-renowned, eavesdropping computer cyber geek, better known to the FBI, CIA, and NSA as a hacker. And, where better to be a hacker than inside the NSA itself.

Alexander had become aware of Sasik one day quite by accident. The general held daily low-level breakfast briefings with various groups within the NSA. On one occasion, he was meeting with a number of his top snoops from a little-known branch called “Signal Intelligence”, abbreviated “SIGINT”.

Within SIGINT was a little subgroup of snoops who tended to overlook little things like the Fourth Amendment, with Alexanders encouragement. They eavesdropped on anyone who they—Alexander—deemed subversive and on leaders of other foreign countries like the Chancellor of Germany, for which they got caught.

The meeting that morning had had something to do with the overthrow of a small country somewhere in Africa called Burundi. Unless it was a high-level meeting, no one payed much attention to a coffee boy coming and going with fresh coffee and donuts.

On that day, Alexander was going berserk, yelling at his top staff of snoops who had been unable to eavesdrop on the President of Burundi. Alexander was ranting and raving that he was tired of excuses and that if he was back in Vietnam, he’d have them all shot, “accidentally” of course by friendly fire. Someone had spilt coffee, and as

Sasik was cleaning it up, he listened to the General's loud remarks.

The problem for Alexander and his eavesdroppers was that, long ago, some do-gooders had added some amendments to the Constitution. One in particular that worried them was about the rights of bad guys. Things had only gotten worse for Alexander when his little group had gotten caught listening in on a not-so-bad guy—the private cell phone of the Chancellor of Germany. Now they were being watched like hawks.

Sasik had actually never heard of Burundi but was curious why the all-powerful NSA could not listen in on the smallest, poorest, unsecured country in all of Africa. For lack of anything better to do, when he got back to his little cubbyhole, essentially a janitorial closet, he tapped into his connection of the world's top hackers. Hackers didn't worry too much about the Fourth Amendment, and Sasik loved this cloak-and-dagger stuff.

It had taken Sasik all of twenty minutes to connect with "Zeus," the current God of hackers, who, after going through a chain of spooks—"Han Solo," the "Mad Hatter," and the "Ghost"—found that the rebels in the jungle already had the drop on the President's office. Alexander's people were trying to eavesdrop on the President when all they had to do was eavesdrop on the rebels.

The following day, Sasik had walked up to Alexander's office. His secretary was not at her desk at the time, so he just lightly knocked on the door. He wasn't sure that the general wasn't going to have him shot, and, at first, it came very close.

The general bellowed out for whoever it was to come in and then called him a "pissant" and asked him who the hell he was. He then told him that if they were back in Vietnam, and a lowly private knocked on a general's door without going through the chain of command, he'd have him shot.

Sasik had apologized profusely, stuttering, "Yes, Sir. I know. I'm sorry, Sir."

He turned to leave, but the general barked at him that as he was already here and had interrupted him, he wanted to know what the hell he wanted.

After explaining that he had accidentally overheard the general yelling at his people about Burundi the day before, he told the him that his people were looking in the wrong place.

From that day on, Alexander had his own little spy satellite orbiting the planet from right here in the NSA. The Fourth Amendment be damned.

Sasik walked in and closed the door behind him.

The general was all ears. "Whatcha got?"

Sasik looked around the General's desk to see if the red phone was still there. Someday, he just wanted to pick that phone up and see who answered. The general had about ten phones on his desk, but only one was red. From the first time he had walked into the General's office, he wondered who was at the other end of that phone—maybe the President or the Pope. He laughed to himself. *Probably his wife.*

"Sir, I've got some chatter."

Alexander knew that meant some ill-gotten eavesdropping. He just prayed to God that it wasn't the Chancellor of Germany again or the big guy's private cell phone in the Oval Office.

"Sir, our ECHELON intelligence gathering network overseas..." which Alexander knew meant Saisk's hacker friends, "...have picked up some chatter about a big meeting of high-level Saudi oil officials at the Aramco facility in Ras Tanura."

The general shrugged. "So what? What kind of meeting? Who's there?"

"We don't know for sure," he said cautiously, "but whatever it is, it's big, and it's hush-hush."

The general leaned forward, put his elbows on his desk and, with hands clasped, stared at Sasik.

"Come on, Sasik. Don't give me any bullshit. I don't care what 'we' know. What do *your* guys know?"

"Well, sir, I have a friend, a cyber-contact in Ras Tanura, and he has a friend in—"

The general sat back in his chair, folded his arms across his chest, and told Sasik to cut the shit. He didn't care about a friend of a friend. He didn't care who found out what, and no one at a Congressional hearing committee would ever think to ask if he got his information from the coffee boy, so he wanted to hear it.

Sasik took out a wadded up piece of paper from his pocket

and started reading the names of the people at the meeting.

"Abdallah Jum'Ah, the Chief Executive Officer of Saudi Arabian oil. A guy named Adil al-Tubayyeb, Saudi Armaco's Vice President of Joint Venture Development, who they flew in all the way from Shanghai, and a woman named Kressmann, Vice President of Research and Development from India."

General Alexander shrugged. "So what? These guys have big meetings all the time."

Sasik waggled his finger. "I'm not done, Sir. That's just the tip of the iceberg. There's a lot more. They also brought in four of the biggest oil engineers they have, including their top guy, Kalid G. al-Buainian."

The general wasn't the most patient man in the world, and he knew Sasik was holding back. "God dammit, son, get to the point."

"Okay, one of my connections accidentally eavesdropped on the King of Saudi Arabia himself."

The general's head dropped. "Jesus Christ."

If it ever got out that the NSA had eavesdropped on the private phone of the King of Saudi Arabia, the Saudies would probably stop all oil exports to the U.S. within days, and he would most likely end up in a federal prison.

Sasik assured him not to worry; this had come from Zeus himself, and no one was ever going to catch Zeus.

The general was very familiar with the cyber code name

Zeus—the current number-one world computer hacker. The FBI's cyber unit had been tracking him for years to no avail.

The general nodded. "Go ahead, let's hear it."

Sasik explained that, two days earlier, some local hackers of a rival political group in Saudi Arabia had listened in on a private three-way conversation between the King of Saudi Arabia, Abdullah bin Abdulaziz al-Saud; Saudia Arabia's Minister of Oil, Ali bin Ibrahim al-Naimi; and Abdullah al-Suweilmy, the CEO of Tadawul, the Saudi Stock Exchange. The King ordered them to be at this big meeting. He told them that there were problems in the oil fields and that it could mean the end of the world.

The general grimaced. The Middle East was a tinderbox just waiting to explode, but even if Israel nuked Iran, Iran nuked Iraq, and Iraq nuked Israel, it wouldn't really be the end of the world. Alexander figured it was just a figure of speech made off the cuff by the King.

"Think about it, Sir," Sasik said, interrupting his thoughts, "why would they have all these bigwigs at a meeting and fly people in from all over the world when they could just as easily do a teleconference link?"

General Alexander got up and walked over to the window, staring off into the distant direction of the White House in DC. "Because they didn't want anyone eavesdropping in on their meeting." The general went back and sat down in his chair. "Okay, so when's this meeting?"

Sasik told him he didn't know. He didn't even know what day it was over there in Saudi Arabia.

The general nodded then told him that he had some phone calls to make. That was Sasik's cue to leave.

Sasik stood up. "You gonna use the red phone, Sir?"

"God dammit, son. Just close the door behind you."

# Chapter 36

***

## Ras Tanura, Saudi Arabia

While General Alexander was making his phone calls, thousands of miles away, a number of black limousines were coursing through the dark streets of Dhahran City. Dhahran City was Saudi Aramco's core administration complex for the giant Saudi Aramco oil conglomerate. By sunrise, no one would be the wiser that inside the secured walls of the complex, the fate of the world would be discussed.

In a room so secured that neither the NSA, the GRU, Russia's Glavnoye Razvedynatel'noye Upravleniye military intelligence service, nor China's 3PLA—The Third Department of the Peoples Liberation Army intelligence—services could infiltrate, Chief Executive Officer of Saudi Arabian Oil, Abdallah Jum' Ah, called the meeting to order.

Jum' Ah thanked everyone for being there and then began. "We are here to discuss a highly sensitive issue that could put Saudi Arabia and the world back into the dark ages."

Despite everyone being tired, many having flown halfway around the world, that comment was like a giant bolt of caffeine—a hundred cups of coffee. Instantly, everyone was awake and sitting on the edge of their chairs.

After explaining that the reason for having everyone there in person was to avoid eavesdropping which could occur on even the most secured teleconference links, Jum'Ah introduced Doctor al-Buainian. Al-Buainian was a stout man, silver haired and in his late fifties. Al-Buaianan was Saudi Aramco's Chief Oil Engineer and Chief Engineer of Research and Development. Jum' Ah asked al-Buainian to please keep it simple—not a lot of engineering, scientific jargon.

Doctor al-Buainain nodded then stood up and walked over to the lectern at the front of the room.

"Over the last eight weeks, we have encountered problems at a number of our refineries, the hardest hit being right here at Ras Tanura, and now rumors of similar problems at refineries around the world—China, India, and Japan."

Al-Buainian could see the growing curiosity on everyone's faces. "I realize that what I'm about to say may sound a little overly dramatic, but I can assure you that the situation we're about to face could be the beginning of the end for the very existence of mankind."

Everyone sat mesmerized. Almost everyone present had learned in high school that the planet had experienced six mass extinctions in the past, but nobody present had heard of any looming asteroids, the sun about to explode, or a Martian invasion. Global warming was a concern but nothing like what al-Buainian was alluding to, like an impending mass extinction within the next few months.

"Our facilities," al-Buainian started, "appear to have been contaminated with a strain of bacteria—a bacteria the likes of which we have never seen before, a strain that reduces crude oil to a smelly sludge within days."

At the far end of the conference table, he saw a hand go up. It was Doctor Susan Kressmann. Al-Buainian knew Susan very well. She was a brilliant chemist, a Cal Tech graduate with a Ph.D. in Organic Chemistry. Al-Buainian nodded in her direction.

She and al-Buainian had shared a number of exciting research projects together and co-authored a number of acclaimed research papers. "With all due respect, bacteria doesn't eat oil."

Al-Buainian shook his head. "Until now."

Doctor al-Suweilmy, the CEO of the Saudi Stock Exchange raised his hand. "Doctor al-Buainian, I'm an economist. I hardly took any science courses in college. What do you mean it reduces crude oil to sludge?"

Doctor al-Buainian explained to the group that the crude oil they pump out of the ground everyday is nothing but the remains of long ago living organisms. Avoiding sounding crass, he explained that the only difference between the waste seen coming out of the backsides of elephants, or a barnyard full of cow or pig manure, was the fact that the decaying waste of long ago had been sequestered thousands of feet down at the bottoms of the oceans. He explained that because of the heat and pressures at those depths, the organic material did not decay, as would have happened to dying organisms topside, but that it had gotten squeezed into a thick, black gunk that we call crude oil.

After a short pause, he continued, "All of that sunlight trapped by those primitive organisms has been lying dormant right here under our feet for billions of years." He looked over at al-Suweilmy, the CEO of the Saudi Stock Exchange. "Without that trapped sunlight, there will be no Saudi Stock Exchange. We'll be back to the 'Middle Ages', burning sticks of wood."

Susan again raised her hand. "So where'd this thing come from?"

Al-Buainian shook his head. "My best guess is that we drilled into a pocket of oil somewhere out there in our oil fields that had the early makings of a bacteria that had started to evolve the necessary enzymes, even at those dark sequestered depths, to degrade that black gunk."

"And now it's topside."

Al-Buainian looked at Susan. "And now it's topside. It has an unlimited food source, a voracious appetite, and it's reproducing at an exponential rate. It's a runaway train."

Essam Farrash, the Director of Civil Defense from Yanbu' al Bahl—a western province of Saudi Arabia—raised his hand. "How long?"

Al-Buainian understood the question.

On the other side of the room, Adil al-Tuboyyeb, Vice President of Joint Venture Development of Shanghai, sat lost in thought. Prior to this meeting, he had gotten word that there were problems at the Port of Zhanjiang in the Chinese province of Guangdong. He had not been given any details as to what the problem was, but now he wondered.

"A matter of weeks," al-Buainian told Farrash. "We have reports of tankers leaving here, and by the time they get across the ocean to their destinations, their oil is already starting to smell. We have to assume that the smell is rotting oil, just like the pig manure that rots and stinks in a barnyard. If we use animal waste as a gauge, a pile of dung is degraded by bacteria in six to ten days."

An Indian-looking gentleman in the back of the room introduced himself and asked, "How do we stop it?"

Al-Buainian shook his head in despair. "I think it'll stop itself when it runs out of food."

# Chapter 37

***

## 1524½ 35th. Street
## Galveston, Texas

Mrs. Hernandez edged to the front of her sofa, her eyes glued to television. She always became excited when they were about to spin the big wheel, more often than not, yelling at the wheel to stop on the one-million-dollar mark as if it had any conscious control over where it stopped.

"Come on. Come on!" she yelled at the television as a mousy lady pulled down on the big wheel. The wheel started spinning, and the little rubber tab clicked, clicked, clicked as it slowed, inching closer and closer to the one-million-dollar mark. Mrs. Hernandez could not believe it; it only had a few more clicks to go and it was going to land on the million-dollar mark. She inched even closer to the edge of the sofa, her fist clenched, yelling, "Yes, yes!" A sudden loud screeching sound filled the room followed by a red ticker tape message running across the top of the television screen:

WE INTERRUPT OUR NORMALLY SCHEDULED BROADCAST FOR THIS BREAKING NEWS ALERT.

Mrs. Hernandez could not believe it. For Christ's sake, this was *Wheel of Fortune*. What was so important that they couldn't wait at least until the wheel stopped? She flopped back on the couch. Unless the world were coming to an end, and even if it were, at ninety years old, she didn't care.

The big wheel disappeared, and a young female newscaster came into view and introduced herself as Kathy Brendt of KPFT News. As Kathy started to introduce her co-anchor, Mrs. Hernandez yelled at the television, "Just get to it, will ya?"

Kathy pointed to a screen behind her showing an aerial view of Galveston. "Over the last week, the city of Galveston has been inundated with an ever increasing foul smell emanating from the direction of our refineries across the bay in Texas City. As anyone living in the Galveston area already knows, chemical odors coming from the refineries are nothing new, but this smell is different, and environmental groups are demanding answers."

Mrs. Hernandez was about to blow a gasket. She couldn't believe that they had interrupted *Wheel of Fortune* to announce that Galveston stunk. Like that was new news.

While Mrs. Hernandez fumed, Kathy continued. "Our radio crew has been across the bay in Texas City all morning with Keith Casey, the director of the complex. Casey would not comment on the nature of the smell, but he did assure the public that it poses no health risk."

Kathy leaned forward slightly and gave a skeptical look. "Although they're reassuring the public that it poses no health risk, there are rumors that the facility has been temporarily shut down." With the aerial view of a haze-filled Galveston in the background, she continued. "We'll bring you more on this breaking news as it becomes available. Until then, we take you back to our regularly scheduled broadcast."

Mrs. Hernandez was about to pop a cork. "Come on, you idiots," she yelled at the screen to get back to *Wheel of Fortune*.

Just as the show came back on, there was Drew Carey standing with his back to the big wheel, telling the audience that he had never seen "that" happen in all of his twenty years on the show. As the credits started to roll, Carey reached over and hugged the jubilant contestant, then the cameras panned out over the audience, who were all standing, clapping and hugging each other.

Mrs. Hernandez yelled at the screen, telling Carey to get his "fat butt" away from in front of the wheel. But before she could see where the wheel had landed, the Univision logo filled the screen.

# Chapter 38

***

## Ras Tanura, Saudi Arabia

After a short break, everyone walked back into the room and took their seats. Ali bin al-Naimi, the Saudi Minister of Oil, walked up to the podium.

"During our break, Mr. al-Suweilmy, as you all know, our CEO of the Saudi Stock Exchange, and I discussed the economic ramifications of our current dilemma. When we finish here, I'm going to go directly to meet with King al-Saud himself. I've asked al-Suweilmy to address the group."

Ali bin gestured to al-Suweilmy.

Al-Suweilmy walked up to the podium, paused, and took in a deep breath. "Thank you, everyone. Within the next twenty-four to forty-eight hours, this news is going to hit the airways. There is no way that we can keep a lid on it, and the immediate shock waves are going to be devastating. The most immediate problem will be for the world stock markets." He paused again, searching for the right words.

"Understand, this is not just going to cause a massive drop in the world markets. If I'm correct, the headlines worldwide are going to read, 'New Bacteria Eats the World's Oil Supply.' If this happens, as I suspect that it will, the world markets in the next few weeks could go to zero."

For a moment, the room stayed silent; everyone was stunned. Then, Essam Farrash, the Civil Defense Director from Yanbu, broke the silence and asked if there were any contingency plans. As a civil defense director, he knew that plans had been made for just about every catastrophic event possible—earthquakes, floods, even asteroids—but no one had ever thought of an oil-eating bacteria.

Al-Suweilmy didn't have the answer. He himself had never even imagined a scenario in which the stock markets of the world could actually go to zero. He looked over at al-Buainian for help.

Doctor al-Buainian nodded, stood up, and walked up to the podium. After thanking al-Suweilmy, he bent down to the little microphone and said just one word: "No."

# Chapter 39

***

## Private Residence
## 1600 Pennsylvania Avenue
## Washington D.C.

Chief of Staff Lenard Robey was jarred from a deep sleep by the flashing red light and piercing sound from the phone next to his bed. Startled, he reached over and picked up the receiver.

"Yes?"

A White House operator told him that she was holding on an incoming high level security call for the president from the king of Saudi Arabia. Robey glanced at his clock trying to figure what time it must be in Saudi Arabia. Then he told the operator to ask the king to hold, and he would be put him through to the president momentarily.

Robey sat up and put his legs over the side of the bed, then he picked up the receiver of the red phone that sat on his bed stand. After two or three bell tones, he heard the phone click.

"Yeah."

"Sir, I have a call holding for you from the king of Saudi Arabia."

The president shook his head trying to figure out where he even was. "What time is it?"

"Here, or there, Sir?"

"Here."

Robey told him that it was two a.m. Thursday morning.

"Okay," the president said, "I'll take the call in the Oval Office. Tell King al-Saud that I'll be with him in just a minute."

"Abdullah, you're up late."

Abdullah laughed. "No, Mr. President, you're up early."

This was President Layton's second term in office, and he and the king of Saudi Arabia had become very good friends.

"Robert, I'm truly sorry to wake you. Believe me, I know what time it is there in the States, but we have a very urgent matter."

Layton leaned forward and rested his elbows on his desk.

"Go ahead. I'm listening."

"Mr. President, it appears that our oil fields have been hit by a catastrophic event that's going to have global consequences."

Layton sat back in his chair. He had known this call was going to come sooner or later. The Middle East was a tinder box. Think tanks in Washington had envisioned every possible scenario—a terrorist group detonating a nuclear bomb, a nerve gas attack, someone setting the oil fields on fire—but no one had ever imagined what the king was about to tell him.

"Mr. President, Robert, it appears that our oil fields have been infected with a bacteria that's degrading our crude oil as fast as we pump it out of the ground."

Robert sat back up, confused. "Abdullah, what the hell are talking about?"

"I know this sounds ridiculous. We don't understand it yet ourselves, but either we have dug into an ancient pool of oil that has long sequestered a primitive bacteria that billions of years ago had the enzymatic fortitude to breakdown the components in crude oil, or someone has genetically engineered a bacteria—a terrorist attack on our oil fields."

Layton sat in disbelief. "How bad is it?"

"Bad. Within days of bringing crude to the surface, this bacteria eats away at it, turning it into a foul-smelling mess. This place smells like a damn pig farm."

Robert sat there, not knowing what to say, when Abdullah added, "It gets worse. I think we've been shipping infected oil all over the world for weeks."

As the president sat lost in thought, he remembered a passing comment made at the morning daily briefing about problems at the oil facilities in Texas City. At the time, it seemed like just another minor item, like many of the topics touched upon at the daily staff meetings. But now he couldn't remember what the problem had been.

"Mr. President, Robert, are you there?"

"Yes, Your Majesty. Abdullah, I'm sorry. I was thinking."

"Robert, the reason I've called you is because we're not going to be able to keep this from the news media for very long. As you can imagine, when this news hits the airways, the world's oil markets are going to plummet, taking the rest of the markets with it. We don't have much time, but fortunately this is a weekend, and that gives us a few days before the markets will open again on your Monday morning."

"What're your thoughts?" Layton asked.

"I think we have to be ready. When and if this news breaks, we have to be ready to close the stock markets worldwide, at least temporarily until the immediate shockwave has passed. There's going to be a massive sell-off."

Robert sat in the silence of the Oval Office shaking his head. "I agree, Abdullah. Let me assemble my staff and start working on this, and I'll get back to you within the next twenty-four hours."

Just as the King was about to hang up, Layton added, "Oh! Abdullah, can you send one of your engineers to sit in on our meetings, someone who knows what's going on over there?"

The king told Layton that he would have a man there in twenty-four hours.

Layton put down the receiver and leaned back in his chair, staring at the ceiling. He could never have imagined the enormity of this problem or the mass extinction that was to follow in the next few months.

Reaching over his desk, he picked up a phone.

"Sir," the Chief of Staff answered.

"Lenard, I want every cabinet member in the Situation Room in twenty-four hours."

Robey looked at the clock. "That's two a.m., Sir."

"I'm fully aware of what time that'll be." Before Lenard could say anything, he added, "And I want you to get hold of Zacharik, Chairman of the Federal Reserve, and Hatch, the President of the New York Stock Exchange." Robey was about to argue, but the president cut him off, "All fifteen cabinet members, Lenard. I don't care where in the world they are. I don't give a damn if someone is having a baby. Have them here. No questions asked. Do it. Absolutely no one except the fifteen cabinet members, Zacharik, and Hatch. No secretaries. No fanfare. No limos. Everyone just slowly trickles in, different entrances; we don't want to tip off the media."

Robey sat on the edge of his bed. "Mr. President, what do I tell everyone?"

"You don't tell them anything. You just tell them to be here. Oh, and find some MIT-type oil expert. Have him at the meeting also," he barked sternly.

Robey took the phone from his ear and stared at it. How was he going to find an MIT oil expert and order him to be at the White House Situation Room at two a.m. on a Saturday morning? But before he could say a word, the line went dead.

Layton stared at the ceiling. "If it comes to this, how the hell am I going to convince Putin to close down the Russian stock markets?"

# Chapter 40

***

## Beacon Hill Bistro
## Boston, Massachusetts

Lucy was in a frenzy as she stood in her white bathrobe, blow-drying her hair, putting on makeup, and baring her teeth to look for any food particles.

Ricky had been on his way downstairs to watch the news and had poked his head into his mom's bathroom to let her know when he saw her, teeth bared, growling at the mirror.

Leaning against the doorframe, he said, "Those are called dental dawdlers, Mom."

Lucy looked over. "What're you talking about?"

"Those little specks that get stuck between your teeth—the ones you're looking for."

Lucy giggled and then scowled, "Go away, I'm trying to

get ready. Aren't you supposed to be watching the news?"

Ricky looked at the time on his iPad. "Not on yet. Still got five minutes."

Lucy, nervous about the evening ahead, scoffed, "There must be something better you can do besides bother me."

Ricky smiled and thought about it. "Not really. This is pretty entertaining."

Lucy loved bantering with her son but didn't have time for it at this point. Doctor Christenson was going to be there any minute.

"Go away, you terrible child."

Ricky grinned and then thought for a moment. "You know, this is your third time in less than two weeks seeing Mr Christenson. Aren't you a little too old to be … you know, all giddy like a teenager?"

Lucy stopped brushing her hair and glared at him, "I'm not to old for anything, mister. And I'm *not* a giddy teenager. You make that comment one more time, and I'll have you shipped out to live with my brother in Patagonia where hopefully you'll be eaten by a bear."

Ricky smiled. "I don't think they have bears in Patagonia."

Lucy frowned, "I think you know what I mean. Now, Doctor Christenson is just a nice man, he's well educated, and I enjoy his company. That's all."

Ricky nodded. "Uh-huh. Yeah, Mom."

Lucy tipped a bottle of hand cream and started spreading some on her face. "Oh dammit. Now see what you made me do. Go away."

Ricky laughed as he glanced at the time on his iPad. "Oops, gotta go." As he turned and was about to head down the hall, he stopped and asked, "What's for supper?"

Lucy stopped wiping the hand cream off of her face and gave a fiendish little smile. With retribution for the old age comment, she said, "Well, I'm not sure what I'm having, but you're having pot roast."

Ricky's eyes brightened. He liked his mother's pot roast, but then a look of skepticism crept over his face. He sniffed the air. The smell of her pot roast cooking usually emanated throughout the whole house.

"I don't smell anything."

With an exaggerated sniff of the air, Lucy smiled. "Huh! I don't smell anything either. Maybe I'm just getting too old and losing my sense of smell."

Ricky rolled his eyes. "Okay, Mom, sorry about the old age comment."

"That's better. Now, your dinner is in the freezer."

Trying to act as though he was terribly surprised, he knew that meant a TV dinner, and he already knew that his mom and Doctor Christenson were going out.

"You're going to leave me here, home alone, on Friday night? Remember that movie where those two bad guys broke into that little kid's house and almost killed him?"

Lucy smiled. "That little kid was all of ten years old, and I think it was called *Home Alone*."

Lucy was already feeling bad enough. It wasn't that she was worried about him being home alone. There were many nights that she had late aerobic classes, and he was home from school long before her. But, tonight, she was having mixed feelings. This wasn't just a late-night aerobics class.

Ricky let out a deep, sorrowful sigh. "Don't worry about me. I'm sure I'll be fine. Of course, the frozen dinners aren't as nutritional as your home-cooked pot roast. Lots of preservatives. Lots of salt. Probably not good for my blood pressure. I'll probably lose weight. Some degree of malnutrition."

Lucy rolled her eyes. "Such dramatics. Maybe we need to get rid of those potato chips, ha?"

Ricky made it into the living room just as the NBC peacock lit up the screen, and he heard the familiar, "From NBC World Headquarters in New York, this is the NBC Nightly News with Lester Holt."

Ricky grabbed his yellow pad and scratched down "Lester Holt". A few days earlier, one of his classmates, Adam, who had apparently not watched the news, had gotten called on, and it had been obvious that he was trying to wing it. Mr. Abernathy, their civics teacher, had let Adam ramble on for a while, watching him squirm. Once it was obvious that he had hung himself, Mr. Abernathy asked him who had been the news caster. Adam said it was Sawyer Clark, who had been filling in for Lester for the last week, but little did he know, not having watched the news, Lester was back.

"Good evening, everyone. In our top stories tonight, for the second week in a row, tornados have devastated the heartland of America, this time heading directly through one of the most populated cities in Texas.

"On the political front, the House and Senate continue to debate the future of health care in America. The President is vowing to continue his fight for affordable health care for everyone. For that story, we'll hear from our White House correspondent Chuck Todd.

"And, on the International front, Aung San Suu Kyi was awarded the Nobel Peace Prize today for her activist activity in Myanmar, 'The Land of the Golden Pagodas.' We'll have a live report on that story from our correspondent in Myanmar."

Ricky jotted down "Myanmar". He had never heard of Myanmar, had no idea where it was, and had never heard of the Land of the Golden Pagodas, but he was sure that Mr. Abernathy would know.

Just as Lester was about to introduce the next story about a gastrointestinal disease, the doorbell rang. Ricky hit the pause button and was about to get up when Lucy flew by. "I'll get it."

A few minutes later, Lucy and Doctor Christenson walked into the living room. Ricky stood up and said, "Hey." Then Lucy told them both to have a seat, that she was almost ready and that she had to get her jacket.

As they sat down, Ricky asked Doctor Christenson, "You ever heard of Myanmar?"

He shrugged. "*Bridge on the River Kwai.*" He could see that Ricky had no idea what he was talking about. "Myanmar used to be Burma. During World War II, the Japanese forced British, Australian, and American troops to build a railroad bridge across the river Kwai. Became a real famous movie. You should watch it. It's good. You'll like it."

Ricky nodded. Maybe he would, that way he could kill two birds with one stone. Home alone on a Friday night. Watch a movie and study at the same time.

Lucy came bopping back into the living room as flighty as a bumblebee. "I'm ready."

Doctor Christenson got up and was about to head to the door when Lucy pulled out a yellow piece of paper and proceeded to go through a long list of instructions that she had scratched down for Ricky. "Don't open the doors for anyone. If there's a fire, call the fire department. If the city's warning sirens go off, go to Channel 13 for information on why the sirens are going off. I have put a flashlight in each room in case the electricity goes out. Oh! And you can always call my cell phone."

Ricky shook his head in disbelief. "Geez, Mom, I never thought of that."

Then she handed Ricky the piece of paper. "I've written down the emergency number in case you forget it."

Ricky looked at it, rolled his eyes, and turned the paper so that Doctor Christenson could see it. "911."

Finally, after a hundred hugs and attempted kisses, Lucy and John headed out. Ricky sat back down and hit the play button, fast forwarding here and there through the stories of the tornadoes in Dallas; they talked about that the day before, and the health care stuff was nothing new. He wasn't going to watch the story about Aung San Suu Kyi because he was going to watch the movie *Bridge on the River Kwai*, but he was going to have to look up the spelling of her name.

As they walked along the brick-covered sidewalk toward the Beacon Hill Bistro, Lucy felt like she was going to faint. She had butterflies in her stomach, Ricky's little song, "I am sixteen going on seventeen," played over and over in her head, and she felt as giddy as giddy could be. There was a chill in the air, the leaves rustled, and John held her hand as they walked under the flickering gas lamps that dotted the sidewalk. It was about the most romantic evening she could ever remember.

Ricky jumped up to go put his pot roast dinner in the microwave. Lester was reporting on some study that found that American women were too fat. Ricky jotted it down but didn't really understand why someone had to do a whole study to figure out that three-fourths of American women were overweight.

By the time he got back, Doctor Snyderman was already talking about the gastrointestinal outbreak that was circling the globe and that it had already caused the deaths of millions. According to her, neither the epidemiologists from the World Health Organization nor the CDC in Atlanta had yet been able to identify the causative agent.

Ricky sat thinking to himself, that might not have been a bad idea for his science project. Diarrhea is definitely inertia; when it gets moving, it keeps moving in a straight line until some outside force acts upon it, like it killing you. If everybody in the world had it, it would shut down the world's work force, and the world's economies would collapse, changing the direction of society. It was too late; he had already submitted his talking-to-plants project to Doctor Christenson. He focused back on the news.

Lester asked Nancy if they had any clues at all, and Doctor Snyderman told him that the most likely culprit was just a common old run-of-the-mill bacteria called E. coli but that no one had figured out what had changed and why it had become so nasty.

A week earlier, Nancy and Sawyer Clark had been discussing gene sequencing as a means of identifying the culprit, so Lester asked if anyone had sequenced these E. coli guys and if they had found anything.

Nancy shook her head, no, explaining that all attempts so far had been fruitless and that just about every bug on the planet had been sequenced.

Ricky heard the microwave beeping. Dinner was ready. He hit the pause button again and headed to the kitchen.

As they approached the bistro on the corner of Charles and Chestnut, a doorman dressed like Paul Revere greeted them, "Good evening, Doctor Christenson."

Lucy was a little taken aback but didn't say anything. Everyone in Boston knew of the Beacon Hill Bistro and that even the President of the United States probably couldn't get a table at this place on a Friday night, and yet the doorman knew him by name. Then she figured they must just be acquaintances from elsewhere.

Inside, the lights were low, and a young lady escorted them to a table next the open fireplace. After she left, Lucy leaned across the table and quietly asked, "How did you get a reservation here at this place, and next to the fireplace?"

John shrugged. "Somebody must've canceled."

Lucy sat back and didn't say anything, but it sure sounded fishy. She knew that if anyone was ever lucky enough to get a table at this place on a Friday night, they sure in the heck wouldn't cancel. She was about to ask John some more questions when a young man interrupted, "Good evening, my name is Matthew, and I'll be your waiter tonight." He handed them both a menu. "I'll give you some time to look over the menu." He nodded to Doctor Christenson. "I'll bring your wine right away, sir," and he walked away.

Lucy leaned forward again and, in a low whisper, said, "He didn't even ask what kind of wine you wanted."

John shrugged and told her that he had already taken care of it and that they were going to have the house special wine. Lucy sat back. This was getting a little spooky. First, they get a reservation at the most sought-after restaurant in the city, then a table by the fireplace nonetheless, and now the maître d' already knows what kind of wine to serve.

Trying to be nonchalant, Lucy looked at the wine list. The house special was a sweet Chardonnay with no price listing, which she knew meant that if you needed to ask, you couldn't afford it.

Lucy started having doubting thoughts. How could a high school teacher afford a million-dollar bottle of wine? This place. The fireplace. The doorman knew him. She had seen some of those television shows where some guy was actually a CIA operative or Attila the Hun or something. She was about to ask John some questions when a crackling piece of wood in the fireplace exploded, startling her.

Ricky was trying to eat his TV dinner and at the same time jot down notes. Doctor Snyderman was explaining that India had been hit very hard by the gastrointestinal infection, especially in the slums, killing millions. To her right, a large projection screen ran a video of the streets of New Delhi, which showed an exodus of people leaving the city. Hordes of flies swarmed over hundreds of dead bodies that lined both sides of the streets.

Lester had not seen this video clip and was truly shocked, "God, it looks like a great plague of the Middle Ages."

Nancy nodded. "It is, and it's traveling around the world at an alarming rate."

Matthew approached the table, set down a basket of bread, and poured each of them a glass of wine. "Have you had time to look at the menu yet?"

John nodded. "I think we've decided."

"Very good, sir. What will it be?"

John pointed at the menu, explaining that they would both have the house special, which was a tea-cured duck breast with roasted chestnuts served on a bed of sage pappardelle and sautéed in an herbal sorrel sauce.

Matthew nodded. "Very good choice, sir," and started to walk away when Lucy interrupted.

"I'd also like a small chopped salad instead of the Caesar."

Matthew stopped and turned. "I'm terribly sorry, ma'am. We don't have any fresh salad tonight. We haven't received any shipments of any fresh vegetables for over a week."

After Matthew left, Lucy leaned across the table. "Isn't it odd that a place like this wouldn't even have fresh vegetables?" John shrugged. He had to admit it was a little odd.

Ricky set down his yellow pad of notes. Lester was introducing the "Making a Difference" story—something about a bunch of women who had knitted quilts for little kids in the Arctic Circle. Ricky picked up the TV remote and pulled up Netflix. Finding *Bridge on the River Kwai*, he hit play.

Lucy was exhilarated, she had never had such a romantic evening and such a delicious meal. She had never dreamed that she would dine at the Beacon Hill Bistro.

After they finished, John stood up, pulled out her chair, and helped her with her jacket. As they approached the maître d's desk, John leaned over, and Lucy heard him say, "Tell the wingman 'thanks'."

The Maître d' winked. "I'll tell him, sir."

Lucy's jaw dropped, raising her eyebrows.

# Chapter 41

***

## Atlanta, Georgia

*The Witching Hour.*

"Are you sure?"

"I'm sure I'm sure. They buried her today. I saw constable Dogberry himself posting a notice on the inn door."

"God," Josephine mused with glee, "old Ebenezer's going to give us the number-one spot at the table. No one has ever gotten a fresh corpse with a full baby still in her, and just buried today."

Ralph set down his book *The Graveyard Shift* and glanced up at the clock. How ironic, it was the witching hour—midnight. Although he hated his night security job, sitting on a Friday night in a Coca-Cola complex on the outskirts of Atlanta, he imagined it had to be better than his forebears sitting in a cemetery all night guarding against marauding medical students trying to find fresh corpses for dissection.

Ralph turned on the little portable television before getting up to do his hourly rounds. An infomercial was claiming that by applying their cream to one's genitals daily for seven days it would give one a sustainable erection and rejuvenate joints at the same time.

Ralph shook his head in despair. He had a wife at home, two kids, and was working a second job all night just to make ends meet. He wasn't going to need a sustainable erection.

Just as he turned to go make his rounds, a piercing sound emanated from the little television. Red letters scrolled across the top of the screen. "THIS IS A BREAKING NEWS ALERT FROM CNN INTERNATIONAL NEWS."

Ralph stopped to listen.

"CNN News has just learned that a commercial airliner flying from Lagos, Nigeria to the capital city of Abuja has crashed into a crowded neighborhood in Ibadan, a city some eighty miles north of Lagos. The plane, a McDonnell Douglas MD-83, took off from Lagos Airport, and sometime after takeoff, the pilot radioed that they were having engine problems and were going to divert to Ibadan. According to CNN reports, twenty minutes later, the plane plummeted into a large apartment complex in the heart of Ibadan. All one hundred and fifty passengers and crew members are presumed dead, and an untold number are buried in the burning rubble in the center of the city. According to the Director of Ground Operations in Lagos, Amos Olajide, the plane is owned by Indian airline Dana Air. Apparently, the same plane was grounded days before, reportedly for problems in its hydraulic systems. An international branch of the FAA, the Federal Aviation Administration, will be arriving to conduct an investigation."

The screen flashed back to its regular broadcasting. Now, a man was putting a whole fish into a blender in an info-mercial for a Fish-O-Matic. After blending it, the man poured it into a glass and drank the grey liquid. After wiping his lips and smiling, he announced that it was not only healthy, but it was cholesterol free and high in vitamin E.

Twenty minutes later, Ralph made it back to his desk and opened his book. He was anxious to see if Josephine and Alistair had dug up the pregnant corpse and gotten it back to the medical school.

# Chapter 42

***

## Situation Room
## 1600 Pennsylvania Avenue

Layton walked from the presidential residence along the colonnade toward the west wing. At the far end of the corridor, Chief of Staff Robey stood waiting.

"Good morning, Mr. President."

Layton nodded. "Everyone here?"

Robey nodded as a full dressed Marine stood at attention.

Layton shrugged. "Well, let's go then."

Just as they got to the Situation Room, Robey stopped. "Oh! And sir, we just received word that a commercial airliner has crashed in Nigeria."

Layton paused. "Terrorism?"

Robey shook his head. "Doesn't look like it so far. Early

reports are mechanical problems."

"Any Americans on-board?"

"From the information we have so far, there were no Americans on-board."

As another young Marine opened the door to the Situation Room, Layton mumbled, "Thank God, that's not our problem then."

After six years, being in the middle of his second term as president, Layton dreaded having to deal with the press and what his administration was going to do about terrorists killing Americans overseas if that's what this had been. Although he felt bad for all of the Nigerian families that lost loved ones in this tragedy, at least it was not going to be his problem.

As the president and Chief of Staff Robey entered the room, it was obvious by the looks on everyone's faces that they were all curious about the unprecedented cloak-and-dagger secrecy. Layton looked around the room and nodded. He recognized everyone except for two.

Vice President Allen stood up. "Mr. President, everyone is here, and we have two new guests."

Allen pointed to al-Buainian first. "Mr. President, this is Doctor Kalid al-Buainian, Chief Engineer of Saudi Aramco's Research and Development at Ras Tanura, and next to him is Doctor Benjamin Armstrong, an oil expert from MIT."

Layton acknowledged each with a nod and thanked them

for coming. Then, with no other formalities, he wasted no time.

"Twenty-four hours ago, I received a call from King Abdullah al-Saud of Saudi Arabia. He informed me of a problem with the Saudi Arabian oil supply. I have very little information on the problem, and that's why I asked King al-Saud to send Doctor al-Buainian here to update us." President Layton turned to al-Buainian. "Doctor al-Buainian, would you please inform us as to the current problem?"

Kalid, a short, stocky man wearing his customary Arabian white turban, stood up and thanked the president.

"I'm very humbled to be here addressing such a distinguished group of individuals. I'll try to keep this very simple and straight to the point. Within the last month or so, our oil fields in Saudi Arabia have been infected with a bacteria that degrades our crude oil as fast as we can pump it out of the ground."

There was no reaction from anyone, just stunned silence. No one could even comprehend what al-Buainian had just said. After an eternity of exchanged looks, shaking his head in disbelief, Thomas Davenport, the Secretary of Agriculture, blurted out, "What do you mean it degrades it?"

Al-Buainian shook his head and said bluntly, "It's eating it. It's breaking down our crude and turning it into a fowl smelling puddle within days."

Being that Vice President Allen and pretty much everyone

else in the room thought of the oil fields of Saudi Arabia as gasoline, he asked quizzically, "It eats gasoline?"

Al-Buainian shook his head. "No, it's worse than that—much worse."

For the next ten minutes, al-Buainian explained that gasoline was only a very minor component of crude oil and that oil refineries were nothing more than huge moonshine stills, but instead of boiling off alcohol, they boiled off gasoline. Then he added with a hint of a smile, "Refineries are the world's largest breweries."

Doctor Armstrong, MIT's oil expert, already knew where this was going, and even he could not comprehend what this would mean for the world. Unconsciously, and louder than he had meant, he mumbled in disbelief, "It's eating the 'petrochemical feed stocks'."

Al-Buainian had a good grasp of English slang. "Yup! Would you like to explain it to the group?"

Armstrong and Kalid knew each other very well and had worked together on a number of research projects. Armstrong stood up hesitantly. He was more used to lecturing to MIT postgraduates than a bunch of sociology majors, but he told Kalid that he'd give it a try.

After nodding to everyone, he began, "Moonshiners in our Appalachian mountains ferment corn and distill off alcohol." He figured that even a bunch of sociology majors understood this much. "The problem that moonshiners have is that after they've boiled off their alcohol, the bottom of their kettles are left with piles of worthless mash, which they spread around the forest floor. To get gasoline, oil refineries pretty much do the same thing, but instead of corn mash, they cook a thick black gunk that we call crude. Crude is long-ago pressurized piles of dead plants, planktons, and maybe a few T-rexes. But the dead organic material that makes up crude was never fermented; it was pressurized at the bottoms of the oceans. The volatile gases and hydrocarbons that we think of as gasoline resulted from high heat and pressures. So, just like our moonshiner friends, when we finish cooking our crude, we're left with a thick black gunk that the industry calls 'petrochemical feedstock.'" Then Armstrong dropped the bombshell—an end of the world bombshell. "Without these 'petrochemical feedstocks', if something were to happen to them, like a bacteria eating them, our world would come to a screeching halt."

Little did the group understand that he meant it literally—"A screeching halt."

Newhouse sat back in the far corner of the room staring blankly. "How the hell did this stuff get over there? I was assured that it would be self-limiting. Dump the stuff in the gulf. It eats up the thick black globs of goo washed up on the beaches, cleans up the pelicans, the news media goes away, the administration gets to drill in the gulf, and when it runs out of food, it's gone. Now its seven thousand miles away in the goddamned oil fields of Saudi Arabia eating the world's oil."

The Secretary of Education, a plump woman in her fifties, raised her hand. "What do you mean the world is going to come to a screeching halt?"

Armstrong shook his head. “I mean just that. In the world of physics, the mother of all evils is friction. Every lubricant, grease, oil and hydraulic fluid in the world is made from ‘petrochemical feedstocks’, and if I understand Doctor al-Buainian correctly, that is what this bacteria appears to thrive on, and it reproduces at an exponential rate. Without lubricants, every moving, spinning thing on the planet is going to grind to a screech-burning halt.”

The Secretary of Education grimaced. “Where’d this thing come from?”

Armstrong shrugged and then looked over at al-Buainian. “You want to field this one?”

Al-Buanian spent the next twenty minutes explaining that no one was sure. Either they had accidentally drilled into a pocket of oil that has for millions of years sequestered bacteria that long ago had the enzymatic capabilities to degrade those long-ago dead plants and animals, or someone, a terrorist group, had genetically engineered bacteria and intentionally dumped it into their oil fields. Then al-Buainian added, “We think this is most likely terrorist related. We’ve been pumping oil worldwide for over a hundred years, and no one has ever drilled into a pocket of oil contaminated with rogue bacteria.”

Gladys Chapman, Secretary of Commerce, raised her hand. “If it was a terrorist group, who would’ve had the capabilities of engineering such a bug?”

Newhouse stared blankly.

Vice President Allen then raised his hand. “Can it be contained?“

Al-Buanian shook his head. "It's too late for that. It appears that we've been shipping the stuff all over the world for weeks, maybe months, long before we had any idea that there was a problem. We now know that, early on, heavily contaminated shipments went to India, China, and Japan."

Finally, after another twenty minutes of discussion, Secretary of Agriculture Davenport asked, "What are we going to do about it?"

President Layton stood up. "That is why we're here. After discussing this with King Abdullah al-Saud, he and his inner circle foresee two global catastrophic events—events that are going to change the very fabric of our society. The first and most immediate is going to be a crash in the global oil markets—an event that's going to devastate the world's economies. That's going to happen within days." He paused. "The second is going to devastate societies. It could bring mankind to the very brink of extinction," he said in a very somber tone.

Everyone sat speechless. This was so beyond confusing that no one could even think of a question. Finally, al-Buainian spoke up. "May I, Mr. President?"

Layton nodded. "Please do."

"This feedstock stuff is our only source of lubricants. We have alternative energies, natural gas, wind, water, solar power, we can even still get some of the gasoline off the crude before the bacteria have time to destroy it, but we don't have an alternative lubrication. We can engineer everything to run on natural gas, solar, wind, and water power, but the moving parts are going to burn up because of friction. The world's food production and distribution depends on moving parts. We have seven billion people on this planet that depend on moving parts."

Al-Buainian paused, broken. "This bacteria is good. It's efficient, and before we have time to develop a defense, we're going to crash and burn." With that, al-Buainian sat down.

Layton stood back up and addressed the group. "We're going to meet back here in twenty-four hours."

Everyone looked at their watches. That was two a.m. on Saturday.

"At that time," Layton continued, "I want a briefing from each cabinet member, an assessment of how this is going to affect your department, and a contingency plan of how your department is going to handle the situation. A three minute briefing each, and no more. No secretaries, and no unsecured lines. There can be no leaks until we have a better understanding of the problem."

Layton turned and walked toward the door. "Twenty-four hours."

# Chapter 43

***

## Situation Room
## 1600 Pennsylvania Avenue

Ralph had finished his midnight rounds, poured himself a cup of coffee, and sat reading his novel *The Graveyard Shift*.

Josephine and Alistair had managed to dig up the pregnant corpse, sneak it past the sleeping night watchman, and get it into the dissection laboratory at the medical school. No one knew what kept a baby in the womb until the time was right, so Josephine pushed a piece of wood between the corpse's legs just to be sure that the baby wouldn't pop out. She was ecstatic. Old professor Ebenezer wasn't too keen on female medical students, but none of the guys had gotten a corpse with a full-grown baby still inside of her.

Six hundred thirty-eight miles away, President Robert Layton sat in the dark silence of the Oval Office.

"Have we finally done it?"

In the previous few weeks, news had been surfacing of major problems around the world—problems with food production in India, a gastrointestinal disease that was spreading across the globe at an alarming rate, killing millions, and now this—bacteria that could devour the world's energy supply in a matter of months.

Layton looked at his watch—a watch given to him as a gift by Vladimir Putin of all people, the one guy that he was going to have to convince that they might need to close all of the world stock markets, maybe within the next twenty-four hours.

Chief of Staff Lenard Robey stepped into the Oval Office. "It's time, Sir."

Layton nodded.

As they walked toward the Situation Room, Layton and Robey could never have imagined that within a few months, they and the core of the United States government would be sequestered in an underground nuclear bunker buried deep in the Cheyenne Mountains in Colorado Springs.

Layton started the meeting with Richard Murphy, the CEO of the New York Stock Exchange, and Randel Belforti, the current Chairman of the Federal Reserve. For the time being, discussions were limited to the immediate fallout that the news of oil-eating bacteria would have on the world's economic markets. Layton asked Murphy for his opinion and a contingency plan.

Murphy, a distinguished gray-haired Princeton economist in his early sixties got up and thanked the president.

"Mr. President, this news is going to have devastating effects on the world markets that we're not going to be able to stop, but possibly what we can and have to do is cushion the initial shock."

Layton nodded. "And how do we do that?"

Murphy paused and ran his hands through his gray hair. "Mr. President, I think we have to make a preemptive news media strike. We can't wait for CNN or some terrorist group to announce some earth-shaking statement like, 'Rogue Bacteria Eats the World's Oil.'"

Murphy handed the president a piece of paper, explaining that it was a statement that he and the Chairman of the Federal Reserve, Mr. Belforti, had worked on earlier in the day.

"Mr. President, this is an unassuming statement that hints of bacteria found in the oil wells of Saudi Arabia that could have future effects on the world's oil markets. It doesn't mention that it eats it. It's vague. After a long discussion, Mr. Belforti and I agreed that we should leak this statement to the news media—our local CNN station right here in Atlanta. As it is written, hopefully it'll be treated as just another unassuming news story, and the news will slowly be filtered to other media outlets around the world. Then, over the next few weeks, we take control of the release of further information. We release bits and pieces, manipulating the media in such a way as to control—control what Randel and I think is, if indeed this bacteria can eat oil at a voracious rate, the inevitable downfall of the world's economies and possibly life on the planet as we know it."

Layton shook his head in disbelief, things were happening so fast that he didn't even have time to think.

Before he could say a word, Murphy interrupted, "Mr. President, we don't have a lot of time for discussion. Now's a good time. It's three in the morning on a Sunday. Sunday morning, three a.m., no one's paying attention. The Sunday newspapers have already been printed. I think we release it now."

Layton looked at the Vice President. "Allen?"

Allen nodded in agreement.

Layton handed the paper to Arnold Jedson, the Secretary of Homeland Security. "Have your boys leak it. CNN. Do it. Now."

After Jedson left the room, Layton turned to al-Buainian and asked him if he really thought that they may have dug into a rare pocket of oil containing a rare rogue bacteria a few hundred-million years old, or if he thought this was indeed most likely terrorist related.

Al-Buainian shook his head. "No, Mr. President, this was terrorism. Someone did this. We've been pumping oil from all over the world for over a hundred fifty years. It's not a million-year-old rogue bacteria."

Newhouse sat back in the far corner and just stared blankly. "Shit. The best laid plans of mice and men."

Vice President Allen raised his hand and asked if it really mattered at this point since it was already out there and what difference it would make if they hunted down some terrorist or not.

Armstrong argued that it could make a difference, not so much in bringing some terrorist group to justice, but, by understanding how they had manipulated the bacteria, maybe they could undo what's been done.

Andria Carpenter, the fiery red-headed Secretary of the Department of Housing and Urban Development, raised her hand. "What if what's done is done?"

Armstrong shrugged. "Macbeth—everyone dies."

***

It was now six-thirty in the morning, and Ralph had only thirty minutes left of his graveyard shift. He looked down at his book. Josephine stood next to Ebenezer as the scalp sliced over the protuberant abdomen of the corpse. A yellow fluid gushed out of the gaping hole, and then a pale wrinkled form, a baby boy connected by a cord of flesh, bubbled out through the open wound and settled between the corpse's legs.

Ralph put his bookmark between the pages and closed the book. He would have to wait until next weekend to see what happens with Josephine and Alistair.

As he packed his things, waiting for his morning relief, he

watched a CNN report about problems in Saudi Arabia and that the problems could have an effect on future oil prices. He didn't pay much attention. He smiled; he had just had the oil changed in both his and his wife's car. He was good for six months.

# Chapter 44

***

## New Delhi, India

With six thousand people per square kilometer, the streets of New Delhi were always chaotic. As a newscaster for NDTV, New Delhi's number-one TV news station, Prannoy Patel was used to chaotic, but today she sensed that something was different—something was wrong.

It was a Monday morning, and traffic on Mondays was always really bad, but this Monday was even worse. A sense of calamity hung in the air. She had left her apartment early, and after winding through the backstreets and cutting across two manicured lawns of private homes and a city park, her driver managed to get her to the news station just minutes before the scheduled seven a.m. broadcast.

As she rushed into the news room, Anaya, her personal assistant, stood waiting for her at the door with a makeup kit in hand.

Prannoy brushed her off with the wave of a hand. “No time, I’m late.” Grabbing the stack of the day’s news sheets from the news director, she rushed over and sat down behind the desk. With only seconds to spare, she brushed back a wisp of her long black hair. Then, just as she looked up, the cameraman was counting down with his fingers: four,… three,… two,… and then the ‘On the Air’ sign stated to flash.

“Good morning, this is Prannoy Patel, NDTV, New Delhi’s number-one television news station.”

Prannoy tried to focus on the news sheets. Her eyes burned; the normal clouds of filth that filled the air of New Delhi had been unusually heavy and foul. With a bit of a squint, things came into focus.

“As we begin the week, two major news stories are impacting not only New Delhi but all of India. The first is a paralyzing shutdown of India’s transit system that extends from the southern tip in the Bay of Bengal, northward, here to New Delhi and beyond. For that story, we’ll hear from our local correspondent Shaili Chopra at the Ministry of Railways and Mass Transit.

“The second is an infectious gastrointestinal outbreak that has been taking a terrible toll especially in New Delhi’s overcrowded slums. For more on that story, we’ll hear from our NDTV reporter Rachid Singh who is standing by on the banks of the Yamuna River at the mouth of New Delhi’s largest slum. And later, we’ll hear more on the terrible accident that killed twenty-three young people at the Parkash Amusement Park this weekend when something went terribly wrong on the ever popular high spinning

'Flying Frisbee' ride. At this time, park officials are only saying that there were mechanical problems."

As Prannoy shuffled to the next news page, a still photo of a large freight train loaded with fruits and vegetables came into view on the screen to her left.

"As everyone is well aware, traffic gridlock is nothing new for the streets of New Delhi as cars, trucks, rickshaws and cattle all compete for the same space, but the recently developing problem plaguing India is in its mass transit system." She turned to the picture. "The survival of India's nearly two billion people depends on this mass transit system. With over ninety-five percent of our population residing in all but a few overcrowded cities, any break in the production and transportation of food and basic goods could result in the death of millions within days, and this is what's currently happening."

Gesturing to the screen, she continued, "As you can see here, this stalled locomotive is reportedly only one of hundreds of trainloads of fruits, vegetables and meats sitting and rotting in the countrysides all across India. Furthermore, it's not only the transit system, but there are reports that much of the heavy farming equipment that produces all of this food has been paralyzed by the same problems. At this point, no one seems know what these problems are, or at least no one is talking."

The screen changed to a live feed with the Ministry of Railways and Mass Transit in the background. "For more on this story, we go live to our local correspondent Shaili Chopra, who is standing in front of the Ministry of Railways in downtown New Delhi."

Waiting for her cue, Shaili stood in the sweltering early morning heat in front of the Indian Railways Headquarters located at the New Delhi Railway Station in the heart of downtown New Delhi. The stench from Paharganj, one of New Delhi's largest slums, which was only blocks away, was overwhelming and making her sick. Finally, the red light on the camera in front of her started to blink, and the cameraman counted with his fingers: four,… three,… two…."

Shaili made one last desperate attempt at swatting away a swarm of flies in front of her face. "Thank you, Prannoy. As you can see, I'm standing here in front of the Ministry of Railways Administration Building, the Grand Central Railway Station for all of New Delhi. This massive system connects the cities and the local farming areas for India's nearly two billion people."

Prannoy was all too familiar with the Grand Central Railway Station, an overcrowded area of filth and stench only blocks from the squalid banks of one of the many slums throughout the city. "So, what's going on?"

Swatting at another group of aggressive flies, she replied, "Well! That's what I'm here trying to find out, and I'm not getting much cooperation. I've been trying to get an interview with the Director of Transit Operations, Rail Bhavan, or the Chief Executive, Mangu Singh, but I'm being told they're not available for comment. But here's what I know so far—this place is abuzz with closed meetings, and no one is talking. There are rumors that the prime minister himself is going to be here later today. That in itself is a rare event and wouldn't happen unless some major crisis was brewing."

"Like what?" Prannoy interjected.

"I don't know, but I suspect that what's happening out there in the countryside is the same thing that we're seeing right here in the heart of the city." Shaili turned and pointed down one of the long streets leading to the railway station. "I can tell you one thing—in the last few days, there's been nothing moving on these streets except hand-drawn rickshaws."

Prannoy nodded. "Tell me about it. My driver had to cut across two private lawns and Jayanti Park just to get me here."

"Exactly." Shaili nodded. "According to the local bus drivers and those with cars and trucks, their vehicles are running fine, then the engine lights come on, and they start banging and rattling. According to one man, he says it sounds like metal grinding on metal, they overheat, smoke, and shut down."

"And no one knows why?"

Shaili shook her head. "Nope, no one knows why."

Prannoy was about to ask another question when she saw her news director gesturing that it was time for a commercial break.

"Shaili, let me take a break, and then I'll get right back to you. I have a lot more questions."

The director signaled to the cameraman to cut the feed, and Prannoy sat back in her chair. She took a sip of water, and Anaya ran over and powdered her face. A few commercials ran, and then the cameraman signaled for her to get ready. Then he pointed to the "On the Air" sign.

"Thank you for staying with us. We are live with Shaili Chopra at the Ministry of Railways in downtown New Delhi, trying to get some information on the current crisis that is plaguing India."

Shaili reappeared on the screen. "Prannoy, while you were gone—let me show you something."

Shaili stepped over to a stalled bus and motioned for her cameraman to zoom in for a close up shot under the bus. A small puddle of oil came into view. Shaili turned to the owner of the bus, a stocky man in his fifties, and asked him what the problem was. Speaking in a Punjabi dialect that she hardly understood, the man lifted the hood of his bus and said, "Itthe. Itthe."

A foul smell billowed out and almost knocked Shaili off her feet. She didn't quite understand what the little man was saying, but from the way he was pointing, she thought it meant, "Here. Here."

The man was pointing to the engine block; the hoses and gaskets were oozing oil. Then he scooped up a finger full of oil from around one of the leaking gaskets and nearly put it up Shaili's nose. "Bashna. Bashna."

Shaili pushed his hand away trying to tell him politely, no thanks and that she got the picture.

Prannoy smiled; she understood the man's dialect. "What's it smell like? He wants you to smell it."

Shaili stepped back. "It doesn't smell like oil."

Just then, there was a commotion in front of the Ministry Building as an excited crowd of reporters pushed toward the steps. Shaili glanced over. "Sorry, Prannoy! I have to go. Let me see what this is. Maybe it's someone from the Ministry."

The live feed went blank, and Prannoy announced that they would be right back after another commercial break. She stood up and stretched as a commercial ran showing a sleek new Indica V2 racing down the open streets of New Dehli. Shaking her head, she wondered where the hell they had found an open street.

Karesh, the news director, walked over and handed her the next set of news sheets. Prannoy took the sheets and, with a cursory glance, said, "What's next?"

"Rachid, he's reporting from Bhalswa."

Prannoy grimaced, "Ouch! God, that must be pleasant."

Along with Shaili, Rachid Singh, as far as Prannoy was concerned, was one of the best on-the-spot reporters that NDTV news had. Both he and Shaili had been graduates of New Delhi University's famed communications program.

His fingers signing, "Four,... three,... two,..." the cameraman pointed to Prannoy.

Rachid appeared on the screen wearing a surgical mask, swatting at the hordes of flies, and doing everything possible not to vomit in his mask.

"God, I'm sorry, Prannoy. The smell here is so bad, and the flies."

Prannoy told him that he had nothing to apologize for and to go ahead and do the best that he could.

He nodding and said, "Thanks, Prannoy."

Rachid turned and pointed to the river behind him. "I'm standing here on the banks of the Yamuna River, which runs, as you know, through the heart of the city of New Delhi. What started as pristine water run-off from the Yamunotri Glacier eight hundred fifty miles away, high in the Himalayas, is now the main sewer system for fourteen million people."

Suddenly, the microphone jerked away from Rachid's face, and he momentarily disappeared from view. "Damn. The thing bit me." He held his hand up for the cameraman to get a picture, and Prannoy could see a large welt bubbling up on the back of his left hand.

She smiled. "Ouch! That must hurt."

Rachid nodded. "As well as being the main sewer system for the city, this three-mile stretch of the river is also the home to over three million slum dwellers. Here in the Bhalswa slums, there's no running water and no electricity, and, in places, the river is so thick with refuse that cats and dogs can walk across from one side to the other. Normally, residents of New Delhi proper either ignore, accept, or just pretend that it doesn't exist."

Prannoy interrupted, "Out of sight, out of mind."

"Not anymore, Prannoy. Normally, hundreds of people die here in the slums every day, and no one ever knows. With over three million people cramped into this three-mile stretch, no one ever really knows that most of these people were ever born. The chances of a baby living past its first few weeks of life here in the slums are pretty slim. Children die here by the hundreds every day from disease and starvation, but now a diarrheal intestinal outbreak has upped that number to thousands a day."

Prannoy interjected, "What are the local officials doing about it?"

Rachid swatted at a huge black fly that nearly filled the lens of the camera. "Well, Prannoy, that's a politically loaded question. Normally, as far as the government is concerned, as long as the problem stays in the slums, everyone just turns their heads. But as you know now, it's a city-wide problem."

Prannoy nodded. For the past two weeks, she had been reporting on the gastrointestinal outbreak that has all but shut down the local economy.

"Prannoy, I have to tiptoe lightly around the political politeness police here, but I'm not sure the government is here to help the people in this slum." He paused and cautiously said, "I think the government is here to protect the city from the slum people, not here to help the slum people."

Prannoy liked that. Say it as it is. It was a risky comment, but that's what a good reporter does. She looked over at Karesh rolling his eyes. As the news director, the shit would fall on his shoulders. He didn't need the whole damned government coming down on NDTV news, but it was a live feed, and it was too late. It was already out there.

Rachid motioned for his cameraman to pan up the length of the Yamuna River. The Bhalswali slums covered both banks of the river—a maze of filth and shanty dwellings.

"As you well know, Prannoy, the Bhalswali slum is a dreadful place."

Before he could finish, Pannoy interrupted, "What are all of those military trucks doing there?"

The cameraman reflexly panned off to Rachid's left where a long line of military trucks stood. Both banks of the Yamuna River were lined with soldiers holding assault rifles. What looked like well over a hundred health care personnel dressed in masks, boots, and white infectious disease outfits were loading bodies onto the trucks.

Prannoy gasped. "What're they doing?"

Rachid explained that they were carrying away bodies. It had been estimated that of the three million slum dwellers, over a hundred thousand had died in just the past week.

"And the guys with the guns?"

"The guys with the guns, Prannoy, are there to stop anyone from leaving the slums and streaming into the city. The people here in this slum are starting to panic. They're agitated like rats scurrying around on a sinking ship. They sense that this place is a death trap. I think that at any time we could see the people storm head-on with the soldiers."

Suddenly, there was a loud burst of rapid gunfire and people screaming. A massive blur of slum dwellers came pushing out of the mouth of the slum behind Rachid and his cameraman. Soldiers, who had taken up a defensive position, started shooting randomly into the crowd. Rachid's cameraman dropped his camera, and he and Rachid ducked behind their news van.

Startled, Prannoy looked over at Karesh, who was anxiously signing a cutting motion across his throat. "Cut the feed."

Prannoy broke into tears. "We'll be right back after this break."

# Chapter 45

***

## 70°19'32"N. 148°42'41"W.
## North Slope
## Prudhoe Bay, Alaska

Mrs. Hernandez sat glued to her television. Ever since Univision started this Spanish channel, she'd been able to watch all of these movies. She liked the curly hair guy in this one; he was cute—actually all three were cute—and they were going to the moon. She remembered when she was a little girl, eighty some years ago, she had watched the movie where a spaceship was shot out of a cannon and landed right in the eye of the moon. Now these guys were really going there.

She watch as they laughed and joked, pushed buttons and floated around inside their spaceship. They looked like such nice boys. Then, suddenly, their spaceship shook, and bells, buttons and whistles started buzzing all over the place. She scooted to the edge of her chair. The good-looking, curly-haired guy looked scared.

"Oh no," she mumbled to herself.

She didn't know much about spaceships and going to the moon, but she could tell something was terribly wrong. Scooting even closer to the edge of her chair, she gasped as a big red alarm sign filled the screen, the red, flashing glow filling her apartment like a giant strobe light.

"Master Alarm.

"Master Alarm."

Throwing her arms up, she flopped back in her chair. She couldn't believe it. Not now. They didn't need a commercial now.

Five thousand miles away, Mike Williams sat behind his desk dreading the call he was going to have to make to Houston. He didn't even know what he was going to tell them other than, "Houston, we've got a problem."

He had just received a call from Rubin, his field operator in charge of Liberty, the largest of the three oil fields on the north slope. Rubin had just told him that he was going to have to shut down drilling operations at Liberty.

Williams just stared at the landline on his desk. There were no cellphone towers this far north, only thousands of miles of tundra, ice, twenty-four-hour a day darkness, unrelenting gale force winds, mosquitoes, and polar bears. A week earlier, one of the drilling crew members had been mauled by a polar bear.

British Petroleum and Phillips would have his ass if

drilling stopped at Liberty. Liberty supplied over ninety percent of the oil flowing into the eight-hundred-mile Trans Alaskan Pipeline and most of the ships that came into Valdez, and Rubin wanted to shut it down.

The problem started a few weeks earlier with the arrival of the latest drilling crew. Because of the extreme isolation, twenty-four hours a day of darkness, and of course the chances of being eaten alive, drilling crews were rotated in and out every three months from the lower forty-eight.

The last crew sent up three weeks earlier had all been sick on arrival, and now that had spread to everyone on all three oil fields, liberty being the hardest hit. Everyone spent their days sitting on the toilets, shitting their brains out and so weak that they could hardly lift their heads. An unrelenting gastrointestinal diarrhea had wiped out the work force.

Williams reached over and picked up the landline. After three or four rings, he heard a click at the other end. "BP Exploration Center."

"Hey, it's Williams up here in drilling."

Houston was the hub for British Petroleum-Conoco Phillips drilling for North America. Adam knew who was calling and where he was, and he was glad he was there in Houston. He didn't envy those guys up there in that shithole. He had once been sent up there for a month; some BP administrator had come up with the bright idea that it would be educational for its operators in the lower forty-eight to have a feel for what it was like for its field crews far north. It had been a bad month. It was at the ends of the world, barren as hell, with windblown rocks covered in seagull shit, and dark.

"Hey, what's up?" Adam asked with a touch of indifference.

"What's up? I'll tell you what's up," Williams blurted out angrily. "This place is shutting down. You guys sent a whole crew of guys up here a few weeks ago that are sick as shit. Now everyone up here is sick as shit. And I mean 'shit'."

Adam knew what he was talking about. The lower forty-eight had been hit hard with a gastrointestinal outbreak of some kind, which had closed schools across the country and had started putting a big dent in the local economy. Adam didn't say anything, but Williams was probably right. They must have taken it with them when they went up a few weeks earlier.

After a long silence, Williams yelled, "Hey! Are you there?"

"I'm here," Adam muttered.

Oil had never stopped flowing through the Trans Alaskan Pipeline since it started in 1977, and he knew that BP and Phillips would castrate both him and Williams if those fields were ever shut down, especially Liberty.

"Have you had your guys seen by the doc?" Adam tried to ask casually.

Because of the distance and isolation, British Petroleum and Philips kept a nominal medical staff at Prudhoe Bay.

Any serious medical conditions were flown out either to Anchorage or the lower forty-eight.

Williams exploded. “Are you kidding me? Have you seen this guy? He looks like Doogie Howser. I think he still wears diapers.”

Adam knew what Williams was talking about. Douglas “Doogie” Howser was a sixteen-year-old child prodigy in a television series set in a Los Angeles area hospital. A number of medical students signed up for a government program wherein the government pays for their medical school training in return for two years of service in under needed areas. So, right out of medical school, most still in diapers, students were sent to some God-forbidden place to play doctor.

Adam had to hold the phone away from his ear as Williams continued to rant and rave. “Do you think any guy in his right mind would come to this place to practice medicine? You know, there’s not a lot of girls up here. This place isn’t a big draw for single women.”

Adam cut him off. “You can’t shut down Liberty. That pipeline goes dry, and every car, truck and train across the country will stop moving, and gas prices will go through the roof. Shit, we’ll have the British Prime Minister and the President of the United States up our asses.” He took a deep breath. “Look, Williams, do something, but you can’t shut down Liberty.”

Mrs. Hernandez could not believe how many commercials they had to show. She was about to have a heart attack as she yelled at the television, “Just get back to the movie.”

She couldn't wait to find out why the big "Master Alarm" was flashing. These guys were flying through space, and something was wrong, and they had to go and have a million commercials. Finally, the good-looking curly haired guy came back on, the red, flashing "Master Alarm" still screeching.

She edged back to the front of her chair as he raised his microphone. "Houston, we have a problem."

# Chapter 46

***

## 86 Pinckney Street
## Boston, Massachusetts

Lucy pushed open the door to Ricky's room and poked her head in. "Hey, let's move it, big day. You have to be at school in two hours, and you're already running late."

Ricky was already wide awake. Doctor Christenson was going to be handing back everyone's research projects on inertia—everyone's scientifically acceptable idea of a theoretical force that would change the direction of society. The key had been that it had to be a scientifically acceptable idea. Things like *Invasion of the Body Snatchers,* the Martians are coming, and making people into "Soylent Green" little green potato chips were out.

Ricky was apprehensive. For twenty percent of their grade, they had to stand up in front of the class and give a five-minute dissertation on their idea. Twenty percent of the grade was a lot, but he was less worried about the twenty percent,at and more worried about what everyone might think of his idea. He didn't want to be the laughingstock of the class.

Despite his mother coming up with some pretty corny ideas, like all the girls in the world killing themselves because their cell phones quit, and with no young girls left to repopulate the world, the world comes to an end, she had come up with a good idea for his presentation.

For dramatics, he was going to project Edvard Munch's painting "The Scream" on the screen behind Doctor Christenson's desk and then stand in the projection of the picture while giving his presentation. Lucy had helped him fill twenty styrofoam cups with nice, fresh, crisp lettuce. Ricky was going to set a cup on each student's desk then outline his idea of the psychological stress of being able to feel and hear what plants were feeling and thinking. Then, after his speech, he was going to have each student take a leaf of lettuce and chew it, all the time thinking, listening and imagining hearing the screaming and the suffering in pain as their teeth ground the poor, helpless, little piece of lettuce to bits. Then, for just one last dramatic effect, he was going to hold his hands to his face and scream just like old Edvard's painting.

Lucy made her way downstairs, hit the light switch in the kitchen, and turned on the little kitchen television that hung in the corner. She tuned into CNN World News and started preparing breakfast.

Twenty minutes later, Ricky came into the kitchen. "Mom, what's for breakfast?" Ricky looked around and saw that Lucy had not even started breakfast. She was just standing, spellbound, staring blankly at the television.

"Shhh, watch this."

Seven thousand miles away, Prannoy Patel was not having a good hair day. She had been forced to ride to the television station in a rickshaw, the only way left to get around New Delhi. Her clothes were covered with foul splotches of urine and feces. As the rickshaw hit another pothole, the remains of someone's intestinal contents splattered up onto her legs. A large irregular mass clung to her right leg and slowly slithered down into her shoe like a leech with a life of its own. Tears streamed down her face.

In a matter of only a few weeks, death had swept through New Delhi. The skies were blackened with dark clouds of swarming flies as their offspring, streaming torrents of maggots, flowed along the streets engorging themselves on the intestinal contents of the once living. The temperature was over one hundred degrees, and thousands of bloated bodies littered the streets. As the rickshaw bounced along, Prannoy wiped a large glob of something off of her face. The foul air burned her eyes, and she sobbed. "How has it come to this?"

The rickshaw ride to work had already taken over an hour, and she still had blocks to go. She had already missed the seven a.m. broadcast, now she was just hoping to make the noon news. Her underarms were stained with sweat, and her legs and dress were covered with human waste. She had never felt so gross in her life. All she wanted to do was stand in a shower for days.

Everything was happening so fast. Only a week earlier,

the more than three million slum dwellers had started overrunning the banks of the Bhalswa slums. Storming into the city proper, they had brought with them a virulent intestinal sickness. Although, as usual, everyone blamed the slum dwellers for any outbreaks, it seemed unlikely that this intestinal debacle could be blamed on just the Bhalswa dwellers. Within a matter of weeks, outbreaks and death tolls were being reported all across the Indian subcontinent—Mumbai, Chennai and Kolkata all reporting hundreds of thousands of deaths.

Adding to the misery, India had been hit with a second, unrelated problem that was even more devastating—one that was aiding and abetting the intestinal outbreak. India's mass transit system, which supplies food, water, and medical supplies to its nearly four billion people, had been crippled with ongoing mechanical issues. These same mechanical issues plagued the streets of New Delhi as the smoldering remains of cars, trucks and buses clogged the streets, foul smelling oil dripping from every orifice of the engines and mixing with the pools of human waste.

Lucy stood transfixed as she watched a CNN news clip of a woman newscaster who had just been pushed down and was being trampled by hundreds of people at New Delhi's Grand Central Railway Station. The crowd, like rats on a sinking ship, desperate to escape the sure death that awaited them in the city, were totally oblivious to the woman under their feet. Lucy watched as the newswoman struggled to keep her face from being pushed down into a pool of waste. Then, someone stepped directly on her face, pushing her deep into a watery pool. The woman struggled, her arms flailing, and then her last bubbly breaths could be seen rising to the surface of the pool of urine and fecal matter. Her body went limp, and the feed went dead.

The cameras switched back to the newsroom, where Prannoy gasped and screamed, "Shaili! Shaili! Oh my God!"

Not taking her eyes off the little screen, Lucy just stood there, shocked at what she was seeing. In a hardly audible mumble, she uttered, "Look at that."

The government had been putting out daily estimates of the number of deaths, but no one knew the real numbers. It was currently estimated that one million of the three million slum dwellers in the Bhalswa slums were already dead, but of the fourteen million in the city proper, no one had any idea of the true numbers. The military, who had set up a defensive line around the slums, had all but given up and gone to take care of their own families. Health care workers sent in by the government had also abandoned any attempt to help. Social order in the city was breaking down fast. Death was not playing favorites. The outbreak did not recognize the Hindu's social class system. The rich, the poor, the untouchables, everyone was fair game. Death hardly had to work at it; it was having a field day. On a continent where it was estimated that over ninety percent of the four billion people lived on the verge of starvation on any given day, for death, it was easy pickings. It had already taken out the weak and the children and now had its eyes set on those who remained.

As Prannoy's rickshaw weaved in and out of the crowds, she could feel that there was an overwhelming sense of panic in the air, like the herds of wildebeest at the end of the dry season, agitated, sensing that it was time to move. Prannoy wasn't sure what it was going to take to spook the herd, but she sensed that the time was near. If the food could not come to the city, the city was going to go to the food.

As Prannoy felt the leech-like slimy glob of intestinal contents slide down her leg, her rickshaw came to a sudden stop. Without a word, her driver set down the rickshaw, hurriedly stepped behind a bus, lifted his long robe and squatted. A watery bout of intestinal contents disappeared into an oily undulating stream of flowing maggots. Before the man could stand back up and drop his long robe, hordes of flies had already deposited a fresh batch of young in the vicinity of his intestinal orifice.

Five minutes later, her rickshaw pulled up to the front of the news station. At the curbside lay a man face down in a pool of human waste. He had squatted in an attempt to rid his intestines of fluid but had been so weak that he had been unable to get back up, collapsing face down. He had drowned in a pool of his own excrement.

Ricky sat eating a bowl of cereal as he watched the little television. He had packed his little styrofoam cups of lettuce into a small box. Meanwhile, Lucy just stood watching the CNN news clips. She gasped at what she was seeing. "My God, look at that poor newswoman. She's…."

Prannoy had splashed some water on her face and had tried to clean her hair. Anaya had not made it to work. She was either sick, dead, or had fled the city. The "On the Air" light started to flash.

"Good afternoon. This is Prannoy Patel for NDTV news."

With tears in her eyes, Prannoy apologized for her appearance. "The city of New Delhi is on the verge of political and social collapse. Food shortages, transportation problems, and an infectious disease has already killed millions. The city is experiencing a mass exodus. Thousands are packing their belongings and attempting to make it to the countryside—the farming areas—their only hope for finding food."

Prannoy brushed an oily wisp of hair from her face. "Provided we can still make the link, we're going to go to Doctor Tarun Kapoor, an Infectious Disease Specialist at the University of New Delhi."

Doctor Kapoor appeared on the screen in a white laboratory coat. Prannoy thanked him for being with them and then asked if he felt that this was like something out of the *Book of Revelation*, or like one of the great plagues of the Middle Ages.

Doctor Kapoor explained that scientists around the world have known for years that this day was going to come, they just didn't know when or who the culprit was going to be—the H5N1 bird virus, Ebola, SARS, or as some yet unknown bug.

"Why now?" Prannoy interrupted. "And how did this bug, or whatever it is, become so deadly?"

Doctor Kapoor nodded. "The word is 'virulent', and I'm not so sure that it's that aggressive of a bug, as you called it. It might just be that it's at the right place at the right time."

Prannoy looked at her notes. "You said earlier in the week in a report that it might just be an ordinary run-of-the-mill garden variety bacteria gone awry. Es—cher—icha, something."

Doctor Kapoor nodded. "Eschericia coli, also called E. coli for short. It's a run-of-the-mill dirt and fecal matter bacteria that's found on every square inch of the planet."

Prannoy nodded. "Why now? Why is it so virulent, as you call it?"

He shook his head and explained that he was not sure it was the E. Coli at all or that it was any different than it had been.

Prannoy interrupted, "Everyone else thinks it is."

Doctor Kapoor smiled, "Everyone else thought the world was flat."

Prannoy felt like saying, "My, aren't we the cocky one?" But she held her tongue.

"The Centers for Disease Control and the World Health Organization have been putting our bulletins and reports for weeks on the E. coli bacteria as the causative agent of a worldwide gastrointestinal outbreak." Doctor Kapoor explained that he felt that the mechanical problems plaguing not only India but the whole world were related but that he just didn't know how. He explained that he wasn't sure it wasn't the old "chicken or the egg" argument. Which came first, the emaciation, the starvation, the weak, and the sick that were allowing a normally friendly bacteria to have a field day; or a friendly bacteria causing emaciation, starvation, and weakness? Doctor Kapoor added that genetic sequencing of every E. coli bacteria around the world had been sequenced and that nobody had found any changes.

Then Doctor Kapoor added, coldly, "Prannoy, I think what we're seeing here is just nature doing its job. The E. coli, just like the flies, the maggots, the funguses, and the slime molds, are all doing their jobs, decomposing organic waste."

As Ricky continued eating, Lucy was watching another CNN news clip, this one the highlights of an interview with an infectious disease doctor in New Delhi. When he referred to the death and carnage of millions as "organic waste", Lucy turned to Ricky, who had just spooned a mouthful of Cheerios, and said, "Boy, that guy. I wonder if he realizes that the organic waste he's talking about are human beings."

Ricky got up and put his bowl in the sink. "Mom, I gotta go."

Lucy turned back to the screen. "Just one second, I wanna hear this."

It was another news clip between the woman newscaster and the New Delhi infectious disease doctor. She asked him, "How are they going to stop it?"

The doctor shook his head. "I don't think we're going to stop it. It's not going to stop until it runs out of food."

Lucy turned to Ricky. "Thank God we don't live in India."

# Chapter 47

***

## 481 Hazel Street
## Wilkes-Barre, Pennsylvania

It was midnight—seven a.m. in Moscow. Chief of Staff Lenard Robey, Vice President Allen, and President Robert Layton sat in silence in the Oval Office, waiting. Layton had spent countless hours on the phone in the last few days with the leaders of every major country in the world. Some had been easy to convince; others, like Russia, had been met with skepticism. Vice President Allen had joked with Layton, "You can take the boy out of the KGB, but you can't take the KGB out of the boy."

Now they sat waiting to hear from Putin, the last player. If Russia was not on board, the other countries would fall like dominos. France, Germany, China, everyone had agreed on closing their major markets providing each of the other countries did the same. If Russia did not agree, the deal was off.

Then, after an eternity of waiting, the red phone started to ring. Layton took in a deep breath, reached over and picked up the receiver.

Peter was up as usual waiting for the early European market reports on CNBC. Being that the European markets were eight hours ahead of the U.S., he had to be up early to put in his buys and sells for the day, well before the U.S. markets opened at nine. Then, it was back to bed, but instead of counting little sheep jumping over a fence, he counted one-hundred dollar bills.

Peter was very proud of himself. He was twenty-four years old, a millionaire, and he had never worked a day in his life. And if all kept going well, he would never have to.

After getting his business degree from the prestigious Wharton Business College in Pennsylvania, which his parents had funded, he had not found a job. Actually, he had never really looked for a job, at least one that required work. He lived off of his parents' money and dabbled in same-day trading.

He found that same-day trading was great for someone like himself who really didn't want to work. He had always found work so tiring. Same-day trading involved watching the news for some socially depressed stock, not for a stock that was depressed for business reasons, which is what that stupid Wharton had taught, but for a stock that was depressed because of some "unbusinesslike" event. In other words, find a company that was getting clobbered by the media for some issue beyond their control, and then take advantage of their misfortune. Like the time that competitors had spread rumors that the

Chesterfield cigarette company had an employee working at their Richmond, Virginia plant who had leprosy.

Thousands of smokers, frightened of getting leprosy, switched brands, and Chesterfield sales plummeted. Meanwhile, Camel, Winston, and Marlboro sales skyrocketed. Of course, three of the four Marlboro Men had already died of lung cancer, but it had been a stroke of genius by someone, although not a business model taught at Wharton. The top-grossing movie at the time had been *Ben-Hur*, and in the movie, Charlton Heston, Ben, crawls on his belly to a leper colony to visit his mother who was rotting away from leprosy.

Wharton's business premise was meaningless to Peter. According to Wharton, the only way to run a successful business was the old fashioned way—you had to earn it. Not according to Peter. According to him, the best way to make money was to take advantage of someone else's misfortunes. Peter thought of it more like being Robin Hood—steal from the rich and give to the poor. In this case, the poor being Peter.

As Peter sat waiting for the reports from the European futures markets, he looked over at the picture he kept on his desk of British Petroleum's Deepwater drilling platform that had exploded in the Gulf of Mexico. He had had it enlarged and framed. It was the most beautiful picture he had ever seen, and it had made him a millionaire many times over without working.

In the weeks after the explosion, the news media had been unrelenting, showing workers with globs of oil stuck to their feet, little birds choking on oil, their little wings weighted down with black tar, and fish on the beaches gasping for air. It was a beautiful sight. As far as Peter was concerned, so what if a few million birds choked on some oil? And Louisiana, who cared about Louisiana? Nothing there but sweltering heat, mosquito-ridden swamps, and crawfish-eating Cajuns.

Peter thought about it many times, how he wished he could just go out to that rig and kiss those BP guys, but, of course, they were all dead. Unfortunately, or in his case, fortunately, they had blown themselves to smithereens and covered the beaches with globs of oil.

In the weeks after the event, everyone had gone around yelling and screaming at how unethical the BP guys had been to cancel a crucial test called the cement bond log test. Had they done the test, the explosion would not have happened. But, at the same time, Peter wouldn't have become a millionaire. Peter mused on the people who were yelling and screaming about the "unethicalnetisity" of it—the same people who wanted their oil but didn't want to have to pay for it.

From a business model standpoint, the BP workers had done the right thing. The protesters had no idea that the delay in getting the Deepwater Horizon rig moved had already cost BP over twenty million dollars, and the cement bond test would have cost millions more, increasing the cost of the protesters' precious oil. So BP took a chance.

Sure, it may have backfired for BP, but for good old Peter, 9:56 p.m. on April 20th 2010 was the day he became a millionaire. Not a bad day considering he had napped all day.

In the months before the explosion, oil stocks had been skyrocketing in fear that Iran would try to block the Straits of Hormuz. News media hype. Peter knew that Iran would never block the Straits of Hormuz because, if they tried, the rest of the world would nuke them. Israel had already been threatening to nuke them anyway and was just looking for a good reason.

In a matter of a few weeks, the news media hype had driven oil prices from $60 a barrel to way up over $110.

Peter had bought futures in oil stocks well below $40 a share a few months earlier when Saudi Arabia had threatened to start pumping and flooding the oil markets.

Peter had never been a religious guy, but now he was a believer there was a God. He had made a mental decision that when oil hit $110 a barrel, he was going to sell. No matter what the futures were, he was going to take his money and run.

*Thank you, God.*

Oil hit $110 a barrel just two days before BP blew up their rig. Five days later, as the news media hype peaked, Peter was sitting on a pile of cash, and he hadn't lifted a finger. The more television coverage by the news media, the more BP's stock price plummeted. Peter had waited a week or two, then when he figured BP's stock was just about at its bottom, he had bought all of his shares back plus a few thousand more and has been sitting and watching them climb back up toward $110 ever since.

Peter's parents thought he was despicable, taking money

without working for it, but he didn't care. They had worked their asses off all their lives, and now they lived on a minuscule Social Security check that they got from the government once a month. To Peter, it was just as unethical not to take advantage of someone's misfortunes if given the chance as it was to take advantage of them.

He had written a paper while at Wharton, which had netted him an F, arguing that if you had a retarded kid who had candy, and you had the chance to take that candy from him, and you didn't do so because you felt sorry for him, that was just as unethical as taking the candy. The conclusion to his paper had read, "There's a sucker born every day. Take the money and run."

The most work Peter had done in the last year was push the "enter" button on his computer. As long as there was oil, and as long as people loved driving their little cars, Peter would be a millionaire.

The European futures markets started opening. Peter watched the oil futures. They were looking great. There were problems in India, people starving or something, but Peter didn't care or worry about India; India didn't have much influence on oil stocks.

Peter turned off CNBC and opened his personal stock account. He smiled. "Four million six-hundred thousand and some loose change."

Peter shut down his computer and headed to bed. His energy-saving icon that he himself had designed bounced across the screen. "Work is for poor people, and it is unethical. Plus, it's a lot of work."

# Chapter 48

***

## Massachusetts Preparatory School For the Advancement of the Sciences Boston, Massachusetts

Doctor Christenson walked into the room, hung his jacket on the hook behind the door, and set the stack of science projects on his desk.

"Good morning, everyone."

Without looking up, he started to finger through the stack of folders. Everyone sat in silence; no one wanted to be first to stand up in front of the class and give their report on their research project. Ricky slowly nudged his box of lettuce-filled cups further under his desk.

As he picked through the folders, apparently looking for one in particular, Doctor Christenson told the class how he had been following everyone's progress for the last few weeks and that he was very impressed with everyone's ideas. Then, finding the folder that he wanted, he pulled it out and held it up. "Katie?"

Katie's head dropped, her pretty red hair falling over her face. "Not me," she pleaded. "Please. Pick Ricky."

Ricky, who was sitting in the seat in front of her, turned and mouthed, "Thanks a lot."

Doctor Christenson had chosen Katie to be first because she was one of the smartest and most self-confident students in the class. She also came from a family of high achievers. Her father had been a key player in getting the Mars Rover, Curiosity, safely on the surface of the planet, and her mother was a renowned fashion designer.

Doctor Christenson nodded. "Okay, Ricky?"

Ricky glared at Katie and said, "I'm going to get you," in an almost inaudible whisper.

Katie winked, but little did she know that she was still not out of the woods.

"Ricky, what was the purpose of the assignment?"

The Massachusetts Preparatory School for the Advancement of the Sciences attracted the best of the best in Boston. For the past three to four years, every student in the class had gotten into the top universities in the country—Cal Tech, Berkeley, Stanford, Harvard, Yale and MIT among them. The teachers at the school, like Doctor Christenson, were paid very, very well but not just to teach facts; those could be Googled by anyone with a cell phone. They had been hired to inspire the thinking creativity of young visionaries, the "movers and shakers" of the future.

Ricky, not sure what Doctor Christenson was looking for, answered cautiously, "To make us think abstractly?"

Doctor Christenson smiled. It was the sort of answer that made him glad he was a teacher. "That's right. While everyone else just saw an apple fall from a tree, Newton saw gravity. And while everyone sat on a train and watched another train passing by, Einstein saw relativity." Doctor Christenson held up Katie's folder. "Let's see how well Katie applied Newton's law of motion, inertia, to a force that could change the direction of society."

Katie's head fell back down. She tried to protest but to no avail. Ricky turned and gave her a curt little smile. Katie stood and, carrying a bottle of water and a small globe, walked to the front of the class.

"Okay," she mumbled, "but this is not fair. I shouldn't have to be first."

Doctor Christenson gave her a reassuring smile. "Bill Gates, Zuckerberg and Steve Jobs were all first."

Katie rolled her eyes at him then focused her gaze on an imaginary point over Ricky's head. "The title of my research project is 'The Wobble: The Force That Changed the Direction of Society.'

She looked around the room to gauge her classmates' reactions, but everyone just sat silently staring at her. She took in a deep breath. "Our society has been moving along in a straight line for a couple hundred thousand years, starting back with Lucy in Ethiopia." She knew that everyone knew who Lucy was; they had been studying her in their evolution-anthropology class. "As we've already learned, there is evidence that there have been five big mass-extinctions on the planet so far, like the meteorite smashing into the Yucatan Peninsula; a once huge solar flare that cooked half the earth; and the big chill that froze the planet into a big Popsicle."

The Popsicle reference earned her a few chuckles, and Ricky nodded with a little smile and mouthed, "You're doing great."

Katie was grateful for the encouragement, especially from Ricky, who she'd always had a crush on. "Humans are the only organisms on the planet that cultivate their own food, other than some little termites that survive through fungal farming. According to Albert Einstein, there are three forces of human nature: fear, greed, and stupidity. I've focused my project on the last one—stupidity."

Katie paused to take a sip of water. "Humans have a voracious, insatiable appetite for energy. According to the laws of physics, energy cannot be created or destroyed, but as far as humans are concerned, it can be wasted. Hence my focus on stupidity. In my opinion, it is the force that changed the direction of society." There was another round of chuckles, but Katie's smile was rather grim. "Actually, it doesn't change the course. It brings it to an end."

For the first time, she had everyone's full attention. "For my project, mankind had to choose between conserving energy, which was not in his nature, or to continue further ravaging the planet of its resources. Needless to say, he chose the latter."

Katie went on to explain that even though for the time being there was plenty of oil, greed drove mankind to want even more. Why conserve? Scientists came up with a plan to drill into the planet's core, sink electricity-producing turbines into the hot molten liquid, and have a never-ending environmentally clean energy source.

Katie paused for effect. "As the old saying goes, if something seems to good to be true, then it probably is. Either that or it's not true."

She reached over and gave the globe a spin. After a few revolutions, she jabbed her finger to a spot near the top of the globe and said, "For geological reasons, engineers chose a spot a few thousand miles from the North Pole—an area where geologists had deemed the crust to be the thinnest. Without taking into account the possible consequences of their actions, the engineers began to drill. The drilling went without a hitch, but when they broke into the molten core, the liquid iron started to bubble out at an alarming rate. Scientists had not taken into consideration that the molten core might be under some pressure."

Then in a more subdued tone, Katie explained, "The molten iron just kept bubbling out, but not erupting like a volcano. Instead, it just kept bubbling up until if formed a huge iron zit on the face of the planet. The engineers attempted to cap the hole, but because of the extreme heat of the molten iron, it vaporized everything that it touched, and then it started to wobble." Katie looked out over the class. "Anyone know why it wobbled?"

Without giving anyone a chance to answer, she said, "The earth normally has a little bit of a wobble, first, because it sits at a little bit of a tilt, and second, because it's spinning like a top on its axis." She looked over at Doctor Christenson and asked him if he knew the name of the earth's wobble.

He smiled. "No, actually, I don't."

Katie beamed with pride. "The earth's wobble is called the 'Chandler wobble'. Being that the earth is pretty round, the wobble is normally pretty small, so we don't wobble off the planet. But as the bubble of iron grew and grew off-center of the spin, the wobble got worse and worse until the planet wobbled to pieces."

She then stepped from behind the podium and bowed. "Goodbye dinosaurs. Goodbye humans."

Everyone sat mesmerized. Katie had surely changed the direction of society. As she was about to return to her seat, she stopped and, with a wicked little smile, said, "Oh, don't worry, in a few billion years, gravity pulls all the pieces back together, and the earth starts all over. Hello, slime molds."

Doctor Christenson congratulated her on an excellent presentation, then he looked around. "Who dares to follow that?"

Just as he was about to pick someone, a woman's voice crackled over the PA system.

"I'm sorry to interrupt everyone's classes, but the President of the United States is about to make an address to the nation on an urgent matter, and the Superintendent of Schools wants everyone to listen. Your classroom televisions will be coming on in a minute. Thank you."

# Chapter 49

***

## 1524½ 35th. Street
## Galveston, Texas

Newhouse sat in his office at 1000 Independence Avenue waiting for the president to appear in the Oval Office.

Meanwhile, fifteen hundred miles to the south, a regular citizen, Mrs. Hernandez, sat waiting for her *Wheel of Fortune.*

Just as the big wheel appeared on the screen, there was a loud piercing sound. Mrs. Hernandez reached up and grabbed at her hearing aid, then a ticker tape message started to scroll across the top of her screen, and an announcer said, "WE INTERRUPT OUR NORMALLY SCHEDULED BROADCAST FOR AN ADDRESS TO THE NATION BY THE PRESIDENT OF THE UNITED STATES."

Mrs. Hernandez threw up her arms. "No! No! Not again."

Unless the world were coming to an end, she didn't want to hear it.

President Robert Layton appeared on the screen, sitting behind his desk in the Oval Office. He nodded. "Good morning." It was obvious that he was very troubled. Taking in a deep breath as if unsure where to even start, he began. "In the past few weeks, there has been a major development that could affect the lives of everyone on the planet. It appears that the world's oil supply has been contaminated by a bacterium that has the ability to degrade oil. This bacterium is having devastating effects on the oil fields of Saudi Arabia."

Newhouse shook his head. "Shit! Shit! Shit!"

"When I say, 'degrading,' I mean that it's essentially eating the crude oil as fast as the Saudis can pump it out of the ground. At this time, it appears that it's isolated to the fields in the Middle East, but there are concerns that it could spread to oil fields around the world. I'm sure that everyone will be wondering where this bacterium came from. At this point, we have no idea, but we're sure that it was genetically engineered; it's not a fluke of nature."

Layton stood up, put his hands flat on his desk and leaned in toward the cameras to make it very clear. "This bacterium was engineered to do exactly what it's doing, and it's doing it very efficiently. This is a terrorist—a terrorist attack on the world. Rest assured that intelligence agencies everywhere are working on it, and we'll find those responsible."

Newhouse dropped his head into his hands.

Fifteen hundred miles south, Mrs. Hernandez was going nuts. Sitting on the edge of her couch, she screamed at the television, “Come on. Come on. Hurry up.”

Mrs. Hernandez wasn’t overly concerned. She was ninety years old. She didn’t drive. Her furnace and air conditioner were run by electricity, and some guys from across the border mowed her lawn, so she didn’t need the oil. As far as she was concerned, the bacteria could have it, she just wanted to get back to her *Wheel of Fortune.*

As she screamed at her television, Layton explained that it appeared that the bacterium had first been introduced into the oil fields of Saudi Arabia, and, from there, contaminated oil had been shipped to a number of ports around the world.

Layton stepped out from behind his desk. “For the last twenty-four hours, my administration has been in contact with every world leader, countries large and small, and plans are being worked out on how we’re going to deal with the short and long-term effects of this news. The most immediate issue is panic. This news has the potential to not only destabilize the world’s banks and economic markets but could result in the total collapse of the world’s infrastructure.”

Newhouse had not been listening to Layton since he had made the comment, “It appears to have been a terrorist attack.” He sat thinking, *As long as they’re thinking it’s a terrorist attack, he’ll have to give them a terrorist. It’ll have to be someone very loyal, someone he can trust.* He sat back in his chair and smiled; he knew just the guy.

"I'm here today," Layton continued, "to announce that the NASDAQ, New York Stock Exchange, and the Chicago Mercantile Bond Exchange will not open until further notice. Leaders around the world have all agreed to do the same—close all of their markets. Banks worldwide will limit withdrawals to a once-a-week minimal withdrawal, enough for basic needs, and all electronic transfers will be halted as of four hours ago." Layton sat back on the edge of his desk. "In two hours, in order to give the press time to assemble, White House Press Secretary Gerald Adams will answer questions."

Newhouse turned off the television; he had heard enough. He booted up his computer and found a red warning icon flashing; his warning system had flagged an email: "kathyluckystarsBP".

Newhouse read the email and then sat back in his chair, rubbing his temples. "Nosey little twit."

An hour later, Newhouse stood dropping quarters into a pay phone on the outskirts of Georgetown.

The television screen went black. Katie raised her hand and asked, "What does that mean, Doctor Christenson?"

Doctor Christenson shook his head. "I'm not sure. We'll have to wait for comments from the press secretary."

# Chapter 50

***

## Texas City, Texas

Doctor Jacobs fumbled through his laboratory coat trying to find his cellphone. He could hear it buzzing, but with a cup of coffee in his hand, the *Galveston Country* newspaper tucked under his arm, pens, pencils, and scraps of paper in every pocket, he had to scramble to find it. Finally, he found it buried in his left pocket next to his ham and cheese sandwich. Flipping it open, he looked at the caller ID. It was Kathy.

"Doctor Jacobs here."

"Did you just hear that?" Kathy blurted out. She didn't give him a chance to answer. "That didn't start in Saudi Arabia."

Doctor Jacobs was caught a little off guard. "What're you talking about?"

"The president. That bacteria. You watched his address, didn't you?"

Then he understood what she was she talking about. "Yes, sure." Kathy was worked up, but he wasn't sure what it was all about. Trying to calm her down, he told her that he had already been on his way to her lab about some other business and would be there in just a minute.

A few minutes later, he walked into her lab, but before he could say a word, Kathy pounced. "The president said, '...in the past few weeks...' We had it here almost two months ago. It didn't start in Saudi Arabia. I think it all started right here with that dirty Coke bottle you bought from Lake Mead."

He set down his coffee and put up his hands. "Slow down! Slow down! Start over. You've caught me off guard."

Kathy didn't necessarily slow down, but she started over. "Okay, the president said in his address that the problems in Saudi Arabia started a few weeks ago, but we had it here over two months ago."

He wasn't sure how she had come to this conclusion, so he just nodded and said, "How so?"

"You remember a few months ago when you bought that oil sample in that old Coke bottle from that spill in Lake Mead?"

He could hardly forget. It had nearly destroyed Kathy's Mass Spec machine, stunk up the lab, and put them behind schedule by a week.

"The oil in that Coke bottle was gooey, but I didn't think much of it at the time. I just thought it was contaminated with some kind of fungus or slime mold from along the shoreline, but now I don't think so." She paused then sternly said, "Doctor Jacobs, that oil had that bacteria in it, right here, months ago."

Doctor Jacobs shook his head; he wasn't so sure. It made no sense. It was hard to make the connection between Lake Mead and Saudi Arabia over 8000 miles away. If terrorists had engineered oil-eating bacteria, putting it in the oil fields of Saudi Arabia would make perfect sense, but why Lake Mead? No, not only did he feel that it was terrorists, but he was concerned that they were still out there dumping their oil-eating bacteria into major oil fields around the world.

He set the *Galveston Country* newspaper down on one of the laboratory counters and motioned for Kathy to come take a look. He pointed to the front-page headline.

"OIL FIELDS—PRUDHOE BAY, ALASKA—CLOSED."

Kathy read the first few lines. "The three main oil fields that keep oil flowing into the lower forty-eight have been shut down due to mechanical issues. Liberty, Kupauk and Alpine, Prudhoe Bay's three largest oil fields on the north slope, have been temporarily shut down." Kathy didn't read any more. She looked at Doctor Jacobs and shrugged, unsure of what his point was.

Doctor Jacobs told her that he couldn't explain the oil in the Coke bottle and that maybe it had just been contamination from up stream of where he had taken the sample, but he doubted that terrorists in the Middle East would have had a bunch of Cajuns in rickety old trucks dump contaminated oil into Lake Mead. Then he shook his head. "No, the north slope of Prudhoe Bay is so extremely isolated that the only way bacteria could make its way there is if someone hand-delivered it. No, it had to have been dumped there."

Kathy nodded. She had to agree; nothing else made much sense.

Doctor Jacobs left to go to a meeting, so Kathy turned on her Mass Spec machine, which started to scroll out reams of reports. But before going through them, she had to check her daily horoscope. Doctor Jacobs had left his newspaper sitting on the counter. She liked the *Galveston Country*'s horoscope writer; he was always spot on, and she loved the tabloid section; it always had really good human interest stories.

She found the tabloid section and her daily horoscope and gasped. "Scorpio. Caution. Those in the constellation of Scorpio must proceed with extreme caution today. Romance is not in the picture. Decisions made today may affect your future."

Kathy sat back trying to think if she had made any major decisions. After assuring herself that she had not, she started reading through the three or four human interest stories. One was about a dog with only two legs—one left front leg, and one right back leg—that had managed to hobble over a hundred miles to make its way back to its master who himself was a double amputee. Then she started reading a story about a lady in New York City who was suing the makers of Vaseline petroleum jelly because it had given her an unrelenting rash on her backside. Apparently, she had contracted the gastrointestinal bug that had hit New York City very hard in the past few months. Because the diarrhea from the gastrointestinal bug had given her so much irritation, she had applied Vaseline to the dry, chafed areas. According to the story, her backside had gotten worse, and her jar of Vaseline had started to smell like pig manure.

The woman was accusing the makers of Vaseline for selling a contaminated product. Then, the color drained from Kathy's face, her reading slowed, and she stared at the article in disbelief. There was no way this could be just a coincidence.

According to the article, the woman lived in Morningside Heights on Manhattan's Upper East Side. The woman's lawyers argued that since she was from Iowa, born and raised on a pig farm, she should know exactly what pig manure smelled like. The makers of Vaseline petroleum jelly refused to comment.

Kathy got up, walked over, and stared out the window, lost in thought. She had sent Doctor Jacobs' oily Coke bottle samples for genetic sequencing to Jennifer, a friend of hers who was a graduate student at Cornell University in Midtown Manhattan. She and Jennifer had both been born and raised on pig farms in Grundy Count, Iowa, and had both gone to the University of Iowa. Jennifer lived in Morningside Heights.

Kathy went back over to her desk, scrolled through her cell phone directory, and texted Jennifer.

"Jennifer, was that you in the Vaseline story in the newspaper? Kathy."

As Kathy sat waiting, she thought to herself, *What if it was actually her? If so, it would all fit.*

Within a week of handling Doctor Jacobs' oil sample, she had been down for the count with a diarrhea bug. No one had thought much of it at the time because it had soon spread around Galveston. The news media had just chalked it up to another food or water-borne bug. The local Galveston media had never made any connection to the fact that millions were dying around the world from a gastrointestinal bug.

Suddenly, her phone started to blink—an incoming text. She stared at the message. "That's me."

Kathy's mind was racing. Without a "hello" or anything, she texted back, "What did you do with the oil samples I sent to you for sequencing a few months ago?"

She sat waiting, staring at the headlines on the newspaper, "PRUDHOE BAY—CLOSED."

Then her incoming text indicator blinked. "They were nothing but regular old run-of-the-mill E.coli. I put some in the freezer and dumped the rest down the drain."

Kathy dropped her head into her hands, then she texted Jennifer back that she would call later.

Doctor Jacobs had said that he thought someone was still dumping contaminated oil into oil fields around the world and that it was being hand-delivered. Kathy sat in disbelief. *It had been hand delivered alright, and it was being dumped.*

She remembered so well her eighty-year-old grandfather who had been a crotchety old fart. Whenever he had to use the bathroom, he would announce to everyone that he had to go "take a dump." Everyone tried to correct him, telling him that maybe he should just say that he had to go to the bathroom, and that saying he had to take a dump was kind of crude. But there had been no changing an eighty-year-old pig farmer from Iowa.

Kathy sat thinking, Doctor Jacob's words echoing in her mind. "No, someone is dumping contaminated oil into oil fields around the world. It's being hand-delivered."

She sat back staring at the ceiling. The gastrointestinal bug and the oil-eating bacteria that the president was talking about were one and the same, and she might have single-handedly delivered it to New York City, and Jennifer might have dumped it into the sewer system in Midtown Manhattan. Meanwhile, Jennifer got the bug, carried it to the Upper East Side and, as grandpa would say, "Dumped it into the rest of the five boroughs." Within weeks of her sending that sample, nine million people in New York City had been hit with an overwhelming gastrointestinal outbreak.

It all made sense. *That's how it jumped.*

She remembered the reports about the increasing numbers of mechanical failures in the big rigs coming across the country. Fresh fruits and vegetable shortages had hit a critical point along the East coast because of transportation issues. At the same time, epidemiologists had been tracking the gastrointestinal outbreak moving across the country. The bug had made its way into the Midwest.

Chicago and the Tristate area had been hit hard. But it had seemed to have stopped or slowed in the Midwest and for weeks had not moved across the rust belt. But then, it had suddenly popped up in New York City, and it had struck with a vengeance. Epidemiologists had chalked it up to air travel.

Kathy sat thinking, *What if the bottleneck of disabled rigs in the Midwest slowed the gastrointestinal bug's movement east? Truck drivers would report mechanical issues in their trucks but not that they were having diarrhea.* She would bet dollars-to-donuts that those same truck drivers also had diarrhea.

She walked over to the window and looked out at the sprawling refineries. What was she going to do now? Doctor Jacobs wasn't going to take her seriously; he just thought of her as his little girl from Grundy Count, Iowa. And she had no way to make the connection with the oil-eating bacteria in the oil fields of Saudi Arabia. That made no sense unless someone infected with the bug flew there and, as her grandfather would say, "dumped it." Then she had an idea—maybe the NH guy would take her seriously. The FBI had been adamant about getting a report on Doctor Jacobs' oil sample, and they were following the terrorist connection. Maybe they would listen.

She went over to her computer and scrolled down through the list of her past emails. She found the NH-FBI email address: NH@JVF1000IA.gov.

"Dear Mr. NH, Kathy here again from Galveston, Texas. I sent you the email a few months ago with the report on the oil sample my boss found in Lake Mead. You guys had told us to send you a copy." Then she sent a long and detailed explanation of what she thought about the connection between the oil-destroying bacteria, the intestinal bug, and the Lake Mead sample. When she finished, she hit the send button.

Just as she was about to start working on her reports, her cell phone started to blink—an incoming text message. It was from her best friend Nancy. "Did you see your horoscope today? Be careful. Mine says romance is in the picture."

Kathy texted back, "Saw it. Don't worry, I'm not going to make any decisions today. Hope romance is in the picture for the weekend. Wink. Wink."

# Chapter 51

***

## 418 Hazel Street
## Wilkes-Barre, Pennsylvania

Peter had gotten up as usual, about eleven, and pulled up his E-trade account to check his daily wealth. Weary eyed and half asleep, he sat staring at his computer screen. "What the hell is this?"

"ALL TRANSACTIONS BLOCKED UNTIL FURTHER NOTICE."

He had just gone to bed nine hours earlier, and everything was fine. Now E-trade, the largest online trading service in the country, was blocked? He logged out and turned on CNBC expecting to see *Squawk Box*, but instead, it was Press Secretary Gerald Gibbs giving a morning news briefing.

Peter shook his head wondering if he had gotten up on the wrong side of the bed. "What the hell is Gibbs doing having a news briefing at eleven o'clock in the morning?"

"Mr. Gibbs," it was Ralph Derricks of the New York Times International Division, "do we know where the bacteria came from?"

Peter raised his eyebrows. "Bacteria? What the hell are they talking about?"

Before Gibbs could answer that question, Blake Conel of International News Line interrupted, "And, can you explain what you mean by 'it eats gasoline'?"

Peter almost swallowed his tongue.

Gibbs put up his hand. "One question at a time, please." He pointed to Derricks. "No, Ralph, at this point, we don't know where it came from, but it's believed to be terrorist related."

"Terrorist related?" Peter actually pinched himself to be sure that he wasn't still asleep. He had obviously tuned into the middle of something because he didn't understand what they were talking about, or could he have imagined it?

"Mr. Conel, as for your question, from what I understand, it doesn't exactly eat gasoline."

Peter listened as Gibbs tried to explain to the best of his ability that each barrel of the stuff that was traded on the open oil markets, referred to as a barrel of crude, was a barrel of flammable hydrocarbons that went into making gasoline, and the rest was a thick, black gooey component that was made into heavy oils and greases—lubricants that oiled every moving part in the world. Then he clarified for Conel that the bacteria was breaking down the grease component of a barrel of crude, not the hydrocarbons. In other words, it wasn't eating the gasoline.

Conel didn't let up. "Sounds like eating to me." All Gibbs could do was shrug.

Next, Alesia Collins of ABC news raised her hand, and Gibbs gave her a nod. She stood up. "Mr. Gibbs, why has the president closed all the world's markets and frozen all of the banks?"

Peter's eyes widened, and an unexpected yelp emanated from deep in his throat, "The banks?"

Peter scrambled to pull up his Bank of America account, where he always kept a few hundred thousand dollars that he used for his cyberspace-style living. Dumbfounded, he stared at the screen.

"ALL TRANSACTIONS LIMITED TO $100 A WEEK. ATM CASH TRANSACTIONS ONLY."

"Cash?" Peter had never even seen cash other than an old jar of pennies that he still had from his college days. Amazon delivered his groceries, online Big Time Pizza delivered his pizza, and a robot from Post-It-All did everything from delivering his toilet paper to wiping his butt for him.

Gibbs reassured Alesia that it was not only the President of the United States but that all of the world leaders had agreed that, until the initial shock had subsided, all global markets and banking transactions would be halted.

This was the first time that it had really hit Peter. "Oil-eating bacteria?" He hurriedly pulled up *The Wall Street Journal* and stared at the headlines:

"COST OF CRUDE EXPECTED TO FALL TO ZERO."

Peter started to panic. He had less than a week's worth of food in his apartment. He had no real money. He bought his food and water with a credit card. He paid his bills by pushing a button on his computer. His entire life's savings was nothing but 0s and 1s flying around in space.

He switched off CNBC and started to scan the cyberspace. There had to be some little war-torn country that had not gotten the word or had not yet closed their markets. There was no listing of the current price of a barrel of crude, but he suspected that the prices had been halted as soon as the news broke, hopefully before they had gone to zero.

He searched, and up popped a little country called Burundi that had not yet frozen its markets. He had no idea where in the hell Burundi was or what currency Burundi used, but if he could dump his BP stocks at the time they were frozen, he actually might have a decent pile of cash. It would be in Burundis, and he had no idea what a Burundi was worth, but it had to be better than zero.

He linked up with Burundi's so-called stock market, put in an immediate sell order for his BP oil stocks, and pushed the button.

"ALL TRANSACTIONS BLOCKED UNTIL FURTHER NOTICE."

# Chapter 52

***

## 40°52'59"N. 119°03'50"W./40.88306°N. Black Rock Desert, Nevada

Hans Euler sat reviewing the lab results from the latest run of recombinant genetic experiments. He was having a hard time concentrating because all he could think about was getting the hell out of this place. Thank God he only had six months left on his contract. The money had been good, but the price he had paid had been too high. He had gone from twenty-four hours a day of subzero total darkness to twenty-four hours a day of Dante's Inferno, roasting like a chicken on a rotisserie.

He checked his emails every day waiting to hear from MIT, where he had applied for a position as a lab assistant. It wasn't much for a guy with three postdocs in recombinant genetics, but even waiting tables in Boston would have been better than this place.

As he sat half reviewing the lab results and half dreaming

about sitting at Quincy's Market eating fresh lobster and feeling the cool breeze blowing off of Boston Bay, the phone on his desk started to ring. He looked at it and hesitated. He thought about not answering it. He knew who it was because it was the only phone access into the complex. There was no outgoing access. Scrambling devices had been buried in the walls of the place, and it was a couple hundred feet underground, which blocked any cell phone activity. Topside, there were no towers for hundreds of miles because they were in the middle of a desert. After letting it ring five or six times, he decided to pick it up.

"Euler! What the hell is going on there?"

Euler was never going to forget that voice. He had never met the guy or even seen who it was, but the guy was an asshole, and Euler knew that the guy owned him.

"What's going on where, sir?"

"Don't give me that shit. You been watching the news for the last month?"

Hans didn't say anything. He just sat and waited, though he didn't have to wait long.

"Don't tell me that this is our bacteria! You're supposed to be in charge of that place. You've been paid millions of dollars, you have a state-of-the-art facility, and you said you guys could make bacteria that could clean up oil spills. *And*, you said when it finished cleaning up a beach, "poof", it would go away. Now there's bacteria, sounds much like ours, *eating* the world's goddamn oil supply."

Hans tried to get a word in edgewise, but before he could, the man barked, "How did this happen?"

"I'm not sure," Hans said submissively.

"Bullshit! Don't give me that shit that you're 'not sure'."

Hans sat back thinking of just how he had gotten himself into this mess. Three years earlier, he had been doing his third postdoc at the prestigious Karolinska Institute in Stockholm, Sweden. One day, he had received an email offering him a job in a newly designed state-of-the-art research lab in the United States. He would have deleted it immediately as just another spam email, but attached was a complete résumé of his life right down to the "Tasmanian Devil" he had tattooed on his butt, which he had gotten while doing his second postdoc in Australia. The email said he would be paid three million dollars, which would be wired to a bank of his choice, tax free, and that the project would last two to three years. Again, he had been about ready to delete the email as some kind of a spam-scam until he had read a comment: "The plagiarism accusations you had while working on your Ph.D. could come back to haunt you."

It had been enough to get him to bite, and, at the time, after sitting for two years freezing his ass off in total darkness six months of the year, he didn't think anything could have been worse. Now he sat listening to the voice at the other end, and he realized how wrong he had been.

"Are you listening?" The sudden booming voice startled Hans out of his trance.

"I'm listening."

"For the last time, how the hell did this happen?"

Hans knew the guy was going to go ballistic, or more ballistic. "A few months ago, there was a mix up. A shipment of barrels that were to be taken to the gulf got lost—mixed up."

The voice at the other end very calmly said, "It didn't get lost, did it? It ended up in Lake Mead. Am I Right?"

Hans took in a deep breath. "Among other places."

Hans could hear him slam his fist on his desk. "Among other places, what other places?"

"We don't know." Hans explained that in order to avoid registering the transportation of hazardous materials with the Department of Transportation, they had hired a bunch of locals with small trucks to transport the stuff to the gulf and dump it.

"Where'd these so-called locals find the stuff?"

Hans hesitated; he knew the guy was going to have a stroke. "We had it shipped from here to a backlot at Armstrong International."

"And?"

"And … I don't know," Hans said.

Newhouse already knew what had happened. He had made sure that the trucks, the barrels, and the Cajuns had all disappeared, he just wanted to hear it from Euler.

He had been able to track down bits and pieces of airport records from Frankfurt, Germany—problems with reserve oil tanks, but no details. But now the Lake Mead thing had become a problem, a loose end, thanks to that little twit in Texas.

"Okay, here's what you're going to do. Are you listening?"

Hans nodded but didn't say anything.

"You're going to put that place on lockdown. No one leaves that place until I can figure out what to do. You got it?"

"I got it."

Before Hans could say anything else, the phone went dead.

# Chapter 53

***

## U.S. Strategic Command
## Arlington County, Virginia

General John McCay, Director of Special Operations, one of the many branches of the Department of Defense, sat at his desk watching a CNN news report out of India. A few years earlier, he had been the Field Commander for Special Operations of the SEAL Team Six unit that had gotten Bin Laden in Pakistan. As a reward for his success in that operation, which had put a feather in the president's cap, he had been promoted to a cushy desk job with a beautiful view of the Washington Monument. Officially, it had been a step up in his career, but now he spent his days embroiled in bureaucratic red tape and longing to be back in the field coordinating clandestine Special Ops teams, taking out the bad guys, and making the decisions, be it right or wrong. But such was the price of climbing the ladder.

"I'm about thirty miles outside the city watching what's left of the twenty million people as they leave New Delhi attempting to make it to the countryside for food."

The newscaster was an Indian woman, tears streaming down her face, her saree tattered and covered in dust. Brushing a swarm of flies from her face, she turned and pointed back toward New Delhi.

"That huge swarming cloud you see hanging over the city are flies—billions of flies thriving on the remains of over fifteen million decaying bodies."

McCay's eyes widened as he stared at the dark cloud of insects undulating with an almost rhythmic beauty.

"The city is a deathtrap," the newswoman continued, "There is no food in the city. There is no mass transit to deliver food. There is no equipment left running to produce food. Every dog, cat, monkey, blade of grass, and even the moss on the rocks has been eaten."

McCay sat and watched as streams of people walked aimlessly past the camera only to disappear off in the distance in a trail of dust. It looked like an exodus of emaciated wildebeest struggling for life at the end of a long dry season.

Suddenly, looking beyond the camera, the newswoman gasped. Covering her mouth in disbelief at the sight, she shrieked, "Oh my God!"

The cameraman swung around, aiming his camera at the approaching stream of people. Not more than twenty feet from them, a woman was carrying a baby, its belly swollen, its eyes eaten away by maggots, and chunks of flesh falling off its little arms. The woman walked past the camera, oblivious to the fact that the baby was dead.

The newswoman wiped tears from her eyes. "I'm sorry about that," she said, apologizing for her sudden outburst. "A few days ago, I saw that mother with her two children at the city zoo. The zoo had been overrun by masses of starving people. Like rabid animals, they broke down the gates to the zoo, broke into the animals' cages, and with their bare hands tore the animals to pieces. The cries from the animals were horrifying." Turning and pointing to the woman with the dead baby, she added, "I watched that mother gouge out the eyes of what was left of the gorilla after it had been torn to pieces by the crowd. She handed an eye to each child."

The woman began crying in earnest, and it was several minutes before she regained her composure. "I'm sorry, but … but that was probably the last food they ever had … I don't know where her other child is … most likely dead."

Suddenly, the door to McCay's office opened, and his secretary poked in her head.

"Your phone has been ringing."

"What?" he snapped, then his expression softened as he realized it had indeed rung several times in the last few minutes. He gave her a sheepish look. "Sorry, I didn't hear it."

She smiled. "It's Robert. Newhouse. Secretary of Department of Energy."

McCay and Newhouse had known each other for years. Before Newhouse got the Cabinet position, they had spent a lot of time together—fishing trips, family functions, and political events. Newhouse was even godfather to McCay's son.

"Robert, what's up? It's been a long time."

Newhouse did not bother with pleasantries. "John, I need your help."

Though Newhouse spoke in his usual curt tone, McCay could hear the concern in it. "Sure, Robert. What's going on? You sound rattled."

Newhouse didn't answer his question. "John, I need to talk to you, not over the phone. Can you meet me on the other side of Pentagon Memorial Park this afternoon, say three?"

"Sure, but what's going on, Robert?"

"I'll tell you this afternoon. And, John, don't bring your cell phone."

McCay knew this meant that Robert didn't want any traceable links to their meeting. There were more phone towers in D.C. than gold in Fort Knox. "Jesus, this sounds like something out of a spy movie."

There was no answer. Newhouse had hung up.

McCay sat back in his chair and stared blankly at his computer, trying to understand what the hell had his friend so spooked.

A sudden commotion on the screen startled him back to the CNN report. A group of three or four men were pushing and shoving as they fought for a beetle that was running for its life across the barren dust. The camera switched back to the newswoman before McCay could see who had gotten the beetle.

"This is Prannoy Patel for NDTV. This may be our last broadcast. As you can see, all around me, the landscape here has been picked bare. There's nothing left but dead bodies, flies and maggots. Millions of desperate and starving people have burned and eaten every living thing in their path."

Prannoy pointed to the ground. "Now that the surface has been stripped bare, they're eating the very dirt off the ground, digging, and hoping to find a worm, a grub, or as you just saw, a beetle."

As she was just about to make another comment, a fly landed on her upper lip, and, before she could brush it away, it crawled up into her nose. She shrieked, reflexively plugged her other nostril and blew. The fly came tumbling out and flew off.

McCay actually gave a little smile; he was impressed with her tenacity.

"All of these people are heading to the countryside—the framing areas—in hopes of finding food." Prannoy paused, a defeated look flashing across her face. "But, inevitably, they're going to collide with the millions from other overcrowded cities—Calcutta, Mumbai, the Delta—"

Suddenly, the face of an emaciated man filled the screen. It seemed he had thrown himself, or had fallen, into the camera, knocking it from the cameraman's grip. A second later, McCay saw a view of the sky, then the landscape, as the camera came to rest in the dust. The feed went dead, replaced by the CNN logo.

McCay blinked several times at the screen, unable to believe what he was seeing. Then he grabbed his coat and headed out the door, grateful he had the meeting with Newhouse to distract him from this horror.

# CHAPTER 54

***

## Won Pat International Airport
## Guam, South Pacific

David and Terry had thought they were the two luckiest students at Northern Michigan University when they had gotten accepted by the FAA for training as air traffic controllers.

A few months earlier, they had finished their training at Louis Armstrong International Airport in New Orleans as they had watched a seasoned controller clear a big DC-10 for takeoff to the Big Apple, JFK in New York City.

Then they had sat and waited with bated breath for their first assignments as full-fledged air traffic controllers. They had requested to be placed together and both felt that no matter where they ended up, it couldn't be any worse than the Upper Peninsula of Michigan or the outer borders of the Adirondacks.

David was raised in a little town in the Porcupine Mountains in the Upper Peninsula of Michigan, and Terry in the Adirondacks only a few miles from the Canadian border in Upstate New York. As a child, while most kids had a puppy, David had an orphaned baby porcupine, and Terry a baby moose.

Now, they sat 6000 miles from California, 4000 miles from Hawaii, 3000 from Australia, and 1000 miles from the Equator in the control tower at Won Pat International Airport, Guam.

It was early morning, and they were expecting only six or seven flights for the day—one from San Francisco, two from Hawaii, and three or four from the Philippines. David sat logging the previous day's flights that had come in and out of Won Pat, and Terry was tracking a flight from Sydney, Australia to LAX.

Suddenly, Terry yelled, "Oh my God! David, come look at this!"

David walked over to the console and looked over her shoulder. She was looking at the Pacific Oceanic Transition Route Tracking System.

"What? I don't see anything."

"Exactly, it's Qantas Flight 2613, Sydney to LAX. It's gone off the radar."

David reached over and hit the reset button, but Terry told him that she had already done that. Then David looked at the original flight path for Qantas 2613 and asked her, somewhat bewildered, "Why are you tracking on an international flight frequency? They should be on a direct frequency track, New Zealand, Hawaii, to LAX. We don't mess with international flight frequencies."

"I know that," Terry snapped somewhat defensively. "The pilot radioed about half an hour ago that warning lights were indicating oil pressure changes in two engines. He didn't sound concerned; they have backup oil reserves. He just wanted us to track him until he got closer to Hawaii in case he needed to divert here to Won Pat. So, I've been tracking him, but he never called back like there were any problems. Now, he's dropped off the radar." She looked at David, as if she already knew the answer. "Do you think they went down?"

David shook his head and told her that he doubted it and that it was probably just a computer glitch. Then he sat down at the console and pulled up the most recent coordinates for Queensland and Northern Territory Air Service Flight-2613. After a few minutes, he sat back. "Aw, shit."

The numbers indicated that sometime after the pilot had radioed Wan Pat, it had descended from thirty-six thousand feet to twenty thousand and had changed headings toward Guam.

David stared at the numbers, then he looked at Terry. "How big a plane?"

They knew it had to be a big plane to fly nonstop from Sydney to LAX. Terry looked over at a separate computer screen to her left. "It's a 747-400, three class layout. If it was full, I would guess 416 passengers and a crew of twenty."

After a number of radio attempts to contact the Qantas flight, David said, "We better call Anderson."

Tears welled up in Terry's eyes. Even the most seasoned controllers with years of experience at places like LAX, O'Hare, and JFK never had to make the dreaded call that every air traffic controller feared—a downed plane, a big one at that.

David picked up the receiver of the phone for the direct line to Anderson. He didn't have to dial. He waited and then heard, "This is General Doucette, Thirteenth Pacific Air Command, Anderson Air Force Base, Guam." After such formality, which was the way Doucette always answered the phone, he asked, "David, what's up?"

Doucette knew everyone on the island, and everyone on the island knew Doucette. The island was only thirty miles long and nine miles wide. He also knew David and Terry very well; he and his wife had taken them under their wing and pretty much considered them their kids.

"Sir, we've lost contact with a commercial airliner, a Qantas flight from Sydney to LAX." After a short pause and with a tremble in his voice, David said, "Sir, it looks like it went down."

"Jesus Christ. Do you have the last coordinates?"

After David told him that he did, Doucette told him that he was scrambling two fighter jets and to give the coordinates to the pilots when they were airborne.

Five minutes later, David and Terry heard two jets screeching overhead.

# Chapter 55

***

## U.S. Strategic Command
## Arlington County, Virginia

McCay sat watching another CNN News Alert before he headed out to meet with Newhouse. Earlier in the morning, he had watched the CNN report out of India. Now, it was China. He sat staring in disbelief, dumbfounded at what he was seeing; the whole world was coming unglued. This report was out of the People's Square in Shanghai. He watched as a young Chinese newswoman was being pushed and jostled around by mobs of people carrying whatever belongings they could, aimlessly heading to anywhere and nowhere.

"This is Chen Lei, with—" A man clutching at a bag of rice that he had just grabbed off of a government relief truck suddenly pushed into her as he tried to escape an angry mob.

McCay flinched as a loud cracking sound flowed through

the microphone as it pushed into the young newscaster's teeth. Chen Lei stumbled back and then wiped at her upper lip where a small drop of blood appeared. Behind her, the crowd attacked the man like a pack of wolves, pushing him to the ground, stomping him to death, and ripping open the bag of rice. Suddenly, there was a frantic scurry of pushing and shoving as everyone did whatever it took to get even one little piece of rice. Then, just as fast as it had started, the rabid fight was over. The crowd calmly shuffled on as if nothing had happened. Behind them, the ground was bare except for the trampled remains of the man, and not one piece of rice was left anywhere.

Gaining her composure, Chen Lei turned and pointed to a tall building behind her that actually disappeared up into the afternoon haze. Wiping another drop of blood off of her upper lip, she said, "The city has been stripped bare. There's nothing left. Thirteen million people lived right here in the central area of the People's Square and another twelve million in the surrounding city."

She looked up at the towering walls of the high-rise building behind her. "People here have been living straight up, one on top of another. The millions in these high-rises have been blindly fed day by day by the few thousands out in the farming areas to the south and central regions. Like animals in a zoo, the zoo keepers in the farming areas have kept the animals in the zoo fed. But now, in a matter of weeks, the flow of food and supplies has stopped. The country's massive rail and ground transportation system and food production equipment have literally come to a screeching halt as oil and oil products are being gobbled up by what has become known worldwide as the 'oil-eating bacteria'. Twenty-five million people here have been living, eating, and existing on little plastic cards. Compounding—"

Chen Lei was again suddenly pushed aside as another brawl broke out next to her, this one over a can of tuna. She managed to stay upright and then continued, "Sorry. As I was about to say, compounding the food problem, the massive gastrointestinal outbreak that has from all reports rocked the rest of the world has also taken its toll here in Shanghai." Her voice was trembling, and she was on the verge of breaking down. "No one knows how many are dead here in these high-rise buildings, and, at this point, no one cares. Millions are already—"

Suddenly, the feed from Shanghai went dead as another red ticker-tape report screeched across McCay's computer screen. "CNN news has just learned that a Qantas Airliner has gone down in the South Pacific somewhere near Guam. We have very few details at this time."

Chen Lei reappeared as the news alert finished. McCay glanced at his watch. It was almost three. Turning off his computer, he put on his jacket and headed out to meet with Newhouse. As he left his office, he wondered how the hell it had come to this.

As he walked across Pentagon Memorial Park, he pulled up his collar trying to shield himself from the late-November winds. The trees were barren, there were no tourists, and the rows of curved memorial benches sat empty, except for one. Ahead, in the direction of the Air Force Memorial, he spotted a lone figure sitting, staring blankly off into the distance.

“Hey, Robert, it’s cold out here.”

Newhouse didn’t say anything, he just turned and looked back in the direction of the Pentagon’s cameras. Then he pointed in the opposite direction. “Here, let’s go this way.”

McCay followed Newhouse and didn’t speak until they were well past the row of benches. Finally, McCay asked, “Okay, Robert, what’s this about?”

Newhouse stared off blankly, lost in thought. “I’m sure you’ve been watching the news for the last few weeks. The oil thing, you know, the bacteria?”

McCay rolled his eyes. “Kind of hard to miss.”

“Yeah. That’s our bacteria.”

McCay tilted his head and grimaced. “What the hell are you talking about?”

Without turning and looking at McCay, Newhouse explained how there had been so much pressure put on the White House to decrease dependence on foreign oil and at the same time increase our own production. He explained how the damned environmentalists did whatever the hell it took to block them at every step and how the damned public wanted their gasoline cheap to run their big cars, but as soon as there was an oil spill with the news media showing some poor little seagull choking on oil, then it was the administration’s fault. Newhouse reminded McCay that, at the time, the next elections were only a few years away, and if gas prices were four dollars a gallon, Layton could kiss his chances of re-election goodbye.

Finally turning to McCay, he said, “Then the goddamn fools blew up that oil rig in the gulf. Fucking idiots.”

McCay continued to listen without saying anything.

“A few years ago, we built a research lab and hired some of the world’s best geneticists to work on bacteria that could help clean up oil spills, enzymatically cleaning a beach.

McCay was starting to get the picture but hoped to God that it wasn’t true. “You mean eat it up?”

Newhouse nodded. “Something like that.”

McCay looked at him skeptically. “I’ve never heard of this research lab. Where’s it at? Who funded it?”

Newhouse nodded. “It’s not on the books. It’s in the desert, and it didn’t go through any appropriation committees.”

McCay just looked at him skeptically.

“I got some money, let’s say, kind of a slush fund. I made some deals with some of the big oil companies—Exxon, BP, Royal Dutch.”

McCay wasn’t sure he even wanted to know, but he asked anyway, “How much?”

Newhouse shrugged. “Fifty million. Or so.”

“Or so!” McCay damned near died. “Let me get this straight. You got fifty million dollars, or so, from somewhere. Didn’t go through any appropriations committees. Built a research laboratory somewhere, apparently in a desert, and genetically altered bacteria that’s now running loose eating the world's oil." Without giving Newhouse a chance to say anything, McCay continued, "Where the hell is this laboratory?"

Newhouse mumbled, "In the desert, in Nevada."

"Where in the desert?"

"Black Rock."

McCay new the area well. When he had been a cadet at West Point years earlier, they had done desert survival training in the area.

"That's an Indian Reservation. Do the Indians know?"

Newhouse told him that they had gotten paid well, so they had been okay with it. He told McCay that they had just been told that it was a project. They have no idea what's there. It's buried.

Finally, it dawned on McCay—why the hell was he here? "Robert, why are you telling me all this?"

Newhouse looked straight at McCay. "We have to destroy that lab."

McCay's eyebrows went up. "We!"

"Look, John, what‘s done is done. The lab, everything, that's all water under the bridge. If the rest of the world finds out—"

McCay could not believe this. "Jesus Christ, Robert, it's not just water under the bridge. There are seven billion people on this planet who eat, drink, and sleep on oil, and your lab has single-handedly fed them to this," McCay rolled his eyes, "this … mold."

"Bacteria," Newhouse mumbled.

McCay started questioning Newhouse on how the bacteria had managed to get around the world, but Newhouse stopped him. "None of that matters now, John. All that matters now is that we contain this. I have it under control. All we need to do is get rid of that lab."

McCay now understood why he was there. "You want me to put together a Special Ops team to go and obliterate that laboratory, right?"

Newhouse only nodded.

"How're you going to keep everyone who worked there quiet?"

Newhouse didn't say anything, he just looked at McCay.

"Oh, no, Robert. No, no. You have to be kidding me."

Newhouse nodded. "The whole lab."

"How many, Robert?"

Newhouse shrugged. "It doesn't matter. One. Twenty. This could start World War III."

McCay was hopeless. "You mean, if anyone lives long enough and has any oil to retaliate with."

Thirty minutes later, McCay was sitting back at his desk with his head buried in his hands. As Newhouse had pointed out, almost two billion people may already be dead. What was thirty more?

# Chapter 56

***

## Palo Alto, California

Adam sat by his window, staring out at his version of Mecca. Although his efficiency apartment was too small and had a musty smell that he could not seem to get rid of, it was smack dab in the middle of Silicon Valley and within a stone's throw of Sun Microsystems, Oracle, Sunnyvale and Hewlett-Packard.

But, today, Adam was focused not on tech giants or institutions of higher learning; nor was his goal to become the king of the proverbial Valley or a zillionaire like Zuckerberg, Gates, Page and Brin. He was pondering his own latest endeavor. It was a theoretical program—a dormant little worm that would be buried in the launch codes of every nuclear missile in the world. But this was not some top-secret government project, nor was Adam an activist who marched the streets. He was just a computer geek with long hair, piercings in his ears and nose and the conviction that mankind was going to annihilate itself. He'd always felt this way on some level, but lately, thanks to his father, it was looking more and more likely.

Adam was sure that mankind was never going to make it to the year 2525. He made no secret of his cynical viewpoint; even the voicemail greeting on his cell was the chorus of the 60's song, "We're on the Eve of Destruction," after which he added, "Please leave a message. If the world's still here in a few days, I'll return your call."

It was inevitable that every nation would one day get its hands on nuclear weapons. And attempting to undo the world's nuclear programs was nothing new. Messing with Iran's nuclear centrifuges had only delayed the process, and a missile destroying another missile up in the sky avoided destruction on the ground, only to kill everyone later of radiation poisoning. Adam had a different plan: rather than trying to mess with launch codes, diverting trajectories, stopping launch sequences, or developing a missile to intercept an incoming missile, he figured everyone should be allowed to build all the nuclear bombs they wanted and let them boom.

To Adam, the logic was as flawless as it was simple. Instead of writing the usual lengthy viral sequences to interfere with other countries' nuclear programs, his program contained only one word: detonate. It certainly avoided the need for retaliation.

He sat there smiling as he thought about it. The moment anyone pushed the button to send a missile flying, the thing would explode right there on the spot, never leaving its silo. By the time the offending country would realize what was happening, they would probably already have pushed five or six buttons. The more buttons they pushed, the more it ridded the world of another nuclear power.

The sudden buzzing of a cell phone startled him from his thoughts. He look down and sighed when he saw the name. It was his father. The word to Adam had become synonymous with stress and inadequacy. This was a man who included in his definition of "slacker" anyone who wasn't striving to become the next President of the United States, working on a Nobel Prize discovery, or studying to be a brain surgeon. No matter that Adam attended Stanford University, home to some of the most innovative minds in the world, to his father, he was just an unkempt geek playing with some very expensive toys.

Adam thought about not answering, then grimaced and reached for the phone. "Hey, Dad, what's up?"

"Not much … I … uh … just had a question. How are things going at Stanford?"

Adam sat back in his chair, suddenly leery. His dad never called just to see how he was doing.

"Everything's fine here," he replied curtly, then repeated, "What's up?"

There was a pause on the other end, then his father continued in a much more somber tone. "Uh, yes, Adam. I, uh … son, I need your help."

Adam's eyes widened. The all-powerful Robert Newhouse, Secretary of the Department of Energy, the man hoping to become the next president, needed help from a lowly, long-haired, ear-pierced, nose-ringed computer geek.

"You need my help? You've got access to the most powerful people in the world. What the hell can I do?"

"I know, Adam, but please, just listen. I need someone who's not part of the establishment here. The assistance I need is a bit more *clandestine.*"

Adam knew he was being manipulated and that by "clandestine" his father really meant that he needed a "nobody". Still, he couldn't help but be intrigued.

"Well, Dad, you've come to the right place. You want me to tap Putin's cell phone? Get the dirt on a senator or congressman?"

His father laughed, a rare sound that never failed to unnerve Adam. "Can you break into North Korea's nuclear program?"

"Already on it," Adam quipped. "Just let 'em push the button."

"Adam," his father said, all business once again, "do you still have that computer program you wrote, you know, the one you said was unbreakable? Untraceable? The one you tried to get the military to buy?"

"Yeah, I still got it." Adam chuckled. "Those assholes should've bought it when they had their chance. Instead, they treated me like I was just some dumb kid. Now they're wondering who keeps breaking into NORAD. The other day, I—"

"Okay, son, I got it. Listen. Are you able to direct a call, say from there in California to a specific cell phone tower somewhere overseas—let's say Yemen—and have your call bounced back to somewhere he in the States?"

"Yeah, sure, Dad. People on both sides of the law have been doing that for some time...."

"In Arabic," his father added.

"In Arabic?" Adam said befuddled. "What the hell is this all about?"

For the next twenty minutes, he sat in stunned silence as his father explained the entire situation, from its allegedly "pure" motive to how things had gotten out of hand.

"What's done is done," he added defensively. "No point in starting World War III. Son, I need to make sure that no one learns of the US's involvement in this."

Adam was silent a moment longer as he tried to search for the right words. As crazy as it sounded, he had to admit his father was right. Even if they were already sitting on the eve of destruction, they didn't need to add a world war to the mix. "I can do it. I have some cyber friends who know Yemen, if that's what you want."

His dad told him that Yemen would be the best, explaining that he needed a legitimate-sounding splinter group, some made-up faction that had a beef with the world. He told Adam to make a call to CNN, claiming responsibility.

Adam heard his dad take a deep breath. "Son, if that call ever got traced back here, you know...."

Adam didn't say anything. He was overwhelmed. He had figured it would be some global confrontation, a nuclear war, global warming, but this? Finally, he sighed. "I'll do it, but Jesus, Dad."

"I know, I know. It was never meant to come to this." He paused. "And, Adam, I need this done *yesterday*."

Adam nodded. "Sure, Dad."

Then he uttered a rare, heartfelt, "Thanks, son."

Newhouse sat in his office and just stared at the ceiling. Adam was a loose end, and he hated loose ends.

# Chapter 57

***

## 86 Pinckney Street
## Boston, Massachusetts

Ricky shivered and pulled up his collar as he watched the rowing team trudge up the Charles River against the frigid December winds. Schools throughout the city had been canceled until after Christmas because of concerns over the availability of fuel and oil in the coming months. Meteorologists predicted the coldest polar vortex ever recorded, expecting the temperatures along the eastern seaboard to drop twenty degrees below normal, with normal already being twenty below zero. Early fuel oil shortages had already sparked a number of hijackings of fuel trucks, and a growing black market for wood was taking its toll on the tree populations in the outlying areas of Boston.

Finally, with his nose dripping, toes frozen, cheeks wind-burnt, and little icicles hanging from his eyebrows, Ricky headed home. By the time he made it to the top of the steps of the old Victorian row house, his hands were so cold that he could hardly turn the door knob. Finally, he pushed open the large wooden door and felt the gush of warm air. "Mom, I'm home."

As he disrobed layer-by-layer: jacket, gloves, ear muffs, and scarf, he heard his mom yell, "In the Kitchen."

As he got closer to the kitchen, he smelled something, and it smelled good. He entered the kitchen and saw his mom standing at the counter opening a can of tomato sauce and Doctor Christenson sitting at the big wooden table. Ricky was getting used to Doctor Christenson; he was becoming a permanent fixture.

"Hi, Doctor Christenson."

He walked over and looked into the pan that his mother was stirring. Without looking over at Doctor Christenson, he said, with a bit of a contemptuous overtone, "Oh! I'm glad you're here, Doctor Christenson. I wouldn't get spaghetti otherwise."

Lucy glared at him. "Maybe you should go and clean up."

After Ricky headed upstairs, Lucy looked over at John. "I'm sorry about that. I think he still feels a little threatened. You're the first person that I've, I guess you'd say, dated. It's always been just him and me."

John got up, walked over and wrapped his arms around her waist, giving her a little squeeze. "You know I can't blame him. Who would want to share you with anyone?"

Lucy melted. It had been such a long time since she had felt the comfort and security of someone holding her. Finally, after an eternity of letting the moment consume her, she wiggled free afraid that Ricky was going to pop in at any moment. She turned to face him. "How do I know you're not just here for a good home-cooked meal? And what about Mr. Morton? Who's going to eat his pot pies?"

John smiled and turned the tables on her. "How do I know that all of these home-cooked meals are not just a well-orchestrated ploy just to have your way with me, and then in a few months, I'll be back to eating pot pies?"

Lucy gave him a little push back as she turned and continued stirring the pot. "Could be. You know what I learned at Bay Community College while you were pondering some theoretical mumbo-jumbo at that high-priced Princeton?"

He sat back down, not sure that he wanted to know, but he had the feeling that he was going to hear it anyway.

"Apparently, they didn't teach you much psychology at that Princeton place. Now, I don't have a degree in Theoretical Physics, but I did get an A-plus on my research paper in Psychology 101 at Bay Community College. Do you want to know what I researched?"

Before he could answer, Lucy put her fingers to her lips silencing him. "Ah! Ah! My research focused on the weaknesses of 'mankind'." She smiled. "Not 'womankind', mind you, just 'mankind'."

When he was younger, he had read the book *The Once*

*and Future King* and remembered the magician Merlin telling the young King Arthur, "Listen to me, young Wart, women don't think very often, but when they do, what is a man to do then?" John wasn't about to interrupt, but he did remember that Merlin, with all of his magical wisdom, never had an answer for the young Wart.

As she continued cooking, she said, "What I found was nothing new, common sense known by womankind for thousands of years. Do you want to hear it?"

John rocked his head back and forth unsure if he really wanted to know. "Maybe it's best I don't know."

"Oh, don't worry. It's not complicated. It's basic. The way to a man's heart is through his stomach and genitals."

John recoiled. "That's a low blow."

Lucy playfully wiggled her backside. "All's fair in love and war. John Steinbeck."

John smiled. Although he got her drift, he said, "I think it was *War and Peace*, and I think it was Tolstoy."

Lucy shrugged. "Whatever."

Their little interlude was cut short as Ricky came into the kitchen asking if dinner was ready.

"Just about. Grab some plates and silverware, and take them into the living room so we can watch the news as we eat."

"I don't have school for the rest of the semester, so I don't need to worry about my Civics class," he protested.

"With everything going on in the world and the oil thing, you might need to know more than you think."

As Ricky left with the plates and silverware, Lucy looked over at John and, with a slight quiver in her voice, said, "What do you think of this oil thing and the millions of people dying all over the world? We've never had enough oil as it is, and now we have to share it with some bacteria."

John shrugged. "It doesn't sound like it wants to share. If we end up with no oil, seven billion people are going to burn through every tree, stick and twig on this planet within weeks."

Lucy stepped over and handed him the bowl of spaghetti and sauce and said solemnly, "It's happening here, isn't it? Right here in Boston."

John only nodded.

Lucy was almost tearful. "I went to the store today, and there was nothing. No fresh fruits or vegetables, and the shelves were almost bare. It's not even Christmas yet, and it's been so cold. Our heating oil tank is only half full. I called, but I doubt the guy will ever come to fill it. Unless we keep this place near freezing, I'm not sure we'll make it to spring."

John nodded. "I know. We might have to leave here."

Her eyes widened. "Leave here, what're you talking about? Go where?"

John didn't know, but if the city came unglued like the rest of the world, Boston and the whole eastern seaboard would become a death trap. Those who didn't starve to death would freeze.

He gave her a little wink and tried to reassure her. "Come on, let's go watch the news."

As they walked into the living room, Lucy stopped and stared at the television. In the center of the screen was a large, darkened circle encompassed by a faint radiant rim of light; like an annular eclipse of the sun, where the sun's center is dark by the passage of the moon and only a faint rim of escaping rays encircle the darkened spot. Then, a brilliant greenish flash of light erupted from the upper corner of the darkened spot, a beautiful fleeting flair of sparks.

"That's pretty. What's that? Is that the solar eclipse that's coming?" she asked excitedly.

"Shhh!" Ricky shrugged. "I don't know, it just started."

Lucy set a bowl of salad on the coffee table and sat down as Sawyer Clark read from her teleprompter.

"Researchers at Northwestern University in Chicago took these pictures of the first moments of life. These photos captured the moment that a human egg was breached by any one of the millions of little packets of genetic material, all vying to be the father. According to the researchers who did the study, the instance that the egg's membrane is penetrated by the winner, an explosion of light erupts in an enzymatic firework of sparks as millions of atoms of zinc interact to produce a fluorescent green flash of life."

Lucy smiled. "Wow! That looks like a solar flare."

Just as Sawyer Clark was about to introduce the next news segment, a message popped up on her teleprompter: "GO TO NEWS ALERT."

"I'm sorry, I've just been told of a breaking news alert. We are going to go to Deputy Director Lyle Atkinson of Homeland Security."

On the screen appeared Deputy Director Atkinson standing outside the Nebraska Avenue complex, headquarters for Homeland Security. He began reading from a prepared statement, "At 4:30 p.m. today, CNN news received an encrypted message from a group in Yemen claiming responsibility for the oil-eating bacteria. The message appears to have originated somewhere north of the capital city of Sana'a. Homeland Security, Scotland Yards, Interpol, and every other major intelligence agency are currently working on deciphering the message. We'll have more on this as it becomes available."

Just blocks from Nebraska Avenue, Newhouse sat in his office in the Forrestal Building on Independence Avenue watching the news alert and praying to God that the thing wasn't traceable. He got up and put on his jacket. He still had a loose end—an idealistic loose cannon.

# Chapter 58

***

## International Space Station

For the ninth time that day, the bright speck in the darkness of space circled over the blue waters of the Pacific Ocean. As Commander Gerald Donaldson of the International Space Station sat in the observation deck, staring down on the devastation below, an infinitesimal burst of sparks and a flash of greenish light erupted deep within a small storage compartment on the station. The burst of sparks went undetected by the most sensitive detectors on the ISS, all except for the primitive storage receptacle sequestered deep in the bowels of the station.

At the exact moment, on the other side of the space station, a second imperceptibly small movement occurred in the recently docked airlocks of the cargo bay. A tiny thread of oxygen squeezed through a small air leak, warming a cluster of ice crystals buried deep in the seals of the air locks.

In a matter of just a few weeks, the thousands of lush, green islands that dotted the blue Pacific waters below had been set ablaze. The millions of inhabitants dotting the islands had been forced back in time to burning every stick, twig, and coconut shell that they could find. Now, from the observation deck of the ISS, the green dots were all brown with small swirling wisps of smoke rising from each like thousands of tiny volcanos.

Luckily, two days earlier, a shipment of fresh supplies had docked with the ISS, which gave Donaldson and the crew at least a year's supply of food, but they feared it would be the last.

Suddenly, Layne, the only female in the crew of six, felt a wave of nausea. She had not felt the little explosion of sparks, or seen the tiny flash of light. She had never had any problems with the nausea of weightlessness. Thinking little of it, the wave passed as fast as it had started.

Layne Rowe, formerly Elaine Annie Parks, and her husband, Allen, had been sent to the space station for one reason—to make a baby. Layne had gotten her MD degree and Ph.D. in Membrane Physiology from the University from Wisconsin, while her husband had gotten his Ph.D. in Electrical Engineering and Microgravity Research from Cal Tech. They had met five years earlier when they both had been accepted at NASA. After getting married, and seeming very compatible—just what NASA was looking for—they had been assigned a joint mission, to say the least, on the ISS.

NASA felt that, sooner or later, if there were going to be colonies on the moon or Mars, it was going to be necessary to see if it was possible to conceive and have a baby in the weightlessness of space. Years of research and ethical issues had been pondered over relentlessly. Experiments with everything from slugs and slime molds to rats, cats, and monkeys had finally assured NASA that it was time. After months and months of dehumanizing compatibility and fertility testing, Allen and Layne were sent to the ISS to make a baby. They had found that conceiving in space was anything but romantic, or easy.

Layne had been following her temperature and cycle closely, and a few days earlier, they had decided that the time was right. Privacy had been arranged, although that was a matter of semantics as they had told the other four crew members, "We'll be right back." Everyone had wished them good luck.

They had been given a small storage compartment on the back side of the space station, and it was anything but what one would call an ideal romantic love nest. The biggest problem had been Newton's first Law of Motion. Layne and her husband found that Newton was definitely right. For every action, there is an equal and opposite reaction.

Little did Layne realize that the fleeting wave of nausea and the little unseen burst of light in her tummy indicated that they had been successful, and soon the single cell would start dividing at an exponential rate.

Meanwhile, in the short time that it had taken for the nausea to pass, on the other side of the space station, in the seals of the life-saving supplies sent to the ISS, the tiny ice crystals were melting, and the single coil of DNA ever so slowly started to unravel.

# CHAPTER 59

***

## Georgetown, Washington, D.C.

Newhouse turned left off Wisconsin Avenue and onto Volta Place, heading toward Georgetown University. As he approached 34th Street, he saw the Circle K on his left, but he continued on for another block. It was only after several glances in the rearview mirror that he made a U-turn and headed back toward the store.

He was always a little edgy whenever he had to drive into this little pocket of Georgetown, especially this late at night. It was a seedy neighborhood and a likely place to get shot, but it was the only place in all of D.C. that still had an old AT&T pay phone.

Newhouse turned into the neighboring dry cleaner then drove around the backside of the Circle K so as to avoid the security cameras that panned the front parking lot. He pulled up in front of the payphone and sat there for a moment with his hand on the headlight switch. In situations like this, he was never sure whether it was better to turn them off and stay in the shadows or leave them on and announce his presence to any would-be perpetrators. It was like being in a cheesy spy movie.

After deciding to leave the low beams on, he got out and walked up to the phone. After one last look around, he lifted the receiver and dialed in a number. An automated operator's voice chimed, "Please deposit two dollars for the first three minutes."

He took a handful of quarters out of his pocket and started slipping them into the coin slot, each quarter leaving a dull bell tone as it fell. When he finished, the automated operator acknowledged, "Thank you. I will make that connection now."

As he stood waiting, a black car pulled into an abandoned parking lot across the street. Two shady-looking characters got out of the car and scanned the dark lot as if expecting to see trouble. Then, two shadows walked out from behind a dumpster on the far side of the lot. They all had guns. Nervously, they slowly approached the men standing by the car. Everyone's guns were aimed and pointing at each other. Then all four stood still and looked across the street at Newhouse.

Newhouse turned his back. This was just great. The headlights of his car illuminated him like a beacon from a lighthouse. Either the guys were going to come over and kill him, knowing he was watching their drug deal go down, or a thousand cops were going to show up, guns drawn, and there was going to be a shoot-out at the O.K. Corral. Either way, everyone was going to be wondering what the hell the Secretary of the Department of Energy was doing at a payphone in one of Georgetown's seediest areas at midnight.

After what seemed like an eternity, a voice spoke over the phone, "Yeah?"

As Newhouse spoke, he glanced over his shoulder toward the lot across the street. After what he assumed had been an exchange of packages, the two men slipped back into their car, and the other two walked off into the darkness behind the dumpster.

With a sigh of relief, Newhouse said, "I have a job."

"I'm listening."

"This one's going to be very high profile—lots of news media. It has to be clean. No mistakes."

There was nothing, just silence. Newhouse was starting to think that the line had gone dead, when finally the cold monotone voice said, "What and where?"

Newhouse hated dealing with this guy; he was one creepy mother. Unfortunately, sometimes one had problems that only creepy mothers could handle. Like when Newhouse needed help with a little problem around the same time a New York City individual needed some help getting some lucrative energy contracts. The New York City individual got his contracts, and Newhouse's little problem had gone away.

"California. Palo Alto. It's all in the folder—pictures, details, addresses, everything you need. Folder's in the same place as before."

"Anything to work with? Drugs, depression, deviant behavior?"

Just as Newhouse was about to answer, the AT&T operator chimed back in: "Please deposit two more dollars for an additional three minutes."

Newhouse reached into his pocket, took out another handful of quarters and started dropping them into the slot. Just as he was about to answer his questions about drugs, depression or other behavior, two black men came out of the convenience store and walked around the corner of the building. They both had huge gold chains around their necks and tattoos that covered almost every inch of their bodies. One had two little tear drops tattooed under his right eye.

They were just as startled as Newhouse. The bigger of the two looked at him and said, "What the hell are you doing here, white boy? You're going to get your white ass shot."

Newhouse shrugged sheepishly, and the two men just walked away.

Turning his attention back to the phone, Newhouse told the guy on the other end that everything in the place had to be demagnetized. The computers, his cloud, everything.

"The money?"

"It's with the folder. Cash."

Just as he was about to hang up, the voice asked, "Why's this going to be so high profile?"

Newhouse hesitated. “It’s a relative.”

There was silence for a few seconds, and then the phone went dead.

# Chapter 60

***

## Bayou Cane, Louisiana

Darryl sat spreading a fresh layer of opossum grease on his arms. The laceration across his chest had healed, and, thanks to the opossum grease, the burns on his arms and legs had stopped oozing and crusting. He had not been paying much attention to the little static-filled radio sitting next to him on the table until he heard, "A group claiming responsibility for the bacteria…."

Setting down the bowl of grease, he fiddled with the tuner knob and bent in to listen.

Since his scrape with death, he had been hiding in his cousin's cabin in the swamps south of Bayou Cane. He had been the only one to survive the explosion. His cousin Eugene along with Silas, Clemet, and the rest of the guys had all been killed.

This far into the swamp, the signal was weak, and there

was a lot of static on the old radio. To compound matters, the announcer doing the broadcast had a strong accent. Darryl couldn't quite place it; maybe Middle Eastern.

"I'm standing here on the outskirts of Sana'a, the capital city of Yemen. As everyone is aware by now, a few days ago, a terrorist group sent an encrypted message claiming responsibility for the development of the bacteria that's currently taking claim to the world's oil."

Someone interrupted and asked, "Osama, is there any word on who this terrorist group is, or where they're located?"

The newscaster, who Darryl assumed was Osama, answered, "No," and explained that there were hundreds of factions of radicals that called Yemen their home, and that as far as their location, they could have been transmitting from anywhere—a moving van, a lab buried in the desert—pointing out that most likely no one would ever know. Then he added, "Probably doesn't matter now; what's done is done."

Seven-thousand miles away, Newhouse sat at his desk on Independence Avenue and watched the news report on his computer screen.

Darryl got up, walked over to the window, and stared into the serenity of the swamps. He had no idea of what was going on. All he knew for sure was that he was supposed to be dead, and it had to do with this oil thing.

All that he could remember were the three FBI agents loading them into the vans at the federal place in Vegas.

They had been driven for hours in the desert heat with no water and had all been on the verge of passing out from heatstroke, when the van stopped, and each had been given a bottle of water. The water had tasted bitter, but, by then, everyone was so thirsty that no one complained. That's the last thing he remembered until he woke up on some kind of a fishing boat, his head in a fog as if he had been drugged. He had just stood up, wobbly, holding onto the boat's rigging when there was an explosion. He remembered being the only guy standing. He had seen Silas, Clemet, and the others still lying unconscious on the floor of the boat. When the explosion hit, it had thrown him dozens of feet into the air and landed him on top of a dense growth of mangrove trees. A broken mangrove branch had cut across his chest, and his arms and legs were burnt.

He remembered coming and going in and out of half consciousness and watching the frenzied feast of alligators fight over the burning bodies. And then that FBI agent—that cold guy with the dark sunglasses, just standing, watching until the boat had sunk. Assuming that everyone was dead, he had turned and walked away casually.

Darryl had just stared aimlessly into the swamp. No matter how drugged he was or how much of a stupor he had been in, he would never forget that FBI agent as long as he lived.

Going back over to the table and sitting down, he scooped up another handful of opossum grease. He couldn't leave the swamps; he knew that he wasn't supposed to be alive.

Newhouse turned off the CNN report and sat back with a sigh of relief. Then, just as he was about to go to a meeting, his computer flashed:

"Mr. NH-FBI, Kathy here. ARMACO Research Labs. Galveston, Texas."

"Mr. NH, I think I have pieced together this oil thing. I got back some results from my friend at Cornell in Midtown. I haven't told anybody yet. I might be wrong, but I'm not sure about that Yemen thing."

# Chapter 61

***

## National Security Agency
## Fort Meade, Maryland

Sasik walked through the expanse of cubicles where over a hundred eavesdroppers sat listening in on every corner of the world. Smiling at a few of the younger girls along the way, he approached the door to the Director of the NSA, Keith Alexander. Alexander was a four-star general, and even the President of the United States had to make an appointment to see him, all except for Sasik.

The door to Alexander's office was guarded by a troll of woman. Her bifocal glasses inched to the tip of her nose, probably for intimidation. A tiny hairy wart just under her left eye twitched with each movement of her eyebrow, and she had a glare that would frighten even Attila the Hun.

She definitely didn't like Sasik, but he figured she didn't like anybody, especially anyone who stepped on her turf or even looked in her direction. Unaffected by her tactics, Sasik approached her desk and matter-of-factly asked, "Is he in?"

She peered over her bifocals, the little wart twitching. "I can check."

Sasik just gave a kind smile as he stepped around her desk. "Never mind, I'll check myself," he said and knocked on the door.

As usual, everyone had watched Sasik walk right past the general's secretary dog without her jumping up. The gossip mill had abounded; maybe they were lovers. Some questioned that maybe he was an illegitimate son, but no one knew the truth. The truth was that he was more than just a lowly coffee boy who cleaned up conference tables after NSA meetings. He was a mole.

Sasik knocked once, waited, and then knocked three more times—it was his and the general's little code.

From the other side, he heard a gruff, "Come in, come in."

Sasik walked in and closed the door behind him.

The general half stood up from behind his large wooden desk, leaned forward, and pointed to the leather chair in front of his desk. "Sit, sit."

Sasik wasn't offended or intimidated by the general's harshness. It was well known in the military that you could take a field general out of the field, but you couldn't take the field out of the general. Sasik had learned this when he was a child.

His grandfather had been a general in "The Big One" (WWII), and for as far back as he could remember, everything was "Yes, sir. No, sir." And, right up until the day he died at age 90, his grandfather never asked people to do anything; he gave orders. So, like his grandfather, Alexander, although no longer in the jungles of Vietnam, didn't exactly ask people to do things.

Sasik walked over and took his seat in the large leather chair. As he sat, he pointed to a red phone sitting on the general's desk. "Who's at the other end of that phone? Anybody call today?"

Sasik asked every time he came in and vowed to someday tap into the infamous red phone. There was nothing more galling for a computer hacker than to have a domain sitting right in front of him and not have hacked it.

He raised his eyebrows. "Is it the Pope? Putin? The president?"

The general barked, "Don't worry about the damn phone." He leaned forward on his elbows. "What do you have?"

Alexander knew that any time Sasik came knocking on his door, either he or one of his sneaky little shit cyberspace friends had some ill-gotten bit of information. He always figured that Sasik probably had more dirt on him than J. Edgar Hoover had on the whole country, but Alexander needed Sasik's anonymity to get around little technicalities of the Fourth Amendment, like listening in on private cell phones of the general public, world leaders, Congress, the Senate; and if need be, the president.

"Sir," Sasik said as he unfolded a crumpled up piece of paper and handed it to the general, "I've been picking up some unidentified signals coming from an unusual spot in the desert."

Alexander looked at the sheet, which had a bunch of latitude and longitude numbers printed on it. And, as usual, he barked, "What the hell do you mean, a *spot*?"

Sasik nodded. "They came from the middle of nowhere."

Like his grandfather, the general wasn't the most patient man, and he didn't like playing ten-thousand questions. "What desert? And what the hell are you talking about, son?"

Sasik held up his hand, trying to calm the general. "A few months ago, while I was just fishing around—"

Alexander stopped him. "You mean eavesdropping on people?"

Sasik wavered a little. "The Air Force, actually, but you don't have to worry, sir, no private citizens."

Alexander flopped back in his chair. "Jesus Christ." He let out a dying breath. He knew someday he was going to end up in front of a firing squad. "And?"

Sasik explained that a few months earlier, by pure serendipity while scanning the Internet, he had run across some chatter in the middle of the desert in Nevada. At the time, he didn't think much of it and had tucked it away in his, what he called, "Keep an Eye On" file. Then Sasik told him that the chatter had continued, so he had tapped into the Air Force's reconnaissance maps—the maps the Air Force updated daily—just to see what was there.

Alexander shook his head in disbelief. "You know, if the Air Force finds out, they'll shoot me."

Sasik smiled with a big grin. "Don't worry, sir, they'll find that it was the Navy."

Alexander smiled. "So, what did you find?"

"Nothing, that's just it. There's nothing there but a shed. Just an old dilapidated barn in the middle of Pyramid Lake Paiute Tribal Reservation—a place called Black Rock Desert."

Alexander didn't have the faintest idea of where this was going or why he was supposed to care about some phone calls in the middle of the desert. He felt like he was back talking to his first wife who used to make everything so confusing that even the NSA wouldn't have been able to figure it out.

"Where the hell is this going?"

Sasik explained that it was curious as to why there would be so much chatter coming from an old shed in the middle of the desert. So, one day, he had listened in expecting to hear someone having phone sex with his girlfriend or some Paiutes shipping illegal booze or who knows what.

Alexander cut him off. "Let me guess, it wasn't just some guy having phone sex with a girlfriend."

Sasik shook his head. "Nope, indeed it wasn't. *And* it was encrypted."

The general dropped his head as he was expecting something big—some earth-shattering revelation. Exasperated, he barked, "Look, I'm busy! So what! Anybody can have encrypted phones."

Sasik nodded, impatiently waiting to drop the hammer. "Not military."

That stopped the general in his tracks. "What kind of military?"

"The highest level encryption the military has," Sasik told him.

Alexander stood up, walked over to the window and looked out in the direction of the Pentagon. "So, who the hell is using these phones?" He turned and looked at Sasik for the answer.

Sasik shrugged. "That's the problem, sir. I don't know who. So, instead of trying to decrypt what they had said, I decided to try to trace the calls back from where they had originated."

Alexander stepped toward him. "And?"

Sasik raised his eyebrows. "It's a bit of a quandary, sir. I couldn't find it exactly."

Alexander's face turned beet-red, "What the hell do you mean you can't find it? We're the NSA for Christ's sake. We tracked down Bin laden in a van in Pakistan. We can take a fly out in Afghanistan, and we could listen in on the president." Alexander paused. "I mean … if we wanted to."

Sasik nodded. "Sure, I mean, if it were for national security reasons." With a hesitant smile, he continued, "But we really don't want to, do we?"

The general didn't answer him, so Sasik continued. "Sir, it took a while, but I did locate the origin of the call."

Alexander's eyebrows rose. "And?"

"It's an old AT&T pay phone in Georgetown."

"A pay phone?" Alexander was taken aback. "You mean like with quarters? I didn't know we had them anymore."

"Here's something else you didn't know. We can't really tap into those old pay phones. It's a little flaw in the NSA's system."

Alexander sat back down, thinking, *It has to be the damn Pentagon. Who else would have access to a high-level military encryption?* He slammed his fist on his desk. "What the hell are they up to now? Did you download the pictures of the shed?"

Sasik smiled. "The Navy did, sir."

Alexander grinned with pleasure then told Sasik to find and get pictures of the AT&T phone in Georgetown, and that he had some calls to make.

As Sasik was leaving, Alexander reminded him, "Be careful. You know we don't listen in on anyone. You know, that Fourth Amendment thing."

Sasik smiled, "We don't waterboard people anymore either, do we?"

Alexander grimaced. “Maybe civilians, but definitely not terrorists.”

As Sasik walked past Alexander’s secretary, he asked snidely, “You need coffee or anything?”

# Chapter 62

***

## Grundy Count, Iowa

While the heat continued to bake the deserts of the Southwest, the Great Plains of the Midwest lay a frozen wasteland as Arctic blast after Arctic blast blew down from the Big Sky Country.

In just a matter of months, the great turbines at Boulder Dam had succumbed to the effects of the oil-eating bacteria, returning the desert to its parched past.

On each pass of the ISS, Commander Donaldson watched as a growing swath of barren land expanded. Glowing pockets of smoldering embers snaked across the Sierras, down the Great Plains of the Midwest and all the way to the eastern seaboard—the last burning remnants of survival.

While Gloria stood in the sweltering heat of her apartment on the Vegas strip, over a thousand miles away, Doctor

Jacobs stood staring at the open grave in Grundy Count, Iowa. Tears cooled by the blustery winds streamed down his face. He hadn't cried since he was a little boy, yet he couldn't hold back his painful feelings of severe loss of a good friend.

As he waited for the service to begin, he thought back to that awful day. It was such a freak accident. He had just finished a meeting when his cell phone buzzed. He remembered looking at the caller ID; it read: "Trauma Center—University of Texas Medical Branch at Galveston". Confused, having no idea why anyone would be calling him from a Trauma Center, he pushed the green button on his phone, accepting the call.

A cold voice asked, "Is this Doctor Karl Jacobs?"

Confused and somewhat caught off guard, he answered, "This is Doctor Jacobs."

Then he remembered so vividly the voice identifying himself as a neurosurgeon and asking if he knew a young lady named Kathy Finley.

Anxiety was churning in his gut. "Yes," he had answered with trepidation, "what's this all about?"

The neurosurgeon explained that there had been an accident and that she had listed him as her local "next-of-kin". The surgeon would not give any information over the phone and suggested that he come to the Trauma Center.

Kathy had been grocery shopping and was carrying a bag of groceries up the stairs to her apartment when she slipped on a patch of icy moss that had accumulated near the top of the steps. Falling back down the stairs, she had sustained extensive head trauma, and the neurosurgeons had been unable to remove the clot that had formed in her brain.

Doctor Jacobs had been apprehensive about driving the thousand miles to Iowa, but even at the risk of dying himself, he was going to be there to say goodbye to the little girl he had taken under his wing—a daughter he never had.

In the previous few weeks, road travel had become dangerous. Cars and trucks blocked the highways all across the country. There were numerous reports of normal, previously law-abiding families hijacking and killing others for their cars, trucks, and the last bits of energy left in the engines. When the fuel ran out, or the effects of the oil-eating bacteria shut down the engines, which ever came first, they then sat and froze.

Doctor Jacobs wasn't sure if he would even make it back to Galveston. So far, his car had held up, but he couldn't tell if it was his car that smelled like pig manure, early signs that the bacteria had invaded his engine, or just a smell carried by the surrounding winds. His trip to Grundy Count had been in the opposite direction of the masses heading south, desperate to escape the cold and sure death of the North.

As the Minister read the Eulogy, Doctor Jacobs wondered if Kathy had checked the Lucky Stars Moon Watch charts that fateful day. She had been such a goofy little girl, never starting her day without consulting her astrological charts.

As the service ended, Kathy's parents came up to him and thanked him for taking care of their little girl in the big city.

He smiled and told them that it was the other way around, thanking them for sending their little girl to the big city to rescue a crotchety old man set in his ways.

He made his way back to his car, the cold wind blistering his face. As he sat waiting for the car to warm up, he couldn't help but think to himself, he had never thought of Galveston as the big city, but then, looking around, he supposed when you're from Grundy Center, Iowa, Galveston probably looked like the big city.

A thousand miles away, in the sweltering heat of Vegas, Gloria stood staring at a plain brown paper bag that she had found on her doorstep. Scribbled across the front with a magic marker, it read, "Grady."

She had been seeing a young man Grady White for well over a year, a paraglider enthusiast and president of the local hang gliding club of Boulder.

A few weeks earlier, after an exhausting sexual interlude, as they lay catching their breaths, he had told her about something that he had filmed by pure coincidence one day while he was hang gliding over Lake Mead. He had not gone into any detail at the time because another interlude had interrupted their conversation, but he had told her that he thought someone was following him. She had not seen or heard from him since, which had been very concerning since they usually got together at least twice a week. She called his cell phone a number of times, but there was no answer.

Reaching into the paper bag, she pulled out a video with a note: "Lake Mead oil spill. Get to Anna Johnson."

She knew Anna Johnson; she had interviewed and gotten an internship with Anna, Las Vegas KXNT TV's number-one newscaster, a few months before the world-crashing, oil-chomping bacteria.

At the bottom of the note, Grady had written, "Be careful."

# Chapter 63

***

## 86 Pinckney Street
## Boston, Massachusetts

Bundled in layers of winter clothes, Lucy and Ricky walked headlong into the blustery winds blowing down from the North. It was only mid-December, and the eastern seaboard had already endured five straight days of subzero temperatures, straining the already critical fuel oil shortages. Lucy and Ricky had gone out grocery shopping, and after hours of scavenging store after store, they returned with only a few meager bags of canned goods. With frozen fingers, Ricky pushed open the large wooden door to 86 Pinckney Street. Lucy felt the gush of warm air and gave a sigh of relief.

Doctor Christenson had been in the kitchen thinking about what they were going to do if things continued to get worse. With dwindling food and energy, major cities around the world had become deathtraps. So far, the government had been able to avoid panic by reassuring the public that by opening the nation's oil reserves and distributing emergency food supplies, the country would be able to make it through the winter. It was reassuring to the public, but like many critics, John was skeptical. No one knew how the bacteria had been able to circumvent the globe so fast. As with any successful infectious disease, an infecting organism has to have a carrier, like a sneezing nose, an infected genital organ, or, unbeknownst to scientists in this case, a colon with a couple trillion oil-eating E. coli bacteria. It was not that the government was being deceptive; the question was, how was the government or anyone else going to stop bacteria that was hitchhiking in the entrails of the very workers who were going to unseal the reserve oil tanks?

Hearing Lucy and Ricky stomping their feet and complaining about the cold, he got up and walked down the hallway toward the front door. As he got close, he stopped in surprise. Lucy had a large goose egg on her forehead, and she was crying.

Putting his hand gently on the lump, he asked, "What happened?"

"A lady hit Mom with a can of chili!" Ricky said excitedly.

John looked at Ricky, surprised by the comment. "What?"

Lucy sniffled. "It's getting bad out there. We spent hours going from store to store looking for food, and all we found were a few cans of beans and chili." She held out the small bag for John to see. "The shelves are bare. People are panicking."

John took her in his arms and held her. Like a little puppy, cold and scared and wanting to be held, Lucy didn't resist.

"How'd you get the bump on the head?"

Sobbing the whole time, Lucy explained that they had gone to a Star Market and found cans of beef chili on a bottom shelf that had gotten pushed way back. No one had seen them. She explained that she was down on her knees handing cans back up to Ricky when a woman with two children came over and tried to take the bag from Ricky. The lady pushed him, and when he wouldn't let go of the bag, she hit him.

Lucy wiped her tears on John's shirt and, with another sniffle, continued, "The woman was like a rabid animal—desperate. As I went to get up, she grabbed one of the cans and hit me." She rubbed the spot on her forehead. "It happened so fast." Then she looked up into John's eyes. "I hit the lady over and over with a can of the chili that I had in my hand. She started bleeding, her kids started crying, and then she just turned and walked away. She didn't say anything."

Lucy shook her head in disbelief. "I've never hit anybody in my life, but she was going to hurt Ricky. I know she's probably just a normal mom doing whatever it takes to take care of her children, but I had to protect Ricky. I didn't mean to hurt her, and now her kids are going to go hungry."

John looked into her sad but beautiful, dark eyes and nodded. "Sometimes it comes down to survival."

John and Ricky sat on the couch to watch the news while Lucy took the meager bag of groceries to the kitchen. She returned a little later with a smile on her face as if she had just cooked up a wildebeest.

"Chili, anyone?"

They watched the news as they sat eating their chili. The president had confirmed earlier in the day that the nation's oil reserves would be opened and that the military would start rationing fuel and oil to homes throughout the northern states. The major airlines had suspended all but a few short, low-level flights throughout the country. Meanwhile, the president also ordered the grounding of all military aircraft after a number of crashes, the most recent a military plane that crashed on takeoff in the oil fields of Alaska, killing the Director of Drilling Operations on Prudhoe Bay's north slope. The Director, Mike Williams, had previously been summoned to Washington by the president to discuss the closing of the Alaskan pipeline.

Ricky held out his empty bowl suggesting that he'd have more.

Lucy looked at John, tears welling up in her eyes. Shaking her head, she said, "No more. We better save it until we see what happens."

John nodded in agreement and then pointed to the television. "Let's listen."

As Sawyer Clark introduced NBC's new nightly news medical editor Doctor Sandra Aarons, a picture of bacteria growing in a petri dish appeared on the screen.

Aarons started by recapping the estimated number of deaths worldwide that resulted from the, as of yet, mysterious gastrointestinal outbreak. Scientists suspected that the two were related, but no one had yet been able to find the connection. She said that, according to estimates, the illness had already been responsible for as many as a billion deaths.

Lucy looked over at John. "We've been lucky so far not getting that gastrointestinal thing, but I hear it's starting here in Boston, and I hear it's really bad out west."

John didn't say anything, he just nodded. But he knew that it was only a matter of time before they would probably have to get out of city. He had been working on a plan for a few days but didn't think that Lucy was ready for the sticker shock. John saw that she was starting to realize that they may need to get out of the city, but six thousand miles and possibly never coming back was maybe a little more than she had been thinking.

"Have scientists made any headway yet in identifying the culprit of this outbreak?" Sawyer asked Aarons. "I mean, it's so widespread."

Aarons shook her head defeatedly.

Sawyer continued with the questioning. "Do scientists think that the oil-eating bacteria and the gastrointestinal diarrhea thing are related?"

Aarons shrugged. "Not at first, but after a while, epidemiologically, it had become more obvious. But, like the oil-degrading bacteria, no one can find how or why these bacteria all of a sudden started eating oil or how they cause such a gastrointestinal upset." She paused. "Scientists now think that the two calamities are related and feeding on each other. At this point, it doesn't matter which comes first—weakness and dying from starvation, or weakness and dying from massive diarrhea. Either way, millions die, flies, maggots, and millions more die." She shook her head. "In the meantime, the few who are left are scorching the earth."

Sawyer nodded.

Aarons continued, "Somebody's missing something. Scientists are sure that someone has genetically altered the bacteria and have narrowed it down to either E. coli, a common dirt bacteria, or a common intestinal bacteria. Both of these guys are normally friendly little bacteria that, for millions of years, have had a mutual agreement with our colons—you give us a place to live, and we'll take care of your colon. But, scientists worldwide have sequenced the genes in just about every E. coli and bacteroid in the world, and no one has found anything."

John sat staring at the television, but he hadn't heard a word Aarons had said for the last five minutes; he wasn't even sure the plane could make it 6000 miles. One little sputter, and they would all be dead. And, he wasn't even sure of what they would find when they got there.

# Chapter 64

***

## National Security Agency
## Fort Meade, Maryland

After making a few notes on the map of Black Rock Desert, Nevada, General Anderson picked up his phone and buzzed his secretary, Martha. After a few rings, she answered, "Yes, sir."

"Martha, see if you can find a Special Agent Michael Kelly. He's with the National Security Branch of the FBI in Vegas."

"I'll find him and buzz you back."

As he waited for Martha, he looked at the pictures that Sasik had sent of the little building in Black Rock. Now even he was curious; something stunk. Someone had to be hiding something. Black Rock was 2500 miles away, and someone was going through all the trouble of dropping quarters into what was probably the last pay phone on earth.

The phone on Kathy's desk buzzed, starling her. Setting down her nail polish and attempting not to smudge her nails, she picked it up. "FBI, National Security Branch, Las Vegas. Agent Michael Kelly's office. Can I help you?"

"This is the office of General Keith Anderson, NSA."

Kathy was about to ask a million questions but wasn't given the chance.

"Director Anderson needs to speak with agent Kelly. Is he in?"

"Yes, I'll get him." Kathy opened the door to her boss' office, and, with a bit of a confused look, holding up two fingers, she mouthed in a low whisper, "The Director of the NSA is on line two."

Kelly straightened up in his chair, eyebrows furrowed, trying to remember who the current Director of the National Security Agency was.

From the look on his face, Kathy could tell that he didn't remember offhand who the current director was. Although he knew, it just wasn't someone who called him very often, like ever. In a low whisper, Kathy told him, "Keith Anderson."

"Ah!" Kelly nodded and motioned for her to put him through.

A few seconds later, the little light indicating line two started blinking. Kelly took a sighing breath. "This is Special Agent Kelly."

"Kelly, this is Anderson, NSA."

Kelly tried to break the ice a little. "Yes, sir. I've heard of the NSA. You're a football team, right?"

Anderson laughed. "That's the NFL. Don't be smart with me, son."

"Sorry, sir, how can I help you?"

Anderson explained that he needed a little local help and hinted that maybe it could be kept between just him and Kelly.

Kelly told him sure, knowing what Anderson was hinting at, and asked again how he could help.

"You know a place called Black Rock? You know where it is?"

Kelly knew exactly where it was, and most of it wasn't under his jurisdiction. He turned in his chair and looked at the map behind him. "I know where it's at. It's about 500 miles from here, Pyramid Lake. It's the Piute Indian Reservation."

Sitting at his desk two thousand miles away, Anderson shook his head. "That's it." Then with a much more toned down, subdued demeanor, he said, "Kelly, I need someone to go there and check something out."

Kelly's head dropped. "Sir?"

"I need someone to go there and check something out," the general repeated.

Kelly was confused. "Sir, why don't you just order up a helicopter or get photos from the Air Force?"

"Too many eyes and ears. You know what I mean, Kelly?"

Kelly knew exactly what he meant. "You don't want your neighbors to know."

The general didn't say anything.

"Sir, what are you looking for? There's nothing out there—no water, nothing. That's why we gave it to the Indians."

Without giving Anderson a chance to say anything, Kelly asked him if he had ever read Dante's *Inferno*, the seven gates to hell, explaining that Black Rock was probably one of the original seven gates.

"You know, Agent Kelly," Anderson interrupted, "I'll bet your chances for advancement in the bureau are pretty slim, being stuck out there at a desk in the middle of the desert." Then, just to make sure Kelly was getting his point, with a Texas drawl, the land of his youth, he said, "Why, hell, I'll bet nobody even knows you're out there."

Kelly didn't say anything; he knew where this was going.

Anderson continued, "You know, Kelly, if you knew the right people, why hell, I'll bet someone could get you moved to a desk right here in D.C., maybe even a desk with a view of the White House."

Kelly knew he wasn't going to climb the ladder any further in the Bureau, and he desperately wanted to get out of this inferno of endless sand and tumbleweeds. "How can I help you, General?" he replied with an upbeat tone.

Anderson laughed. "Thata boy, Kelly. And they say our departments can't work together. Why, hell, we're a team," he said, again with a twinge of Texas drawl.

Kelly just rolled his eyes.

Anderson spent the next ten minutes explaining the encrypted phone calls from D.C. to the little building in Black Rock, and that he needed someone to more or less go there under the radar and check it out.

Kelly had been born and raised in the beautiful green hills of New Hampshire and longed for the cool, fresh air, the trees and flowing streams.

"I've got a pen. You have the coordinates?"

Kelly told the general that he would send a couple of agents, and the general asked him if he had a car or truck that he was sure hadn't been contaminated by this oil bacteria thing. Kelly told him that they had essentially quarantined the carpool area, and he felt comfortable enough to send a couple of agents.

The general read off the coordinates and told Kelly he'd forward pictures of the building. Then he gave Kelly a phone number and told him to have his guys call him when they were there at the site and that he wanted them to send some pictures back to his phone.

Kelly wanted to make sure the general got the picture. "It's really hot out here, sir."

The general understood. "Don't worry son. You wipe my ass, I'll wipe yours. That's how we get things done here in D.C. Now you better go start packing."

As Kelly put down the receiver, Sasik leaned forward and

pushed the button disconnecting “voicecast”.

Two thousand miles away, Kelly folded his hands behind his head and leaned back in his chair. He stared up at the ceiling feeling like he had just made a pact with the devil.

After a few minutes of thought, he yelled, “Kathy, get me agents Shields and Whitbolt.”

# Chapter 65

***

## Black Rock Desert, Nevada

Hans walked along the dimly lit corridors of the research facility towards the residential complex. The facility had been build underground with state-of-the-art laboratories, individual living quarters, kitchens, a movie theater, an exercise complex, and a swimming pool, but nothing could change the prison-like chill of the gray cement walls. Hans had sold his soul to the devil.

There was an elevator to take one topside, but there was little to see, only endless miles of baked desert and a few rock outcroppings; no cacti, no tumbleweeds, no jackrabbits, just miles of flatness.

Hans found Lidia sitting alone in the theater room, staring blankly at CNN. Some newscaster was updating the estimated death toll worldwide to now over two billion. In a matter of just a few months, minuscule little bacteria with no arms and no legs had managed to traverse the globe and tip the ratio of the biomass of the planet in its favor, and it wasn't over yet.

Hans walked up and put his hand on Lidia's shoulder. She didn't move; she just stared, then, numbly pointing at the television screen, she said, "We did that, you know?"

Hans nodded but didn't say anything.

With tears in her eyes, she said, "From dust we came, and dust we shall return," in a low, almost inaudible mumble. She looked up at Hans. "You know that, right?"

Again, he didn't say anything, but he could see that Lidia was loosing it. Between the guilt and the isolation, she was going stir crazy. Taking her hand, he said, "Let's go topside. We have to get out of here for a while."

Lidia pulled back on his hand. "We can't. We're on lock-down."

Hans smiled; that had never stopped them before.

"What if we get caught?" Lidia protested.

Hans grimaced, "What're they going to do, shoot us?"

The place had more security cameras and alarms than Fort Knox, but despite all of the wisdom of the security engineers, the alarms, the cameras, and the sensors, Hans had found a flaw in the system.

A few months after arriving, he and Lidia had become an item. They enjoyed each other's company, but no matter where in the facility they went, they always had the creepy feeling of being watched, which they were correct. And, going topside was no better because the elevators required a retinal scan.

Hans had been determined to find a way around the system. It had become his passion. Not being able to access the schematics of the facility, which the makers had made sure of, he had spent his time off walking every corridor, every nook and cranny, and drawing his own blueprints.

In his wanderings, he had found a large air vent that ran parallel to a steep driveway, which led down into an underground garage beneath the complex. The entrance to the garage itself was secured by two large steel doors, but just inside was a maintenance door into the shaft of the air vent with steps leading up to the top. There was a steel gate at the top, but it had not been secured. One security guard probably assumed another had secured the door at the bottom—the flaw Hans had been looking for.

Lidia shrugged and stood up. Hans was right; they probably weren't going to shoot them, and they were already in prison, so what the hell else could they do?

Hans took her hand and told her to go pack a little picnic basket, some wine, cheese, and to bring a couple of blankets.

Lidia looked at him wearily. "Why do we need blankets?" she asked as if she didn't know.

Hans gave her a fiendish little smile. "The Tasmanian devil needs a little sunlight?"

Lidia rolled her eyes, "Tasmanian devil, my ass."

Hans' face brightened. "Exactly."

Twenty minutes later, they made their way up the vent and stepped into the desert heat. The midday sun was scorching, but for Hans and Lidia, just getting out of the place felt like heaven.

With basket and blankets in hand, they walked a few hundred yards from the complex up a small knoll to a large outcropping of rocks, most likely deposits from some prehistoric glacier. On one side, a large overhang of granite boulders formed a nice little cave-like nook. The opening to the cave faced east, blocking the afternoon sun and any cameras from the facility below. With the desert winds, it left a fairly cool little enclave—Hans' and Lidia's little getaway.

Lidia rolled over. "Is the Tasmanian devil happy now?"

Hans grinned. "For the time being."

She gave him a playful slap, but then she started to cry. Staring up at the ceiling, tears streaming down her face, she said, "That bacteria didn't come from Yemen."

Hans took a napkin and wiped her eyes. "I know."

Lidia rolled over and put her head on his chest, sniffling. "Do you think whoever runs this place is just going to let us walk away?" Before he could answer, she lifted her head and looked into his eyes. "Do you even know who runs this place?"

Hans had no idea who ran or built the place. He had never seen whoever was supposedly in charge, but he knew the voice—a voice that he would never forget as long as he lived.

Lidia sat up and started rummaging through the picnic basket. She got out some cheese and crackers and poured some wine.

Hans lay watching her backside with a devilish grin. "You ever thought of getting a Tasmanian devil?"

Lidia turned and gave him a pathetic look.

They lay on the blankets, the desert winds blowing across the front of the cave, sipping wine and nibbling on the cheese and crackers. Lidia was reminiscing about her childhood upbringing in Prague when, suddenly, Hans sprang up.

"Shhhhh! Be quiet. What's that?"

At first, Lidia didn't hear anything, then as she lay quietly listening, she heard it—a low hum far off in the distance. "I think it's just the wind," she reassured herself. But then the hum got louder and louder, and, within minutes, it turned into a rhythmic chopping sound.

Hans got up and looked out around the outcropping of rocks, back in the direction of the little shed that lead down into the complex.

Lidia propped herself up on her elbows. "What is it?"

Hans shrugged.

Lidia got up and walked over. Putting her hands on Hans' shoulders, she got up on her tiptoes and peered out around the corner.

"There." Hans pointed to a spot way off in the distance.

"What is it?" she asked excitedly.

"Helicopters."

Within minutes, two huge helicopters, blacker than the ace of spades and with no identification markings, landed only yards from the little shed.

Gripping his shoulders tighter and pushing further up on her tippy-toes, she said, "Those are funny-looking helicopters."

Hans nodded. "They're stealth."

As the rotors slowed, the doors flew open and at least ten ninja-looking military guys flooded out of each helicopter, fanning out around the area as if they were looking for bin Laden's compound.

"What're they doing?" Lidia asked.

Hans looked at her just as confused. "How do I know! Do you want to walk down there naked and ask them, 'Hey guys, what's going on?'"

Lidia slapped him on the shoulder. "Don't be funny. It was just a rhetorical question."

As they watched, one group poured into the little shed where the elevators were that went down to the complex. Meanwhile, another group circled around to the entrance that lead down to the underground garage. Although the entrance down had been well camouflaged with mounds of natural looking desert sands and a smattering of the prehistoric rocks, they seemed to know exactly where it was.

Two men disappeared into the depths of the driveway while the rest waited topside. A few minutes later, the two returned, and the group scattered. Then, suddenly, a huge explosion boomed, and billows of smoke belched up from the entrance to the underground garage.

Lidia screamed, "What's that?"

Hans turned and covered her mouth.

Below, one of the men turned and looked up toward the outcropping of rocks. Gripping his gun, crouched, he started walking up the hill toward them until what appeared to be the leader of the group screamed at him, "Come on. Let's go."

He turned and headed back toward the rest of the group, and then they all disappeared down into the complex.

Hans shook Lidia. "Are you nuts?"

"Sorry," she whimpered.

Hans knew that they had blown the doors to the garage, and then they heard it—the rapid bursts of gunfire coming from within the complex. He mumbled to himself in disbelief, "They're killing everyone. They're destroying the lab."

Within minutes, the ninjas poured out of the complex and climbed back into the helicopters. The rotors hummed to life, picking up speed, and slowly lifted into the air.

Because of the sand and dust whipped up by the powerful rotors, Hans temporarily lost sight of the helicopters. Then, suddenly, one appeared directly overhead. Hans pushed Lidia as far back as possible into the cave, then he reached down and pulled the blankets back out of view.

Lidia cried, "What're they doing?"

"I think they're scouting the area, being sure there are no survivors."

Pushing as far back as possible into the little cave-like nook, they waited in shocked silence. After what seemed like an eternity, the helicopters lifted, banked to the west, and flew off.

Hans and Lidia inched to the front of the cave and peered out, watching the helicopters until they were only distant specks on the horizon. Lidia was about to say something when there was a sudden succession of massive explosions. The ground thundered under their feet. A fireball with a plume that looked like a nuclear explosion blew straight up the elevator shaft, lifting the little shed hundreds of feet into the air and disintegrating it into shrouds of splintered wood.

As she gasped, two or three more explosions belched up from the underground garage, and a fireball of heat blasted past their little hideaway.

Then, there was nothing—deafening silence, only the low hum of the desert winds.

Hans and Lidia stood naked in the doorway of their little cave, staring straight ahead at the nothingness.

Lidia whimpered, "What're we going to do?"

Looking into her tearful eyes, he replied, "We're going to walk away. We're just going to walk away."

# Chapter 66

***

## Belle Haven, Virginia

Newhouse sat in his living room in Belle Haven, Virginia edging evermore forward in his chair, quietly cheering on the television as if he was watching a football game.

"Way to be, Lipton. Way to be."

He was watching *60 Minutes* as Scott Pendleton was interviewing a Professor of Biochemical Engineering from Cal tech, Doctor Angela Lipton, a well-respected researcher in the field of oil.

A few weeks earlier, he had seen Lipton on a weekend CNBC news special, a round table discussion with some of the world's top researchers on the current oil issues. She and a group of other well-respected scientists were a fringe group that had doubts about the origins of the oil-destroying bacteria, arguing that it may not have been the results of genetic manipulation, and just as likely that it was a mere fluke of nature. Lipton's group argued that after months of every research group in the world sequencing just about every bacteria in the world and finding nothing, sooner or later the scientific community had to start considering other possibilities. She argued convincingly that Homeland Security, Interpol, Scotland Yards, and everyone else might be chasing ghosts.

This is exactly what Newhouse needed—someone articulate and with authority to divert the attention of Homeland Security at least until he was sure that the lab and everyone in it had been destroyed.

After dangling the possibility of some research money from the Department of Energy in front of Lipton, he had made sure that *60 Minutes* heard about a researcher at Caltech who might be getting a large government grant to study the origins of the bacteria involved in the oil debacle. Since the oil thing was all the rage for any television show, *60 Minutes* took the bite, and now Lipton was on prime time Sunday night television.

Newhouse couldn't inch any closer to the edge of his couch. "Come on, Lipton. Don't let me down. When I'm president, I'll give you a Cabinet position."

"You're suggesting," Pendleton was asking Lipton, "that this may have been something that was just waiting to happen, a fluke of nature as you called it, and that it might've had nothing to do with human involvement?"

Lipton nodded. "That's right, Scott. In the beginning, I was just as sure as the rest of the world that someone had genetically manipulated this bacteria and most likely for terrorist reasons, but after months of research, we're just not finding that."

Lipton explained that it was possible that a few billion years ago, some primitive little bacteria had evolved the necessary enzymes to break down the complex organic components of what we call crude oil, and that the genetics of this bacteria have been lying dormant for all of these years.

Pendleton interrupted, "So you're suggesting that this bacteria has stayed alive for billions of years hundreds of feet underground?"

She waggled her index finger. "No, I'm suggesting that some little genetic fragment of this early bacteria survived and that we drilled into a pocket of oil containing these fragmented sequences, brought it to the surface, and it got incorporated into the genome of our everyday, normally friendly bacteria."

Pendleton questioned her, pointing out that these fragments had not been found, and Lipton agreed that it was a quandary but that no genetic manipulation of the bacteria's chromosomes had been found either.

Pendleton nodded in agreement. "So, you don't believe this group in Yemen?"

"No," Lipton replied shaking her head, "this would've taken an extremely sophisticated lab with some of the world's top geneticists. Unless we find such a lab, I think we're just chasing ghosts."

Lucy was laying on the couch with her head on John's lap.

They had also been watching *60 Minutes*. Ricky had gone up to his room to text some friends. Without looking up, she asked, "Do you think that's true?"

John ran his hands through her hair. "I don't know. I don't think it matters anymore."

Things along the East Coast were deteriorating fast, and people were starting to die. The winter was brutally cold, and fuel oil for heating homes was almost nonexistent. Lucy's fuel oil tank was nearly empty. When that day were to come, her old Victorian home would be plunged to twenty below zero. The few remaining cans of chili would freeze solid. There was a small fireplace, and they could start pulling the wood off the walls and burning everything in sight to keep alive, but that would only last a few days. They were going to have to leave. John didn't say anything; he just continued to stroke her hair. He was going to wait for another day to tell her about his plan.

Lucy picked up the remote and started flipping through the channels. She was tired of hearing about the damned oil bacteria. Just as she was about to hit the "off" button, a newscaster on WGN was announcing that Adam Newhouse, the twenty-seven-year-old son of Robert Newhouse, the Secretary of the Department of Energy, had been found dead in his Palo Alto, California apartment from an apparent drug overdose.

"Oh my God," Lucy gasped, "only twenty-seven. That's not much older than Ricky."

John nodded; it was terrible, and it had become all too common in the past few years. Shaking his head, he mumbled, "Live fast, die young, and leave a good-looking corpse."

Lucy rolled over onto her back and looked up at him. "What's that supposed to mean?"

With a painful smile, he said, "Kurt Cobain, Amy Winehouse—the twenty-seven club."

# CHAPTER 67

***

## Walker River Indian Reservation
## Schurz, Nevada

Shields' back was killing him, his ass was numb, he had to pee, and Whitbolt wouldn't shut the hell up. Riding in the car with him was worse than with his first wife.

They had been riding for over four hours, the gas gauge was pointing towards empty, the temperature gauge was pointing toward boiling, and Whitbolt was babbling on that if they broke down out here in the middle of the desert, their rotting bodies would probably be scavenged by coyotes or some shit, and no one would ever find them.

Shields had just about had it. He thought of taking out his gun and shooting Whitbolt. He was sick of the FBI, sick of the Bureau, and sick of Kelly and his political bullshit.

"Goddamn," Shields slammed his hand on the steering wheel, "I can't believe Kelly got us into this shit."

"Here, we're there. Straight ahead." Whitbolt was pointing at the map on his lap. "Y'all better slow down, son. You don't wanna get busted by the local sheriff. We're heading straight into Main Street USA."

Shields looked straight ahead through the dust-covered windshield and turned on the wipers. "What the hell are you talking about? I don't see anything," he said, squinting.

Whitbolt pointed to an upcoming welcome sign. "There. Right there. 'Welcome to Schurz, Nevada. Population 742.'" Whitbolt told him that they better stop here, gas up, and spend the night.

Shields just shook his head and asked him where the hell they were.

Whitbolt consulted his map. "We're two hundred fifty miles from Vegas and two hundred fifty miles from Black Rock in the middle of the Walker River Piute Indian Reservation." Then, all bubbly as if this were a Sunday morning ride in the park, he said, "Here's an interesting fact, Shields," reading something off of his map, "there's only one person here per twelve square miles. Isn't that interesting?"

Shields reached down to see if he had his gun. He knew he could get away with it; he'd claim "justifiable homicide". No one was going to argue that. "That goddamned Kelly," Shields mumbled to himself, "just looking out for his own ass."

Shields had gotten the scoop from Kelly's secretary, Kathy,

who he occasionally slept with. After an evening sexual encounter, she had told him about the call from Anderson, the Director of the NSA, and that she had listened in and heard Anderson suggest that if Kelly did him a favor, maybe he could do Kelly a favor and get him out of Vegas.

Whitbolt looked out his passenger side window and pointed. "Over there! Slow down."

Shields slowed and looked over. He didn't see anything, only a pile of abandoned cars, three rabid-looking dogs, and a tiny adobe building with a sign above it: "Hotel."

"You've gotta be shitting me," he protested.

As they drove around the pile of abandoned cars, the three mange-ridden dogs barked, and they could see an elderly, heavyset Indian woman sitting in a rocking chair watching them approach.

Shields pulled up in front of the office and edged the nose of the car up to what appeared to be a hitching post. Strapped to the post with cowhide was the head of a long-horned Texas steer, the horns spanning the full width of the post.

Shields cut the engine. The old Indian woman just sat and stared, and Whitbolt, looking at the skeletal remains of a long ago dead steer, said, "Wonder what that damn thing died of."

Shields looked at him as if he were nuts. "What the hell do you think? Maybe thirst."

As Shields opened the door and turned to step out, sand

and dust poured down the back of his shirt. He cursed. Brushing the dust out of his hair, he told Whitbolt that he'd talk to the old woman, and, in the meantime, maybe he should tie the car up to the hitching post.

Whitbolt smiled; somehow, he was enjoying this shit. "Man, this place is just like Tombstone. Expect to see old Doc Holliday, Wyatt and the boys shooting it out any time now."

Shields reached for his gun.

# Chapter 68

***

## Weill Cornell Graduate School of Medical Sciences

## New York City

Doctor Adolf Gustafsson had been trying for over a week to review a research paper sent to him from the Netherlands on the genetic alterations made in nematode worms that increased their lifespan fivefold. Between endless meetings, teaching a medical school genetics class, and the damned phone ringing constantly, he couldn't get past the abstract. As he made another attempt, the phone started ringing again.

Not allowing his secretary time to answer the call, being as cantankerous as ever, he yelled out, "Ms. Krause, hold all my calls for one hour."

Elfriede Krause uncomfortably smiled at the young

woman who was standing in front of her desk and told her, "Don't worry, he's actually in a good mood today."

Elfriede had been Gustafsson's secretary for over twenty years, starting back in Germany at the Berlin Institute of Technology before he had received his Nobel Prize. Although he had always been better at communicating with his snails, slugs and nematodes, as he had gotten older, he became a little bit of an old grouch.

Jennifer Chambers shrugged. "Tell him that I'm a post-doc from the Belfer Center. I need to see him, and I'm not leaving until I do."

Elfriede raised her eyebrows. "Yikes."

Gustafsson was old-school German. He wasn't too keen on women in research or anywhere else other than at home, and he wasn't used to being confronted.

Elfriede held up her hand, said, "Just a minute," and stood up and went to Gustafsson's door. Knocking, but not waiting for a reply, she opened the door.

He peered up over his half-framed reading glasses. "What?"

Undeterred, Elfriede replied, "There's a young lady here to see you, and she says it's *very* important."

Gustafsson scoffed, "I can't afford the time to see anyone right now. Make an appointment for her for next week. And close the door behind you when you leave."

Elfriede turned and looked back toward her desk.

Jennifer, who couldn't help but hear the discussion, shook her head and mouthed, "No ... now."

Elfriede stepped into Gustafsson's office and gently closed the door. "The young lady says you can't afford not to see her, and she's not leaving."

That got Gustafsson's attention—the great Adolf Gustafsson, Director of the Weill Cornell Research Medical Center in New York City, Nobel Prize winner, and a man that researchers around the world bowed to.

Taking off his reading glasses, he said, "Who is she?"

"She said she's a postdoc from the Belfer Center."

"What does she want?"

Krause tilted her head and replied, "Why don't you talk to her and find out?"

Gustafsson took a breath and gave a pronounced exhale. This bantering back and forth was taking more time than just seeing the woman.

"Fine! Five minutes. Tell her five minutes, no more."

Elfriede smiled. "Be nice."

A minute later, the door opened, and a young woman walked in wearing a white research lab coat, heels, and a Belfer Center identification badge.

Before Gustafsson could say anything, she said, "My name is Jennifer Chambers, and I'm a second-year postdoc from the Belfer Center. I need to talk to you."

Gustafsson wanted to chastise her intrusion but had learned long ago, after being married for thirty years before his wife had died of ovarian cancer, that you don't get into an argument with a headstrong woman.

Gustafsson pointed to a chair. "Fine. Sit."

Jennifer didn't budge. "That's okay. I can stand." She held up a computer printout. "I'm from the Department of Mammalian Studies. My area of research is the evolutionary transfer of Prokaryotic plasmid analogs and the comparative genetic anatomy with Eukaryotic mitochondrial DNA. I work in Bittar's lab, and he's on sabbatical at the Karolinska Institute in Sweden."

Gustafsson was caught off guard and could do little more than nod before Jennifer reached across his desk and handed him the printout. "I found it."

With his bushy eyebrows raised and a confused look on his face, he took the sheet. "Found what?"

"I found how the bacteria is eating the oil."

Gustafsson just about had a stroke, not sure he had heard her correctly. Every laboratory, researcher, and Nobel Prize winner in the world had been trying to figure out for months how normal run-of-the-mill bacteria had suddenly acquired the ability to destroy the world's oil.

Gustafsson pointed to the chair again, this time a little more civil. "Please … sit. Now, what're you saying you found?"

Jennifer took a seat and told him the story about her

friend Kathy, who worked at the Amaco PC oil refineries research labs in Texas. She explained that she and Kathy had gone to high school together in Grundy Count, Iowa and then to the University of Iowa for biochemistry.

Gustafsson didn't interrupt; he just sat twirling his glasses and listened for something relevant.

Jennifer told him the bizarre story that Kathy had told her about the relation between the oil spill in Lake Mead, an FBI agent, and samples that her boss, Doctor Jacobs, had taken from the spill.

Gustafsson nodded that he knew Doctor Jacobs, another Nobel laureate. "Yes, Jacobs has a Nobel Prize in the field of Oil Fingerprinting. But what're you—"

Jennifer cut him off, "Kathy sent me the samples because she wasn't able to fingerprint the origin of the oil from Lake Mead. This was strange since that was their area of expertise." Gustafsson stared blankly, losing his patience.

Jennifer spoke as fast as she could, "Kathy knew I had access to a Mass Spec machine with forensic toxicology capabilities. Kathy thought something was wrong with the samples, like they were tainted."

Jennifer reached across Gustafsson's desk and tapped her fingers on the printout. "Keep in mind, I got those samples a month, if not longer, before the outbreak of bacteria in the Middle East."

Gustafsson held up his hand. "I'm not sure I get it. You don't do Mass Spec. How'd you get from a toxicology report to solving the world's oil dilemma?" He leaned forward, looking at her doubtfully. "…as you so claim you've done!"

Jennifer held her ground. "I never ran it through Mass Spec. I never got a toxicology report." Jennifer explained that when she had received the samples, they smelled awful, like being on a pig farm in Iowa, which she knew very well. She told Gustafsson that she was so busy, she'd put them in her lab freezer but never got around to sending them to the Mass Spec people.

She continued, "Almost two months later, I was watching the news, and one of the reporters made a comment that one of the telltale signs of contaminated oil was that it took on the smell of pig manure. I remember just staring at the television. That comment hit me like a brick wall. I had gotten Kathy's samples long before anyone had ever heard of oil-eating bacteria, and her samples had already smelled like," she wrinkled her nose, "you know … pig shit."

She went on telling Gustafsson that she had wondered where the heck Kathy had gotten this bacteria seemingly before anyone had ever heard of it.

Reaching over and taking back the printout, Jennifer continued. "So, the next day, I pulled the samples out of the freezer and, just out of curiosity, ran the stuff through my own Gene Machine."

Gustafsson barked, "So did everyone else in the world."

Jennifer nodded and gave a little smile. "I know, but I was the lucky one in a billion." She went on to explain that she had found the culprit in a plasmid, a small snippet of DNA that was independent of the bacteria's circular chromosome.

Again, Gustafsson scoffed, "Every lab in the world has looked at every segment of the circular DNA, every plasmid in every E. coli and any other bacteria they could find in the world, and nobody found anything." He pointed to the printout in Jennifer's hand, and being more than just a little skeptical, he said, "So? Yours is different?"

"Yup! This is the sequence of a segment of commands attached to the tail of a common run-of-the-mill plasmid found in every E. coli in the world. And it codes for some remnant evolutionary prokaryotic loops and coils of RNA. It has a 'kill gene' in it. I don't know how they do it, but these loops and coils act like turbocharged USB flash drives that direct a bunch of commands to the cell's machinery, like, to eat oil. And then, within microseconds, poof—the DNA tail and RNA coils self-destruct."

She could see that Gustafsson was about to interrupt. Holding up her hand and stopping him before he could say anything, she said, "But, here's the beauty of it; only the segment of commands hooked to the tail end of the plasmid self-destructs, leaving behind normal-looking plasmids. So, there's something in the plasmid code that tells the rogue end to start running, and then as fast as it transcribes, it does its thing, and boom, it self-destructs. That's why no one has ever found anything."

Gustafsson leaned back in his chair and opened his hands like he was the Pope giving Benediction to a crowd in the Vatican Square. He just couldn't believe that she, a second-year postdoc, had found what the greatest researchers in the world were unable to find.

Jennifer could see that he was just chomping at the bit to interrupt, but she stopped him again. "Just listen. I don't know how or why, but I started thinking that somehow, just maybe, I had some of the original genetically altered oil-eating bacteria."

Now Gustafsson really started looking at her doubtfully, and Jennifer knew that he was starting to think she might be a bit of a nutcase. He shook his head, letting her know that this discussion was close to being over. "So, you think some terrorist from Yemen came over here and dumped some genetically altered bacteria into Lake Mead to destroy the world's oil? Don't you think that sounds a little off, like maybe they would've picked the Middle East, where the planet's main supply of oil is? Why would you think you had some of the original bacteria?"

Jennifer stammered, "I know. I—I don't know. I know it doesn't make much sense, but just listen. I decided, just out of curiosity, to look at Kathy's oil samples. I was just randomly sequencing different plasmids, I guess like everyone else did, when suddenly at the tail end of one of the plasmids, after a short pause, this strange sequence started coding." She pointed to the printout. "This sequence right here. But then, within a millisecond, the sequence of DNA that codes for the RNA loops and coils just disintegrated, and I couldn't ever find it again."

Gustafsson didn't interrupt. He was still unsure whether she was a screwball or not, but she had his attention now.

Jennifer burst with excitement, almost in tears at the very thought of the one-in-a-billion chance of what had happened. "It printed. Somehow, it printed. I got the rogue DNA sequence on paper before it destroyed itself."

Gustafsson sat back in his chair, spellbound at the thought. If this was true, that she had found it, it would be the discovery that could save mankind, if it wasn't already too late. He gestured for her to continue.

Jennifer told him she thought that maybe, through pure serendipity, somehow in that one-in-a-billion nanoseconds she had caught the rogue snippet of DNA just as it had started to code and that she had gotten a physical copy of the thing on paper. With a big smile on her face, she continued, "Having a copy of the original, I thought it was going to be simple. I'd just run off a copy or two, then using polymerase chain reaction sequencing, I make a few thousand copies, and—" Her big smile turned to a frown. "But the darn things kept self-destructing immediately."

The intrigue was killing Gustafsson. "So, what did you do?"

Jennifer told him that she had searched the sequence over and over, each time removing little segments of code here and there until she found the "kill gene". After removing the "kill gene", she told him she had been able to make millions of copies that didn't self-destruct. "So, I went to Ace Hardware and got a can of grease. I put my snippets of DNA in the grease and let it sit." Jennifer was beaming. She had made it this far and hadn't been kicked out.

Gustafsson leaned forward in his chair, waiting, knowing

what the answer was going to be but wanting to hear it from her.

Jennifer could see the anticipation on his face and nodded. "Yup, within two days, it started smelling like pig poop."

Gustafsson was speechless. After all of these months, after all of these researchers worldwide, this little girl from Grundy Count, Iowa had found the culprit that was threatening to bring mankind's domination of the planet to an end.

He was about to tell her that she had probably just won herself a Nobel Prize, but then a very concerned, almost scared look came over her face. Gustafsson shrugged. "What?"

She was almost tearful, or maybe scared to death at the thought. "I know this might sound crazy, but I don't think I just caught it by chance. That one-in-a-billion nanoseconds, I think it paused ever so slightly."

"Paused?"

Jennifer nodded. "I think it was thinking twice about just letting itself be killed. I mean, self-destructing." She leaned forward in her chair and, with a tremble in her voice, said, "What if it's trying to rewrite itself, trying to get rid of the 'kill gene'? I know it's only a snippet of DNA, but what if it's trying to take on a life of its own?"

Gustafsson scoffed, "That's ridiculous. DNA isn't living."

Jennifer just looked at him. She knew it sounded ridiculous, but she didn't have any other explanation.

Gustafsson stood up and was about to end the meeting when Jennifer blurted out, "And, within one week of working with those samples, I had that gastrointestinal illness—that thing that's killing millions of people."

Gustafsson plopped back down in his chair and shook his head. "My God!" he yelled with a halfhearted chuckle. "It's not about which came first, the chicken or the egg. They're one and the same. It's the chicken *and* the egg." After a short pause, lost in thought, he told Jennifer that he needed some time to think. As she went to get up, he stopped her. "Young lady, phenomenal work. I think you've just won yourself a Nobel Prize."

With a sigh of relief and tears in her eyes, Jennifer stood up. "Thank you. Thank you so much." Just as she got to the door, she turned. "You know, whoever did this was pretty smart. They reprogrammed a billion years of evolution. They must've had one hell of a lab." Then she closed the door behind her.

Gustafsson dropped his head into his hands. "That list. That damn list."

After a few minutes, he reached over and picked up the phone. "Ms. Krause, get me Heilbronner, Eberstark, Department of Genetic Research at MIT."

# Chapter 69

***

## 40'52'59"N. 119'03'50"W./40.88306'N.
## Black Rock, Nevada

After five hours in the car with no radio reception, no trees, fence posts, jackrabbits, nothing but flatness, Whitbolt pointed to a spot on the map that was sitting on his lap. "We're here."

Shields slowed the car and looked out through the dusty windows. "What the hell are you talking about?"

To Shields, it didn't look any different than the last 300 miles. Whitbolt pointed to what had once been a green highway sign before it had been sandblasted by the desert winds. Shields squinted to read it. "Black Rock. Unincorporated. Population 75."

Shields and Whitbolt had gotten up early for the continental breakfast that was part of the package deal at the hotel in Schurz. The old Indian lady had cooked up some eggs and some kind of mystery meat. Shields knew that there were no cows out here, so it wasn't beef. There were a few scrawny chickens, one mangy-looking goat, and the rabid-looking dogs. Shields had pointed out across the field and held up two fingers. Whitbolt nodded. The night before, when they had arrived, there were three rabid-looking dogs. Now, there were only two. They had politely passed on the meat.

Shields looked at the weather-beaten sign. "I'm going to kill Kelly when we get back." Whitbolt nodded, but before he could say anything, Shields exploded, "I don't see any damn black rocks. Do you see any black rocks?"

Whitbolt told him that it was just the name of the desert as a whole and that at each end, a few hundred miles to the north and a few hundred to the south, according to the map, there were black rock mountains or something. Then Whitbolt pointed to another spot on the map. "There's a town here—Gerlach."

Shields shrugged as if that made any difference in this fiasco. He looked down at the temperature gauge on the dash, and it was slowly rising. "Shit! So what the hell are we supposed to do, search this whole goddamned desert for a shed?"

Whitbolt held up an Air Force reconnaissance picture of the little building with the coordinates of its location scrawled across the top. "Looks like it should be near a big outcropping of rocks—big bunch of boulders. Shouldn't be hard to find a pile of rocks out here; it's flat as shit."

Whitbolt had been wrong. Because of the distortions

caused by the waves of shimmering heat rising off the desert sands, it took over twenty minutes to find the place. When they finally did, Shields pulled up and stopped the car on the far side of the outcropping of rocks. He stepped out and looked around. "Not a building anymore."

Strewn from the base of the outcropping to the front bumper of the car were shards of splintered wood and ashes. In the center of the debris was a deep crater.

Shields and Whitbolt sidestepped their way across the charred splinters of wood until they came to what looked to be the remains of an old mine shaft, probably remnant from the days of uranium mining. Carefully making their way to the edge, Whitbolt shined a flashlight down into the shaft.

"Jesus," Shields said, "what the hell happened here?"

Inside the dark hole, they saw what looked like elevator cables twisted and melted like one of Dali's paintings of melted clocks. The rocks on the walls had been turned to glass, and the gondola portion of the elevator at the very bottom of the shaft looked like a molten puddle of glass and steel.

With his cell phone, Shields snapped a few pictures, and then they began walking around the area. Fifty yards or so from the center of the crater, between the little mountainous outcropping of rocks and the burnt-out mine shaft, they came to a long cement ramp leading downward into what appeared to be an underground garage.

Whitbolt pulled out the reconnaissance photos from his

pants pocket. "Man, you'd never be able to see this in aerial photos."

The opening to the ramp had been set flush with the desert sands, and scattered rocks had been haphazardly laid from the foot of the natural outcropping to the opening of the ramp.

Whitbolt turned to Shields. "What the hell is this?"

Shields shrugged. "Got me. Probably an old underground research lab from the forties. Lots of uranium research out here. Would've been hidden like this to keep it from the eyes of the Russians."

As they walked down the long ramp, Whitbolt muttered, "We're gonna get our balls fried off down here. Maybe we should've brought a Geiger counter."

As they got to the bottom of the ramp, they could see where a huge hole had been blown through a set of double steel doors that had secured the entrance.

"Shit," Whitbolt said, "must've been a nuclear explosion in there."

Shields shook his head. "No! The hole's blown inward."

After snapping another picture, they stepped through the hole and found themselves in a large underground garage. Everything in it was burnt to a crisp. Four raggedy old trucks were melted beyond recognition, and hundreds of oil barrels were strewn about, half melted from intense heat.

For the next half hour or so, they wandered through the

blackened maze, going from what looked like living quarters to laboratories, snapping pictures as they went. Then Shields yelled, "Hey, over here." Shields was in a room that looked like it had been a small gymnasium. Whitbolt stepped in, and Shields shined his flashlight around the room.

"Oh shit!" Whitbolt could not believe what he was looking at. Shields was shining his light on what looked like ten to twenty piles of bones, skulls, and teeth essentially reduced to ashes.

Whitbolt shined his flashlight onto one of the piles. "Who the hell were these guys, and what the hell were they doing here? What is this place?"

Shields stood shaking his head. "I don't know, but someone didn't want anyone to know." Pointing to the way back, he motioned to Whitbolt. "Let's get out of here."

When they reached the top of the ramp, the sun was so bright that it almost fried their retinas. Squinting, Shields felt around for his phone and was about to dial when Whitbolt stopped him. "Wait, look over here."

Whitbolt was pointing to some footprints that were heading up the hill to the outcropping of rocks. Shields snapped his phone closed. "Let's check it out, then I'll call."

They followed the footprints up the hill and around to the opening of a little cave-like nook, where they saw a few empty wine bottles, an old blanket, a dried up banana peel and an apple core.

"What do you think?" Whitbolt asked.

Shields shrugged. "Looks like someone had a picnic, probably one of those poor bastards down there. I doubt anybody lived through that."

The midday sun was directly overhead as they made their way down the hill and back to the car. The heat was overwhelming, and Whitbolt was sweating like a pig. "Man, this is such a nice piece of property. I can't believe we just gave it to the Indians."

Shields rolled his eyes. "Yeah, I think we traded it for the crop land in Iowa."

When they got back to the air conditioning of the car, Shields dialed up Kelly's office, and Kathy answered.

"Hey, it's us. Where's Kelly?"

"Just a minute."

Kelly picked up the phone, but before he could say anything, Shields told him,"I'm going to kill you when we get back."

Kelly told Shields to hold and that he was going to patch the call through to Anderson of the NSA.

Anderson's secretary took the call and patched it through to her boss, who was in his office. Back in the cubbyhole on the far side of the expanse of eavesdroppers, Sasik's computer Icon started to flash.

Shields did the talking, explaining that they had found some kind of an underground complex and that it had been had incinerated beyond recognition.

Anderson barked, "What the hell do you mean, 'incinerated'?"

"I mean just that." Shields explained that whatever the place had been, it had not just been destroyed; it had been incinerated beyond recognition. Then he told Anderson that he had not seen this kind of stuff since he was in the military.

Two thousand miles away, Anderson got up and looked out his window in the direction of the Pentagon. He knew that nobody but the military had these kinds of incendiary devices.

Then, as Shields was telling him about the bodies, the phone went dead. Shields looked at his phone. "Ha! Lost the connection."

Whitbolt shrugged. "Good, let's get out of here before whoever did this finds us here."

Anderson sat at his desk, rubbing his temples. "Fucking Pentagon. It has to be the Pentagon."

Sasik turned off his computer.

# Chapter 70

***

## Wilkes-Barre, Pennsylvania

Peter was one day from starving, two to three if he rationed his last package of little kids' meals. He had been doing pretty well living off of baby food, little meals, and formula milk that he was getting through a program run by the "Sisters of Charity", a religious organization that provided food for children and infants. He didn't particularly like baby food, although the kids' meals chicken and rice wasn't bad, but it was better than trying to eat his credit cards.

He had run across the program one day when he was searching around on his computer. It was a program that was handing out baby food to parents who had children five years and under. The thing that had caught his attention was not the headline, "SAVE THE CHILDREN," but instead the words, "FREE FOOD."

There had only been one little glitch; he didn't have

children. But as luck would have it, he knew of a single mom down the street who had two little kids—a boy of four and a little girl of about three. He had seen them occasionally as she walked the kids down his street before the weather had turned cold. Being that ethics was not an issue for Peter, he had come up with an idea to help the mom get signed up for Sisters of Charity, as well as himself.

Printing up a few official looking Sisters of Charity flyers, his laptop in hand, Peter went door to door getting the word out about the free food program. Being that it was cold, he had actually only managed to make it to one door, the mom with the two kids. With his computer expertise, he got her signed up for the program. All it required was a picture of each child and a picture of the person—the mom or dad who would be picking up the food.

Luckily for Peter, the nuns trusted in the goodness of mankind and never thought that anyone would be such a low life as to take the food from the mouths of children.

With Peter's help, and to the glee of the mother, he downloaded pictures of the kids and the mom and got her signed up to go Mondays, Wednesdays, and Fridays to pick up baby food.

Once back at his apartment, he replaced the mom's picture with his, doctored up the kids' pictures in Photoshop, and signed himself up to go on Tuesdays, Thursdays, and Saturdays to pick up his allotment of food for his two starving little kids.

All's well that ends well. The mother thought Peter was

God's gift to the world. Peter felt good about himself in that he had helped two starving kids, and the nuns blessed him over and over each day that he came to pick up his food, not that Peter felt he needed blessing. Of course, being that Peter lacked any moral fiber, it never bothered him that maybe two other kids might be starving on his behalf. But in the world according to Peter, it would have been just as unethical not to take advantage of the situation.

Now, Peter sat staring at his last kids' meal of chicken and rice. He had gone a few days earlier to pick up his allotment, which had been pretty substantial for two kids, especially for one that had a "methylmalonic acidemic metabolic disorder," something that required a double allotment of nutrition just to stay alive. The nuns had found it so sad that his little guy had this disorder that they told Peter they gave a special prayer every day for his little boy. After a while, even Peter had started feeling a little sad for the kid.

Now he was about to starve. When he had reached the program a few days earlier, there was a sign: "Program Discontinued." The Sisters of Charity was out of food. The program had been subsidized by the government, but due to the country's transportation problems and the fact that there just wasn't any food being produced, the Sisters were no longer getting help.

Peter had been livid. "What was this world coming to when the government and those chosen by God to spread his word were willing to let little kids starve?"

Peter had to come up with a new plan. In the past few

weeks, things in Wilkes-Barre were getting close to the boiling point. People were freezing and starving to death. There were numerous reports of family pets missing, mostly dogs, and unsubstantiated rumors were flying around town that they were being eaten by the local Vietnamese population.

After the Vietnam War, a number of Vietnamese families had been resettled throughout the country by various church groups. On the outskirts of the city, there was a commune of Vietnamese farmers who pretty much kept to themselves, tilled the land, and were self-sufficient. Back in the day, when Peter had jogged a little, he used to run past the settlement.

Now, as he sat thinking, he remembered back to a few years ago seeing a local television report on the commune, how they raised their own crops, canned their own fruits and vegetables, raised chickens, and lived off the land. Peter remembered that during one of these news reports, an old Vietnamese farmer had taken the reporter down into one of their root cellars, pointing out shelves of glass jars full of meats and vegetables, strips of salt-cured rabbit, and piles of walnuts, hickory nuts, and potatoes. At the time, Peter had thought of them as stupid people who needed to get with the times. He found it disgusting to think of eating dried rabbit when all he had to do was pull out his credit card, pick up the phone, and order a pizza.

Thinking back to his jogging days, he remembered seeing along the edge of the woods at the back of the complex a set of double doors that went down to one of the root cellars. The back line of the commune was only surrounded by an old, broken-down wooden fence. Now that he was desperate, a nice chunk of dog or a dried piece of rabbit might not be so bad.

He put on his coat and boots and headed toward the outskirts of town in the direction of the Vietnamese enclave. It was cold as hell, and it had snowed. He soon stood at the edge of the woods, looking across an open field at the old, broken-down wooden fence. He figured they were just poor dirt farmers who probably didn't have guns and would never miss a few jars of pickled dog, chicken, or beans.

The ground was covered with about a foot of snow, and, in the subzero temperatures, it had become as hard as ice. He walked ever so slowly across the field because with each step there was a crunching noise as his feet broke through the crust of icy snow.

He finally made it to the fence and peered through the broken slats. He didn't see anyone. He could see in the distance, maybe forty yards from the fence, the double doors that opened down into the root cellar. He walked along the fence until he came to an old broken gate. It wasn't chained or locked. After looking around again, he pulled off one of the old dried boards next to the latch of the gate. After waiting to be sure that the sound of ripping wood had not alarmed anyone, he took off his glove and reached in and around to unlatch the gate from the inside.

Suddenly he heard a snap and then he felt a sharp, fiery pain at the end of his wrist. At first, he thought that he had been stung by a bee, but when he pulled his arm back, all he saw was a bloody stump where his hand had been, and blood was squirting with each beat of his heart.

Peter looked back in through the hole in the fence, and there, down on the ground, he saw his hand, as pale and white as the snow, his fingers twitching. Then he looked up, and there stood an old Vietnamese man holding a blood-stained axe. The old man never said a word, just stared at Peter. Then he bent down, picked up Peter's hand, and threw it over the fence.

Peter backed away and picked up his severed hand. Cupping it over the bloody stump, he turned and started walking back across the open field, leaving a trail of blood in the fresh snow.

As he got closer to the edge of the snowy clearing, he started to feel weak and dizzy. He stumbled and fell to his knees. Throwing the severed hand down, he cupped the bloody stump even harder as he tried to stop the flow of blood.

He looked back and could see the old Vietnamese man just standing, watching, and waiting. The pool of blood grew larger and larger, and then Peter fell forward, face down in the snow.

The old man watched until he saw no more motion, then he turned and went back to the root cellar. With more snow predicted for the day, it would be spring before anyone found Peter's remains.

# Chapter 71

***

## Boston, Massachusetts

John sat in the empty classroom of the Boston Preparatory Science Academy staring at his laptop. He had just watched a CNN special report, and the eastern seaboard was becoming a deathtrap. Reviewing for the last time the coordinates for their destination, he closed the lid to his computer. It had been a long time since he had flown blindly, instruments only, and without a wingman. Slipping off his stool and tightening his jacket, he headed to the door. It was time. It was time to go.

The Atlantic coast from Canada to Georgia was starting to unravel. The Boston Gardens was as dark and barren as the surface of the moon. Every tree, bush, and shrub had been cut and set ablaze in a last-ditch effort to ward off the cold, unrelenting Arctic winds. The famed Boston Gardens lagoon was a frozen depression—a mirror image of the "Lake of Death", a prominent crater on the moon's eastern seaboard.

John stepped out of the Preparatory Academy for the last time. A thick, black haze blanketed the city. The air hung heavy with the smell of burning tires, furniture, and the very wood paneling that once lined the walls of people's homes. Now, like a rush of lemmings heading for a cliff, the instinct of survival was pushing people to the edge. There was nothing left to burn, nothing left to eat, and the only chance of not freezing to death was to head south.

The CNN report had been a live address by the governor of Florida. He had announced that he was ordering the Florida National Guard to establish a line across the two-hundred-mile border between Florida and Georgia. He was ordering the National Guard to shoot to kill anyone trying to cross into the state. The governor claimed that it was his responsibility to the people of his state and that he could not allow ninety million starving, freezing people to push into Florida. According to the CNN report, it was estimated that there were already twenty million people pushing down Interstate 95 heading toward the Florida-Georgia border. President Layton had countered that he would take whatever action necessary if Florida's National Guard started firing on civilians.

John turned his back to the wind and snapped open his cell phone. "Where are you?"

"Home," Lucy said.

"Good," John told her, "stay there. I'm going to my place to pick up some supplies that I've been gathering for the last few weeks. I'm going to get them and be over there in an hour."

Lucy had not given it another thought, assuming that he meant stocking up on supplies that they would need to make it through until spring. Little did she know that he meant 6000 miles away.

In the last month and a half, it had become obvious that the U.S. was not going to be immune to the massive number of deaths that had already rocked the rest of the world. At the rate that the bacteria was devouring the world's energy, when this was over, there would only be pockets of humans left in small encampments around the world, struggling to rebuild.

John had been taught at the academy that a downed pilot that survived for the first month had a high probability of further survival. And if he survived for one year, he had an almost one-hundred percent chance of eventual rescue, although the waiting period would lack the comforts of home.

For downed pilots, one-month survival rested on a tiny 22-pound bundle attached to the undersurface of their ejection seats. The packet was known as the "Hit and Run" kit, but for John, Lucy, and Ricky it was going to be a "Hit and Stay" kit.

The biggest commodity in the little 22-pound kit was space, and the most important survival item was food. It was assumed that a downed pilot would find enough roots, berries and water, but the hardest item to come by was protein. The military had solved this problem by essentially squeezing a whole cow or wildebeest into half-ounce sticks of rock hard protein that had to be soaked in water before eating. John had calculated that for their

6000-mile journey and a shot at survival for the first month, they had to carry the equivalent of three dried up cows or wildebeest, and it had to be the size of a 66-pound packet that would essentially fit under the seat.

He had spent over a month scouring every convenience store, gas station and vending machine he could find, buying sticks of dried everything. Down on the harbor, he had managed to find shops that had dried alpaca, alligator, snake, ostrich, kangaroo, as well as turkey and beef jerky. Space for the three of them in the small plane for the 6000-mile week-long journey was going to be a commodity, but John had managed to gather enough dried protein to last the three of them a whole year, and it essentially fit into a large suitcase. Along with the stash of protein, he had bought as many compact cigarette lighters as he could find, and with the help of a pharmacist friend of his, he had obtained bottles of antibiotics, vitamins, and minor first-aid items. He had stored all of this in his apartment, and now with his van loaded, he headed to 86 Pinckney Street.

When John arrived, Ricky was in the living room watching the news, and Lucy was in the kitchen. Lucy had just opened a can of chili. When she saw John, she held up the can and almost cried. “We only have three more.”

John nodded. “I know. We have to leave.”

Lucy hadn’t been ready for that response. With a confused grimace on her face, she said, “Leave? Leave where?”

John took her in his arms. “We can’t stay. We’re going to die here. We’re leaving.”

Lucy gave him a push back, "What are you talking about? Leaving? Where?"

John took in a deep breath. "Patagonia, the tip of the world where your brother is."

Lucy's eyebrows shot up. "Are you nuts? Patagonia? Do you realize it's over 10,000 miles from here?"

"Actually, it's only 6000." Immediately, John realized that had not been the best of comments. He had been given an instruction manual on how to handle the explosive thrust of a thirteen-ton flying piece of metal, but for this 110-pound package, instructions were not included.

Lucy looked at him, bewildered. "How did you think we were going to get to Patagonia?"

After a slight hesitation, John said, matter-of-factly, "We're going to fly."

Lucy's head dropped. "You're just going to call up an airline and tell them you want to book a flight to Patagonia. Maybe we could just walk since planes aren't flying anymore. It's not far. Just down across the States, down Mexico, Central America, all of South America, and we're in Patagonia," she said facetiously

John interrupted, "I have a plane."

Lucy looked at him, dumbfounded. "You have a plane? Where, in your apartment?" Lucy doesn't give him a chance to answer. She couldn't believe how things were unfolding. It was like one of those television shows where a woman is married to a guy for twenty years, and then she finds out that he's a serial killer. She shook her head. "I suppose you know how to fly?"

John nodded.

Just as Lucy was about to explode, Ricky popped his head into the kitchen. "Mom, they're shooting people in Florida, and the president is being moved out of the White House."

Lucy started to cry; she was emotionally spent.

John looked at Ricky. "We're leaving. You, me and your mom."

Ricky looked at his mother, confused. "What does he mean, Mom?"

Lucy cried, "We can't stay here anymore, honey. A lot of people are going to die."

"Where are we going?"

Lucy looked at John. "Patagonia."

# Chapter 72

***

## Belle Haven, Virginia

Newhouse sat in the silence of his Belle Haven home staring at the ceiling, it was the first time in months that he felt like he could actually breathe. Earlier in the day, he had taken a chance and had made his way to the pay phone in Georgetown. He had been assured that all of the loose ends had been taken care of, all of the Cajuns had been disposed of, the Palo Alto thing, the nosey little girl in Texas, and the cameraman in Boulder. Furthermore, General McCay had assured him that the lab and everyone in it had been destroyed beyond recognition.

Suddenly, the ringing of his cell phone broke the silence. He looked at the caller ID, and it was Eberstark Heilbronner from MIT. Looking at the time on his cell phone, it was after seven. As he straightened up in his recliner, he tried to think back. It had been at least five years since he had talked with him. Suddenly, the suffocating feeling was back. "Now what?"

Newhouse pushed the little green button accepting the call, but before he could say, anything Heilbronner barked, “Do you know who I got a call from yesterday? Adolf Gustafsson at Cornell.”

Newhouse had heard of Gustafsson. He was some Nobel laureate guy who worked with sea slugs or something, but he had no idea what this had to do with him or Heilbronner. Before he could ask, Heilbronner interjected, “Do you know what he told me, Newhouse? He says that they found the genetic alterations in the bacteria that’s currently responsible for killing over three or four billion people.” Then, being intentionally flippant, he asked, “You know anything about that, Robert?”

Newhouse took a deep breath and stared back up at the ceiling. He couldn’t believe this. *How the hell did this get to Cornell?* Then he remembered that girl from the research labs in Texas. She had mentioned that she had sent samples to a friend of hers at Cornell. Trying to calm Heilbronner down long enough to find out how much he knew, he asked him why he was in such a tizzy and what this had to do with him.

Heilbronner was not about to be appeased. “Don’t give me that shit. You know goddamn well what I’m all in a tizzy about.”

Newhouse stayed silent.

“You know what Gustafsson just happened to ask me during our little conversation? He asked me if we were working on writing computer programs in genetic code and then slipping them into bacteria. I damn near shit my pants, Robert, but then everything fell into place."

Newhouse waited for Heilbronner to take a break and finally jumped in, "Look, Eberstark, I don't understand what this has to do with you."

"You know damn well what this has to do with me. I'm just not sure what it has to do with you."

Newhouse dropped his head into his hands. He knew, and now he was sure that Heilbronner knew.

Heilbronner continued, "You remember five-six years ago, you called me and asked me if I could come up with the names of some postdocs that were working in the field of computer programing in genetic code? I gave you a list of about ten to fifteen names that I knew of at the time—one bright fellow, Hans, from right here in my own labs at MIT. I didn't think much of it at the time until Hans got an incredible job offer to work at a new 'startup' research lab. At the time, something seemed a little fishy; I couldn't find anything about this new lab or who was running it." He paused, giving Newhouse time to think. "You know where this is going, don't you, Robert?"

Newhouse didn't say anything.

"A few months after I had given you those names, I found out that each of them got the same phenomenal offer. I've never thought much of it since, until yesterday when, out of the blue, Gustafsson asked me if we were still doing research in genetic programming, like the kind that might've changed this bacteria. That's when the light went on. So, just out of curiosity, I went back and did a little research of my own. You know what I found, don't you, Robert?"

Newhouse had a pretty good idea, but he needed to know just how much Heilbronner had figured out, so he just sat and listened.

"According to the names on the list I gave you, presumably two of them went to the Max Plank Institute in Germany, two went to the Karolinska Institute in Sweden, one young lady from Prague went to Caltech, and the list goes on and on. But I called every one of those labs, and they've never heard of these guys. They're not at those labs, are they? They worked for you. Am I right?"

Newhouse could not believe this. "Yeah, they've been working for me on a classified government research project."

Heilbronner exploded, "What, making a bacteria that eats oil?" That was about the size of it, but before Newhouse could comment, he continued, "And where the hell is this classified government research project?"

"Don't worry about that," Newhouse told him. "This is none of your business."

Then Eberstark went berserk. "Look you son of a bitch, if any of this gets traced back here, to me, what do you think the penalty might be for killing four billion people? Ha! Go ahead, take a guess. Maybe the electric chair, a firing squad? This kind of makes the World Trade Center thing look small, don't you think?"

Newhouse spent the next twenty minutes doing his best

to calm Heilbronner down, telling him to just sit tight and that he had everything under control. Then he made the point that it was in his best interest to keep his mouth shut.

After Heilbronner hung up, Newhouse opened his desk drawer and took out a prepaid disposable cell phone. He dialed and waited for the flat monotone voice at the other end to answer.

# Chapter 73

***

86 Pinckney Street
Boston, Massachusetts

"When?"

"Now. Tonight."

Lucy stepped out into the cold and pulled the big wooden door of the old Victorian house closed. Rummaging through her small fanny pack, she found the key. As she went to insert it into the lock, John took her hand gently. "You don't need to lock it. We're not coming back."

Tears welled up in her eyes. "Ever?"

John shrugged.

Lucy nodded and tossed the key into the snow.

Getting out of 86 Pinckney Street had gone anything but smoothly. After hearing of the military standoff along the

Florida-Georgia border and that the president and entire Cabinet were temporarily being moved to a secured facility at Mount Wealth in Berryville, Virginia, Lucy had slowly come to accept the fact that they were going to have to leave. But when John had said, "Now. Tonight," she almost had a stroke.

The straw that broke the camel's back came that day when Con Edison, the huge conglomerate that provided electricity for the eastern seaboard, announced that it was cutting power to only a few hours a day. That was all it took to spook the heard. Within seconds, the electrical connections in the normally dormant bundle of nerves of the primitive reptilian brain snapped to life. Rage, panic, and self-preservation circuits overpowered the evolutionary advanced synaptic connections of the neocortex.

Once John had gotten Lucy calmed down long enough to listen, he tried, with countless interruptions from an ever skeptical Lucy, to outline his plan. He started by telling her and Ricky about his uncle who had been a pilot in World War II and how he had restored an old 1941 twin engine Beechcraft military plane to mint condition.

Lucy interrupted, "Oh no. Let me guess. You're planning that *we* fly 6000 miles to Patagonia in a 1941 refurbished military airplane?"

John nodded. "Yeah!"

Lucy's eyebrows shot up. "And where is this plane?"

"In a barn. On my uncle's farm. In Pennsylvania."

Lucy's jaw dropped. "Pennsylvania?"

John had driven to the place during the summer, and the plane was still sitting in the barn in perfect condition. Despite it sounding rather old, it had been one of the military's most reliable planes, and his uncle had refinished it to perfect condition. John was confident that they could make it with a lot of luck, and a wing and a prayer, an old saying they learned during flight training when a pilot with a disabled plane had to land with one wing and a prayer.

Now Ricky interrupted, "How do you know it's still there?"

Lucy looked at John, waiting for an answer.

John reached out and took her in his arms. "I don't."

Lucy didn't struggle, she just collapsed in his arms, emotionally spent.

"I don't know. We're taking a big chance. If we get there and the place has been ransacked, burnt to the ground, we might not survive, but we can't stay here." John gently straightened Lucy up. Holding her at arm's length, he looked into her tear-filled eyes. "It's going to be a one-way trip."

Lucy sniffled and nodded.

After a lot of, "What ifs," John explained that the place was extremely isolated and that if no one had been there, the plane wouldn't be contaminated with the bacteria, and it should be safe to go.

Lucy reluctantly agreed.

All went well for the next hour until Lucy came down the stairs with three suitcases. John, being as sensitive as possible, explained that space on the small plane was a commodity and that this wasn't going to be just a short warm summer trip to the mountains. The fur started to fly when John told Lucy that she could not have the three suitcases—as a matter of fact, no suitcases, just her clothing and everything stacked in little flat piles.

Lucy stood fuming as John rummaged through her suitcases. She accused him of being insensitive, a tyrant, a bully, and a dictator. Things had gotten extremely dicey when he rummaged through her intimate items, unfolding her neatly folded underclothing and laying them all in one flat little pile, throwing out those that were frilly, silky, skimpy, and those designed to create a sense of bustiness. Then he told her to go back up and pack heavy, thermal, flame-retardant clothing.

"What? Flame retardant?"

John smiled. "Just in case the plane goes down."

Lucy was in no mood for humor and stomped off telling him that she wasn't going and that she would just as soon die here.

# Chapter 74

***

## Welcome
## You Are Entering Pennsylvania

Lucy watched as the key sunk into the snow, then she turned and took Ricky's hand. "Let's go."

As they headed out of Boston into the darkness of the night, Lucy sat in the passenger seat sniffling. She couldn't believe that only a few months earlier she had been dining at one of Boston's most famous bistros, maybe in love for the first time in her life, and now she was leaving for God knows where with everything she owned in the back of a van, her life reduced to three piles of clothing about the size of a peach box each. No dresses, blouses, jewelry, or cosmetics, only heavy cotton underclothing, spots bras, heavy coats, flannel shirts, denim jeans, heavy socks, a few pairs of tennis shoes, a couple pairs of hiking shoes, and a number of winter boots. Her toiletries had been reduced to a toothbrush, one tube of toothpaste, a bar of soap, and one hairbrush.

As Lucy squirmed in her seat trying to get comfortable, her hand slipped off the armrest and fell between the seats. There, she felt something cold—something metal.

Looking down, she saw that it was a gun. She looked over at John quizzically. "Are you intending to shoot someone?"

Not taking his eyes off the road in front of him, he shrugged. "If we have to."

Lucy looked at him in shock. "We! What are you talking about, 'we'? I'm not going to shoot anyone."

Lucy had never even touched a gun in her life, let alone shoot one. Expecting that the answer would be no, in that most sane people have never shot anyone, eyebrows furrowed, she asked, "You ever shot anyone?"

John nodded. "Yeah. Once."

Lucy's eyebrows shot up, and her jaw dropped. She couldn't believe this; it was like *A Nightmare on Elm Street*, and she was riding with Freddy. "You've shot someone?" she asked just to confirm that she heard him correctly.

"Yeah," John nodded, "a kid in eighth grade took my baseball glove. I shot him with my BB gun."

Lucy looked at him in disbelief. "You shot another kid because he took your glove?"

John shrugged. "Yup. Had to. Had make an example of him, you know, for the rest of the kids in the neighborhood."

Ricky, sitting in the back seat, piped up, "Wow, that's neat."

Lucy turned and gave him the evil eye, "It's not neat." She turned back and slumped in her seat. She was mentally exhausted. She just sat in silence staring out the window at the passing carnage—people huddled around fires, fighting over cans of food—and then an ironic smile came over her face. As she looked up, there in the light of the few remaining streetlights, she saw a street sign. They were on the corner of Washington and Elm. It was midnight, and they were on Elm Street.

It had taken over an hour, but they finally made it out of Boston. Lucy and Ricky had fallen asleep, and John drove along in silence. As he made his way across the blackness of New York state, little did he know that the International Space Station was passing directly overhead.

Ironically, little did Commander Donaldson, the crew of six, and baby makes seven know that they were all heading for the same destination.

Suddenly, Lucy felt a little jerk, and the van slowed down. Sitting up, sleepy eyed, she looked at John. "Where are we?"

Without taking his eyes off the road, he told her they were a little more than halfway across the state of New York heading toward the Pennsylvania border. Then, intent on what was in front of them, John bought the van to a stop.

Lucy could see the concern on his face. "What is it?"

"I don't know. Just be quiet."

Ahead, in the beam of the van's headlights, a man was standing in the middle of the road waving his arms in an obvious gesture of trying to flag down someone for help. A few feet off to the side of the road was a stalled car. John assumed it belonged to the man standing in the middle of the road.

Through the back window of the car, the van's headlights silhouetted the outline of what appeared to be the man's family sitting huddled in the freezing cold. It was ten below zero, and John could see that the headlights of their car were very dim. They were freezing to death.

Then, John caught a glimpse of movement. He reached down between the seats and pulled up the gun. Subconsciously, deep in his brainstem, the synaptic connections of evolution, his reptilian brain came to life.

Lucy gasped. "What're you doing?"

In the dimness of the stalled car's headlights, John could just make out a figure crouched down in front of the car. Then, suddenly, out of the corner of his eye, he saw a flash, a movement. Someone was coming out of the darkness toward his door. As he turned to look, the window shattered. In that split second, all he could make out was someone with a tire iron smashing at his window. Luckily, the safety glass held before the person could take another swing.

Reflexively, he pushed the accelerator to the floor. The van lurched forward gaining speed and then hit the man standing in the middle of the road waving his arms. The man flew up over the hood, and his face smashed into the center of the windshield. Lucy screamed as his face flattened, blood splattering like a paintball hitting a wall, and the man's eyes popped out of their fractured sockets.

Lucy gagged, then the body catapulted over the top of the van landing in a crumpled heap behind them in the middle of the frozen road.

As they sped away, John could see through the rearview mirror the man's lifeless body lying in the road. Then, as the scene grew more distant, he could just make out a woman and three children getting out of the car and rushing over to the lifeless form.

Everything had happened so fast, and Lucy had been so weary eyed from sleep that she had never seen the man crouched in front of the car, nor did she comprehend the person with the tire iron smashing the window. It had all happened so fast that it was just a blur. Looking at John, she screamed, "You killed him!"

John slid the gun back down between the seats. Without looking at her, he said, "It was a trap. They're desperate, they're freezing, and they're going to die."

Lucy, wiped her nose with a tissue. "Doesn't that bother you?"

John didn't say anything, he just stared at the road ahead. It bothered him, but it was survival.

It had been easier in his F-18, pushing the little red button on the plane's control stick and watching the missile on the computerized screen vaporize a building, a convoy of trucks, or a family in an adobe hut. In the F-18, there was no emotional connection between the vaporized object and the fact that someone had just died. As a fighter pilot, it was just mission accomplished.

John looked at Lucy. "Did it bother you when you hit the lady with the can of chili?"

Lucy nodded. She understood.

Then, suddenly, a violent, heaving gasp erupted from deep in Lucy's throat. "Oh my God. Oh my God," she said as the sounds of repeated dry-heaves echoed throughout the van. There, frozen to the windshield, was one of the man's eyes staring straight at her.

Lucy's retching had finally stirred Ricky, and he leaned forward between the two front seats to ask what was happening. John told him, "Nothing. I think we might've hit something—a cow or a deer in the road."

Ricky nodded. "I'm hungry."

They rode on in silence for another few hours until a faint brightness started to creep up on the horizon behind them, then John pointed to a small road sign. "We're here."

Lucy looked out her window at the sign: "Highway 17C. Susquehanna River."

John could feel his heart pounding; he had no idea what they were going to find. If the place was not there, burnt to the ground, they were going to die.

After a few miles on 17C, John slowed and pointed to an old hand-painted sign nailed to a tree: "Locust Hill."

John held his breath as he turned onto a snow-covered dirt road and wound his way through a dense growth of woods, then a clearing. Letting out a sigh of relief, there in the dimness of the early morning light, he could just see the outline of the old barn.

# Chapter 75

***

## Locust Hill, Pennsylvania

John stopped the van at the edge of the clearing. "That's it."

Lucy sat forward and looked out her window. It was so beautiful, so serene, like something out of a winter postcard. On the other side of the clearing, the early morning light shined on an old, abandoned barn with a rust-stained tin roof and long strands of icicles hanging from its edges. Next to the barn sat an old pickup truck sinking into the tall, overgrown grasses.

"It's so quiet, so peaceful," Lucy said with a faint childlike pleading. "Can't we just stay here?"

For a moment, John didn't say anything. He just sat staring ahead in his own cataleptic trance, his mind looking back into the past—back to the times with his uncle, the old barn, the farm, and the trees. And then, just at the threshold of consciousness, he heard a soft, "No, it's only a matter of time."

He looked over at Lucy, his mind drifting back to the present.

"They're already burning their way down from Canada, and soon they're going to burn all the way to Boston," she said.

Reaching over and taking her hand, he said, "There's going to be a war here—a war for every tree, twig and blade of grass, and when it's over, there's not going to be anything left." He gave her hand a gentle squeeze. "We can't stay here. It's you, me and Ricky now."

A little smile came over her face as she thought back to one of Ricky's favorite little story books *Lucy's Baby*, a story about the first Lucy and how she and her baby started the whole world three million years ago. Ricky would sit on her lap as she told the story and point to the frizzy-haired little baby. "Me!"

In the story, Lucy, her baby and her mate were trapped in a tree on the open, windblown savannas of Africa, and the big bad lions were about to eat them when a bolt of lightning saved their lives. Ricky would always laugh and give her a big hug when she read the ending of the story: "And they lived happily ever after."

Lucy looked at John and nodded. "Let's go then."

John pulled up and parked in front of the old farmhouse—a nineteenth-century stone slate building mortared with an earth-gray Pennsylvania mud and a snow-covered stone chimney clinging to its side.

Lucy stared at it. "It's beautiful."

John nodded. "I'll build you one just like that in Patagonia."

Lucy's eyes brightened. "Really?"

John smiled and, with a bit of hesitation, said, "First, we've got to get there."

John opened his door, and a blast of cold, brisk air filled the van. Lucy and Ricky both opened their doors, and Lucy stepped out and tested the morning air with a puff of breath. A soft, white cloud of condensed moisture filled the air. "It's cold."

John pointed to the house. "There's a fireplace inside." Then, pointing to an old woodpile, he said, "We'll get a fire going, get some sleep, and start packing the plane. We'll leave day after tomorrow."

Lucy stood with her legs half crossed like a two-year-old. "First, I have to go to the bathroom, bad."

John pointed to a small, wooden building with three horseshoes arching over a crescent moon carved into the door.

Lucy looked at him. "You've got to be kidding. Do you know how cold it is?"

Little did Lucy know that this was to be as good as it gets—the Taj Mahal of bathrooms compared to the bucket she would be using in the back of the plane or the fallen tree stump with the wind blowing up her backside on the open plateau in Patagonia.

John smiled. "Ricky and I are just gonna go behind the barn."

Lucy walked toward the little shed mumbling, “It’s not fair. It’s just not fair.”

While John and Ricky got a fire going in the fireplace, Lucy looked around the house. The kitchen had an old wood stove, a small brick oven carved into the wall for baking bread, and stairs leading down to a root cellar.

When John and Ricky walked into the kitchen, Lucy pointed at the little brick oven. “I want one of these when you build my house.”

John nodded. “Okay. Anything else?”

Lucy smiled. “I’ll let you know.”

John started a fire in the old wood stove, and Lucy heated up the last of the cans of chili.

It was mid-afternoon before everyone woke up, and Lucy was already up and about carrying in firewood from the woodpile. John looked at her with a big smile. She was becoming a real frontierswoman. “I like your hair,” he said facetiously.

Lucy gave him a snide smirk. She had her hair wrapped up with a scarf and tied with a big knot in the front. She did look a little like a rough and tough frontierswoman on an early wagon train heading west. With her hands on her hips, she gave a little wiggle and said, “You like it?”

John gave her a hug. “You’re so beautiful.” Then, after a long kiss, he said, “I’m gonna go out and look at the plane.”

As he turned the key to the old Yale lock of the barn doors, he prayed to God that the plane was there and untouched. He took a deep breath, closed his eyes, and pulled open the big doors.

"God, I can't believe this."

John could hear Lucy muttering as she walked through the snow heading toward the little wooden outhouse, carrying a roll of tissue that she had found in a cabinet in the pantry.

John had never seen such a beautiful sight—the old twin engine Beechcraft with its huge Pratt and Whitney engines sat perched nose up in the doorway, the sun glistening off the windshields. He walked in and caressed the propellers. "You've got to get us there, baby."

He and Ricky spent an hour carrying wood to the barn and starting a fire in the old potbellied stove. If they were going to leave in few days, he had to get the plane warmed up above freezing.

It was late afternoon by the time they carried in enough wood. The sun was setting, and the temperature was dropping. John sealed the barn as best as possible to keep the heat in and would go out a few times during the night to keep the stove burning. Lucy, in the meantime, had a big fire going in the fireplace and had found some canned goods in the pantry and cooked up a hearty meal.

As they ate, John explained that they had a big day ahead of them the next day. They had to get the plane packed and clear the runway of snow and ice.

Lucy looked at him, confused. "I didn't see any runway."

John explained that it was just the open grassy clearing and that his uncle had carved out a makeshift runway.

"What about the trees at the end?"

With his mouth full, he motioned with his hands, "Up and over."

Lucy's eyebrows shot up. "And if you don't," making the same motion, "make it up and over?"

Again, he motioned with his hands, this time diving them downward, then he gave a half-garbled, "Boom." Lucy looked at him unsure if he was serious or just kidding, then he smiled affirmatively. "Don't worry, I've flown that thing out of here a million times."

Actually, it had only been once, but he didn't want to make Lucy nervous, and he felt pretty confident. It really was no different than flying off the end of an aircraft carrier. He remembered that great feeling. You just head into the wind, wait to feel the plane drop off the end, push the throttles, gun the big turbos, lift and bank hard to the right. He took Lucy's hand. "We'll make it."

Ricky sat trying to use his laptop, but there was no signal. On the mantle of the fireplace was an old fifties-looking radio. "Does that work?" he asked pointing to the radio.

John shrugged. It was battery operated, so he gave Ricky a nod and said, "Give it a try."

Ricky turned it on, and it crackled to life. Turning the tuner back and forth, he picked up a number of static-filled stations until he finally hit one with fairly clear reception. It was WGN out of Chicago. Being that the old radio only had AM reception, it was still pretty broken up, but, compared to his high-tech laptop, at least it worked.

Lucy had never felt so at peace in her life despite the world outside spiraling to an end. How she wished this moment could last forever—the fireplace crackling, John holding her cuddled in a blanket, and Ricky spiraling to manhood. Staring at the open fireplace, she mumbled, "I wonder what's going to happen."

Little could she ever have imagined what lay ahead. Her brother would die at her hands, she'd have a baby girl, Ricky would have his twins Angus and Braveheart, and they would be the beginning of a brave new world with a crew of six space men, and baby makes seven.

# Chapter 76

***

## 39.7545°N. 79.8692°W.
## Locust Hill, Pennsylvania

The sun was just peeking over the horizon, and the early morning rays were shining through the open doors of the barn, lighting up the nose of the plane like a beacon. John sat uneasy as he stared at the controls, unsure of what they would do if the plane didn't start. He didn't have an alternate plan. Finally, he took a deep breath and put his fingers on the ignition buttons for the big Pratt-Whitney engines.

After two days, the barn had warmed up nicely thanks to his uncle's drywall on the inside of the building and the old potbelly stove. There had been enough fuel in the storage tank to fill the plane's tanks to the brim. Now, it was just a matter of the twin engines turning over.

John pushed the start button for the right engine. It coughed, choked, and sputtered a few times and then stopped. Taking another deep breath, he waited for a few seconds and pushed the button again. "Come on, baby … start."

This time, the old engine coughed, backfired, and belched out a large cloud of black smoke before settling into a smooth hum. John let out a sigh of relief, put his finger on the button for the left engine, and pushed.

After letting the plane idle for a few minutes, he eased it out of the barn and taxied it to the head of the makeshift runway. Sitting with the sun's rays warming his face, he looked down the long, frozen path cut out of the countryside and smiled. "Here comes the sun. It's alright now."

John and Ricky spent the morning walking the length of the makeshift runway inspecting it for any rocks, twigs, or branches. Luckily, there had only been a dusting of light snow in the past few weeks, and the winds had blown it off, exposing a straight, frozen path of dark Pennsylvania earth. It had taken him and Ricky a few hours to carry the red indicator flags from the barn and place them on either side of the dirt runway, which came to an end at a large looming oak tree.

Lucy spent the morning packing the plane as efficiently as possible; bedding, canned goods that were in the old pantry, kitchen utensils, knives, forks, spoons, pots and pans, and a large boiling kettle.

Once John and Ricky finished with the runway, John loaded a number of guns from his uncle's gun cabinet into the plane: a couple of twenty-two caliber rifles with over twenty boxes of shells, a thirty-aught-six high-powered rifle, a few handguns, and a twelve-gauge shotgun, along with a bunch of fishing equipment. Meanwhile, Ricky had been assigned the job of collecting some basic tools: a machete, screwdrivers, wrenches, hammers and nails, and a small handsaw. At one point, Ricky came to John with a huge wrench-type tool and asked what it was and if he wanted him to pack it.

John took it, looked it over, held it up, and handed it back to Ricky. "No, it's too big and heavy. I don't think we'd ever need that. Leave it behind."

Ricky threw it off to the side.

It was almost noon, and Lucy was packing the last of the items into the plane when she saw the tool Ricky had tossed. Assuming that Ricky had forgotten to put it into the plane, she picked it up and slid it under some of the bedding. Little could she have ever known how that snap decision would come to mean the difference between life and death for the crew of six of the ISS.

It was now high noon, and the plane's engines purred like a pair of baby kittens. John reached over and took Lucy's hand. "It's time to go."

Lucy sat buckled into the copilot's seat and looked down the long dirt runway at the huge oak tree at the end, "I think I'm going to wet myself."

John gave her hand a little squeeze and smiled. "It's alright now, little darlin'." Then he pushed the throttles forward. The plane picked up speed, quickly moving down the runway. Just as the plane lifted, Lucy felt her stomach drop. "Oh God!"

John felt a rush of adrenaline. It was just like dropping off the end of the *Nimitz* super aircraft carrier when he flew in the Navy.

Ricky was excited but apprehensive about the giant oak they were quickly approaching.

At the end of the dirt runway, just to the right of the big oak tree, was a steep rock cliff. John felt the plane lift, and just as the big tree filled the view of the windshield, he banked it hard to the right and caught the updraft coming up over the cliff. The plane floated like a bird out over an open field.

As he leveled it off, he looked over at Lucy who looked a little pale. "You okay?"

Lucy was gagging into a vomit bag that John had anticipated needing. "No, I'm not okay. I want to go home."

"Wow, that was neat," Ricky gleefully announced from the back seat. "That was better than the Yankee Cannonball," a turn-your-stomach roller coaster ride outside of Boston.

It had been a few hours after the harrowing takeoff, and Lucy had fallen asleep, but something woke her up. She sensed the plane was going down.

Sitting up, sleepy-eyed with the vomit bag still in her hand, she looked out her window. "Where are we?"

John was bringing the plane down to a remote dust-covered landing strip at the tip of Texas. One of his military friends from the *Nimitz* aircraft carrier had an uncle who had a crop dusting service, and John had made plans with him to refuel. Being that it was winter and there were no crops to dust, his uncle had a full tank of aviation fuel.

As John slowly pulled back on the throttles, he said, "This is McAllen, Texas. We're going to refuel before trying to make it across the Gulf."

Lucy peered at all of the dials and lights on the console trying to find the fuel gauge. "Did you say *try* to make it?"

John was looking straight ahead as the dirt landing strip got closer. Without looking at Lucy, concentrating on getting the plane on the ground, he said, "It's not gas. It's aviation fuel."

"Are we going to make it?"

Just then, the plane gently touched down on the runway, stirring up clouds of Texas dust. John pulled the throttles completely back and the engines slowed to a quiet hum.

He looked over at Lucy. "I'll let you know when we get to Honduras."

"We're going to Honduras?"

John winked at her. "On a wing and a prayer."

# Chapter 77

***

## La Esperanza, Honduras

It had been over three hours since they left McAllen, Texas. Lucy sat staring out her window, mesmerized by the blue sky above, the silent hum of the plane's engines, and the sparkling blue waters of the gulf below. Three hundred miles overhead, in the darkness of space, Layne felt a little kick as the newest member of the International Space Station stirred.

John looked over at Lucy. "Penny for your thoughts."

She smiled halfheartedly. "What're we going to do if my brother's commune doesn't let us in?"

John shrugged. "I don't know. We'll figure it out. We'll find shelter … a cave … whatever. We'll have to make the best of it."

Lucy less than cheerfully rolled her eyes. "I've always wanted to live in a cave."

John smiled. "We have a lot more going for us than little Lucy did from three million years ago in Ethiopia. We have guns, fishing equipment, and a couple hundred little gas lighters to make fire." Reaching over, he gave her hand a gentle squeeze. "Hey, we'll make it. And someday, we'll make it all the way back up to Boston."

Lucy smiled. "I love you."

Ricky was playing games on his laptop. Luckily, John's uncle had installed a power port for electronic devices into the plane. Ricky leaned forward and looked out the plane's front windows. "How much farther?"

John glanced down at the dials on the console and did some mental arithmetic. Glancing back to Ricky, he said, "A few more hours—three or four."

Lucy's eyebrows shot up, "Three or four hours? I can't wait three or four more hours. I have to pee."

John smiled and pointed to the back corner of the plane, which was a little less than thirty-five feet away. Lucy looked back. "Oh no! No, no. No way!"

John's uncle had installed a small military-designed bathroom facility in the far corner of the plane. It was essentially a modified five-gallon bucket with a toilet seat. Being that there were no females in the military at the time, the design was not female friendly, and being that John's uncle normally flew alone, it was not well-adapted for privacy.

Lucy adamantly refused and continued to squirm and fidget for the next hour. Finally, begrudgingly, she unbuckled her seatbelt and started crawling toward the back of the plane. John and Ricky could not help but laugh.

As Lucy crawled past Ricky, he grinned and, with a curt little smile, said, "Don't forget to flush it. Oh, and put the seat back up."

Lucy gave him a despicable look but was too preoccupied with the more pressing matter than scolding her incorrigible son. She continued to the far corner of the plane, mumbling all the way how unfair it was that men had it so easy and that someday women were going to rule the world and that they would pass a law making it mandatory for men to sit down to pee.

John looked back at Ricky and raised his brows as they both strained to keep their laughing to an inaudible level knowing perfectly well they were treading on thin ice.

A few minutes later, Lucy crawled back to the front of the plane and strapped herself into her seat. Looking out her window at the ocean below, she thought, *I want to go home.*

A few hours later as the sun had set, everyone was sitting quietly in the darkness of the plane. Ricky pointed out his window at some dim lights off in the distance. "What's that?"

John looked at the latitude and longitude dials on the console. "That should be Honduras. We're about forty miles off the coast, so that should be a small town called Trujillo."

Looking at the fuel gauge, Lucy asked, "Are we going to land there?"

"No. We've had strong tailwinds and have enough fuel to make it across Honduras to Las Esperanza. That way, we won't be cutting it so close on our flight to Bolivia.

Lucy's eyes shot up. "Bolivia?"

Weeks earlier, John had pulled up Air Force reconnaissance images of airstrips at both Trujillo and La Esperanza. Their next stop after Honduras was actually going to be Ecuador. But Lucy was already stressed out enough, so John thought it best to keep things on a need-to-know basis. The plane's range without tailwinds was at best 1100 miles; 1200 or 1300 with favorable winds. According to the military reconnaissance, both Trujillo and La Esperanza had fuel storage facilities on or next to the airstrips. John's concern was that Trujillo's appeared to be government storage tanks of some kind, although not military, while La Esperanza's were civilian. He knew they would probably not be welcomed at either place but would much rather deal with civilian authorities than government.

He wasn't too worried about trouble at La Esperanza or Ecuador, but Bolivia's stopover was a military refueling outpost, and John knew those guys would have guns.

After another few hours, the dim lights of La Esperanza could be seen twinkling off in the distance.

John looked at Lucy. "That should be it."

Lucy looked at the fuel gauge and asked, "Is it safe? Are

the people there going to be like the rest of the world—desperate?"

John was hoping that it was not going to be a problem. He explained to Lucy that La Esperanza was very rural, and the people there lived off the land and weren't very dependent on oil. Also, he was planning on getting in and out as quickly as possible. The plan was to land in the cover of darkness, refuel and gather supplies as early as possible in the morning, and leave before much of the town woke up to realize what they were up to.

Lucy halfheartedly smiled. "It's kind of ironic. The poorest people in the world are now the richest … and the richest are now the poorest."

John nodded. "For now, but it's not going to stay that way for long. It's only a matter of time for these poor people before millions start funneling down from the United States, down through Mexico, and into the lush, narrow strip of Central America. And, at the same time, millions more will push up from South America." Shaking his head, he said, "There'll be nothing left." He banked the plane to the right. "Here we go."

# Chapter 78

***

## La Esperanza, Honduras

"What're you doing?"

Lucy didn't know anything about airplanes, but after sitting for over twelve hours in the copilot seat, she at least knew which dial on the dashboard was the altimeter—the up and down dial—and she could see that they had dropped to less than 2000 feet.

Without looking over at her, John said matter-of-factly, "We're landing."

Lucy's eyebrows shot up. "Landing!"

She looked out the front window of the plane. "I don't see an airport. I don't see anything. It's dark."

Glancing back at the altimeter, it now read 1480 feet. Just as she looked over at John, he reached down between the seats and pulled a lever. Moments later, Lucy heard the grinding of motors and recognized the sound of the landing bay doors opening below her. The plane suddenly slowed down.

John could see that Lucy was turning a little pale. He smiled and said, "Don't worry, that's only the drag from the landing gear."

Pushing the throttles forward a little, the plane picked up speed, and the weightless sensation went away. Lucy took a deep breath and exhaled—a momentary sigh of relief, but it was only to be short-lived.

John reached down and pulled another lever. This time, the plane slowed so much that it seemed like it was actually going to stop in midair.

Lucy's stomach started to turn. "Oh my God!"

John had put the flaps down, and now the plane was truly floating. Again, pushing the throttles forward to keep his air speed above stall speed, the big engines whined, and the plane picked up speed and floated forward.

Lucy looked at the altimeter and shrieked as if giving warning, "1000 feet."

Frantically looking back out the front window of the plane and still seeing nothing, Lucy screamed, "What are you doing?"

John slowly pulled back on the throttles, and the plane continued going down. Calmly, he said, "We're doing a blackout landing. This is an airstrip without any lights."

Lucy was about ready to have a stroke. She looked at him

wide-eyed. "What's a blackout landing?"

As he focused on the nothingness in front of him, he explained that there were night landings on aircraft carriers in combat areas where all of the lights on the carrier were off so that it could not be spotted by enemy planes. He continued that the latitude, longitude, and speed of the carrier deck appeared in a pale, green print in the upper right-hand corner of the pilot's face shield. All the pilot had to do was match his latitude, longitude, and air speed to that of the carrier deck.

He began to think back to the adrenaline-rushing days of landing his F-14 Tomcat on the deck of the *Nimitz*—the exhilarating feeling when his thirty-five-ton machine touched the deck's cold, metal surface, the heart-pounding tension of pushing the throttles full forward at the exact moment the wheels touched the deck, feeling the thrust of the huge engines pushing him back in his seat. Then the milliseconds of terror, waiting and praying the tail hook caught the carrier deck's cable. If not, he and his wingman were off for a second try.

Though he wasn't letting it show, he was uneasy for a couple of reasons. One was, being that his plane was built in 1941, it would have to be landed the old-fashioned way with a copilot verbally reading out the airspeed and altitude. That was not an insurmountable problem because Lucy, little did she know, was going to be his wingman. But his biggest concern was whether the coordinates for the runway were correct.

He had gotten the coordinates for the exact spot that his wheels had to touch down from what he hoped had been the most up-to-date Air Force reconnaissance numbers. Providing that Las Esperanza hadn't changed anything in the meantime, like moving the runway, he should be okay. But, if for some reason they created a new runway, the one he was about to land on could be riddled with potholes.

Lucy was sitting at the edge of her seat, her shoulder harness pulled tight. She continued to glance back and fourth, first out the window at the darkness in front of them and then back at the altimeter. It now read 968 feet.

Ricky had his head poked between the seats. "Wow! This is exciting!"

Lucy looked at him, then at John. "Are you both crazy?"

John didn't have time to argue. Pointing to the airspeed and altimeter instruments, he told Lucy, "Keep reading the numbers on these two dials—first the airspeed, then the altimeter."

Lucy's voice quivered, "What?"

They were about to touch down at any moment. John looked over at Lucy and, with a hard stare, said, "Now! Start reading now! Airspeed."

Lucy looked at the two dials. "Okay! Okay! The airspeed is 184, and the altitude is 840 feet."

John sat forward intently peering through the front window, hoping the plane's landing lights would bring the tip of the airstrip into view while at the same time listening to Lucy read out the numbers.

Lucy cried, “I’m scared. 460 feet.”

“Don’t fall apart on me now. You’re my wingman. Air-speed?”

Suddenly, time stopped. The wheels in Lucy’s mind echoed, “Wingman?”

The first time that she and John had ever gone out on a date, he had taken her to the most expensive, most impossible place in all of Boston to get reservations—the Beacon Hill Bistro. And, he had not only gotten reservations but also had gotten the most highly sought-after table in the whole place, right next to the fireplace. At the time, she had wondered how he could afford such a place as well as get reservations. As if it were yesterday, she remembered how on the way out, John had leaned over and quietly said to the maître d’, “Tell the wingman thanks.”

Coming out of her momentary reminiscence, she turned and looked at John bewilderedly and said, “Wingman!”

They were only feet from touching down, and John didn’t have time to explain. “The numbers. What’s the altitude?”

Lucy looked at the altimeter and again shrieked, “Oh my God, 100 feet!”

Before she could even take another breath, there was a hard thud. John reached down and pulled the throttles all the way back and then stepped on two pedals on the floor. The nose of the plane dipped down, and Lucy felt herself being thrust forward, the shoulder harnesses pulling tight across her chest. The plane coasted to a stop, and Lucy flopped back in her seat. “I have to pee.”

As they sat in the dim light of the cockpit, Ricky grinned. "Wow, Mom! That was neat."

Lucy just looked at him, shaking her head.

Letting the plane idle, John looked around. With only the dim light from the landing gear, he spotted the fuel tanks that he had seen on the reconnaissance pictures. As Lucy sat hyperventilating, he taxied the plane over to the area where four fuel storage tanks stood. As he got close, he could see that the third tank was not locked and that he would not have to cut the hose. He was going to refuel the plane tonight and then get it turned around at the head of the runway in case they had to make a quick getaway in the morning.

Lucy sat as pale as a ghost. "How did you know how to do that?"

John smiled. "The U.S.S. *Saratoga*."

Lucy looked at him, dumbfounded. "You flew in the Navy?"

Lucy knew what the U.S.S. *Saratoga* was. When she was little, her family had vacationed in Pensacola, Florida. She remembered how she and her father use to watch young Navy pilots practice landing jets on an old decommissioned aircraft carrier anchored in the gulf.

"Yup," John nodded, "went to the naval academy in Annapolis."

Ricky sat forward. "Told you, Mom. Remember when I told you there was something fishy about him?"

Lucy was still shaking but managed to break a little smile. Looking over at John, she said, "The class had a conspiracy theory about you. There was a gap in your résumé between high school and your physics degree at Princeton."

John laughed. "I knew about the conspiracy theory. It ranged from serial killer to government spy."

Lucy just sat mentally drained. "So, is there anything else I should know, other than you shot a little boy for taking your baseball glove, you went to the naval academy in Annapolis and flew jets off of aircraft carriers, and you got a Ph.D. in physics from Princeton?"

John shook his head matter-of-factly. "No, that's about it."

The next morning, they got up early, and, as expected, things were quiet. It appeared that no one was the wiser or seemed to care that a plane was sitting on their runway. Just after sunup, an old man came walking by with a donkey, said good morning, and went on his way. So far, everything was going okay.

They still had some room left in the plane for supplies, so John told Lucy he was going into town to see what he could find—things that they might need. He tucked a small handgun under his shirt and handed Lucy the shotgun.

Lucy looked at him. "What is this? I'm not going to shoot anyone."

John explained that she and Ricky were going to guard the plane while he was in town, telling her that she wasn't going to have to shoot anybody, only to stand in front of the plane, hold the gun, and look menacing. He told her that if anyone approached, they would most likely only be locals that were curious, and seeing someone with a shotgun, they would just walk away.

Lucy started to argue, but John cut her off, "Just stand tall, aim the gun chest high, and let them know that if they come any closer, you'll shoot."

Lucy looked at him like he was nuts. She had never done anything more than played with Barbie dolls as a little girl. "And if they don't stop?"

"Point the gun in the air, and pull the trigger."

John spent the next twenty minutes showing Lucy how to hold the gun to look intimidating, explaining how not to hold the gun at her side with the barrel pointing at the ground. "You gotta look like you know how to handle a gun, like Anne Oakley in a wild-wild west show."

Lucy rolled her eyes. "Yeah, that's me … Annie Oakley."

John continued his instructions on how to look intimidating and fearless. "Gun to your shoulder. Finger on the trigger guard. Right foot back. Left foot forward. Upper-half of your body turned slightly to your right, bringing the left shoulder and gun forward."

Pointing to a little bead on the tip of the barrel, he said, "Look straight down the barrel, aim at the center of their chest, and tell them, 'Don't take another step or I'll shoot.'"

Lucy looked at him, shocked. "And if they don't, I point the gun in the air and pull the trigger?"

John smiled. "You got it." Although he knew it would knock her on her pretty little butt. As a backup, he handed Ricky an unloaded handgun and told him to wave it around and to also look menacing.

After a few more instructions, John headed for town. As he looked back, he couldn't help but smile. Lucy was standing in front of the plane between the two propellers, shotgun in her hand, her hair tied up in a bandana, and looking menacing as hell.

As he headed down the hill toward the little town, Lucy yelled out to him, "If you're looking for trouble, young fella, I'll be glade to accommodate you."

# Chapter 79

***

## Ecuador

"Don't come any closer, or I'll shoot."

John stared in awe, unsure of what he had created; a Tania Bunke, the revolutionary female in Che Guevara's-Argentinian guerrilla gang that helped overthrow the Cuban government; Bonnie Parker, of Bonnie and Clyde fame, who robbed banks across Kansas; or frontierswoman Calamity Jane scouting out the wild-wild west.

Lucy was standing in front of the plane wearing a slightly tilted beret beanie. The butt of the shotgun was resting on her left hip, her left hand tightly gripping the walnut gunstock, and the barrel aiming straight up. "I wouldn't come any closer."

John held up his hands. "Don't shoot, it's only me."

Ricky was standing behind her by the left wing. "I'd do what she says, Doctor Christenson. I think she's losing it."

Lucy lowered the gun and smiled. "Don't worry, I took the bullets out. I'm just practicing looking menacing."

With a sigh of relief, John took the gun, checked the chamber, and set it up next to the plane. Then, brushing a wisp of hair out of her eyes, he smiled. "Where'd you get the beret?"

"Same place all the revolutionary girls got theirs, Boston's Newbury Street."

John laughed. "I've always wondered where Che got his."

It was already mid-morning by the time John got back to the plane. He had spent as much time as possible looking around for items that they might need, especially if they were not allowed to join Lucy's brother's commune.

At the general store, he had found a trove of things. He'd found mosquito netting that he knew they would need during the warmer times of the year to ward off swarming hordes of insects. He also found a large canvas tent that he thought might come in handy to cover the entrance to a cave, should they end up living in a cave like little hominid Lucy three million years ago. And, lastly, he'd found a large, iron boiling kettle that was big enough for a cannibal's cookout. He figured it would make a nice heated bathtub for Lucy.

Behind him were four young boys who had been lingering around the general store looking for work and for a few American dollars. Although up in the states, paper money was currently more valuable as kindling, here, to these boys, the American dollar represented power, being really rich. They could buy anything with American money.

John motioned to Ricky. "Help us pack this stuff."

It had taken some time to pack and repack, especially the large kettle, but now they sat at the head of the runway, the big propellers humming.

John looked over at Lucy and then back to Ricky. "Ready?"

Everyone nodded.

Minutes later, as the plane lifted and the sounds of the bay doors locked into place, John let out another sigh of relief. "One down, and three to go."

Things had gone surprisingly well in Las Esperanza, but they had three more stops to make before Patagonia. He felt good about his plans for the next two stops—Ecuador and Lake Titicaca on the Peruvian-Bolivian border—but he wasn't so sure about their last stop, which was an Argentinian military refueling outpost high in the Andes Mountains. The outpost would be manned by soldiers with guns, which was a lot different than local civilians with machetes.

Lucy sat staring out her window, mesmerized by the countryside below—the small villages, the lush, green hillsides, and the clusters of banana trees. She sat dreaming, wishing that the world could stay just like that. It looked so peaceful; there were no roads, no stoplights, just an occasional farmer and his donkey loaded with bananas.

Without looking over at John, lost in the serenity of the beauty below, she asked, "How far to Bolivia?"

John thought some and then said, "About twenty-five hundred miles, give or take. But we have to make a quick stop in Ecuador first."

Lucy turned her head with a bit of a snap. "Ecuador? I thought you said we were going to Bolivia?"

John pointed to the fuel gauge. "We can only go 1200 miles without refueling, so we have to make a stop somewhere before Bolivia."

Lucy looked at him, disheartened. She knew what "we have to make a stop" meant.

She looked out her window at the ground speeding by below. "We're going to rob another gas station, aren't we?"

For a moment, John just sat quietly, not saying anything. He didn't like what the world had become, and he wished it could go back to the way it had been, but that wasn't going to happen. Reaching over, he took Lucy's hand and gave it a little squeeze. "We're going to ask nicely."

Lucy rolled her eyes.

John's plans were to ask nicely in Ecuador and Bolivia, but he wasn't so sure that "nice" was going to work in Argentina.

He turned and looked back at Ricky, who was sitting silently, staring out his window. After a short pause, he looked back at Lucy and, in a somber tone, said, "We don't really have a choice."

Lucy nodded; she understood. "You either hit the lady with the can of chili, or you and your offspring die."

Resigned to their fate, Lucy asked, "I assume you have a plan?" John did and was about to explain, but Lucy stopped him, "No, no. Let me guess. We're going to stop in and ask those nice people for some gas, which we don't really have the money for, correct?"

John kind of smiled and replied, "Exactly!"

Lucy looked at him, flabbergasted. "You know there's a bug out there eating the world's gas?" she asked, somewhat unsure whether he remembered.

John nodded. "It's actually eating lubricants, oils and grease, not gas." But he understood what she meant.

He didn't bring up the grim circumstances they were facing—the danger and ruthlessness they might be forced into. There was no reason to make things any more stressful than they already were, but he was just as concerned. In reality, their chances of making it all the way to Patagonia in a 1941 airplane and being accepted into a commune, possibly already overrun by thousands, were slim, but all he could do was hope.

"So," Lucy said with a fiendish smile, "we're not really going to rob anyone, we're just going to hip-hop across South America asking people nicely for gas."

John shrugged. "Yup, that's my plan. And it's aviation fuel, not gas."

Again Lucy rolled her eyes. "Tomato tomata."

Either way, that was John's plan, except for Argentina.

"And if they don't?" Lucy asked with a sinking feeling.

John turned and looked back at Ricky again and then at Lucy. With a dispirited nod, he said, "We'll have to take it. We don't have a choice."

***

Over three thousand miles away, another dispirited nod came from deep in the Cheyenne Mountain Military complex known as NORAD. Robert Newhouse had just been handed the latest reports for the United States and the world: "Number of dead-UNKNOWN. World population-UNKNOWN."

Setting the reports down on the desk, he leaned back and stared at the ceiling. "How did it come to this?"

***

Lucy looked at John, eyebrows raised. "So, what's your plan?"

John had started working on a plan six weeks earlier as it had become obvious that Boston was spiraling into chaos. The city and the whole eastern seaboard were going to be a death trap, and he knew they were going to have to leave.

He had spent nearly two weeks planning out a route from Locust Hill, Pennsylvania all the way to Patagonia, South America. Calculating wind speeds, tailwinds, the weight of the plane's load, and, with the help of reconnaissance pictures lifted from an Air Force database, he identified isolated airstrips with refueling tanks at 1200-mile intervals.

Las Esperanza had been perfect—a sleepy little town with an airstrip on the outskirts, fuel tanks next to the airstrip, a quick and easy in-and-out. His next planned stop was 1200 miles away on a banana plantation in Ecuador.

John reached under his seat, took out a sheet of paper and handed it to Lucy. She took it, not sure what it was, turned it over and then back. "What's this?"

It was a Chiquita banana requisition form with the Miss Chiquita banana girl and her brightly colored Chiquita banana fruit hat printed in across the top.

John explained that there was an airstrip on a banana plantation sixty some miles outside of a city called Machala in southern Ecuador. He explained that the airstrip was owned by the Chiquita banana company and that they had fueling tanks alongside the runway for their planes and trucks transporting bananas to the coast or flown throughout the country.

Lucy didn't say anything. She just listened, content.

John went on to explain that there were hundreds of these rural airstrips all across South America—airstrips owned by huge conglomerates like Chiquita. He explained that these airstrips were usually manned by little more than locals—poorly paid peasant farmers who gathered bundles of bananas, loaded them on donkeys, and delivered them to the airstrips.

Lucy, looking a bit skeptical, said, "Somebody must run the airstrip other than guys with donkeys?"

John nodded. "True, but they're still just local workers armed at most with machetes."

Pointing to the requisition form in Lucy's hand, John said, "Look, if someone shows up and has a requisition form to get bananas, these guys couldn't care less. They're drowning in bananas."

Lucy looked at him a bit confused, thinking that somewhere along the line she must have missed something. Turning the form over and back, she didn't see a requisition form for gas.

"So, we're just going to stop in with a requisition form telling them to give us some bananas and then just matter-of-factly mention that we need gas, for which we don't have a requisition form."

John was elated. "Exactly!"

Lucy looked at him in disbelief. "Let's say they give us the bananas but don't want to give us the gas?"

John grinned. "I still have a few crisp, new twenty-dollar bills left."

Lucy let out an exasperating breath. "You know money's not worth much anymore."

"I know, to you and me," John said, "but these people don't know that. They're isolated. Their daily currency is bartering with chickens, eggs, and goat's milk. Here, it's not the gold the money is backed with; the value here is the bill itself. Even though the world's monetary system has collapsed, they view the dollar bill as the ultimate commodity. For years to come, it'll be accepted like gold to buy and sell anything. It's the perception. They see the United States as too big to fail."

Lucy gave in. “So you think that by slipping some poor local guy a few American dollars, he’ll let you fill the plane with gas?”

John nodded confidently. “Yup, the gas isn’t his, and he’s probably the guy that keeps the records for Chiquita. He’ll write in one of the ledgers that one of their planes landed, took a bunch of bananas, and fueled up.”

A few hours later, after Lucy had dozed on and off, John broke the silence, “There it is.”

Lucy sat up straight and looked out her side of the front window. Ricky leaned forward and poked his head between the seats. Ahead in the distance was a long runway carved out between miles of banana trees. Leaning forward, as if to get a closer look, Lucy said, “Are you sure this is the right one? Wouldn’t that be just great to accidentally steal some gas from a drug cartel?” she added with a bit of sarcasm.

A short time later, they were taxiing down a roughly paved strip. John looked around and spotted the fuel tanks to the left of the runway just as he had seen them in the reconnaissance pictures. As he got to the far end of the runway, a man stepped out of a metal building to his right and started walking toward the plane. John gave the man a friendly wave and turned the plane around, aiming its nose down the runway just in case they had to make a quick getaway.

Shutting down the engines, he tucked a small handgun under his shirt, opened his door, and told Lucy and Ricky to stay in the plane. As he stepped out onto the wing, he cautiously looked around before jumping down onto the tarmac. Back in the metal building, he could just make out three or four shadowy figures standing in the dim light of the open doorway. After being sure that things looked fairly safe for the time being, he jumped down and approached the man with his hand extended.

The man appeared to be non-threatening—a short, elderly Spanish gentleman, who took John's hand. "Sí Senior."

John nodded, shook his hand, and asked him if he spoke English.

The man nodded. "Sí, Poquito."

John didn't know much Spanish, but he knew "poquito" meant small or something. He handed the man the requisition form, which he had printed in Spanish. The man looked at it and pointed to a large stack of green bananas piled a mile high next to the metal building. Then John pointed to the fuel tanks and then to the plane. "Poquito?"

The man looked at him a bit confused, and John sensed that he may be getting a little suspicious. The man walked around looking the plane over and then looked up into the cabin.

Lucy looked down, smiled, and waved. "Hola," she yelled, which was the extent of her Spanish vocabulary.

The man smiled back. "Hola."

John reached into his pocket and took out a few of the last twenty-dollar bills and then pointed to the fuel tanks.

The man smiled, took the money, and put it into his pocket. Then he pointed to the tanks. "Sí."

A short time later, John was standing on the wing, refueling the plane when he became aware of an uncomfortable silence. He looked around. "Uh-oh."

The man had disappeared, and the shadowy characters in the shed were gone. John nonchalantly edged over and looked into Lucy's window. "Get the shotgun and some shells. Don't load it, just get them ready."

The shotgun was a pump-action twelve-gauge with a three-shell magazine. John had shown Lucy how to load the shells into the magazine. Then looking back at Ricky, he said, "Do the same. Get your handgun, and be ready with some bullets."

"What is it?" Lucy asked anxiously.

John wasn't sure and didn't have time to explain. He still had the second tank to fill. Then, at the far end of the runway, an old woman came walking out from behind a clump of banana trees with a young girl about 10 years old, pushing some kind of cart.

Lucy stepped out onto the wing next to John and handed him the shotgun and shells. Looking down the runway, she asked, "Who's that?"

"I don't know," John said, handing the gun back to Lucy. "Listen, that thing is loaded. The safety's on. Don't put your finger on the trigger. Just hold it up and look menacing."

Lucy handed the gun back. "Hold it for a minute." She putt on her Che Guevara beret and took the gun back. "Okay! I want to look menacing."

John couldn't help but smile, and with a bit of a John Wayne drawl, he said, "Ain't nobody going to mess with you, little lady."

The old woman and young girl stopped about forty yards from the plane, said, "Hola," then pointed to her broken-down cart.

It was a typical roadside food and fruit cart pushed by locals selling roadside goods. The old woman pointed to some homemade bread, most likely made from bread-fruit, some goat cheese, and a chunk of dried meat with flies swirling around it.

Lucy waved, smiled and said, "Hola."

The little girl was gorgeous—long, beautiful black hair, golden skin, and as cute as a bug's ear. With a big smile, the little girl waved back.

John was now on the other wing filling the second tank. Meanwhile, Ricky had climbed into the front of the cabin and was sitting in the pilot's seat. "Hey! Look!" he yelled, pointing out the front window down the length of the runway.

John looked up, and at the far end of the runway, from where the old woman and girl had come, three men with machetes could be seen moving about in the clump of banana trees.

John told Ricky to come out and take over refueling the plane. Keeping his eyes on the far end of the runway, he and Lucy jumped down and walked out to meet the old woman and her food cart.

The little girl was so cute that Lucy just wanted to hug her. She curtsied and said, "Hola."

Lucy's heart melted. Little could she know that it wouldn't be long and they'd be a family of four—the newest member a beautiful blacked-haired, golden-skinned, Argentinean beauty from the Pantanal.

The old lady pointed to the cart. "Comida, you want?" In a little less than a month, as they would learn from their newest member of the family, "Comida" meant food.

John took out a five-dollar bill and pointed to a loaf of bread, the cheese, and a chunk of the dried meat.

"Hey! Look!" Ricky was pointing down the runway. At the far end of the runway, three men with machetes had stepped out from behind the banana trees and were walking toward them. John reached under his shirt and took out the gun. He motioned to Lucy to take the bread, cheese and dried meat and to head back to the plane. By the time he looked up, the three men had picked up their pace.

John grabbed the little girl by the shoulder, twirled her around, and pointed the gun at her head. Then, with the girl in tow, he started backing up toward the plane.

The old woman screamed, "No! No!"

Midway down the runway, the three men stopped. When John got back to the plane, he handed the girl a five-dollar bill and gave her a little push. "Go! Go!"

The little girl ran back and hugged the old woman. John, Lucy and Ricky climbed into the plane.

# Chapter 80

***

## Argentina

As the banana plantation dwarfed into the background, Lucy looked over at John. She could not believe how her world had become so unraveled, so surreal.

In a low, disheartened whisper, she asked, "Would you have shot that little girl?"

John looked over at Lucy and smiled. "No, I'd probably have shot her food cart, that huge papaya she had sitting on top."

Lucy didn't say anything. She just turned and looked out her window. Little could she know that things were going to get worse—much worse.

Refueling on the Bolivian side of Lake Titicaca, their latest stop on the way to Patagonia had gone more smoothly than it had on the banana plantation in Ecuador. This time, they landed on a parched dirt runway that belonged to the Corocoro United Copper Mining Company in the most sunbaked, desolate terrain that Lucy had ever seen. Again, with the Bolivian currency, the Boliviano, being worth about fourteen cents on the dollar, the workers at the mine had no qualms about exchanging a few gallons of fuel for some American dollars, especially since it wasn't their fuel.

As the plane took off from the arid mining strip, Ricky pulled himself forward between the seats. "What's next?"

John looked over his shoulder and, with a bit of hesitation, said, "Argentina."

Lucy could feel by the tone in his voice that he was a little concerned; it lacked the air of confidence of Ecuador and Bolivia.

"You're worried about Argentina, aren't you?"

John nodded. "A little."

Actually, John had high hopes that their stop in Argentina would go without a hitch. But, this time, they were not going to ask nicely. This would be more of a "hit and run" gas station type stickup.

Their last stop before dropping into Patagonia was a remote refueling station high in the Andes Mountains. During his research, John had identified a number of small military outposts that dotted the ridges of the mountains. They were isolated facilities manned by teams of two low-level privates. There was actually very little there to guard. They were there to be little more than "eyes in the sky" so to speak.

John was very familiar with such outposts. When he had been stationed on the U.S.S. *Nimitz* in the South Pacific, he had seen a number of these low-level grunts being rotated in and out of isolated island camps. Inevitably, the poor guys returned with little will to fight after spending three months bored out of their minds on a rat-infested island in the middle of nowhere.

From the reconnaissance pictures, John had identified one such outpost that had a set of refueling tanks. It was perfectly located 1100 miles from their last stop in Bolivia and about 1100 miles from their final destination in Patagonia. It was midway down Argentina, three hours west of a small city called Mendoza, high up on Mount Aconcagua, on one of the mountain's higher peaks.

"Why are you concerned about our next stop?" Lucy asked.

John looked over with a little twitch of his eyebrows. "It's a military installation."

Lucy's jaw dropped. "You think a military installation is just going to give us fuel?"

John shook his head. "No, we're probably gonna have to be a little more forceful."

Lucy let out a deep, exasperated breath. "Oh God!" She hated to even think what that meant.

John's plan was to land at the military airstrip using an SOS distress signal. The base was an Argentinian Air Force refueling station used by small military planes that hopped around the Andes delivering supplies to various outposts. From his research, he'd found that these small outposts consisted of a housing facility, two soldiers, and a communications radio. Their job was to call in if they ever saw anything out of the ordinary, which was unlikely halfway up a snow-covered mountain.

John planned to start sending a mayday signal when they were about fifty miles out, giving no details of their problems. He would continue with a distressful sounding mayday until they landed. He was pretty sure that the two guys assigned to the place would be little more than kids and first-class privates. And, most likely not perceiving it to be any kind of a threatening situation, they would just come walking out without guns to see what the problem was. His plan was to explain nicely that they ran out of fuel and needed just enough to make it to the nearest commercial airport. If that didn't work, he would hold them at gun point and take the fuel.

Lucy was too numb to even argue about it. She just turned and stared out her window.

After a little more than an hour of silence, again Ricky poked his head between the seats. "Doctor Christenson, how do you know that Mom's brother's commune hasn't been overrun by all kinds of people?"

That caught Lucy's attention. She turned from her semi-conscious gaze out the window. "Yeah, what about that?"

John shrugged. "I don't know. We can only hope and pray. It's an extremely isolated and hard to get to place other than by air. There are no roads, and the terrain to get there is unforgiving."

As they flew on, John explained that most of the people in the northwestern half of South America would most likely push west into the sweltering, insect-infested Amazon basin where millions would die from disease. Then, shaking his head at even the thought of the horror that would ensue, he said, "Millions of decaying bodies will kill millions more. It will be a terrible, vicious cycle."

Lucy sat listening, thinking back to the pictures of India—the millions of decaying bodies and the black clouds of swarming insects. Then, for some reason, an image reappeared from somewhere deep in her memory. It was the Indian newswoman. Looking over at John, she said, "I wonder what ever happened to that newscaster lady—the young Indian girl. Remember, I think her name was Shaili?"

John could only wonder. Either she had survived and now lived among a small subgroup of humans scratching out an existence from the bare earth, or she had died along with the millions.

Lucy mumbled more or less to herself, "It's terrible. It's like a mass extinction, except this time it's not the dinosaurs."

John didn't say anything, but he knew that their survival, as terrible as it was, depended on millions of people dying.

As they continued south along the mountain ridges, John explained that the Andes and the Atacama Desert would stop migration down along the West coast of South America and that most people in the center of South America would either push up into Central America or to the East coast to hopefully survive off the oceans.

Ricky poked his head between the seats and asked, "Why don't people just go down the center, straight down to Patagonia, where we're going?"

"They'll try," John said, "but the Pantanal, a huge wetland in the middle of the country, is cold and wet this time of the year. People won't make it through."

Little could they have known as they flew overhead that, below, a young cowgirl was trudging through the Pantanal toward Patagonia, and in her basket of eggs was the future Angus and Braveheart.

Everyone sat silent for a while until John broke the silence. "Okay, here we go."

Reaching over, he pushed a small, red button. It started to ping. "What's that?" Lucy asked.

"It's an automated SOS single." John picked up the radio receiver. "Mayday! Mayday!"

A few minutes later, the airstrip and military base came into view. John circled a few times and then landed the plane, purposefully taxiing up next to the fuel tanks.

As John had hoped, two young men who had no doubt heard the mayday call were standing outside the housing facility, watching. As nothing appeared threatening about the plane, they meandered nonchalantly across the tarmac. As they approached, John gave a little friendly wave.

Lucy looked at John. "They don't look any older than Ricky."

John nodded in agreement then tucked his handgun under his shirt. He told Lucy and Ricky to get out and stretch their legs and make it look like just a nice family in distress.

When the young men reached the plane, John asked, "Do you speak English?"

Both young men nodded. "Yes, we went to English school," one of them said, turning and pointing in the direction of Mendoza.

John pointed to the tanks. "We need fuel."

One of the young men shook his head. "No! We have strict orders. There's a fuel problem. We can't give you any fuel. We'll get in trouble."

John knew how the military worked and that these were just kids, first-class privates in no position to disobey orders. As he reached under his shirt, he said, "I understand," and pulled out his gun.

Both young men stepped back, surprised. "No! No! What're you doing?"

John motioned for them to sit on the tarmac. Then he crawled back into the plane and took out the shotgun. Getting back out of the plane, he handed it to Lucy. "Guard them."

The two young men sat petrified. Lucy felt sorry for them; they couldn't have been over eighteen. She gave a motherly smile and said, "Don't worry. I won't hurt you."

It took John over half an hour to refuel the plane. When

he was done, along with Lucy and Ricky, John marched the two young men into the housing facility. They had a nice stash of supplies. After scavenging around, he found four one-gallon cans of cooking oil and a number of canned foods. He asked one of the young men, "When do you get supplies again?"

He told John that he didn't know and that there were problems with the military supply planes and trucks—oil problems.

Lucy put her hand on John's shoulder. "We can't take all of their food. They'll die up here."

John nodded and then walked over to the radio. The last thing he wanted was the soldiers to call in an Argentinian fighter jet to shoot them out of the sky.

He was about to smash it when one of the boys yelled, "No! Please! We don't have a way to call for help. We promise we won't call anyone. You just leave."

John knew they were just kids who really had no idea why they were even there other than that they had been assigned there, and it was not for them to question.

John nodded. "Okay, but if you call anyone, I'll come back." He pointed his finger at them. "You understand me?"

Both nodded.

John knew damned well that there was really no way he'd ever be back. Then John looked at their guns. Knowing that they may never receive supplies again and could possibly survive by hunting for rabbits, snow foxes, or mountain goats, he said, "Don't shoot at us as we leave."

They nodded. One replied, "We won't. Just leave."

John motioned to Lucy and Ricky to take two of the cans of the cooking oil and a few canned goods.

Ten minutes later, as the two young men stood at the door of their building, they watched as the plane took off.

# CHAPTER 81

***

## International Space Station
## Where have all the flowers gone?

Commander Donaldson wasn't able to sleep and went up to the observation deck to have time to think. As the last vestiges of light dropped below the curvature of the earth, the International Space Station started its journey into the darkness of night. Donaldson sat in silence.

As only a few dim lights blinked on the deck's consoles, he stared down at the nearly black surface below. Gone were the huge pockets of blinking lights, the millions of little artificial suns that, only months earlier, had lit up the night skies of the eastern seaboard. As he stared in disbelief. With a bit of an ironic smile, he mused, "Where have all the flowers gone? Gone to graveyards everywhere."

Earlier that afternoon, he had received news—news that was going to force them to abort the station. But what a dilemma: who would stay, and who would go? Though there was no guarantee that their plunge into the darkness would offer a safe landing, whoever was left behind was certain to die.

In his mind, his decision was made a little easier by knowing that he would stay, and Layne would go, but—

"Hey! It's supposed to be sleep time."

Startled out of his ponderous thoughts, Donaldson swiveled in his chair to see Layne Rowe, NASA's ultimate on-board baby experiment, floating her way up into the observation deck.

"Couldn't sleep," Donaldson told her.

Layne made her way into the chair next to him. "Why not?"

With a disheartened look, he replied, "We've got a problem, a big one."

She lifted her eyebrows. "Like?" Layne wasn't overly concerned. They had problems of one kind or another all the time. A few days earlier, one of the crew members had gotten sick and thrown up, spewing food particles into a carbon dioxide cleanser. It had taken most of a day to catch all the droplets of some kind of mystery meat that floated around the cabin.

Donaldson turned away from her and stared out the observation window, back to the black surface below. With a somber nod, he said, "Like, our resupply payload capsule was broken into today by workers at the Cape in Florida."

Layne was taken aback a little. She knew it meant they would have to go back to the surface, and she knew there was nothing to go back to.

She put her hand on Donaldson's shoulder. "How long? How long do we have?"

"With rationing, maybe five … six months."

Now it was Layne's turned to stare out the big windows at the nothingness below. "So … when do we go?" When there was no answer, Layne turned back to Donaldson, who was just staring at her blankly, lost in a fog of thought. Then it hit her; she understood his blank stare. "Oh my God! Oh my God! No!"

Looking at him wide-eyed, spewing from somewhere deep in her subconscious, she yelled, "My God! Sophie's choice?"

Donaldson nodded. Giving her a deep, somber look, he said, "It only holds three—the Descent Module."

Layne shook her head. "And baby makes seven."

# Chapter 82

***

## Patagonia

The two boys stood in the doorway of their building watching as John positioned the plane at the head of the runway. After a quick look at the instrument panel, the oil pressures in each engine, temperature gauges, and positions of the flaps, John pushed the throttles forward. The engines whined, and the plane slowly moved forward picking up speed, the huge propellers kicking up a dusting of snow along the way. Just as the plane was about to lift off, they passed the two boys. Lucy had been sitting silently, staring out her window, when she suddenly gasped. Tears welled up in her eyes as the plane whizzed past them. For a split second, she saw two Rickys standing side by side, bundled up in their winter coats, ready to head off to school. She couldn't suppress the sniffles; they were just kids, just like her beautiful son.

As the plane lifted off, Lucy stared back and watched

until the boys disappeared into the distance. With the tears blurring her vision, she looked over at John. "Do you think those boys will survive?"

John could only shrug. He knew deep down that their chances were slim, but he could only hope. Seeing the hurt in Lucy's eyes, he reached over and gave her hand a little reassuring squeeze. "They'll do just fine. They have shelter, and we left them with their guns, so they can hunt." Although, he doubted that they had ever really shot their guns in anything other than a few training sessions. With a reassuring nod, he continued, "There's wild game there: rabbits, snow foxes, hawks. And if they're lucky, they'll get a mountain goat."

Lucy turned back and gave a last look out her window, trying to see the boys standing in the doorway, but they were gone. The building was only a dot in the far distance. Looking back at John, she said, "We should've taken them with us. They're going to die there."

John didn't say anything. He only looked at her and, with a nearly imperceptible shake of his head, gave a silent "no".

Lucy nodded knowing that it wasn't possible.

John only wished he could save everyone—the whole world—but he couldn't. God, nature, fate, whichever had dealt the cards, things were the way they were now. Ironically, little did he know it had not been any of these things that dealt this fatal hand.

In the short time they were on the ground, Ricky had

developed a kind of emotional bond with the two boys. They were just like him. It sounded like they had gone to the same preparatory school as he had, although 5000 miles apart, and maybe they had even dreamed of going to Harvard someday.

Unhooking his shoulder straps and leaning forward between the seats, he looked over at his mom and said, "Why couldn't we take them with us?"

Before Lucy could answer, he turned and looked at John. "They might die there, won't they?"

John just sat for a silent moment and stared out his window. What a quagmire, a philosophical dilemma. The issue wasn't why they couldn't take them. That was simple; they had no choice. The issue was having to decide—to choose who goes and who stays, who lives and who dies.

Looking back at Ricky, who was obviously very troubled, John gave a somber shake of his head and replied, "If we took them, we'd all die. We didn't have a choice."

Ricky didn't say anything. He just nodded and sat back in his seat. He understood, although it wasn't fair. Life wasn't fair, but he understood.

Months earlier, his civics class had taken a field trip to the Holocaust Memorial in Boston. There was a story there about a mother named Sophie who came to the front gates of one of the concentration camps with her two children—a beautiful little girl, and a blue-eyed little boy. The Nazi commander at the front gate stopped her and told her that she could only keep one, the boy or the girl. And if she couldn't choose, they would both die.

As Ricky stared out his window, his mind lost in a huge subconscious void, a nearly inaudible mumble unwittingly escaped, "She chose the little boy." Looking over at John, he said, "Sophie did."

John looked back, confused. "What?"

He sighed and said, "Never mind."

Thirteen thousand miles away, above the other side of the planet, Commander Donaldson nodded to Layne and said, "And baby makes seven."

# Chapter 83

***

## Patagonia Plateau

For the last five hours, they had slowly dropped from over 9000 feet, their last refueling stop at the military base on Mount Aconcagua, to 1300 feet. Behind them were the barren, windswept tundras of the Alpines as they now skirted along the foothills of Mount Piltriquitrón, Patagonia.

Lucy stared out her window, amazed at the untouched expanse of rivers, streams, and open grassy plateaus in the foothills below. There were no roads, no buildings, just flowing green valleys studded with low-level rock formations and an occasional waterfall. Ricky sat in the back excitedly pointing out a group of condors flying high above the Alpine tree line and then a herd of Andean deer resting on a windswept outcropping of treeless rocks. John, meanwhile, sat quietly concentrating on the fuel gauges with periodic checks out his window, assessing the terrain below.

Lucy could see that he was tense. Reaching over, she put her hand on his shoulder. "You look worried."

John nodded and replied, "A little." Then he pointed to the fuel gauges. "We don't have much time."

Lucy looked at the gauges. Both were quickly approaching the empty mark. Then peering out her window for any signs of human habitation—a commune, a road, an airstrip—she asked, "How are we going to find them?"

John reached down and grabbed an envelope that was stuffed between the seats. It was one of the letters that Lucy's brother had sent to her a year earlier. He handed it to Lucy. "In this letter, your brother apologized for not writing more often, explaining that it was a three-day hike from their commune to the nearest post office."

Lucy took the envelope as John pointed to the post office stamp in the upper right-hand corner. "El Bolson. That's where he mailed it from."

"I remember him talking about that place. We were so young. He got into the hippies movement: antiwar, anti-government, anti-everything and said that someday he wanted to live a handmade, sustainable lifestyle. When Mom and Dad were killed, it tipped him over the edge."

Lucy had only been sixteen, but she remembered that day vividly. It was the worst day of her life—the breaking news "Pan Am Flight 103 Explodes over Lockerbie, Scotland."

Her pain of that awful time resurfaced from long-suppressed memories. Lucy mumbled, "He never even stayed for their funeral. He said he was going to move to the 'ends of the earth' as he called it."

John reached over and wiped a tear from her cheek. "You can't blame him for dealing with his pain the way he did. And looking at what's happening, he might have been right."

Lucy's thoughts slowly returned to the present. "So how are we going to find him?"

"Since he said it took three days to walk to the nearest post office, and figuring that at most they could only make it eight to ten miles a day hiking in this terrain, they must be within a thirty-mile radius of this El Bolson."

John had searched reconnaissance images of the southern tip of the Andes and found a settlement called El Bolson nestled in the foothills of a small mountain range called Piltriquitrón.

As they flew, he kept reviewing the coordinates he had downloaded for El Bolson. And after about ten minutes of searching, with the plane running on fumes, he pointed, "There! Up ahead … that should be El Bolson."

Ricky popped up between the seats, and they all looked out the windshield at the small village, their hope beginning to build. Just then, the right engine began to sputter. John tensed and looked at the fuel gauges. "We're running on fumes!"

Banking the plane to right, he started circling in a thirty-mile arc with El Bolson at its center. Within minutes, the right engine quit completely, and the huge propeller cranked to a stop.

For the first time since she had met him, Lucy saw fear in

John's face. Reaching over with a consoling touch to his shoulder and a concerning look of her own, she asked, "Are we going to find it in time?"

"I don't know, but we've got to find a place to land, and soon!" Pointing to the left engine, he said, "If that engine quits, we're going to drop like a rock. This thing isn't going to glide far with the load we've got."

Lucy looked down at the steep, wooded terrain below and then at the altimeter. "820 feet."

Suddenly, Ricky burst out, "There! Over there!" pointing out his window. It was an encampment.

John stretched across Lucy's lap and looked out her window. "That's it! That's them."

Lucy looked at him, confused. "How do you know?"

"There, in the middle of the page." John pointed to the letter that Lucy still had in her hand. "Your brother said they had just finished building a kiln and were making their own bricks from clay and grasses from a nearby boggy area and that they were going to build twin smoke-stacks for their ovens."

Just as Lucy glanced and saw a set of twin smokestacks, the left engine started to sputter. She gasped. John grabbed the yoke and flattened the plane into a glide position.

John pointed to a flat, grassy plateau about ten miles ahead. "There!" Now, the left engine was sputtering continuously. John sat bolt upright in his seat, intently looking ahead at the plateau. "Come on! Come on!"

Lucy pulled forward in her seat, her restrains tightening across her chest and her fingernails digging deep into the dashboard of the plane. Looking at the altimeter, it read "602 feet." She then noticed the jagged outcropping of rocks below—rocks that had been slowly pushed up over millions of years by the ever-rising mountain peaks of the Andes. Pulling even tighter against the restraints, she asked, "My God, are we going to make it?"

They were now flying up a narrow valley with steep, rising embankments on both sides and, straight ahead, at the far end of the valley, a dead-end ridge of rocks and trees.

As they got closer and closer to the looming ridge, it looked as though they were going to crash headlong into the rocks.

John shouted, "Hang on!"

While pushing the throttles forward as far as they would go, John was praying to God that there was enough fuel left to lift the nose of the plane up and over the rocky ridge.

Holding his breath as the rocks loomed ever closer, he heard the engine slowly picking up speed, and then he felt the nose of plane lift ever so slightly. The rocky cliff filling his windshield began to disappear only to be replaced by a tall stand of pines.

Pushing even harder on the throttles, his knuckles nearly white, John gave out a last desperate plea, "Come on!" as the view of the pines started filling the windshield.

Then, for a short moment, the engine roared to life. Just as the nose of the plane lifted, the thin film of fuel remaining in the bottom of the tank sloshed back into a small puddle, bathing the feed line to the engine. Clear blue sky stared to fill the windshield, and the tops of the pines scraped the underbelly of the plane. Letting out a deep breath, he reached over and pushed the lever for the landing gear.

Lucy sat petrified, looking out of her window. Ahead laid a long, flat plateau of grassland. To the left ran a small river, and to the right about a hundred yards away was a tall stand of birch trees. The plateau was a few hundred yards wide and at least three hundred yards long, ending at a huge lake.

John's knuckles were slowly returning to their natural color, and he mused to himself that at least the plateau was wider and longer than the U.S.S. *Nimitz*. John's moment of relief was short-lived. He tensed up again as he could see that they were going to hit the tall grasses. Again, he yelled, "Hang on."

Within seconds, the wheels dug into the soft dirt of the plateau, abruptly slowing the plane. The nose dipped forward lifting the twin tail fins high up into the sky. John held steady on the yoke, praying that the plane didn't flip over onto its top.

Lucy screamed as dirt and grass flew, completely blocking their view. The big right propeller snapped off, flying miraculously just over the top of the plane. Then there was an earth-shaking thud as the twin tail fins slammed back down onto the ground. The plane bounced and fishtailed wildly for a few yards, then a loud crack was heard beneath the plane. Before Lucy could even scream again, the right wing dropped into the dirt, throwing her head against her window.

There was nothing John could do at this point. Their fate rested in the laws of physics. The landing gear on the right hit a rock and snapped off, plunging the tip of the right wing into the dirt.

With the left propeller still spinning, no power to the right, and tip of the right wing in the dirt, the plane started a violent 360-degree spin.

Although hardly able to keep his eyes focused because of the merry-go-round spinning of the plane, John managed to reach over and cut the power to the left engine.

Suddenly, everything stopped. For seemingly an eternity, no one said anything. The plane was sitting at a 45-degree angle with its nose facing the ridge that they had cleared only seconds earlier. John reached over and pushed the landing gear control button. With a thud, the left landing gear collapsed, setting the plane flat on the ground.

Lucy looked back at Ricky with tears in her eyes. "Are you okay, honey?"

Ricky nodded. "I'm okay, Mom."

With a small goose egg over her right temple where she had hit the window in the spin, she looked over at John. "Are you okay?"

He nodded. "I'm fine."

“Now what?” Lucy asked.

John smiled, reached over, and gave her a little kiss on the forehead. “I don’t know, but now it’s you, me, and Ricky makes three.”

# Chapter 84

***

## The Commune

"I know the last few weeks have been very difficult for all of us, last week more so than others." A tortured look distorted Dietric's face. "They were young, struggled so hard, and having children made it all the more painful."

Thomas Dietric was a former Wall Street executive who lost everything when his wife and daughter were killed by a truck driven onto a crowded sidewalk in Central Park, all in the name of some idealistic crap. Unable to cope in the weeks and months after the loss, he rejected everything—the establishment, the money, the house on Long Island—and made his way to the tip of Patagonia. Now in his sixties, his belly a little more rotund and his white hair pulled back in a ponytail, he stood addressing the commune.

The commune was made up of just over twenty members, all who, for various personal reasons like Dietric, had dropped out of mainstream society.

Glen Letchworth was a former Harvard professor of political social issues who, having gotten caught up in the aftermath of the Timothy Leary psychedelic drug craze, drummed out of Harvard for less than ethical experimentation with LSD and students. Philip Jorckowski was a wayward student of the arts who had lost his parents in a terrorist bombing over Lockerbie, Scotland. Leonard Bradly was a disgruntled environmentalist. But the commune's enigma was Arnold Driscoll.

Driscoll was a shady character who had stepped out of the shadows early in the commune's history. Little was known of his past other than he had been a former CIA operative involved in disbanding—though rumors implied essentially eliminating—key U.S. personnel who had sensitive knowledge of the failed Bay of Pigs invasion of Cuba. He had been one of the masterminds behind the exploding cigars sent to Castro and rumored to have been personally responsible for the untimely deaths of a number of news reporters digging into government issues that were deemed, "Close to Presidential Level."

Driscoll's roll in the commune was to deal with problems that no one else wanted to deal with—problems that everyone just wanted to go away but didn't want to have to dirty their own hands with, such as the young couple a week earlier who had arrived with two children.

In the past few months, the oil issues to the north had started putting extreme pressures on the survival of not just the commune but on each and every individual member in the commune.

The collective cooperative was now an aging group of old

men content on living out their last years in the peace and quiet of nature. They had no desire nor the ability to compete with an influx of stronger, younger "warriors" as Driscoll called them.

The commune had always been well isolated from intruders to the north by the unforgiving Andes Mountains along the western ridge, the impassable wetlands of the Pantanal in the center, and the allure of the ocean's resources along the eastern coast. For years, the group had lived off the land in stasis with the natural resources, but now their status quo was in jeopardy. In the past few months, a number of stragglers had managed to survive the nearly impossible trek, landing on the doorsteps of the commune.

The commune's recycling of the available materials was meticulously kept in check by Leonard Bradly. Bradly was a former statistician and environmentalist from the University of Michigan who had warned of mankind's eventual demise, arguing that stealing from Peter to give to Paul was a risky way to live. Disgruntled, after years of his warnings falling on deaf ears, he had retreated to the "isolation of nature" as he called it.

Bradly kept a day-by-day log of the commune's impact on the environment right down to the grass, the number of fish in the streams, every stick of wood used, and the time it took their waste products to return to nature. Taking into account all of the environmental factors, he calculated the turnover time for the commune's resources. From these calculations, he determined that the commune needed, at a minimum, a seventeen-mile perimeter of natural terrain to keep the status quo for twenty-one individuals. Adding any more, he warned, even one more individual, would tip the balance to the negative. Then, as he often pointed out, the only way to get back into the positive would be to keep expanding the seventeen-mile perimeter, which they had no means of defending. Therefore, as cold and difficult as it seemed, turning away new members was deemed a matter of survival—Darwinism.

But, as the members were finding, the matter of survival worked both ways. Survivors were just as determined to survive as the members of the commune. In the past few weeks, the number of people who had beaten the odds of making it over the rugged terrain was reaching an alarming number. At first, it had been enough to just turn people away. Weakened by the cold, disease, and starvation, all had succumbed in a short time to the environmental pressures beyond the seventeen-mile radius.

Although, as psychologically stressful and heartbreaking as it was for the group, the deaths occurred out of sight. Out of sight, out of mind made it a little more palatable. But now there were growing concerns that just forcing people away was not going to be enough. Survivors were going to start surviving, amassing on the commune's perimeter. Knowing mankind's disregard for controlling his own populations, living beyond his means, and the inevitable border wars that always arose, the decision had been made by the commune to definitively deal with new arrivals. With heads turned and no questions asked about the issue of "definitively dealing" with new arrivals, the matter had been left all to Driscoll.

John, Lucy, and Ricky spent their first night in the plane. After John's less-than-perfect landing, he and Ricky had unloaded the bulkier items: the big cooking kettle, fishing equipment, the canvas tarp, and other nonperishable items and had laid a nice cushion of blankets, making a more than comfortable bed.

Early the next morning, just as the faintest rays peaked over the ridges of Mount Piltriquitron, John and Lucy headed out toward the commune. Ricky stayed behind with the unloaded shotgun to guard the plane.

They knew the commune's location was downstream of the little river that ran alongside of their new home. When they circled over the commune only minutes before their crash landing, John had looked at the dials and was now able to calculate that the commune was about fifteen miles from their location. Walking along the gravelly river's edge was smooth going, and they reached the commune by noon.

It was well after dark by the time they returned to the plane.

Ricky was sitting by a small campfire that he'd started. "How'd it go?"

Lucy answered as she heavily exhaled and kicked off her shoes, exhausted. "We won't know till tomorrow," she said as she rubbed her blistered feet.

After a meal of dried beef jerky, goat cheese, and a mango, Lucy took a quick dip in the cold river.

As the campfire burned down, they closed the doors of the plane and went to sleep.

# Chapter 85

***

## The Commune

Dietric stood before the emergency meeting of the members of the commune. "I know everyone is aware that we had five new arrivals yesterday—a mother carrying a baby, and three who flew in an old plane that landed about fifteen miles from here. They've approached us asking for help, which means allowing them into the commune, at least temporarily. They're coming back the day after tomorrow for our answer." He looked around. "Any comments?"

A voice came from the back of the room. "The girl with the baby won't be a problem. The baby is dead. She's just in a state of shock carrying a dead baby. She's already so weak she can hardly stand up. She'll be dead in a few days," Driscoll said in a cold, heartless tone, "but the other three are going to be a problem."

"Leonard?" Dietric looked over inquisitively at Leonard Bradly.

Bradly shook his head. "We don't have the resources to take in more people. We'll be tipping the balance, using more than we have."

Driscoll spoke up in his harsh, brash manner, making it perfectly clear what had to be done. "Let's be realistic; the other three are already within the commune. They're maybe fifteen miles from here. They're strong, they have shelter, and they have survival equipment. They're likely to survive."

"Molothrus," a loud outburst came from the middle of the room.

Dietric looked over at Robert Fogerty, the head of the commune's energy waste disposal and clean water systems. Fogerty was a philosophical nut case who drove Dietric crazy, always talking in riddles that no one understood.

With a quizzical lifting of his eyebrows and a little tilt of his head, Dietric asked, "Robert, you have a comment?"

"The cowbird, Molothrus, you know," Fogerty blurted out. "They live in the trees right outside our doors. We see them every day and think nothing of it. They do what they have to. That's how they survive."

Dietric had no idea what he was talking about. "Do you have a point to make, Robert?"

"The mama cowbird, man. She kicks out the eggs of other birds from their nest, lays her own in their place. She eliminates future competition. Her babies hatch and get taken care of. She doesn't do it with any ill-intent. It's matter of survival, man. It's evolution."

Dietric nodded. “You’re saying we need to kick the new arrivals out of the nest—our commune—and break the eggs?”

Fogerty nodded adamantly, “Exactly, man! It’s nature at its best survival.”

Hoping to change the subject, Dietric looked over at Philip Jorchowski. “Phil, I’m not sure everyone knows.”

Philip nodded, stood up, and looked around the room. “The woman … with the three in the plane … she’s my sister.”

A silent awe filled the room.

# Chapter 86

***

## The Commune

Lucy sat on the edge of the wing putting on a second pair of socks, hoping it would cushion her blistered feet, preparing for the long walk. Today was their meeting with the commune. She hardly slept, tossing and turning all night wondering what they were going to do if the commune said no. Ricky was already up and about, having gathered wood and started a small fire.

"Morning."

Looking up, Lucy saw John standing in the doorway of the plane tucking a handgun under his shirt. A little surprised, she asked, "Why the gun?"

John stepped down, walked the length of the wing and sat down next to Lucy. "I don't know, I've been thinking about it all night. Something just doesn't feel right."

Lucy was trying to pull on her shoes over the double pairs of socks. "Like what?"

John slightly shook his head and thought for a second, not sure in his own mind what was bothering him. Then he said, “Didn’t you notice there weren’t many members?”

Lucy shrugged, lacing up her shoes. “I guess. I never thought of it. So what?”

“I don’t know, but in all this time, we’re the only ones to arrive here?”

Lucy looked at John, bewildered. Half jokingly, she said, “What, you think they’re doing away with new arrivals?”

John sat staring blankly as if he was actually considering it.

Lucy’s eyebrows shot up; she couldn’t believe he was actually taking her seriously. Grabbing his arm, she turned him toward her with somewhat of a frantic jerk. “What! You do?”

John shrugged. “I don’t know.” Then he turned and looked out toward the little river. From somewhere deep in his subconscious, he mumbled, “The path. It’s the path.”

“Breakfast is almost ready,” Ricky interrupted. He had cooked up an international meal of some eggs they took from the old woman in Ecuador, a little cooking oil they took from the two boys on the military base, and some bacon John got from the little store in La Esperanza.

Lucy turned and said, “In a second, honey.” She turned back to John. Confused, she asked, “What path? What’re you talking about?”

Snapping out of his momentary trance but still in deep

thought, he shook his head. "The other day! While you were talking to your brother, I was walking around the commune, just looking. I came across this path. I don't know why it caught my eye, but for some reason it did. Just out of curiosity, I followed it, and it opened into a field."

Lucy sat listening, confused. The whole place was one big, open field—a couple hundred thousand miles of fields. Putting her hand on John's shoulder, she turned him toward her. "You're losing me … so what?"

John looked very deeply into her eyes. "It looked like a cemetery. Rows of fresh mounds."

Lucy didn't understand. She wasn't sure how he had come to the conclusion that it was a cemetery. Standing up and wiggling her toes in her shoes to see if they were comfortable, she said, "Maybe it's where they bury their waste every day. They have to put it somewhere." She gave a sarcastic grin. "You know, they're a fastidious bunch of old farts. They've been out here for years with no women to lead them. They probably have a meticulous ritual for everything, even burying their waste."

John nodded. "You're probably right, but I'll bring the gun just in case we come across a bear or something on the way."

A few hours later, John and Lucy were about half a mile from the commune. They were met by three of the members in a small, wooded valley. John was immediately wary that something wasn't right.

The shorter of the three men stepped forward, putting out his hand. "Hi, I'm Adam. I'm the head of the New Member Welcoming Committee."

Lucy put out her hand feeling a little more relaxed by the name, thinking that maybe they were going to be accepted.

John wasn't sure about their motives. It was a little odd that they had a welcoming committee but no new members. Looking up at the hillsides all around them, the memories from "Military Strategy 101" echoed in his mind: "Never be lured into a trap. Always keep the high ground." His gut feeling was that this meeting place wasn't by happenstance but was more of a calculated plan.

Suddenly, something splattered on Lucy's face, and John's head snapped forward as he fell to the ground. During their warm and fuzzy welcoming, Arnold Driscoll had come out from behind a bush and hit him with metal pipe across the back of the head. John lay on the ground moaning. A gaping wound on the back of his head oozed with blood.

Lucy shrieked, "What're you doing!" She dropped to her knees and cradled John's head in her arms. He was awake but stunned. As she looked up at the men, she saw Driscoll standing over her, starting to bring the metal pipe up over his head.

Lucy's primeval reptilian brain kicked in. There, just below John's waist, she saw the handle of the gun. Reaching down, she pulled John's shirt back, grabbed the gun, and rolled onto her back. Holding the gun with two hands, her arms fully extended and locked at the elbows, she pulled the trigger twice. Pop! Pop!

Driscoll staggered back, dropped the pipe, and grabbed his belly. Looking down, blood seeping between his fingers, he fell to his knees and then sat back on his legs. He started to say something, but the sound was muffled by a gurgling gush of blood that flowed up his throat and then started to trickle out the corners of his mouth. The other men backed away.

Lucy stood up, an animal rage in her eyes. Her hands trembling, she bought the gun up and pointed it inches from Driscoll's forehead.

Driscoll looked up into her eyes.

Then, a wet, bloodstained hand gripped her wrist. Blood running down his face, John took the gun. "No!"

Lucy nodded.

Getting up, staggering, John took her hand. "Let's go."

TO BE CONTINUED.

*SIX BILLION COUNTS OF MURDER*

A wise writer, comedian, and philosopher once told a young group of graduates about life:

“You are at a crossroads in your lives. The path to the right leads to despair, destruction, and utter hopelessness. The path to the left leads to total extinction. Choose wisely.”

# About the Author

Dr. James D. Tesar was born and raised on a large dairy farm in Wisconsin. He never missed a day of getting up at 4:30 a.m. and milking fifty cows from age five until the day he left for college at seventeen.

Dr. Tesar has majored in biology and chemistry, has a degree in Nuclear Medicine, a Masters in Bionucleonics, a Ph.D. in Membrane Physiology and a Medical Degree.

Dr. Tesar's understanding of biological life forms and chemical compounds has spurred his imagination to write fictional stories that are, in actuality, just a few degrees away from reality. His writing amalgamation of bizarre situations and realism makes for awe-inspiring, page-turning books.

Dr. Tesar is currently an Emergency Room Physician and teaches emergency medicine at the Orlando Regional Medical Center in Orlando, Florida.